Whitechapel

IAN PORTER

authorHOUSE®

AuthorHouse™
1663 Liberty Drive
Bloomington, IN 47403
www.authorhouse.com
Phone: 1-800-839-8640

First published by AuthorHouse 5/12/2009

ISBN: 978-1-4389-5250-5 (sc)

*Printed in the United States of America
Bloomington, Indiana*

This book is printed on acid-free paper.

To Ruby & George, my parents & inspiration; and to Jenny, my partner, saviour & muse.

"*The success of poorly-paid women of the lower working class is revealed in their willingness to take any task which might feed their families and maintain their unity and independence. The haggard, worn, tired faces of the working women of the urban poor are to be seen in this light; they were signs of victory not of failure.*"

Dr Carl Chinn, They Worked All Their Lives 1989

"*I went to the street solely to get a living for myself and my child. If I had been able to get it otherwise I would have done so… It was the low price paid for my labour that drove me to prostitution.*"

Unknown to Victorian social explorer.

"*The result justifies the deeds*"

Ovid c.10BC

CHAPTER 1:

"Born in slums, driven to work while still children, undersized because underfed, oppressed because helpless, flung aside as soon as worked out, who cares if they die or go to the streets provided only that Bryant & May shareholders get their 23 per cent"

Annie Besant, White Slavery in London

Saturday, September 29th 1888, Whitechapel:

'Long Liz' Stride began the last day of her life by putting the money she had earned from selling her body to filthy sailors at Limehouse docks, into buying some flowers from the Colombia Road flower market. She had saved the money it would have cost to share a bed with some body-lice in a common lodging house by walking the streets all night. She would be the first customer at the flower market, and would have her pick of the best, most saleable flowers that way, before investing the profit from hawking the flowers on the streets, into gin to drink herself to oblivion; to escape.

She had been at it all day, selling all but one puny bunch which the costermonger had passed off on her without her noticing. Nobody was going to buy them, and her profit margin, as puny as the remaining bunch, had gone. She was about to call it a day and head for the Ten Bells, when one of the women from Toynbee Hall came along. Liz had never met her before, but she had been pointed out on more than one occasion. She had caused quite a stir in the local community. Tongues had wagged. The woman stopped and smiled. She had the best teeth Liz had ever seen.

The memory of the worst moment of Liz's life thrust itself into her mind, deep from the mire where she had tried to bury it without success. In her teens, Liz's greatest physical attribute had been her fine row of gleaming white teeth. She was proud of having the best 'ivories' in the neighbourhood. But her parents had decided a plain, weak-looking 'streak of piss' like her would struggle to find herself a husband unless she could offer something tangible to a prospective young man. She was good for nothing except taking food off the table and keeping them in poverty as far as they were concerned. They decided low maintenance was to be her great matrimonial asset. The common occurrence of tooth problems due to the poor's preference for all things sweet in their diet, not to mention a lack of calcium-bearing food, and the exorbitant cost of dentistry meant that a young woman who could guarantee not to be a dental burden on her husband had a certain attraction, even if that attraction was not physical. On her seventeenth birthday, without being warned of what was about to happen to her, Liz had been taken to the local dentist. An hour later the dentist was sweating with the effort of having removed every tooth in Liz's head. It was her birthday treat from her parents. She never recovered.

Before the woman had a chance to speak Liz thrust the flowers under her nose.

"Smell 'em. Fourpence ta you lady. Always keep the best of the bunch till last, they lasts longer see."

She was trying to sell flowers she was about to throw away for double what she usually charged for the best bunch.

I seen you comin' a mile orf.

Sookey Parsons had stopped to offer to take this poor wretch to Henrietta Barnett's coffee room around the corner in Toynbee Hall. The woman looked in dire need of a warming beverage and a rest. But the offer of the flowers made Sookey hesitate. She was desperately trying to be accepted in this new slum world she had recently chosen to live in full time, and this was awkward. Did she refuse the woman? She had no need of flowers, especially such an ill-looking bunch, because she bought flowers herself regularly direct from the market. Refuse her and then offer her a free cup of coffee instead? Would that be the typically unwanted behaviour of a slummer? Did she try to buy the flowers for less than was being offered, as appeared to be the norm when marketing? Fourpence did seem rather excessive. The apparently wealthy charity worker, knocking down the price on a woman who needed every penny to keep out of the clutches of the dreaded workhouse. How could she?

"They do indeed have a fine bouquet," she lied. "Fourpence you say."

She rummaged in her purse and found a thruppenny piece and a penny but brought out a sixpence.

"I have er I ain't any thruppeny pieces or pennies. I have a sixpenny."

She was pleased to have remembered to say ain't, albeit with too much emphasis on the t, as she was trying to speak in the local dialect, so she would be more accepted, trusted and liked. She was blissfully unaware that so clearly enunciating some words made people wince, if not snigger. Liz gave a toothless smile, her lower cheeks caved in by the lack of support, and bent close enough to Sookey for her to smell a pungent mix of gin, tobacco and sick. Liz whispered conspiratorially.

"I ain' got no thruppeny bits or coppers. Got a tanner mind."

Sookey had lived in India as an army doctor's wife, and had seen slum life there, even if it was through the protective gaze of imperialism, enabling her to deal with the sights and smells of life in Whitechapel better than other slummers. She didn't flinch at Liz's breath, simply smiling and nodding her appreciation for the tip. Nonetheless she was relieved to extricate herself from the near-embrace and proffered a fingerless-mittened palm with a shiny silver coin on it to her new English tutor. Soon after arriving in the slums she had taken a knife to her best pair of gloves and cut the fingers off. She saw many costermongers wear such things so she thought she would too. Liz handed over the flowers and started to delve in her skirts for the change.

"Oh, I can't abide penn..coppers, big dirty heavy things," said Sookey.

She had picked up on how people would offer drinks as a sort of currency.

"Perhaps you could buy me a cuppar some time."

Liz smiled briefly at the overly perfect pronunciation of 'cuppa' but her expression quickly changed.

I don't take no chari'y. Seein' someone comin's one fing, that's business ain' it, but I don't takes no 'and outs from no one, an' scarce from no slummer an' there's the troof.

Liz studied the woman intently. Sookey simply looked back at her pleasantly, raising her eyebrows ever so slightly in requesting an answer. Liz decided the woman was playing straight with her.

"Yeah, a cuppa some'ime it is lady."

A young woman joined them. She had white powder on her face, big lips covered in the brightest red lip rouge, well tended long carrot-coloured hair and a tight bodice that did more than hint at the ample bosom beneath. She was no more than moderately pretty in the understood fashion, but she radiated sex. She was a head-turner. Men crooked their necks in lust, women in disdain, envy or jealousy, or perhaps all three.

The confident young woman made the opening gambit.

"Didn't know you two knew each ovver."

"We have just met. Helloo, Mary," replied a smiling Sookey. "This lady here was good enough to sell me these lovely flowers at reasonable price."

She turned her body as she spoke so she was square on to her friend Mary with her back to Liz. She glared at Mary, hoping to transmit to her without a word, 'please do not say anything!' Mary caught the stare and made no comment on the pathetic excuse for a bunch of flowers.

She knew Liz from their days when they used the same common lodging house; both of them bent over the same fire in the living room, sharing it with the dregs of humanity. Haggard old Liz was still living in such places, whilst Mary had been able to afford her own hovel thanks to her greater physical attributes; youth, breasts and best of all, a luscious mouth rather than one that crumpled. They were both part-time prostitutes, both had about the same amount of clients in any given week, but Mary could charge a lot more for her services.

The three women exchanged gossip and discussed the horrors of the murders which dominated most conversations in Whitechapel these days, before going their separate ways. Sookey practised using the odd glottal stop as she attempted a version of estuary Londoner.

She made her way to her improvised art gallery, in a building down a narrow alley close to Toynbee Hall. Her dream was to the make it a proper gallery one day.

The other two women were on their way to work. It was a Saturday, their best day of the week for clients. Apart from one local regular who she serviced every time he had money in his pocket, usually at the weekend, Mary had given up working late at night after the last murder.

The late September nights were drawing in, and although the first green pea-souper smog of the winter was still a couple of weeks away, the chocolate coloured pall of autumnal fog had already arrived on one occasion. The earlier darkness brought men the cover they needed, and some of them seemed as petrified of the Whitechapel murderer as the prostitutes, so Mary started in the afternoons these days and finished by eleven, both for her own safety and that of her customers. It was not the murderer himself, of whom her clients were afraid, rather the fear of being arrested by the police. The place was swarming with them nowadays. And it was full of newspaper reporters too. Any respectable man was only a bit of bad luck away from having their name in the notebook of a police officer, or far worse still, in the notebook of a reporter. Consequently there was not the money around any more. Gentlemen looking for release, stuck to the West End, so even the cream of East End whores such as Mary had to make do with the lower paying 'respectable' working man.

Much later than her planned eleven pm finish, Mary slumped onto her bed, soaked to the skin by a sudden downpour, exhausted and aching from the fumbling, groping and thrusting of a long series of eager customers. She had grazed knuckles from the delivery of a right cross to the mouth of one man. It had been the high point of her evening.

Liz had the same plan for the evening as Mary but soon after leaving her, she had slumped down with exhaustion and the weakness of starvation, and fallen asleep in a doorway for several hours. It was the rain and cold that had revived her. She dragged herself to her feet and raced to the shelter offered by the doorway of the Bricklayers Arms in Settles Street. She sheltered in the doorway for a few minutes before spotting a likely looking gent. The flower selling profit was her bed for the night. The gent's money would be her next meal.

A gent walkin' 'round 'ere at this time a night in this wevver, 'e must be keen.

Unfortunately for her, he was. She stepped out of the doorway and into history.

⌒ ◆ ⌒

Whoredom was the only trade where the optimum income tended to be paid to the newest apprentice. A girl could earn more in one night than a week in a sweatshop. But her high earning potential was for a limited period, before the evils of disease took their hold.

Kitty Johnson was fifteen years old. After three years on the game she was still beautiful, her outstanding features being her long dark hair and unusually faultless skin. It was Saturday night and she had been excited about going to the penny gaff that had just been set up in an empty greengrocer's shop in Court Street. Her excitement was attributable to the fact that she was going to see a mermaid.

A man with no arms, who could shave and play the violin with his toes, was top of the bill, but experience told her to doubt his credentials. Her last job before going on the game was on the Whitechapel Road, as the smiling little girl who turned the handle of the organ to keep the audiences amused before the Elephant Man appeared. She still felt privileged to be involved with the only time, before or since, that a gaff had been able to get away with charging tuppence instead of a penny as the entrance charge; such was the demand to see the beast. During her time there she had seen the gaff get up to all sorts of trickery to first attract, and then fool, their clientele. In the dim light of a barely lit gaff, a pig had once been passed off as a half-man half-beast from darkest Borneo. The wretched creature had been drugged, roped in to sit upright and kicked from a hidden spot below the stage when a response was required. A dog with lion's claws was a poor mutt which had had its fore-feet split. The medicine man's cure-all wizard oil was black treacle, formaldehyde, charcoal water and condensed skimmed milk; the first three ingredients to make it dark and disgusting like all good medicine was, and the last was a nod to the working man's sweet tooth.

Nah, the violin-playing cripple sounded right rum, but the mermaid were werf a copper ov anyone's money right enuff.

Kitty's Saturday night ritual on the rare occasions she was not forced to work the streets by her procurer, was to 'ding' her hair out. After the awfulness of the working week, it made her feel like a human, a woman; an attractive woman; attractive not to men, but to the mirror. She would plait her hair, coiling the plait around the side of her head, and then cover it in coconut oil to make it glossy. Her procurer was, as was so often the case, also her fancyman. She was clinging to the false hope of dignity through marriage and wifedom to even this most debased of ponces.

At the moment she should have been staring a fifteen year old's wide-eyed amazement at seeing a mermaid, she was sitting on her usual bench in Brick Lane, waiting for trade. Her ponce had turned up unexpectedly, having previously said he had a little business to attend to in Hackney. He was in a foul temper because his caper had fallen though and on finding her about to leave for the gaff with her mate Vi, had given her a beating (vicious body blows so as to not mess up her face for clients) for not working on a Saturday night when trade was at its busiest. She was sent out into the night.

Kitty's hair now hung down wild and disordered, her beauty tarnished by a scratched and bloody left cheek. The ponce had not reckoned on his target hitting her head on the table as she collapsed from his punches.

Being young, she could at least be choosey. She sat and waited to service a young wealthy popinjay who would pay much more than the filthy drunks the older members of her trade had to pleasure. Her customers were to marry late when they had reached a position as commended by bourgeois Malthusians, political economists and social reformers. Until that time arrived, they found their release amongst the prettiest of the poor.

Kitty passed the time by bubble-blowing. This pastime was all the rage since Millais had painted his famous picture. Earlier soaps had not provided the right surface tension, but the new stuff provided a fifteen year old girl with lots of innocent fun.

Despite enjoying her bubbles, she was uncomfortable. She did not usually work when she had her period and it was due soon, which was why she had planned to have a rare Saturday night off. She was now wearing a sanitary towel of clean rag made from bed linen, which she had used last month but had washed through well. The trouble was that it was rubbing against her pessary – a home made compound of lard and flour. She dreaded starting with her pessary still in place. She had once paid two shillings for a manufactured one - a small piece of oiled sponge on a string soaked in quinine, which was more comfortable, but the tapes must have detached because she had fallen pregnant. She had tried everything to get rid of it – massive doses of Pennyroyal syrup; gin, water in which pennies had been boiled; slippery elm, hot very soapy water; aloes concoctions, vigorous use of turps and even a fall down stairs; all to no avail. She had been about to go to a woman who used knitting and crochet needles, when an abortifacient used by vets seemed to do the trick.

A likely customer turned the corner so Kitty forgot about her troubles downstairs and quickly hid the bubble blower away under the bench. Out of her eyes shot bolts of wrath, contempt, meanness and hatred for the man in the Derby hat approaching. The feelings were reciprocated.

Kitty was wearing a dirty linen dress, torn open to reveal her still child-like breasts. As she approached, she realised the man was no young whelp, rather a man in his 40's or 50's, but he was a gent alright so she continued up to him. Her large eyes sparkled with apparent desire as she pressed herself against him. She pulled him to her and pushed herself back against the wall of a warehouse stuffed with riches from all over the Great British Empire. She expected to feel the man's randy member start to grow, but repelled by her youth the man pulled himself away, turned and quickly disappeared into the night. Not a word had been uttered by either party. She returned to her bench, slumped down and buried her face in her hands.

꘎　◆　꘎

Catherine Eddowes started the night with a trip to the pop shop. It was a filthy evening more in keeping with November than late September. The rain was coming down like stair-rods and it had turned cold too. She had to queue in the rain as being a Saturday night the pawnbroker was busy handing back the pathetic best possessions of the poor for their weekly outing. A threadbare old 'weasel', a shiny pair of trousers and a ragged waistcoat would be redeemed for the loss of the pawnbroker's commission, for a Saturday night out at the boozer or penny gaff and the weekly bit of meat for Sunday dinner. The clothes might even get an airing on a Sunday too. A walk or church was free at least. The items would be back in the shop first thing Monday morning to pay for the owners' rent or next meals.

But Cath, as she was known, was trading in the opposite direction to the crowd. As the pawnbroker handed Cath her redemption ticket and a couple of coppers for the pair of battered old boots she had just pawned, he asked where she was off to.

"Gunna get meself a nice cuppa tea. Warm me ol' cockles up."

She had no intention of drinking tea. It was just the expected response. The part she played. Good old Cath; salt of the earth. Behind the heavily painted cheeks, toothless grin and cheery banter was a woman at rock bottom. She had not eaten for days. She was pawning the better of her two pairs of boots on a Saturday night, the time above all else when she needed to look her best.

Saturday night had always been her busiest time of the week but she couldn't see herself getting much trade because, apart from the weather, the streets had been deserted during the increasingly long hours of darkness for the past three weeks since the last murder. And there wasn't much chance of picking up trade at closing time either, because the pubs were near-empty too. Even some of her roughest trade, who raised the money for her services by various illegal nocturnal means, dare not commit street crimes for fear that their next victim might be an undercover policeman after the killer. She had heard in her local, the Crown, down the Mile End Road, that a lot of street thieves had become snakesmen because burglary had actually become safer since the murders, with so many of the police just looking for the killer. But they went to ground afterwards rather than look for the services of an 'old tail', and now their new professional successes meant they could afford a younger, more expensive whore. Only the most desperate sought good old Cath out.

Cath cursed the rain. But for that, she thought trade might have picked up. Three weeks ago there were gangs of vigilantes roaming the streets looking for the killer, and woe-betide any Jew caught out on the streets at night. They were under curfew if they knew what was good for them, which they did. So she hadn't even been able to get a few coppers for a fumble with an old blind moneylender. But things had settled down. It seemed ages ago that she had joined the throng of hundreds who paid a penny to view the backyard of the house where 'Dark' Annie Chapman had got sliced up in Hanbury Street in Spitalfields.

"Did you know 'er?" people would ask.

"Course I did; soppy as a box a lights she were, but none the worse for that, and she were always good ta me. She'd see yer alright".

It was all lies. She had never met Annie Chapman. But she had to play the part. People seemed to think that old prostitutes were members of some sort of whores' social club. They didn't want to know any different. In reality, it was lonely. She drank with other whores in rough pubs sure enough, and there was laughter along the journey, but all they were doing was sharing the same route out of London; the quickest, the only route. They were fellow travellers. Not friends. You worked alone; got hacked to pieces alone.

Cath was wandering along a slum street, her imagination being allowed free reign to escape her reality for a few seconds. She remembered fondly skipping down the streets with her fellow young girls when their twelve hour shift at the Bryant & May factory in Bow had just ended. The only thing she missed about such a terrible job was that sense of freedom and joy when a shift ended; the excitement as she and her mates pushed through the crowds to get outside those factory gates as fast as their legs would carry them. She used to skip down the street, singing the latest shocking dirty ditty, belittling and flirting with lads on the other side of the street; ruining a crossing sweeper's work and returning his swearing with interest; stealing something from a market stall that she didn't want just for the devilment of it.

A strand of heavy wet hair fell into an eye, the pain bringing her back to the present with a jolt.

"I am fuckin' satura'ed!"

The shout was loud and angry for the world to hear.

She was wearing an old alpaca skirt that now weighed a ton, with a filthy ragged deep-pocketed blue skirt underneath, a white vest and a pair of tatty lace-up boots. She was not wearing any drawers or stays. They were not only a hindrance in her line of work but a luxury she could not afford. Her clothes stuck to her like glue.

She could walk to the Saturday night stalls and do some marketing. There were bargains to be had from the stallholders who had food 'goin' 'ome'. They would sell if off cheap. Unsure if she had enough money to both eat and get drunk, Cath rummaged in the deep pockets of her underskirt for a count up. She took out her knife, which was sufficiently large to ward off anyone, clients or otherwise, who started any rough stuff; a small tin box containing tea, another with sugar in it, a small fine-toothed comb, a piece of old white apron, a mustard tin in which she placed her pawn ticket for safe keeping, an empty tin matchbox, the coppers the pawnbroker had given her and two specially shined up farthings which she always kept on the off chance she could pass them off as half-sovereigns. If she was lucky enough to attract a gent, she offered to give him change if he wanted to get rid of a sovereign on her. They were always surprised by such business acumen, and the greener of them fell for it. In the pitch darkness of an unlit alleyway, anything was possible.

She was not going to get far on that little lot. There was one thing about starving – drinking on an empty stomach got you drunk quicker. A pub beckoned. She would spend all her money in the one pub so that with a bit of luck she might be able to cadge a few more drinks 'on the mace' from a friendly landlord. If she could drink till closing time, she should be three sheets to the wind, and if it stopped raining a bit she might even get a bit of trade afterwards from one of the costers. They would be setting up their stalls for the early Sunday morning market in Petticoat Lane by the time she rolled home.

Cath was very drunk and penniless long before the pubs closed, and was staggering along the street when she heard bells ringing. They were actually cow bells, a herd being taken through the empty streets from Liverpool Street station, where they had just arrived on a train from Essex, on their way to the Aldgate slaughterhouses.

"Blimey a fire engine!" Cath started whirling around with arms stretched wide, shouting at the top of her voice. "Clang, clang, clang, where's the bleedin' fire then?! I'll piss on it and put it out for ya!"

PC Spicer hove into view. He was very pleased to see Cath. He didn't enjoy his job at the moment, spending as he did, eight hours a night looking into the darkest courts and alleys looking for a madman. The only man he had had the nerve to confront this night had been a smart-looking gent complete with expensive looking gold watch and chain, wearing a Derby hat, carrying a large leather bag.

Friendly chap. Doctor, 'ence the bag. They might charge the earth, but you 'ad to 'and it to 'em, coming out on a night like this riskin' life and limb in the foulest of rookeries, with a madman on the loose to boot. Nice leather case. Didn't look in; wouldn't a bin right. I leaves that sort a fing to me sergeant.

Spicer had arrested him as a matter of course, as per his orders to arrest anyone he came across in the early hours, but after a few questions at Bishopsgate police station by his sergeant, he had been allowed to go on his way, leather case unopened.

Spicer could have hugged Cath. The easiest of collars, and if he played his cards right, he could spin the arrest out till it was nearly the end of his shift. She collapsed in a heap just as he got to her. He had the devil's own job half dragging her to his police station, and normally he would have been furious. He would have been quick to give her a good tap with his tightly rolled up raincoat, which served as a soft truncheon for clipping children and drunks around the head when they were guilty of minor misdemeanours. But he was patience personified on this occasion – the longer it took the better as far as he was concerned, and she was making such a din that no self-respecting knife-wielding madman would come near or far.

Cath was let out of a Bishopsgate police station cell at 1am, when she would not be able to get a drink anywhere. She had sobered up a little but was still in cheeky mood as she bade farewell to the release constable, PC Hutt.

"Good night old cock."

Ten minutes later she was at the entrance to Duke Street, at the bottom of which was a covered alley called Church Passage, which led into Mitre Square, which was on her way home. She saw a man looking at her and recognised him.

"Want some business Joe? You're taking a bit of a chance ain't ya? On the streets at this time a night."

The man was a Jewish cigarette salesman called Joseph Lawende. He scuttled away without answering her. A couple of minutes later there were two more men on the street, twenty yards apart. She never did see one of them. The other approached her and after a short negotiation, agreed a price and what was to be done. He was a gent; she might be able to change a sov. She felt in her pocket for her shiny farthings; he looked forward to opening his leather bag.

CHAPTER 2:

"The story is full of hope for the future, illustrating as it does the immense power that lies in mere publicity."
William Stead, Pall Mall Gazette

1871 Whitechapel:

The world's oldest profession was never entered into lightly. It was the last port of call for the desperate women whom society had failed. A prostitute would become an outcast, treated with contempt by all. Many were part-timers, spending some of their time earning a pittance for long hours of tortuous work in the sweated labour of respectable jobs. Some attempted to live a double life of apparent respectability, keeping their night work a secret.

Maud Nash was such a woman. She kept her ex-stevedore husband, unable to work after a bad injury from a fall into a ship's hold, and their seven children, out of the workhouse by spending every spare minute of the day working in the sweated industries, before dragging her aching body onto the streets to pleasure rough trade. She walked an exhausting mile each evening before applying her rouge; her 'for hire' light, to make sure she was not spotted by any neighbours. Nobody knew, least of all her husband. Such women did not use a ponce to protect them, and even seventeen years before the grim reaper appeared in the guise of Jack The Ripper, disappearing down a dark alley with some filthy specimen was fraught with potential danger.

Maud had just serviced such a man, who gave her a gratuity of a punch in the face after an argument over payment. She staggered into the light and was soon the subject of unwelcome attention from the local policeman on his beat. In her highly upset state, she made the mistake of telling him who she was, and it was obvious to the bobby what had happened and why. Wheels were set in motion and before she knew where she was, her husband had been informed of everything.

He might not have been fit to work twelve hours a day in a back-breaking job, but he was certainly able enough to beat his wife within an inch of her life. Or he would have been, but for the intervention of their oldest child, the thirteen year old Alexander. He was a big boy for his age, already a gang-member with a score of crimes under his belt, and he wasn't scared of anyone or anything.

His father had already rained a number of blows on his mother. Alexander had heard the gist of the story and along with the other children had made himself scarce, out in the yard. His father regularly hit his mother so it was nothing new. There were the usual shouts and abuse, screams of panic and pain, the noises of fist on face, scuffling boots on floorboards and furniture being flung to all parts. But then there was a sudden eerie silence. It wasn't right. Young Nash crooked his head round the door to see his father strangling his mother; his two thumbs pushing into her throat as she gurgled, tongue lolling out, staring bug-eyed back at her attacker.

The entire boy's weight hit his father at speed; his right shoulder thundering into the man's back, knocking the breath out of him. The three of them fell to the floor. The woman rolled away heaving as she tried to get her breath, while the father and son fought on the floor. The bigger man was getting the better of it until young Nash caught him with a straight-fingered jab to this throat. It was now his turn to fight for his breath. The boy got quickly to his feet and waded in with his boots, aiming at the man's head. He would have killed his father that day but for his mother flinging herself on the prone body of her husband, screaming hoarsely at her son.

Young Nash left and never saw his parents again. He joined a kidsman's pickpocket gang. He planned to go back and see his mother some time, but it wasn't long before he heard that his family had been packed off to the workhouse.

Like all families entering the workhouse system, they were split up, Nash's father going to the men's ward, his mother to the women's and the children sent to the pauper's school miles away after a short period in the probationary ward to ensure they weren't carrying any infections. The two parents never saw each other or any of their children again, the physical health of the father and mental health of the mother, having faded fast within the debilitating inhumanity to man.

One of young Nash's fellow boy pickpockets told him from first hand experience what happened when his own father had presented himself to the workhouse, in the forlorn hope of receiving outdoor relief. He had faced the Guardians of the workhouse in a meeting that resembled a criminal trial, standing in the dock of a board room, a large horseshoe table of men surrounding him on all sides.

"The House!" had been the lofty decry of the chairman, before the man had even stated his case.

"They don't look, they don't listen Nashey," complained the little urchin.

"They will do one day boy, you mark my words, you see if they don't," came the determined answer.

☞ ◆ ☜

September 29th 1888:

Being tall and broad-shouldered with a countenance which transmitted menace was very useful in Alexander Nash's world. And he optimised his potential. He looked after himself; didn't drink alcohol to excess, other than when he needed to down a few 'tighteners' in a pub to glean some information from someone. He even trained his body like he had heard those public school boxers did when they were about to take on an East End boy in front of a baying crowd of drunken costers down the Radcliffe Highway on a Saturday night. Plenty of meat; push-ups; even some running. As a boy he remembered his father telling him the story of how Tom Cribb, the unbeatable back in the old days, once almost lost to 'sum black American fella 'alf 'is size cos 'e 'adn't looked after 'isself properly'. He had looked after himself after that scare and won the rematch comfortably.

But in Nash's world you could not afford to make one mistake. There were no second chances. You wouldn't just lose a fight; you would end up dancing on the end of a rope, or worst still in prison for the rest of your life.

The menace had come naturally. He had always been able to impose his will on people with a glower and a slight lowering, deepening or raising of the voice according to the situation. Even when he was simply chewing the cud with drinking mates (he had no true friends), just a slight enthusiasm for the subject about which he was speaking could have tough mean men cowering in submission. You didn't argue with, or show disrespect to Nashey. He was a nasty bit of work.

But this had its drawbacks. Menace drew fear, demanded attention. People kept their eye on him. They averted their gaze but they were watching nonetheless. He was noticed. This was a problem when one of your many pieces of business was following people with a view to relieving them of their valuables when an opportune moment occurred.

Nash was well aware of this. He always made sure that when he committed a crime, it was unseen. He couldn't simply give someone a 'facer in the chops' on a busy street and make off with their Hunter pocket watch. There must not be any witnesses.

Nobody who knew him would say anything to the police; the poverty stricken had no liking or respect for authority, and besides, who would dare say anything about Nash. But there were all sorts on the streets these days, thanks to the Whitechapel murders. People who lived part-time in the East End, but whom were not of the East End. There were plain clothes, as well as uniformed police, and middle class charity workers all over the East End in general, and Whitechapel in particular. It would only take a bit of bad luck; a soup kitchen helper perhaps, or a plain clothes crusher to be looking his way at just the wrong minute, and he could have his collar felt.

From a professional point of view, Nash did not like the increase of policing in his neighbourhood, and he thought many of the philanthropists such as the Salvation Army did more harm than good, but on balance he greatly approved of what was happening in the East End at the moment. The success of the Match Girl's Strike, the first ever success of a woman's trade union, just two months before the murders had began, had shown him the importance of publicity. One little story highlighting the appalling working conditions of the girls in an obscure little ha'penny newspaper, and public support for the girls' grievances grew apace. And that was as nothing compared to the fuss being stirred up by the press about these murders. The newspapers were sensationalising everything, but that was no bad thing as far as Nash was concerned. Every gory detail of the murders and the conditions in the area they were being perpetrated in, 'Darkest Whitechapel', forced the middling classes to sit up and take notice. Nash didn't care whether it was middling class guilt, or fear of uprising that was causing the East End to be the focus of national attention; he simply knew that people couldn't look the other way any longer.

Nash was thus content to overcome his more difficult working conditions. He followed potential targets for as long as it took, till they disappeared up an alleyway, and nowadays he only worked at night or when the foggy miasma came down. But that had inherent problems too. Noise travelled at night. It was even worse in the fog when there were few cabs rattling over the cobbles to drown the sound of footsteps. And people were more aware, their every sense heightened by the need to find their way whilst fearful of the unseen; of what might be lurking in the shadows. The sound of a single pair of footsteps following them sounded every bit as sinister as indeed it was in this case.

He had made-to-order boots of soft kid-like leather that didn't make any noise when he walked. The boots gave him no support and felt paper-thin. He could feel every crack in every cobble. He would curse, 'me dogs a barkin' by the time he got home after a night walking the streets.

Nash lived in a model dwelling, just off the Commercial Road in Berner Street, Whitechapel. Model dwellings had been built for the poor but the charitable trusts who owned them were profit-making, and as land prices rose, rents were raised to ensure profits, which made the housing unaffordable for most of the very people for whom they were built. And even those who could afford to pay were not prepared to put up with the list of regulations; no homework allowed in case it was an offensive trade such as fur-pulling or gluing; no dogs, no paintings, no wallpapering or pictures on walls, no washing hung outside, no children playing in corridors or stairwells, no sharing or sub-letting, curfew – main door locked and gas supply turned off at 11pm.

The Peabody Trust, who owned this property, barred tenants with earnings over thirty shillings a week or under twelve shillings a week and they had to pay in advance and provide an employer's reference. Middle class female charity workers were used to collect the rent. They were nicknamed the 'petticoat government'. Nash wasn't eligible for such a place, but he was on friendly nodding terms with the local vicar at St Judes, Samuel Barnett, who put a word in, and as they couldn't fill the places anyway and he could be relied upon to pay the rent…

He got a good quality forged employer's letter written by a screever, and everyone was content. Perversely the curfew was ideal for a nocturnal animal like Nash. He paid the manager to look the other way, and had a key made so he could come and go as he pleased. He had few neighbours due to the unpopularity of the place, and those who did live there were safely tucked away for the night by the time he crept home from a night's work. He never saw anyone from one week to the next, and more importantly nobody saw him.

Saturday night was Nash's busiest and most profitable time of the week. He slid quietly out of his abode as usual, but as he turned from locking the main door behind him, an affluent-looking man, in a hurry, almost bumped into him. The man was glaring down the street and barely noticed the large man just alighting from his door who had to dodge adroitly to avoid him. Nash peered quizzically at the man's back as he sped off.

There was something not quite right about this man. In the brief moment he had seen his face, Nash had noted that he was distinguished, with a slightly puffy florid face, from overindulgence perhaps; expensive shoes, a neat haircut beneath a smart Derby hat and the complexion and general look and swagger of a man who certainly didn't live or work in the degradation and squalor of the East End. He was carrying a good sized leather bag; a doctor's bag perhaps? It wasn't a Gladstone, which was their usual type of bag, but it was close enough. Nash had also noticed from a professional's sharp glimpse of the clothes beneath a flapping open overcoat, a middle-class man's suit complete with gold watch and chain. It was raining stair-rods now, a filthy night. But not an hour earlier it had been a warm Indian summer's evening, on which someone with even the most delicate constitution would not wear such a coat. And this man may have left his distant well-to-do neighbourhood when it was still dry. The man was striding out, almost at a march, with his eyes peeled, continually scanning the ground ahead of him. He was far too preoccupied to notice anyone following him. Nash's curiosity was aroused.

A simple plan was hatched.

Foller 'im till 'e's well away from me own doorstep, which at the rate 'e's goin' won't be long, wait for 'im to get in an empty unlit part a the street, give him a facer an' make orf with wot I can lay me 'ands on. The gold watch an' chain first job a course.

But Nash wanted to see what the man might be up to first. There might be more profit in waiting. A little blackmail perhaps if he saw the gent involved in something untoward. Nash then spotted that the man was doing some following of his own. He was on the prowl for prostitutes. Nash smirked with contempt. The man was just a customer, nervously trying to decide which poor wretch he was going to use. The man had approached one, a pretty young thing, but suddenly moved away from her as if horrified.

Poor lit'le cow not good enough for 'is lordship ay? Doin' 'im when the time comes will be a right pleasure. Even if it were blackmail, not robbin', I'll do 'im any'ow.

A minute later the gent homed in on another street-walker, who seemed to be more to his liking, and they moved off together, looking for a quiet alley or court.

The doctor's case and its contents could be valuable. Nash had robbed men with their trousers metaphorically down on many occasions; literally down once or twice. Easy pickings; and it was always good to rob such men. He would use a little more force than was necessary and give them one extra kick in the ribs as he left. This neat little man with his neat little suit would spend a little time kissing the cobbles. The gentleman would eventually stagger home to tell his wife and cronies of how he went to the aid of a poor respectable girl being attacked by some ruffian and succeeded in saving her from a fate worse than death, but only at the expensive of a bloodied nose, broken rib and much mauve skin. This hero would write to the self-appointed eugenics mouth-piece Arnold White, about the growing problem of the underclass; an inferior race of the undeserving poor; the residuum that should be gradually eradicated by sterilisation so that respectable people could walk the streets at night. Such a man would not see the irony.

Nash's thoughts returned to the matter at hand. He had to be careful with this crime. He didn't want the woman seeing his face. Most men, when robbed in such a situation, would scuttle away into the night with their tail, amongst other things, tucked between their legs. But occasionally one of them might accuse the girl of being an accomplice to the crime and start knocking her about. Voices would be raised and before you knew it, a policeman's Bullseye lantern was lighting up the sorry scene. The only chance the girl had to extricate herself from the situation without seeing the magistrate the next morning was to tell the crusher who had perpetrated the crime. Nash was a well known face in those quarters – either the prostitute would recognise him, or the policeman might from her description. If the former, he couldn't rely on the normal rule of not telling the police anything. The girl would have to do what she had to do. That's why she was selling herself on the streets in the first place.

The couple disappeared into a dark alley. Nash was quickly on the corner looking on, with just his head crooked around the wall of the alley, well hidden in the darkness. After a short negotiation, the prostitute and client moved into a dark slum court off the alley, out of sight of Nash. They had moved because they had been standing beneath a street lamp; a little more privacy was needed. This was awkward. If Nash moved towards them they would see him under the street light long before he saw exactly where they were, and the court was overlooked by two-storey slums. Somebody looking out of a window could see him commit the robbery.

He decided on a different tactic. He would wait for the man to finish his business, after which he would be in a hurry to get away, and would leave the girl to attend to herself. She would want to take out her sponge in the privacy of the court as soon as the client had gone. There would be time for Nash to cosh and rob the man in the dark part of the alley just after the man had passed by the gas lamp. By the time the girl appeared he would be gone. He would not have time to give the man the extra kick in the ribs, but maybe the girl would as she stepped over him on her way to rinse out his residue. Nash liked to think so.

The time dragged.

Blimey 'e's taking his bleedin' time ain' 'e. I'm standin' 'ere like two ov eels!

Nash's mind wandered, thinking of the most recent occasion he had himself been attacked. It was an occupational hazard for anyone in his line of business. There were always others out there looking to wreak violence for exactly the same reason as him. The hunter became the hunted. There had been two of them. He had left them both lying in much pain on the cobbles. It would have been worse for them, but he saw how young and poverty-stricken they looked.

Jus' lads with their arses 'anging out their trousers, tryin' to earn a crust.

The memory made him angry.

There was movement. The man had re-entered the alley and was coming towards him. Nash's fingers curled around the cosh inside his right pocket. While his mind had been wandering he had not been his usual alert self, but instinct now told him to have a quick 'butcher's' along the street before making his move.

Christ almigh'y, a soddin' crusher!

A policeman was walking towards him. He wasn't taking any particular interest in Nash and would soon pass by and be gone, so the attack was only postponed for a minute or two. Turning towards the officer, Nash felt in his left pocket for a dog-end and a Lucifer match, both of which he kept there for precisely moments like this, struck the match on the brickwork of the street wall, curled both hands around it and lit the cigarette remains. He then walked towards the policeman, looked straight ahead till almost in front of him before glancing his way casually, momentarily as he passed. It was exactly what an innocent man just going about his business would do. The uniformed man returned the glance but no more than that, and carried on making his way down the street. Nash feigned the cigarette going out, clicking his tongue with irritation as he stopped to relight it, turning his body slightly as he cupped his hands again, and glanced back.

The constable stopped suddenly. Nash cursed to himself, but then let out his breath in relief when he saw why the uniformed man had stopped. He was unfurling his raincoat. Nash pitied the poor drunk who stumbled across this crusher's path in tonight's rain. Suitably attired against the elements, the policeman turned the next corner and was out of sight. There was thankfully no sign of the gent. Nash surmised his quarry had obviously spotted the crusher too, and retreated back into the hidden court with the prostitute waiting for the coast to clear.

Nash would have to move quickly now to catch him before he exited from the alley. He started to retrace his steps but within a second the gent appeared from the alley, looking about him in all directions, eyes wide open, staring wildly. He made eye-contact with Nash, who immediately averted his gaze, put his head down and carried on walking past. He felt the man's stare burrowing into the back of his head, before he heard footsteps moving off in the opposite direction.

Nash crossed the street at once, so he had an angle to look in the direction of the footsteps without actually turning around. The man was scuttling away quickly, head down just as Nash would have expected. But suddenly he slowed to a stroll and straightened, stretching his neck out like a clerk in a collar a size too small. He then loosened his vice-like grip of the bag in his right hand, as if making a conscious effort to return his countenance back to the dignified look of a man of letters. He was now apparently on a Sunday afternoon stroll in the park, a man at ease with the world and his place in it. Nash looked on with a grim expression on his face.

Bleedin' amazin' wot a quick bit a tail can do ain' it.

The immediate moment to strike had gone, but Nash was determined to get this smug respectable bastard. He would follow him till the moment was again right to pounce. Nash re-crossed the street so he was back on the same side as the gent. In the lit main street, he was too close for the moment, so ducked down the same alley where the man had just had his pleasure, to wait a few seconds to give some leeway before starting to follow his target again. There was no sign of the woman. She should have been out by now.

'as that bastard 'urt the poor ol' cow?

Nash decided to quickly run along the few yards of the alley to the court and check on her. He had time to return to the street before losing his slow moving prey.

If 'e's 'urt 'er, 'e won't be comin' back 'ere again in 'urry. I'll see a that.

Nash quickly dived down the alley and turned into the court. It was pitch-dark but he could just about make out the dim outline of what appeared to be a pile of scattered old clothes. He took another few steps closer and saw it was the body of a woman. Her clothes had been partly removed. She was dead.

Nash struck a match. The woman had been gutted; sliced open from vagina to breast plate. Her internal organs had been cut out and left in a pile by her side. Her eye-lids had been slit;   lips and jaw sliced; both breast nipples sliced off, as had the tip of her nose and ears. A replacement match of light enabled Nash to note that whilst there was blood, given the horrendous damage done to the body, surprisingly little of it.

He had seen many terrible things, instigated some of them, but this was unlike anything he had ever seen or even imagined. This wasn't right. This was pure evil. He staggered back into the alley, barging into the wall as he went. His legs were weak and his hands trembling, though not as badly as his stomach muscles which were twitching uncontrollably. He got back to the street and stopped to look along it in both directions. No crushers. Nobody else either, except at the very far end of the street, a slow strolling figure in a Derby hat was turning the corner and about to disappear out of sight.

❧　◆　❧

Nash's head was spinning. He started to run after the figure, but he couldn't get his breath. It was like he normally felt at the end of a run round the marshes. He couldn't make any sense of it. What was the matter with him? He had to slow to a fast walk; his head started to clear and his lungs started to fill. He started to feel very uneasy and angry, but he couldn't think straight. This was all too much.

People notice runners, 'specially at night. If yer running, yer bin up ta summin' ain't ya. Dogs bark; chase after yer. Crushers get int'rested. Seen running away from a murder, me neck 'll be stretched for sure, and not like no clerk's in a tight collar neiver.

He stopped at the corner and peered into the next street. The distance between himself and the Derby hat had been halved. A deep lungful of putrid air later, he was on his way after the figure. Nash followed his man along a haphazard route. The man seemed to be doubling back on himself at one point.

Where the 'ell's 'e goin' now? 'e'll be caught for sure if 'e keeps up this lark.

The man then ducked through a doorway and up some unlit stairs. Nash was close on his heels now. The killer stopped under a gaslight and took a piece of rag and a large knife from out of his bag. He used the rag to wipe his hands and then the knife-blade and handle, before tossing the rag, quite deliberately, on the ground.

Nash noticed the man was smiling as he bent down to pick something else out of his bag. It looked like a piece of chalk. The man started to write on the wall by the stairwell. Nash was incandescent.

Bugger me if he ain' started whitewalling! Writin' the poor cow a review is 'e!? I've seen it all now!

It took all Nash's self-control not to march straight into the gaslight and cosh the killer right there where he stood, chalk in hand. The man's large knife was, however, still in his left hand, and Nash wasn't about to march into the light and give the killer any chance to use the weapon on him. He would wait for the man to finish his scribbling so he could attack him in the darkness as soon as he stepped out of the gaslight.

The graffiti artist finished his work and calmly tossed the chalk and the knife into his bag, closed it, picked it up and started on his way. A thought struck Nash like a lightning strike. He allowed his quarry to pass by, no more than a few feet away, untouched.

He had made a profound decision.

Nash's thin shoes took him silently across to the wall. It seemed to read:

'The Juwes are the men That Will not be Blamed for nothing'.

It made no sense. He squinted and got closer. The loopy writing on a wall whose mortar and brickwork was crumbling, and the poor lighting, made it difficult to tell.

Were it James or Juwes? Juwes, that's not 'ow yer spell Jews. But the rest's spelt right enuff so 'e knows what 'e's about when 'e were writin' alright. All very queer and there's the troof.

He peered after the man disappearing back down the stairs. Nash's blood was pumping rapidly round his body and into his head; he felt strangely hot, almost giddy, and could hear his heart pounding as if it was trying to leap out of his chest. He nipped down the stairs and for the third time that night, started following the man in the Derby hat. He reached a street-corner and for the first time since leaving the stairwell, such had been his concentration on following the killer, he became aware of his surroundings. He was at the corner of the market and could see coster stalls along the length of the street, full of prone costermongers asleep on their stalls, with their wares scattered around them, though even this early there was already sign of life, with some of them starting to set up. It was Middlesex Street, otherwise known as Petticoat Lane, the main thoroughfare through this part of Whitechapel to Liverpool Street Station.

The station...

Nash's thoughts turned away from his prey. This end of Whitechapel, known as Spitalfields, was remarkably close to Liverpool Street station. One moment it was possible to be in a low common lodging house full of the dregs of humanity, or tripping over the body of a hacked to death prostitute, and the next you could be walking past a growler which dropping a party with first class tickets to Frinton-on-Sea.

But there would be no cabs full of the well-heeled at this time of night. The station would be deserted save for the human flotsam and jetsam who lived, worked and slept in or around the station. Once the body was found, there would be police all over the place, but Nash doubted they would make enquiries at the station before daylight. He would head for the station; get a couple of hours' sleep in amongst the human misery, before sliding off home in the safety of the crowds that daylight brought.

The Derby-hatted man was making his way oh so calmly down the middle of the street rather than the pavement so as not to have to pick his way through the stalls. Nash was close behind. Too close. He stopped and waited, staring after the retreating figure until he realised he was lit up under a gas lamp for the world to see. This brought him back to his senses, his trained response to get out of the light and into the shadows got him moving again. But he was still drawn to the figure like a moth to a flame. He could not take his eyes off him. Nash was now moving much quicker than his target but was sticking to the pavement for cover, so had to hop over and around various stalls, stock and appendages, so he was only closing the gap between them slowly. The Derby-hatted figure reached a front door, took out a key, and whilst putting it in the lock of the shabby old slum, casually looked back along the street. The man was too determined to act nonchalant to make the look more than just a cursory glance, so the dark shape of a large man in the shadows, thirty yards from him wasn't seen. The man bent down to check something on the floor just inside the room for a brief moment.

Now what the 'ell's 'e doin'?

His quarry seemed satisfied and disappeared inside.

It was time to walk on. Liverpool Street station was no more than a couple of minutes walk away. A police whistle was bound to pierce the air any minute and then all hell would break loose. But Nash stayed where he was. He slid down onto his backside, his back leaning against a shop frontage, put his legs up on a costermonger's stall to rest his ever-aching feet, and started to ponder.

It mus' be the Whitechapel murderer. 'e ain't but firty yard away. That tat'y old door's on its last. Wouldn't stop me would it. I'd 'ave to watch that knife ov 'is mind, but I could 'ave the Whitechapel murderer by the froat an' that'll be that. Top the cowson right there where 'e stood, quiet – cosh 'im, strangle 'im, then scarper in ta the night?

That would have ended the reign of terror over East End women who had long been degraded, abandoned and ostracised by the respectable classes, the men of whose ranks did not want to know about prostitutes, though when it suited, knew very well where to find them. But this maniac was grabbing Victorian hypocrisy by the chin and thrusting its face into the mire.

Open door, dead body covered in blood not its own, doctor's bag with a blood-stained knife in it, less than a quarter mile from a gut'ed 'ore. Even the crushers an' Abberline's tecs runnin' round after their own tails lookin' for the killer should be able to work that one out! And who did fer the killer any'ow? What a mystery that'd be if yer please! Or praps I jus' gives 'im a little tap to subdue 'im and then shouts out for a crusher?

Nash smirked at this ridiculous idea. No crushers.

He thought about the information he now possessed. It was gold dust.

I keeps it to meself and uses it when I needs it. If I gets me collar felt, or has some other big reason to make a bargain about anyfin' with any cove, I gives up the man in the Derby 'at. Nah, that ain' right. There's only one reason not to top the bastard this second.

And Nash most certainly had it.

He would pay a few noses to keep watch on the place and follow its occupant to collect information about the man and keep Nash informed of his comings and goings. In no time he would have a name, place of work and all sorts of useful knowledge on the killer.

James, Levi or whatever his bleedin' name were.

The murderer's behaviour sprung back into his thoughts.

What were that whitewallin' all about? Juwes or James would not be blamed for nuffin'.

Everyone in Nash's world agreed that a Jew must be responsible for the murders. Hadn't the first suspect, Leather Apron, been a Jew, and it was said no true blooded Englishman could commit such crimes. It was about the only thing the people of the East End did agree with the police about.

Why would a Jew-boy murderer tell the weld the killer's a Jew, and then spell the word Jews wrong? An' any'ow, it could a said James, not Juwes. Jim's a used enuff name but nobody round 'ere's ever called no James. But the middlin' sorts used the name and the Derby-topped devil firty yard away 'ad the stamp of a middling feller alright.

The shrill blast of a police whistle sliced through the darkness.

Sod it, the body's bin found.

Nash was up and walking as casually as he could in the direction of the railway station. Casual walking when the heart was pumping ten to the dozen and the brain was saying 'run!' was quite a skill. He had seen a master of it a few minutes ago, and a couple of seconds later he approached the door behind which stood that master.

There was no number on the door but Nash noted that there was a coloured rag on a stick above the entrance. This was effectively the address for the postman and from now, Nash's noses too. He noted that the next door had an old boot in the window, the next a hieroglyph on it. They couldn't fail to find the right place. There was no need for him to risk returning there to point it out to them. The dullest of light, probably a single candle, peaked through a gap in the newspaper-curtained window, but the glass was so caked in filth, there was nothing to see. And even if there had been, Nash would not have noticed it. He had crossed to the other side of the street, eyes averted. He had just let the Whitechapel murderer go, and he felt content about it.

CHAPTER 3:

"In a room perhaps 12 feet by 10...we find several girls and women packed together, stitching without a moment's pause... while the tailor heats irons at a coke fire and presses the seams, filling the air with steam;...too often, the room in which the trade is carried on is that in which the family eats and sleeps also."

The Evils of Home Work for Women in Investigation Papers, Women's Co-operative Guild

Sookey Parsons lived in dark, narrow little Widegate Street, next to the Jewish Band of Guardians, opposite the ale and pie house. Just fifty yards from the Bishopsgate thoroughfare, it was the closest she could live to the prosperity of the City of London and Liverpool Street station, yet still be in what had just started to be called 'slums'. The term was an improvement; she had never cared for 'rookeries', and what it implied. Sookey had money; not a great deal after her recent financial debacle, but she certainly didn't need to live in such surroundings. But she wanted the anonymity of the poverty stricken and even more importantly wanted to be of the slums, not merely a visitor to them, as she had in the past, both in India and here. She wanted to be accepted by the local populace as one of them, and in so doing, cease to be what she had always been.

Though she chose to live amongst the poor, she also felt the need to be able to escape quickly to her old world, albeit just for the odd hour or two, when life got unbearable. She allowed herself one great luxury when life got on top of her. The one thing she missed of her old life was drinking best quality coffee. She couldn't abide the pond water that passed for coffee in Whitechapel. So on occasion she ventured out of the slums, in her one clean dress, to a fine coffee house on the Strand. She would meet an old acquaintance, Nora. This woman was not really a friend, but all her so-called friends had deserted her or she had chosen to drop them because she would have felt awkward in their company. Sookey felt more comfortable with Nora, partly because she wasn't close to her but also because this woman had never judged her. They would pass a pleasant hour making the sort of small talk middle class ladies were so well versed in, without ever venturing onto the sort of ground that real friends might discuss. This suited Sookey very well. And there was never any question of visiting each other's homes.

Nora knew Sookey had been financially ruined, but she also knew Sookey had an army officer's widow's pension and had not had to seek a position, so she assumed she must still be at least comfortable. Sookey lied about her circumstances and lifestyle, but it was important to her to bend the truth or exaggerate rather than tell outright lies when she could, and when she did have to tell lies, she kept them as white as possible.

Sookey lived in the City close to Liverpool Street station (the second part was true); she spent a lot of her time in the slums helping people (true); she was a close friend of Reverend Barnett and his wife Henrietta (more just friendly work colleagues really); and lectured at the reverend's centre for the help and improvement of the poor, Toynbee Hall (she handed out soup and coffee, had set up an impromptu art gallery, and did some literacy classes rather than lectured as such). At the end of the hour, Nora returned to her eight-bedroom house in Barons Court which she shared with her husband, two children and six servants; Sookey returned to a one-bedroom slum in Whitechapel, where she lived alone. There were eight bedroom houses in the neighbourhood, where over fifty people lived, up to eight to a room. Sookey appreciated very well how lucky she was.

Even though she kept her room relatively spotless, it was impossible to keep anything completely clean and fresh in the grime of slum life. There was filth in the air, and her room was damp. She had a reciprocal arrangement with an illiterate Jewish tailor. He kept a dress for her in immaculate condition at the back of his workshop, and she in return wrote anything he needed. Advertising-related mostly, though she also wrote the odd private letter for him, and read him any answers received.

The first time she took the dress from the tailor she changed into it in the public washhouse in Goulston Street. There was a little drying room there that she could pop in and out of very quickly, and it was the cleanest place in Whitechapel. She did not want to risk getting the dress dirty or picking up any foul odours back in her rooms. But leaving there in the dress was a mistake. The dress turned heads and lost her some of the trust she had built up over the preceding weeks since her first arrival. She was not one of them after all.

Sookey had used the facilities at the washhouse regularly. It had soap, hot water, towels, laundries with washing troughs; boilers, irons, drying horses and mangles. Although provided by a philanthropist, it was not free, so the poorest women were unable to use it, but it was nonetheless an important social as well as work centre. Many women in Sookey's neighbourhood did their laundry and socialised there. Sookey had hoped it would be a place to interact with some of these women. To build, if not friendships, for she appreciated she had little in common with them and completely failed to understand their ribald humour, at least an acceptance, a fellowship.

She found this very difficult at first. The women were friendly enough amongst themselves, the endless gossip and double entendres, none of which she understood, helping pass away the hours of tortuous steamy drudgery. But Sookey had been just as big an outsider as she had always been; worse in fact. When she had been a lady charity worker, a 'slummer', women of the slums had at least been respectful to her, if not particularly communicative.

But lady slummers did not do their own washing in the public washhouse. The women now viewed her with great suspicion. Their initial reaction was to be taciturn with her, and she noticed the atmosphere of the place change dramatically as soon as she walked in. Banter was replaced by glances being exchanged; words were mouthed silently, rather than spoken, behind her back. If she asked a question about how things worked or enquired if anyone was using a piece of equipment, it was met by a curt reply.

"Everyone's finished with it so you can 'ave it but yer too late for 'ot."

But her inability to work much of the equipment, and her obvious general ineptitude, gradually changed the suspicion to amazement and savage sarcasm, and over the weeks eventually to a warmer amusement.

One woman, her next-door neighbour Rose, started helping her with a mix of exasperation and camaraderie. When Sookey failed to grasp how to work a simple mangle, tangling the clothes so the thing was jammed, she was castigated.

"You're an awkward sod ain't yer?! I've never seen anyfin' like it in all me life. Soppy as a box o' lights you are gell!"

She acquired the nickname 'Soppy Sookey'. She occasionally had someone shout across the street to her.

"'ere, SoppayAY!" with the second 'ay' higher pitched and louder than the first, boneman shout-style, that was a common form of friendly greeting from afar.

She had never been spoken to like this in her life before but a moment of shock and effrontery was immediately replaced by a feeling of well-being.

The acquisition of a nickname, albeit derogatory, was a badge of honour. Better called soppy than what she was called in the witness box at the trial. Better the butt of good-natured humour than the barbs of a barrister, playing to the baying crowd up in the gallery, some of whom were supposedly her friends.

Now, here, in this slum, she felt accepted. But some of the women were still suspicious of her.

"She's more ar than eff that one," was said knowingly.

They were convinced nobody could be that stupid. She was putting it on; being crafty; and for what purpose? When she appeared from the drying room wearing a 'hoity toity' frock, and quickly disappeared without so much as a by-your-leave, even the friendliest of the women started to doubt their acceptance of her.

Sookey was keen to explain about the dress, so even though she didn't have much laundry to do, she made a point of returning to the washhouse two days later at a time she knew most of the regulars would be there. She was naïve enough to tell the truth about the dress, explaining she kept it for trips to the West End.

"Cor, you're lucky ain't ya!" was the sarcastic reply.

But the barb flew over Sookey's head. A couple of the natural comedians in the group then started a conversation between themselves using high-pitched approximations of middle-class voices.

"Oh it's so nice to take the air up West at this time of yar, don't you think my dar?"

"Yes indeed my dar, I often pop up to Hampstead Heath for me 'ealth don't yer know."

Sookey giggled at the dropped aitch, but as soon as she had done so realised that the women may take this amiss and frantically hoped they would think she was laughing at herself being mimicked. Luckily the women didn't spot the irony and the moment passed in good humour. But Sookey didn't have the social understanding to quit while she was ahead. She went on to explain that she only kept such a dress so she could take coffee with a friend in the Strand on occasion. It had taken several weeks before she was to be as accepted again.

Sookey now changed in a toilet in Liverpool Street station. She entered the station by the east entrance a pauper and left by the west a lady. She wrapped her ragged clothes in some fine paper and ribbon she kept precisely for this purpose, and passed it off to Nora as her latest frippery purchase. She wondered if Nora ever thought it strange that she never wore any of these purchases, just the same black dress. Did she know of Sookey's life in the slums? Nora did not know; Nora did not want to know.

❦

Prostitution had been the last resort for Mary Kelly. She had run all the errands and done all the jobs expected of a small child. Her first adult work at the age of ten had being doing little jobs for Jewish people on Friday nights such as lighting fires or cleaning their homes in time for the Sabbath. Over the next decade she tried her hand at whatever came along for as long as it lasted or until she missed a day's work through illness and found her job given to someone else. This was a common enough occurrence – the poverty in which she lived and the appalling conditions of most of the sweated labour she did, meant she was permanently suffering from one ailment or another and it was only a question of time before she became so ill that she couldn't get out of bed one day.

Mary had been a feather worker, cinnamon washer, India rubber stamp machinist; she had made cigarettes, magic lantern slides, ties, portmanteaus, surgical instruments, spectacles. 8am to 7pm; 10 or 11 if she could get the overtime. Half day Saturday. Some of the best jobs in terms of the working conditions insisted upon a genteel appearance. Mary had stinted on underclothes and food to meet such a demand, but had fallen ill from near-starvation, and lost such jobs.

The steadiest work was at the Bryant & May factory in Bow, but it involved working with phosphorous. It was nasty stuff and it got everywhere. Food was eaten at the workplace and the caramel gunge that made Lucifer matches was ingested as part of lunch. When a shift ended, pools of fluorescent vomit were deposited by the factory gates by escaping workers. Bryant & May workers also suffered from Phossy Jaw. The jaw decayed with pea-sized fragments of bone falling off. It caused a horrible smell in the mouth, and teeth had to be pulled to arrest it. If workers didn't get it done themselves, a Bryant & May dentist would do it for them if they wanted to keep their job.

Mary suffered with necrosis before she had a chance to get Phossy Jaw. She had swollen cheeks, lips, neck and throat, closing eyes, and her nose and forehead were an area of florid intumescence. Her skin emitted dirty black/grey pus, and she suffered intense fever with delirium, affecting the actions of her mouth, plus nausea and vomiting. She recovered intact, but vowed never to enter the factory again.

She escaped the factory by becoming a home worker in the same industry. She did the 'ins an' outs', making the trays and covers of matchboxes, pasting together strips of magenta paper and thin pieces of wood by brush. They were then put on the floor to dry, forming piles of trays and lids which would be made into matchboxes, tied up with string and returned to factories for tuppence-farthing a gross. She had to work sixteen hours a day just to keep out of the workhouse so she changed to being a canvas worker making blinds for shops; tents and coal sacks. She was paid two shillings for twelve sacks, five shillings and sixpence for ten hammocks, four shillings for large navy sacks. This was fifteen hours a day to keep out of the workhouse. Her last job before becoming a prostitute was a fur-puller. A shilling and a penny for five dozen rabbits skinned. It was filthy work, with fluff everywhere, and when a friend died of consumption brought about by this job, Mary decided anything was better than this. It was ironic she had been too ill to last long enough in the Bryant & May factory to get Phossy Jaw – she still had her looks, so was well placed to become one of the unfortunates, the scorned, the ashamed, the expendable.

She swopped Phossy Jaw, necrosis and consumption for the probability of rheumatism, gout, syphilis and the risk of death at the hands of a maniac.

◈

Sookey and Mary were opposites who attracted. The fiery young prostitute from the East End and the middle class middle-aged West Ender had little in common. Mary's intelligence had seen her learn to read and write a little, despite limited educational opportunities, whilst Sookey was highly educated but she had been a poor student for all that. Mary was shrewd and street wise; Sookey had the naivety of a small child.

They had first met when they had literally bumped into each other buying face powder. A liking for visually striking make-up and hair was something they did have in common. It had been Mary's fault, but she wasn't the sort to apologise to anyone about anything, and rounded on the woman she had absent-mindedly barged into, ready to give as good as she got. But all she saw was a genteel smile.

"I do beg your pardon. It was entirely my fault," Sookey had said earnestly.

Mary had looked her up and down suspiciously with chin pushed forward.

She takin' the rise?

But the look of apparent genuine concern in the woman's face suddenly changed to the warmest of smiles.

"It would seem we share an interest," said Sookey, looking at Mary's make-up and then her own, in their respective hands.

It was the same.

The ice broken, they began the first of numerous conversations together. Sookey had marvelled at Mary's striking lip rouge and asked if she could borrow some until she acquired some of her own. She wanted to rid herself of the look of her previous life.

Yeah, I can see that from that cheek rouge yer got plastered on yerself like sum doll, thought Mary, but she kept those thoughts to herself.

"Give over. This ain' fer the likes a you. There's only two types a women who uses lip rouge, an' them's brasses an' actresses."

"You tread the boards Mary?" It was honest, naïve interest.

She takin' the rise again?

"I do plenty ov actin' alright." There was disgust in Mary's voice.

The two women intoxicated each other. Mary was drawn to Sookey's neediness. Mary had never had any responsibility in her life. She was always the new young girl, in the factory, in the sweat shops, on the streets. The one who had to be shown things; the pretty one to be put in her place, to be jealous of, to resent, to be left out or belittled whenever possible. She was an only child; the still-birth of what would have been her little sister causing internal problems that ended her mother's ability to have children. The distraught woman never thought so, but she had been lucky in one way. Having only one child to feed had kept her family out of the extreme poverty of the rest of the people on her street. As a result Mary had not grown up as malnourished as many, so her inherited good looks had not been withered by starvation.

Mary had thus never been anyone's big sister, but Sookey, though thirteen years her senior and far more sophisticated, which made the age gap appear greater in many ways, brought out Mary's big sister instinct. Sookey was someone who needed protecting; to be looked after; educated in the ways of the world. And she so lacked confidence, but Mary had enough confidence for the two of them. Not that she would allow Sookey to stay as she was. She needed to learn. A day wouldn't go by without Mary good naturedly mock-berating Sookey for some misdemeanour.

"Gawd 'elp us gell, what yer bleedin' gone an' dun now yer daft mare."

The first time Mary had sworn at Sookey, the older woman's flash of effrontery and embarrassment was immediately overridden by warmer feelings. She saw in the sparkle in Mary's eyes that it was Mary's way of telling her that she liked her, accepted her.

Sookey's medical skills had led her to save the life of a little boy with diphtheria. She thought it would break down the barriers she had encountered in the slums, but although the parents were very grateful, and it led to her becoming the unofficial doctor of the neighbourhood, she was disappointed to find that people still didn't award her the acceptance she desperately sought. She remained an outsider to all but her great friend Mary.

Sookey was in awe of the young woman's vivacity in the face of the most appalling poverty. She had to sell her body, which Sookey knew she hated doing with a passion, just to keep herself fed and housed. But she fiercely refused any hint of financial assistance from Sookey.

On a dark drafty Sunday afternoon when Sookey was attempting to take her friend to task for not trying a more respectable line of work, Mary had told Sookey her life story over a bottle of sherry.

Sookey had been given the alcohol by one of her clients in payment for some writing she had done for him, when he hadn't had any money to pay her. Although pleased to see the bottle, especially as sherry was so expensive and therefore quite a luxury item, Mary had been quick to give Sookey one of her many lessons.

"Bleedin 'ell, gell, get their gelt first. Don't do nuffin' till they pays yer. None a my lot 'ould pay me if I let 'em 'ave their way first. They'd scarper an' fetch me a facer fer me trouble if I said summin'."

Sookey was repaying her life skills tutor by providing her with more formal education of her own. She gave her lessons in the three r's. She tried history and geography too, but Mary didn't enjoy those. Sookey had started with the Tudors, thinking her pupil would enjoy, if nothing else, the profound, romantic and bloody tales of Henry the Eighth's wives, the lady Jane, the two Marys and Elizabeth. She was wrong. The only positive remark Mary made was about Lady Jane Grey, although she thought her stupid.

"Soppy cow should 'ave jus' pretended she were one ov us Cafflicks shouldn't she. I 'av to pretend every day or it's me neck in a manner speakin' ain' it. No 'ead or the work'ouse, it's all the same I says."

And although she thought Henry a 'cowson', her greatest vitriol was for his eldest daughter.

"She were a wrong un and there's the troof. Wernt there enuff men choppin' our 'eads orf wivout 'er startin' up. An' all so as she could have a bit a Spanish cock. Women dieing cos a cock, fings don't change much da they?"

No, she couldn't see what the point of knowing about a load of dead coves was. Sookey wasn't sure what the point of history lessons were either if the truth be told. It was just something one always had to learn. Sookey went on to tell Mary where Spain was amongst other things, and she guessed from Mary's name that she might be interested to know something about Ireland, but again she was wrong. Mary's Irish roots must have been a couple of generations or so back because she made a less than flattering comment about her ancestor's country of origin. Xenophobia was one of the many survival techniques of the starving. Our street against the next; our neighbourhood against theirs; the East End, London, England against the world. The country which was failing them, starving and working them to death, received a fierce allegiance from the voteless of the slums.

"I ain' never been furver than a mile out a Whitechapel. Tell a lie, farver took me a King's Cross once ta see the trains when I was lit'le. Filfy 'ole. Come 'ome smovvered in soot! Looked like a bleedin' sweep if yer please! Could a grown turnips in me ears after that! One day I wanna go a Soufend ta see the sea when I can pays for it, but I won't never go a no alien places so I don't see why I should learns about 'em."

Sookey stuck to literacy and arithmetic from then on.

Mary's life story had finished half way through the bottle. Although not always the most tactful of people, she didn't ask Sookey to reciprocate. She surmised that her rather odd friend had some sort of secret she must be running away from, but it was obviously too painful for her to talk about.

CHAPTER 4:

"The gentleman who occupies his spare time in mutilating and murdering in the neighbourhood of Whitechapel, has quite unintentionally done Society a service."

Commonweal

Before she had time to catch up with the gent, Liz Stride had been accosted by Aaron Kosminski, a violent man who wished to sample her wares without paying the requisite sum. Kosminski threw her to the ground, then dragged her back to her feet and was pushing her towards an alley when he spotted another man appear out of the shadows, which was sufficient to send him running off into the darkness. The other man was James Maybrick, wealthy Liverpool cotton merchant down in London on business, who was quick to go to Liz's assistance. He bought the upset woman some grapes from a shop that was still open despite the late hour. When she was sufficiently recovered, he fondled her as he made a financial offer. Maybrick led her into Duffield's Yard, where he throttled her with her own scarf. His business was murdering women.

Witnesses had seen Liz with both men shortly before she died. The police received descriptions that were obviously of a Jew and a gent. Aaron Kosminski became the prime suspect in the case; no description of Maybrick was ever circulated within the police force or in the public domain.

Stride was already dead when Maybrick slashed her throat as she lay, still clutching a small packet of the Nigerian cachous that smokers chewed to conceal the habit. Maybrick was about to start his work, as he called it, in full, when Louis Diemshutz, a seller of cheap jewellery, arrived in the yard with his pony and cart. He interrupted the attack, and the pony veered towards the left wall to avoid an obstruction in their path – the body of Stride. Maybrick lurked in the shadows as a terrified Diemshutz drove his horse off. Maybrick quickly followed, turning left into Commercial Road, then left into Whitechapel High Street.

Maybrick almost bumped into a man coming out of premises at the end of Berner Street, before he continued on into Aldgate, deliberately crossing the boundary between the Met and City police forces. It had been just fifteen minutes since he had left Duffield's Yard when he met Catherine Eddowes.

Within seconds of meeting Cath, he strangled her, cut her throat and with frenzied uncontrolled fury, slashed and mutilated her face, carving the letter 'm' into her eyelids, before moving on to the stomach and internal organs. He also deliberately left a strand of cotton as a joke clue as to his profession but in his frenzy he accidentally dropped a red leather cigarette case by the body; something a poverty stricken woman would never have in her possession. Even if she had pickpocketed such an item, it would have immediately been taken to the nearest pawnbroker shop or receiver. The 'm', the cotton and the cigarette case were all missed as clues by Inspector Abberline's detectives.

Maybrick could not take the direct route back to Middlesex Street because costermongers were already making preparations for the Sunday market. He would be seen for certain. He took a roundabout route into Stoney Lane, across a main road into a parallel side street into Goulston Street and doubled back. He dodged into an arched doorway and up unlit stairs to an out-of-sight landing. He wiped his blood-stained knife and faeces-stained hands on a scrap of material torn from Eddowe's apron and purposely dropped it on the floor to be found later by the police.

Goulston Street was in the Met Police area; Eddowe's body lay in the City. Maybrick was enjoying himself running rings around the police.

He checked his clothing for bloodstains and was surprised, not for the first time, to find few traces. He had mixed emotions about this, being thankful it made him far less vulnerable in those few minutes between leaving the body and reaching the safety of his bolt-hole in Middlesex Street, but also a little disappointed.

I would have liked to see the whore bleed like the pig she was, he thought to himself on more than one occasion.

Maybrick threw the knife into his bag, alongside a piece of chalk.

Remembering why he had brought the chalk, he grinned. His hand dipped into the bag for the little white stick and he wrote on the wall of the landing:

'The James are the men That Will not be Blamed for nothing'.

He took great care to write his name so that it could just as easily be read as Juwes, and had deliberately made a few errors in the writing to compound the apparent miss-spelling. He tossed the chalk in his bag and thought about his handiwork.

Everyone thinks it must be a Jew, because 'no pure blood Englishman could possibly do such a thing' so I have made it so. I do not suppose for one moment that one half of Inspector Abberline's policemen will even spot the spelling mistake on Jews.

⟱ ◆ ⟰

Nash remembered the fuss when Annie Chapman's body was found. Just after the discovery, he had been pulled once by the City police and then again by the Met's boys, just making his way home in the early hours from a night's ratting. He had been lucky he had not been up to anything illegal so he had nothing incriminating on him, least of all blood from assaulting someone. Otherwise he would have been arrested and taken to answer questions in Liverpool Street police station.

There were twice the crushers on the streets these days mind, and that weren't coun'in' gawd knows 'ow many plain cloves were about an' all, and this time I does 'ave summin' to 'ide. 'oo knows what nose-aches might a seen me leavin' that alley where the dead woman were.

To get home Nash would have to cross the City and Met police boundaries again, so it would have been doubly dangerous. The Metropolitan police controlled the whole of London except the square mile of the City, which had its own force. Middlesex Street was the boundary.

The boundary! Blimey! Were that chance or were the killer being a clever bastard? Live in the City, kill in the Met? 'ome to Middlesex Street while one lot a crushers is runnin' round chasin' shadows and the other lot ain't got a clue what's goin' on first up.

The thought that the killer was not just some madman, probably escaped from an asylum somewhere, but a clever, calculating man, was a chilling one. And Nash had just let this man go. Nash did not like the way his thoughts were going. Better he addressed the matter at hand. He considered knocking on someone's door. Who did he know in Middlesex Street? Polly Nathan, who ran the fish & chip shop; Solran Berlinski, a rag-trader; George Bolam, a cow-keeper; Isaac Wolf, a dealer in playing cards; and Samuel Barnett, the vicar, who also ran Toynbee Hall, the library, the EE Dwelling Company and the local coffee rooms for the poor with his wife Henrietta.

They're all law-abidin' 'cept ol' George. 'e might be keen to earn a few bob as a nose. I could cross 'is palm wiv silver so as 'e keeps 'is lugs and eyes open for the gent 'oo lives in the 'ouse wiv the coloured rag over the door. 'e'd see 'im soon enough, follers 'im an' tells me wot 'e's about. I can get proper noses on the pull then. An' I won't need to make up no tale ta ol' George.

It would be assumed Nash was up to no good, and the gent was about to be relieved of something dear to him, but that was as far as George would think about it. And there certainly wouldn't be any thoughts about linking it with the Whitechapel murders.

Give over!

Nash scolded himself for his stupidity.

If 'e's some gent 'e don't live there does 'e? Course 'e don't. It's a bolt-'ole thas all. Somewhere a dive into ta wash the blood orf, get a new set a cloves on an' lie low while the crushers chase their tails for a while. 'e scarpers orf back to the West End as soon as 'e can. I needs noses 'oo knows the West End an' can 'ang about the gent's 'ouse wivout being moved on.

Nash needed the Middlesex Street bolt-hole and the gent's home, wherever it was, watched every minute of the day from now on. But he could not undertake any of the surveillance himself, just in case the man recognised him from their brief encounter.

Nash decided on second thoughts not to give George a knock. Under normal circumstances George could be relied upon to ask no questions and keep his mouth shut.

But this was not normal. As news of the Whitechapel murderer's latest escapade began to spread, even the most trustworthy might get a little loose with their tongue. Not necessarily even to get a reward, or get the police off their own backs for some misdemeanour. Nash had noticed how people were gaining some sort of glory from association by living in the murder area. They loved talking about it to strangers from outside the area, even with newspaper reporters, implying that they knew something, passing on the latest snippet of rumour as if it was absolute truth. And according to them they all knew the latest victim.

"Known 'er all me life I 'ave. I slept in the next cot in the same lodging 'ouse only larst week I did."

People like his drinking mate Will Roud were actually making a nice little living out of such tale-telling for a few bob, especially out of reporters and apparently nosey bystanders who were probably undercover police. No wonder the completely innocent Leather Apron, a local butcher, was at one time wanted for questioning by the police and for stringing up by vigilantes, on the say so of rumour-mongers.

Nash was delighted with the interest being shown by the newspapers in particular. It was his big opportunity.

But now he needed to get off the streets, without any fuss or anyone seeing him. He slipped into Liverpool Street station and settled down amongst the human misery, just one more anonymous, filthy pile of clothes amongst many others.

He thought back to the mutilated body he had just seen not an hour ago. It was strange that there wasn't much blood given the cuts, gouges and slashes inflicted. And come to think of it, the last time he was in the Ten Bells, Will Roud, had told him that he had bribed a couple of young constables guarding the murder scene whilst Annie Chapman's body still lay there under a sheet, waiting to be taken away by the morgue wagon, to let him ''ave a quick butcher's.'

Will had been surprised too, not to say had his gruesome interest disappointed, by the lack of blood.

"There were so much may'em goin' on, what wiv most ov the coppers being used to push the crowds back, I was able to slip in sharp. Course, I could 'ave been the murderer back to swipe something back, but the two crushers right in front were so green they let me in for a couple a bob. And I don't mean green like they were wet behind the ears neiver, though they were right enuff – it would have been their jobs if I'd been caught gawpin', and I'd 'ave paid more. Got me money back and some, charging the weld an' 'is wife tuppence for the gruesome de'ails. 'ad to make a lot ov it up right enuff; there weren't nuffin' much to see. Any'ow, green ta the gills these young crushers were. Seen the body they 'ad, before the sheet were put over. I couldn't but take the rise out ov 'em. Said to 'em after, two bob for that? Blimey yer see worse down the Highway most Sa'urday nights! Don't spose you been down there yet 'ave ya boys? I did larf."

This memory left Nash pondering.

So 'ores don't bleed much? Why not, they're 'uman after all. They're 'uman all right. More 'uman than most of their customers and there's the troof.

Should he have apprehended the killer? He did not like this subject. His thoughts returned to the subject of blood. Syphilis?

Praps if you've got syphilis yer blood don't run as quick or summin'? Ol' Rev Barnett's an educa'ed man. Wonder if he knows summin' about blood? But what a subject ta put ta the vicar I arst yer!

Nash had a better idea. He had heard of a middling slummer woman who now lived full time in Whitechapel.

Fallen on 'ard times by all accounts. Ain' we all gell? 'elps out at Toynbee 'all for nuffin', and earns a livin' as a scribe, copying documents for lawyers, signwritin' an' all sorts.

Sid Beamish, a pickpocket Nash had worked with on occasion, had once told him that she was also being paid well below the going rate as a screever by assorted villains to forge credentials and certificates, write letters of recommendation, hard-luck begging petitions and the like, without her knowing she was involved in any kind of chicanery. She amused Sid no end.

"Does doctorin' for free if yer please an' speaks wiv the queerest voice you've ever 'eard. She's tryin' a put on some sort ov Whitechapel talk 'alf the time, and forget'ing 'erself an' talkin' like lady muck the other 'alf. 'as a rum name an' all. Sookey. What sort a name's that ay?!"

The crucial piece of information about her as far as Nash was concerned was that she did doctoring. If she has medical knowledge, she should know about blood, and from what he had heard, it should be easy enough to wangle information out of this gullible woman on the telling of some tall tale she would swallow hook, line and sinker. He would make his way over to the Ten Bells later. Even if Sid wasn't in there, someone would know where he might find her.

It was getting daylight now and Nash was just starting to think about making his way home, when the first murmurings of murder arrived in the station. The amorphous huddle of snoring, torpid humanity had burst into animated life within seconds. The news spread through numerous souls before an excited little urchin ran up to him with eyes wide open.

"e's only gone an' done two of 'em this time! Over in Whitechapel again!"

Nash cuffed the boy hard round the ear. He waited for the boy to ask him what he had done that for, but the boy simply looked sheepishly at him. Perhaps he understood, but Nash doubted it. The boy moved away to inform the next stinking pile of rags of his news. Nash resisted the temptation to call the boy back to explain his news.

Two? Woss the soppy little sod shoutin' about?

Within minutes the station was abuzz with hysteria, fear, horror, disgust, anger. Nash was the only person registering bemusement.

A few city policemen came into the station and started asking questions, which Nash took as his prompt to disappear; not all the exits had yet been manned. He sauntered away from the station, mingling in with people making their way to Petticoat Lane Sunday morning market.

He was stopped several times by people he knew, eager to discuss the latest horrors. They were quick to fill him in with all the gory details, only some of which he knew for a fact, were true. The lad had been right. Two murders, the first clearly just a few seconds before he had first set eyes on the killer. And now everybody in the area was being asked if they had seen something. Woe-betide him if they had.

Nash needed to get his head down for a sleep but living in the very street, off which, the first murder of the night had taken place, meant that he was sure to be stopped by the police if he wasn't careful. He had a story ready but who knows what they might already know and missing a night's sleep was not a good preparation for answering awkward questions from suspicious policemen. It was decided to take a round-about route home which took him away from the murder sites for a while. Word would spread like wildfire and a crowd was sure to gather soon enough, as close to the bodies as the police allowed. On nearing home, Nash could blend into the Berner Street crowd trying to gawp into Duffield's Yard, before easing off into the safety of his lair.

But before that, he had to act quickly. His quarry might be leaving his bolt-hole any time. He needed him watched and, when the time came, followed straight away. Nash thought of two men who both lived the other side of the hospital, on his planned route home. He would knock them up. One was just the man he needed in one way; one was ideal in another. He would use them both.

Nash took a long but far from haphazard route home, via whatever roads looked the quietest and least likely to have the police running about. This turned out to be through Shoreditch, past the Jewish burial ground and round the back of the London Hospital, before stopping off to knock up his valued accomplice, Khan, and someone he was far less well disposed to, an old acquaintance of his, Shanks. He had given Shanks some orders, before stopping off at Will Roud's to tell him that if anyone from the law asked, he was with him all night. Will and Nash went back years together. Will was the closest Nash had to a male friend.

"I was 'ere indoors on me own all night. If I tells 'em we were 'ere togevva all night they're fink we's a couple a brown'atters," Will had complained.

Nash had told him in no uncertain terms that he didn't want any arguments. The story was they were playing cards all night.

Nash had tried to catch up with some sleep whilst he laid low on Sunday morning, waiting for the dust to settle. He hadn't lit a candle, lest some light would escape under the door, telling the outside world someone was home. There had been several knocks on his door, one of which had been by the police, but he hadn't stirred from the darkness. When not in a fitful sleep, he had spent the time mapping out in his mind his course of action; and inaction.

He drifted quietly out on to the street at noon and made his way to The Chimney Sweep, a faded relic of an old gin palace of the lowest order, in Church Lane, a main street bordering Brick Lane. There were always some noses in there of his acquaintance at any given time, and he wanted to sound them out about this odd middling woman he had heard tell of. But he had to be artful about it. If you showed interest in anything, people asked themselves why. And if they thought you needed information, they were in a position of power over you.

'Wass it worf?' 'Why d'ya wanna know?' 'Lets me in on it.'

Glances were exchanged, mutterings made. Need was weakness. You never showed need. The information he wanted had to come out as a natural consequence of conversation.

There were a couple of shellfish stalls outside the pub, as well as several Salvation Army people selling the War Cry newspaper and doing their best to intimidate those who looked like entering The Sweep. A couple of noses were just starting to tuck into some oysters. Nash wasn't particularly hungry but saw it as a good opportunity to get talking to the men. He motioned to the stallholder.

"Gis 'alf pint a them whelks, I'm bleedin' starvin'."

Men in Nash's world tended not to use words of greeting. There was no 'good day' or 'how do you do'. Not even a curt nod. They simply started speaking when they wished to start conversing, and would appear to ignore each other until they did. Nash paid for his whelks and turned to look at the Salvation Army people.

"Look at them amen faces," he said with disdain.

He spat on the ground and then raised his voice so the amen faces could hear him.

"What does it matter if a man dies in the workhouse, if his soul is saved!" he called sarcastically, putting on a middle class accent.

"Amen to that brother," came the naïve agreement.

Nash looked at his fellow shellfish eaters with contempt on his face.

"I'll give them ar fuckin' men."

Nash had been impressed by the work done by the Reverend Barnett at Toynbee Hall; Frederick Charrington and Dr Barnardo, but he was bitterly opposed to the Salvation Army because of its acceptance of society and its indifference to the causes of poverty.

"You tell 'em Nashey," chuckled one of the men enjoying his oysters. In an attempt to further ingratiate himself with Nash, he continued. "Mad cowsons the lot of 'em, they ought to put 'em all in the loony bin!"

Nash glowered at the man.

"Nobody should be put in places like that!"

"No, no, course not Nashey, just er..."

Though not anywhere near as annoyed as he appeared, Nash gave the man his most withering stare. He could now move the conversation whatever way he wished, and the men would be only too pleased to go along with it to ease the tension. Nash held the stare for a second, before moving his gaze to a small child playing by the door of the pub. The little lad was filling a Woodbines packet with a mix of dirt and sawdust that had been trodden out of the pub door. Nash tossed the child a farthing.

"Go and get yourself some pop, boy."

Nash turned to the men with a grim smile.

"Got a keep in wiv 'em ain't yer? Little bleeder'll be part of the Adelphi Street gang in a few years time just as I'll be getting weak and feeble!"

The men silently exhaled their pent up breath in relief at the thawing of the atmosphere.

"Yeah, you can say that again Nashey, they breed 'em tough round 'ere all right," said the man who had hitherto been silent.

His mate, the one who had passed the remark about lunatic asylums, simply nodded in agreement and uttered a safe "Yeah".

Nash looked up at the advertising signs pasted across almost every square inch of the pub yard wall. One read:

'Wine Spirit Vaults Fine Cordials Gin'

"That 'ow yer spells vaults? They got that wrong ain' they?"

Given that both men were illiterate, spelling wasn't a subject that interested either of them but they saw Nashey was offering an olive branch; a way of starting a new, friendlier conversation.

"Yeah, I fink you're right Nashey, they ought to go back ta school, them sign wri'ers," said one of them.

"Chance'd be a fine fing round 'ere," said the other.

He had not been sure whether to say it with a slight chuckle or with grim contempt. He chose the latter given Nashey's mood. He chose well.

Nash made the move he had been angling towards since he first spotted the men enjoying their oysters.

"They should go to that 'oity-toity piece I've 'eard about. Some funny rich woman's livin' 'ere somewhere pretendin' to be one of us, ov all fings. Does a bit a wri'in' and teachin' an' all."

"Yeah I knows 'er," said one of the men. "She's a queer one all right. To look at 'er you'd fink she were a gyppo straight off a fairground. Long greasy black 'air, loads a rouge, but she talks well proper 'cept some words she tries to speak like us. Queerest fing you've ever 'eard. She does anythin' like writin', readin', doctorin' and such – fancy wri'in' for law stationers is her paid job, but she never turns no cove away, does let'ers, in'raductions, all sorts, mostly for nuffin' if she gets a sob story, which she always does a course. She does forging for coves like us without even knowin' she's doin' it!"

"An' yer say she does doctorin' an all?" queried Nash.

"Yeah, when ol' granny Betts died, the area where she lived, Chequers Yard an' round there, were wivout nobody 'oo could 'elp out when people were taken, so this Soppy Sookey, as they calls 'er, starts rollin' 'er sleeves up. 'er old feller were an army surgeon they says. Dead a while back since. The doctorin's 'elped 'er become accepted. Up to a point any 'ow. She ain' never gonna be one of us is she. But she'll do anything to 'elp with that see."

"Soppy Sookey?" laughed Nash.

The nose was enjoying himself now. He continued with enthusiasm.

"Yeah, you ought to see 'er try and do certain 'fings. Fings all women can do – washin' an' the like. Ain' got a bleedin' clue. So big Rose Martin, started calling 'er Soppy Sookey and it's stuck like cobbler's wax. Sookey's 'er name if yer please."

"Blimey, I'll have to give 'er a knock meself," said Nash in a cheerful throwaway manner. "I got some gip from this finger since I stiff-fingered some toff in the throat last week. Serves me right for trying a be too easy on 'im. Used me monkey's fist when I should 'ave used me cosh.

I mus' be get'in' bleedin' soft in me old age or summin'. 'e didn't go down an' rounded on me. It was over in Frying Pan Alley an' yer know 'ow bleeding' narra' that is. Didn't 'ave room to fetch him a facer so just gave him the straight fingers. Caught some pawsey tie-pin 'e were wearin' or summin'. Fought it were just gonna be a black man's pinch but it's gonna go septic if I ain' careful."

Nash showed them his right ring finger, which was black and swollen with the nail soon to come off. The story had been true. But it was an occupational hazard. He was always carrying some injury or another. He never bothered with medical treatment.

"Looks nasty that do. Why don't you go round an' see 'er. If she's not 'ome she'll be round Toynbee. She does a bit of teachin' round there an' all. Lives next door a big Rose in Widegate Street she do."

Most people in the neighbourhood knew, or knew of, Rose Martin. It was difficult not to. She was six feet tall, nineteen stone and had arms like sides of mutton. Her husband once made the mistake of complaining to her about the poor quality of the sandwich she had made him for his lunch. The next day, in full view of his fellow workers, he unwrapped his lunch to find the rent book between two slices of bread.

Nash had caught the tail-end of what had happened when Mr Martin arrived home after an afternoon being the butt of all his workmates' jokes. Mr & Mrs Martin had a full, no holds barred, fight that spilled out onto the street. The image of slum women scratching and pulling hair in a fight was false. They fought like men, and Mr M had a black eye from a right cross to show for it.

A crowd had gathered round and there was a row of excited boys seated along the wall looking down on the skirmish. Adult and boy wags alike had a field-day making fun of the man who couldn't control his wife. But he was fitter than her and after a while started to get the upper hand. When a left hook landed on Rose's chin, Nash decided it was time to step in, much to the chagrin of the crowd, who were having a fine old time. But Rose didn't appreciate his help, and gave him a verbal volley that no man would dare have done. Nash was mightily impressed by this woman but feigned offence.

"'ere! Any more a that an' you'll get my boot, now fuck off indoors before I frow you in that 'orse-troff there!"

Rose's husband wanted to round on Nash.

No cowson talks to my old lady like that.

But he knew that was very unwise, so simply put his arm round his beloved.

"Come on ol' gell let's get 'ome away from this lot."

With the common enemy of Nash to glare at, the husband and wife had made it up.

That was several months ago, but although Nash had seen Rose about here and there on the street since, he hadn't had occasion to speak to her. He wondered what his reception would be. There were few people whose approval he craved, but this woman was one. It was ironic that he suspected the feelings were far from mutual. He nodded curtly.

"Rose."

"It's Mrs Martin ta you."

"Very well Mrs Martin" he said formerly, keeping the amusement he felt out of his expression and voice.

"I 'ear you're mates with a woman who does a bit a doctorin'. Sookey ain' it?"

"I ain' no mates with 'er. I puts up with 'er more than most, thas all. After a bit a doctorin' are ya? Dear o' lore, don't tell me someone's given yer a good 'iding, I'd 'ate to 'ear that. Or is it a nasty disease," said Rose with mock concern.

"Don't worry yerself Mrs, I'll breeve," he retorted, this time allowing a smirk to escape as he held up his black finger.

She made it clear from her expression that she wasn't impressed.

"Don't look much ta me. You get'ing' soft or summin'? Want me ta pull that nail off for ya. I'll do that with pleasure."

"I'm sure you would," Nash said knowingly.

He decided it was time to end the banter and get on with the job at hand. He changed his tone to one he would use when speaking to men.

"Where is she gell?"

Rose spotted the change and knew it was time to tell this man what he wanted to know.

"She lives there," nodded Rose, at the house next door. "But she ain' 'ome. Said she were going up the 'all to see Henrietta as she calls 'er."

Rose made pains to over pronounce the H in Henrietta, mocking her next door neighbour, both for her accent and her relationship with Reverend Barnett's wife. Everyone else in the neighbourhood referred to Henrietta Barnett as 'the reverend's wife' or Mrs Barnett. It didn't help Sookey's desire to be accepted as 'one of us' when being on first name terms with the wife of the vicar made her more like 'one of them'.

"Mrs Parsons is helping her chum to give a lecture on Sir Walter Scott." Rose had used a sarcastically high-pitched well-mannered voice before returning to her usual speech. "'oo ever the bleedin' 'ell 'e is. I'm sure it'll 'elp the young servants they're tellin' it to, no end when they're black-leadin' tomorra'."

Nash understood very well Rose's sarcasm, as Toynbee Hall could be condescending at times, and some of what they did certainly lacked common sense. What was the point of lectures on aesthetics or chemistry; orchestral recitals or debating societies for the poverty-stricken? But in general terms he greatly approved of the place. At least it was trying to do something for the poor, which was more than could be said for most.

It provided useful classes in shorthand, arithmetic and book-keeping, and ran a company which provided much needed basic but decent homes for working men and their families. The accommodation would have a walk-in living room, front room, two bedrooms and a distempered scullery, with a toilet on the stone landing, which was lit by gas jets. There was a black iron sink, cold water and a large coal box.

Events, societies, clubs, exhibitions and a library were also worthwhile things, but most crucial of all, it did more than anything to focus middle class attention on East End poverty. Though Nash thought the nocturnal habits of a man in a Derby-hat had superseded it in this respect.

The lecture had already finished when Nash arrived at Toynbee Hall. One of the helpers told him that Sookey had just left for her art gallery around the corner, so he strolled along to it. It was quite a shock. He had never been in an art gallery before. Amongst the dirtiest, filthiest part of London, was what must have been the cleanest, brightest interior in the East End. He immediately felt ill at ease. The place was empty save for pictures on the walls. So much space; so much silence; he wasn't used to this. His footsteps echoed on the shiny, spotlessly clean, polished hardwood floor.

I'd never be able ta creep up behind no cove 'ere, and there's the troof.

The gallery was empty of people but he could hear someone rummaging around in a back room. It must be Soppy Sookey. He decided to look around at the pictures and wait for her to appear.

It's bloody clever what some a these ar'ists ov painted 'ere. Some of the likenesses is almost as good as them camera pictures I seen in shops up the West End, but these pain'in's is bet'er cos they're coloured. They're much better than the pictures yer sees all the time on advertisin' boards. 'cept for the Pear's bubbles picture a course. Nuffin' can beat that.

One picture made him stop in his tracks, because it was so different from the rest. It wasn't very good at all as far as he was concerned.

It ain' a proper likeness is it. A picture ov a London music 'all but it's all false lookin'. The people don't look real, and everyone in it's gesturin' and pointin', all stoopid. Why would yer wanna paint summin' like that? The real fing's only just down the road, and if you're gonna waste yer time paintin' it yer might as well do it right.

He looked at the caption at the side:

'Walter Sickert, on loan from the New England Art Club'.

On loan? Blimey, glad ta get rid ov it more like. An' where the bleeding' 'ell's New England when it's at 'ome? Couldn't be any worse than old England mind.

"I could paint a better picture ov a music 'all than that," he said out loud.

"Could you indeed sir? I look forward to seeing your work."

Nash spun round to see a woman of indeterminate years, perhaps thirty five or thereabouts, smiling warmly at him. She had white powder on her face, as well as perfectly round discs of rouge on each cheek. Her hair, complete with mid-forehead parting, was pinned up at the lowest possible point allowing the loose-bundled, long thickly glossed hair as much licence as custom allowed.

Gawd 'elp us if she don't look like sum doll. No, a puppet. Mrs Punch? No, too fair by 'alf. Bleedin' fine rouge I must say an' 'er 'air's the shiniest I ever did see. It'll be falling down over 'er shoulders if she ain' careful, them pins don't look too clever, an' then she'll look like sum lit'le gell if yer please. An' gawd knows what potions she's got on it. What a queer stamp ov a woman. But fair mind.

Nash was lost for words. He blurted out something just to end the silence.

"This Sickert, young local Jew lad is 'e?"

Sookey was getting used to people in Whitechapel simply starting conversations without the usual greetings or introductions in place. She smiled and answered confidently.

"He is something of a friend of mine. That is how I was able to secure the loan of such an important piece all the way from the United States of America. He resides part of the time in Camden Town, and part of the time in Dieppe in France presently. He is London-born but not local to Whitechapel. Yes, he is young, though no lad. He is a young rake of some five and twenty years. As for his religion, I could not say. It is the rarest of names is it not?"

Sookey had a wealthy woman's voice all right, but it was unusually attractive and friendly. In Nash's limited experience of the middling type, they had two modes of address to the poor. One was a kindly, condescending form in which each word, mostly kept to one syllable if possible, was clearly enunciated; the second was a loud, self-assured hectoring note. Law staff, doctors, judges, magistrates, officials and clergy were experts at this social intimidation. This voice was neither.

Nash tried to be on his best behaviour.

"I didn't mean to take the er, to be rude about the lad. It's just that all the ovver paintin's seem so much better to my eye," said Nash in a defensive, unconfident tone he was unused to affecting.

"There, you have it sir. To your eye. Beauty is in the eye of the beholder is it not?"

Nash had vaguely heard of this phrase before. He was thinking about a reply when Sookey carried on.

"But some art appreciation can only be determined by education. And the raison d'etre of Toynbee Hall is education," she beamed.

Raisons? Debt? Eh? Blimey, praps it were bet'er when the middling types spoke in a clever manner after all! Least I can understand wot they're goin' on about then.

Thankfully she carried on again so Nash didn't have to summon a reply.

"You see, Sickert is an impressionist," she said with great enthusiasm. "It is a new form of painting. Yer paints yer own impression of somefing, not an actual likeness of somefing. So it can appear amateurish at first, but given time people come to appreciate it for its artistic thought as well as its artistic skill."

Yer? Somefing? Nash now realised what they meant when they said her accent was all over the place. She said the odd word wrong, in a working woman's accent. Nash was flummoxed by art, but he was impressed by Sookey not using a condescending tone towards him when trying to explain something that was clearly beyond his understanding. He was not sure he would be so considerate if he tried to explain to her the subtleties of the thieving, dishonesty and general skulduggery of his world. Or

God forbid, when trying to explain why the Whitechapel murderer was still at large, courtesy of him. He wasn't sure he could explain that fully to himself, come to think of it.

He felt that he should reply but wasn't sure what to say. He thought it safest to stick to a subject he knew.

"I take it these pictures are worth a bob or two, being on show so ta speak? You should be careful not to leave 'em unguarded. They might walk."

This was said in his usual gruff tone.

"Walk?" queried Sookey.

Her eyes flickered a little as her right hand moved up to touch the top of her blouse for a moment. Her breezy confidence had evaporated. She was aware she was alone in an enclosed space with this huge, rather aggressive, dangerous-looking man.

Course, she ain' gonna understand me 'alf the time if I talk normal is she. We're from different cun'ries, or might just as well be. An' I can sees as 'ow I've gone an' frightened 'er now. I gotta speak more friendly ain' I, like I do some'imes to little perishers. And try a use proper words and phrases an' all.

He remembered the slight smirking smile that came naturally when he was talking to Rose Martin. Rent-book sandwich indeed. The smile returned at the thought, and he kept it there as he changed to a softer tone.

"My apologies madam. I didn't mean to offend. It's just that there is rather a lot ov crime in this neighbour'ood and I would 'ate to see your fine pictures stolen. Alexander Nash…"

He hesitated.

Do I say 'at your service' or 'by your leave' or summin' like that now? He tried to remember what he had heard those greasy clerks say down the chancery. He decided to keep it simple, offering his hand.

"'ow d'yer do."

My, he has a fine smile, thought Sookey, relaxing somewhat. He seems quite personable after all. She gazed at the huge, surprisingly clean hand proffered to her. It had rather taken her aback, but she didn't want to insult him by not responding appropriately. She had spotted immediately (you couldn't very well miss it), his badly injured ring finger.

"Helloo Mr Nash. I would shake your hand but I fear you would not thank me for doing so," she smiled, nodding down at the blackened finger. "My name is Sookey Parsons, I am the curator here at the gallery, and Henrietta Barnett's assistant for the remainder of Toynbee Hall." Her hand briefly held his two healthy middle fingers. "It would appear my tiny hand is just able to make acquaintance with two of your fine fingers at a time sir," she said in a self-deprecating voice, leaning her head slightly to one side as she smiled.

Hello? Wot the bleedin' 'ell's that mean?

Sookey had barely sounded the second 'o' of the old hunting cry, helloo, which some middle class people had started using as a term of greeting, mostly on the new telephone invention. Sookey's pronunciation was closer to 'hello'.

I've 'eard the ice cream seller use funny words like that, ending in o all the time. Praps it were Italian talk for 'ow d'ya do. What she speaking I-tie for? Mind you, I do 'av dark, fick 'air dun I, so I spose I might 'ave the stamp of an I-tie to 'er.

He certainly had the idea that she liked the look of him. The unfunny joke about the little fingers and the coy sideways look she gave, told him so. This was useful. This could be used to his advantage.

"It's jus' occupational 'azard in my line a work," he responded.

He was pleased with 'occupational'. He didn't know too many long clever words like that. But he was annoyed for dropping the aitch off hazard.

"Indeed sir, and what is your position?"

Christ I should a seen that comin' a mile orf. Talk about walkin' right inta somefin'.

He chose to ignore the question. Usually, if he was asked a question he didn't like, he would ignore it, stare at the questioner for a second, and an unspoken agreement was made between them to move the conversation on in a different direction. He replaced the usual stare with an even broader smile than the one he had been using.

Am I overdoin' it? I don't wanna come over like one a them smarmy Sally Army bastards.

He answered her question, with a question.

"You ever had anythin' pinched, er stolen, from 'ere?"

"Oh no, it is very safe here," Sookey explained earnestly. "Nobody would steal from us. Everyone has too much respect for the reverend and what he's trying to achieve here." Her eyes suddenly narrowed with suspicion. "Are you a policeman sir?"

Nash burst out laughing. He had never heard two good jokes in such quick succession. He wasn't sure which was funniest.

People 'aving too much respect for slummers to steal from 'em, or me bein' a bleedin' crusher. She's green as them noses said she were.

He forgot his soft tone and attempt at speaking correctly for a moment.

"Gawd 'elp us no!" He heard his voice echo around the all but empty gallery. "Beg pardon my lady." He had recovered his composure. "I meant no disrespect to you. It's just that the police are not well received 'round 'ere. It's the last position you'd seek to 'old."

All gawd, I called her 'my lady'. Is that some'ing you only say to yer fancywoman or is it all right? The police are not 'well received'. It's the 'last position'. Blimey, I ain' got a clue 'ow a speak ta this woman.

Sookey wasn't sure how to react.

Was this man making sport of her?

If so, she rather enjoyed it. She enjoyed being the butt of a joke. It was a means by which she felt she was transported from the excepted to the accepted. She never felt better than when her friend Rose was being sarcastic at her expense. But as far as she was concerned, it wasn't an expense; rather a benefit.

She felt that her medical work was crucial in gaining respect within the neighbourhood, but she had noticed that doctors throughout the slums were respected but never accepted or even liked. It was through humour that Sookey felt truly part of the neighbourhood. It was clear to her that humour was an intrinsic part of life in the slums. It was the only thing that kept people going at times; the one possession which could not be taken away from them. How often had she heard the expression, 'Got a laugh ain't ya gell. Otherwise you'd bleedin' cry.'

The big handsome man in front of her looked a little uncomfortable. She threw him a smile to reassure him no offence had been taken. Nash thought she was probably about to ask again what he did for a living; a question he needed plenty of time to mull over before deciding what his answer would be. So he quickly got a question in first.

"As yer can tell, I ain' someone 'oo visits art places normal. I were looking for ya. The people down the 'all told me you were 'ere. I 'ear tell you do sum doctorin' and I were wonderin' if you could 'ave a look at this finger fer me. Well, you've already looked at it so to speak ain't ya?" he laughed, hoping for a similar response.

Sookey duly laughed. It seemed genuine enough.

"Certainly sir, though I have nothing here with me. Can you come to my lodgings? Perhaps in one hour?"

There she goes wiv that sir again. Keeps callin' me sir; cur more like.

If any other woman he knew asked him to come to her lodgings, he would immediately make a crude double entendre with a wink. Not that he enjoyed music hall humour, but like it or not, it was expected.

"That'll be good, right enuff."

She started to give him directions but he interrupted her.

"Thas all right, you live next ta Rose Martin dunt ya?"

He knew that there was every chance that sometime in the next hour, Rose would tell Sookey that he had been there looking for her. He thought it would sound better if he told her first that he had been there.

"I were there earlier see, lookin' for ya. As soon as I did me finger the ovver day, people kept saying you ought to go and see ol' Sookey. You're well known round 'ere yer know."

Sookey glowed. Not only was she going to see this interesting, handsome man again, but she was, 'well known round 'ere.'

CHAPTER 5:

"The exclusive culture of those whose sensibilities are so shocked by the brutality, the responsibility for which their greed and cowardice evades....and when the dark side of this inglorious inequality is thrust on their notice, they are shocked and read moving articles in the newspapers."

William Morris

Immigrants were easy prey for con-men. As soon as Naseer Khan had stepped off the train at Fenchurch Street station he had been accosted by a couple of apparently very friendly men claiming to be porters. He had an address in Aldgate, which unbeknown to him was just a mile away, but the con-men took him on a roundabout route on the Great Eastern railway and relieved him of £1-17 shillings. They then put him in an accomplice's growler and the cabman was very pleased to relieve him of his last thirteen shillings for what should have been a one shilling cab ride to his address in Aldgate.

The tall, thin ebony-skinned man had journeyed from the Punjab to look for his daughter. She was a sixteen year old servant who had accompanied her British employer back to England with the promise of a return fare on arrival. The one subsequent letter he had received from her, written in English, had told him that her employer had not made good on their end of the bargain and she had been cast adrift without a penny as soon as they had arrived in England. Her employers now had plenty of English servants at their disposal. As a result she was marooned in England until she could find a position with an India-bound employer. Having been told that nannies were always popular, she was hopeful of getting home soon via such a position. The young woman had been illiterate in her own language, let alone English, when she left, and the spelling, grammar and syntax was so unlike the English she spoke that he suspected that someone had written it for her.

Khan had nursed his ailing wife whilst waiting for his only child to walk back through the door. Khan was initially unconcerned by the time it was taking for his daughter to find her way home. She had probably got a position with a British army family and would no doubt be indentured to the position for some time to recompense her employers for the cost of her passage. And even when she was in a position to leave, she would be penniless and could be as far off as Bombay, for he was realistic enough to appreciate she may not have had much choice as to where in India she could get employment. It would be a long journey to get home. But the years had passed with no further word, his wife had died and he was now at a low ebb. He needed to find his beautiful daughter. Of course she could return to the village whilst he was away in England, but he left behind a large family network who would take her in awaiting his return.

The address he had was the Ayahs Home in Aldgate. The problem of marooned Indian women had become so acute that this home had been established as a shelter for Ayahs, the collective term for Indian servants and nannies. But to the people of the East End they were more generally known as lascars. The term had originally been for any dark skinned Asian, Arab or even Chinese sailors who had jumped ship to swop the appalling conditions on board for the horrors of the East End. But now anyone with a complexion darker than a Jew or Italian and lighter than a Negro was called a lascar. Khan had made all the obvious enquiries but his search had come to nothing.

Having had his life savings conned out of him on arrival, he had eked out a living doing whatever was necessary. Slum life was the same whether you were in Whitechapel or Delhi. In fact the two places were remarkably alike in many ways. You did whatever kept you fed and, if possible, dry. You existed. He had experienced how the British in India treated Indians, so the level of racism in England was no great surprise to him, and his lesson about trusting strangers had been quickly, painfully learned.

Khan settled into his new life quickly. His first job had been assisting a glazier. This skilled man padded the streets clutching glass in a wooden frame, shouting "winders!" On one cold winter's day, cramp had locked his arm rigid to the glass after hours of walking the streets without a customer. The glazier was too old and weak to do this any longer; the workhouse beckoned. But he remembered what his father always used to say.

"There's always some poor bugger worse orf than you boy."

And sure enough there was. He was approached for a job by someone who appeared to be an old lascar.

"Ain' see you about 'ere before. You just orf the boat are ya?"

"Yes sir. I am strong as ox. Need work. Place to sleep."

The old glazier had a room to himself in a nearby slum. He only really needed a corner to sleep in, but had to pay for a whole room so he could store his glass and tools in safety. There was room for another straw palliasse next to him. He couldn't afford to pay anything, but the man looked desperate enough to work for nothing.

"Can't pay ya nuffin' but I got a bed for ya and you can eat what I eat. I'll see ya alright there. Wassyer name?"

"Khan."

"Jus' Khan?"

"Yes sir."

"Alright by me boy. Some of you coves 'a' got some right queer names. Can't get me laughing gear 'round 'em at all."

Khan had passed his first job interview with flying colours, and he kept the old glazier out of the workhouse by carrying the glass for him. As the old man's health faded and as his own English accent improved, Khan started to do the shouting as well. One morning the old glazier didn't wake up and Khan needed to look for another job. Various ones had come his way. He had been a sand-bone man, selling sand for floor covering; hawked brownstone for cleaning and colour-stoning the doorsteps and pavements outside houses; general dealer of old boots and clothes; egg vendor – eggs came over from Ireland un-cleaned, in crates packed with straw. They were sold sixteen for a shilling, but some were broken and bad, and these, plus cracked eggs, were sold to the poor at a cheap price by the old lascar egg-man.

But Khan came to appreciate that his appearance could, in the right circumstances, be a help rather than a hindrance. He had been to a fair and spotted that many of the people making a living as fortune tellers, mystics, potion sellers and anything considered the least bit exotic or occult, had a similar complexion to his own. Slum life in England had also taught him the popularity of gambling.

He had an idea which was against his religious beliefs, but after much soul searching, not to mention a much grumbling stomach, he put his idea in to practice. He grew a full beard and moustache, used kohl around his eyes to make them appear wider and brighter, and bought a striking outfit in Petticoat Lane market – a filthy old sergeant's overcoat and soldier's hat, not unlike a policeman's, probably a relic of the Crimea; and changed his name to Khano, The All-Seeing. Decked in this garb, he went to all the horse race meetings at Alexandra Palace, Hurst Park, Epsom, Ascot and the other race meetings within easy, cheap travelling distance of London. He sold tips; the exotic, mystical man with the big bulging eyes and the sixth sense, who knew the winners. Of course he knew nothing about racing, but enlisted the help of a man he once helped in the street to escape the police.

The man had obviously just committed a crime and had been surprised by an unseen policeman. He was making a run for it with the policeman in hot pursuit when Khan casually walked straight into the pursuer, knocking him down. Khan quickly dropped on the uniform apologising most profusely whilst hindering the man from getting up.

He did not know the man he had just helped escape at the time, but he knew that any action against the loathed police was viewed with appreciation from those around him in the slums, and it was important to gain their acceptance if he was to live among them in peace. And he had no liking for the police in any case. They harassed him at ever turn. He called them bobbies, because he once called them peelers but his accent made it sound like 'pillars'.

"They ain't pillars a this communi'y," growled the big brooding man he had once helped escape them.

"Very well Nashey, I call them bobbies now."

"Bobbies, crushers, coppers, Old Bill, they're all the same whatever yer call 'em," was the curt reply.

Nashey wasn't a friend. Nobody was friends with Nashey, but Khan liked him. Unlike most people, he treated Khan exactly the same as he did everyone else. Khan once relayed this thought to him. Nash grunted.

"Everyone's the same in my book. You're all some muvver's son ain't ya? Till yer cross me a course. But until then I jus' treats all men with the same contempt."

Khan saw the merest hint of a twinkle in the man's eye, but knew not to show Nashey that he knew he was joking.

"'cept bobbies Nashey eh?"

"Yeah, 'cept bobbies Khan, and wrong uns."

The two men met up regularly so that Nash could give him tips he could use at the race course. Khan always bought his adviser a drink, though he insisted he give Nash the money to actually buy the drink himself, but other than that the big man seemed content to help him just as a continuing thank you for his one time assistance. Nash could only speculate on the best bets, but at least he followed 'the form' and could make educated choices. He left the exotic reasoning as to why a horse was sure to win to Khano. The All Seeing gave his clients knowing reasons for each tip.

"This horse looked me in the eye. Oh, and what a look it was. I am going to win today. I will run like the wind."

And then he would add something more concrete gleaned from Nash.

"The horse tells me, this is my course. I win here last time I run. I no like that left hand course las' time and it was too wet and boggy. I like the sun on my back and the rattle of my hooves on the hard ground, like today."

The punters accepted the idea that horses spoke broken English with an Indian slant without exception. One huge slice of luck was that the very first tip Nashey had given him, Doleswood at Ascot, won at long odds - 16 to 1. Since then, like all tipsters, he lost his customers a little more than they won overall, but he won enough to keep the faith of some clients at least, and there were always new ones impressed enough by this striking looking lascar to hand over some cash.

When he wasn't at the race course, Khan was a look out and general information gatherer – a nose. His very incongruity as a black man in a sea of whiteness actually made him strangely effective at blending into the background; the most important of all a nose's talents. Every one saw him, yet didn't see him. They didn't want to see him. They saw a lascar but paid no heed; he was no doubt just selling something they didn't want, and wouldn't buy off him even if they did.

If you told Khan to do something, he did it to the letter, without query, without complaint, and would carry on doing it until you told him otherwise. He was ideal for the job that Nash needed someone to do. Nash had rapped on Khan's door very early on Sunday morning. Khan didn't mind; he was going to the market early in any case.

Khan was to stand across the street from the door with the red rag in the window in Middlesex Street. Nash would get another man to alternate with him, doing shifts. Nash suggested they sell matches as a cover, and gave Khan some coins to buy them with. He told him to rig up a tray from a box-side with strings attached that he could hang round his neck. Nash would pay him good wages and he could keep whatever he made on the matches as well. This was on the understanding that he didn't tell a soul who he was working for; that he was working for anyone in fact. He was just selling matches because the race-course work wasn't paying much at this time of year. It was always the same with racing in October – 'the flat' was finishing and 'over the sticks' hadn't got started properly yet.

As soon as a man left the house, Khan was to follow him to wherever he was going. It would be a gent with a fair moustache, and he might be wearing an overcoat or suit, gold watch and chain and a Derby hat, though these weren't certain. Nash was in a hurry to get off the streets, and in his rush, he didn't make himself clear as to the extent he wanted the man followed. 'Where 'e's goin'' had been ambiguous and Khan always did exactly what he thought he had been told. Suitably decked out in the garb of a match-seller, Khan stood across the street, right outside the house where the Whitechapel murderer was ensconced. When he alighted, Khan would follow him.

⁀ ◆ ⁀

There was a knock on the door. Nash didn't give out his address to just anyone and even those who knew it preferred to meet him on more neutral ground whenever possible. Nash had been about to have a wash. He was bare to the waist, his large belt several inches below the top of his corduroy trousers. He slipped it off and held it by its thin end, the buckle dangling just above the floor. That was the only trouble in living in a new tenement; he didn't have front windows to peer out of. It could be anybody out there.

"'oo is it?"

"It's me, Khan, Nashey."

Khan was green. He could have been duped into bringing someone with him who Nash didn't want to have at his door.

"Yer on yer own?"

"It's Khan."

Christ almigh'y I could be 'ere all day.

"Are you on your own Khan?" said Nash enunciating each word deliberately through clenched teeth.

"Yes, yes Nashey. No one here. No one here."

Nash opened the door. No words of welcome were offered but he moved his body sideways to allow Khan room to pass by him. Khan hesitated, so Nash jerked his head towards the room and Khan scurried in.

"I was just about to 'ave a sluish. Sid down."

Khan hesitated and then motioned to sit on the floor.

"On the chair yer soppy sod!" barked Nash with obvious exasperation.

There was only one chair in the room, a decaying rickety little wooden affair. Khan had thought he had better not sit in Nashey's only chair.

"It's on it last legs but it'll probably 'old your weight if yer lucky," said Nash with that slightest of glints in his eye that Khan had come to spot. "I'm goin' out the yard wiv me bucket."

Nash disappeared out the back, leaving the back door open which let in daylight as well as a harsh, biting westerly wind. Khan sat down and looked about the room. The chair was at a table, fashioned from fruit crates. On it was the stale, unwanted crust of one of last night's pie-man's sales, and a selection of strange looking implements; a flat cap with small razors sewn into the peak, a metal spike, a thick rope, a leather cosh, several large rings and a small knife which rested on a thick book. Khan couldn't read English (he had to have his daughter's letter read to him) but assumed it must be the Christian bible. A thick walking cane rested against a crate. In one corner of the room was an empty coal sack. In another corner was a single iron bedstead with a horse-hair mattress; with hair protruding. Along the wall opposite was a shelf, on which was a blow lamp, a tin of condensed milk, the lit gas lamp which was enabling him to see these things, and a blue sugar bag. Beneath the shelf, on the floor, were a pile of newspapers and a tin of paraffin. On the opposite wall was a fireplace, complete with grate, surrounded by a fender, on which lay a cat, asleep, with its head using one of Nashey's boots as a pillow. By the boots was a pair of shoes with very thin soles and a chipped and cracked enamel teapot, and next to this was another blue sugar bag, filled with tea leaves. A single heap of clothes had been piled on the floor closest the fender. A vest, a muffler, two old shirts, two waistcoats of different sizes, two pairs of trousers, a tatty billy pot bowler hat and a huge black overcoat.

Nash would wear the whole lot, even both pairs of trousers, in all but the hottest months, a psychological defence against the world. These scraps of human habitation sat on a hard splinter encrusted wooden floor, with brown walls rising from them to the ceiling. Khan picked up the book to see if it had any drawings in it, and to his delight there were, though not of the sort he had expected.

Nash walked in, his head and huge muscled torso dripping wet. Khan started to get up.

"Stay where you are," ordered Nash.

He then picked up his bed mattress, took it outside, gave it a good shake and beat it with his walking stick.

"That should've got rid of most of the lit'le bleeders. I had to paraffin me 'ead to get rid of 'em last week."

He rolled the mattress up into a bolster and threw it down next to Khan, then started to rub himself dry, first drying his hands on his trousers and then drying his chest and stomach with his hand.

"Didn't know you read Khan. What yer fink of Old Moore's Almanack then?"

"Good pictures Nashey."

"Yeah," said Nash, now realising the Indian couldn't read, or certainly couldn't read English.

Why should 'e? 'ardly any other poor cowson round 'ere does da they.

He sat down on the bolster and changed the subject.

"Wot yer got for me boy?"

"I waited in Middlesex Street like you told me Nashey."

"Good boy, and?"

"I sold matches. Good ay Nashey?"

"Yeah, bleedin' wonderful," came the sarcastic, increasingly impatient reply.

"I only had to wait a couple of hours and the man you told me about came out the house. He was wearing a suit, the same hat and gold watch and carried the same case you told me. I followed him to Liverpool Street station. He got in a taxi cab at the rank."

"Where to?"

"Dunno Nashey. I run after for a while but couldn't keep up."

"Didn't yer follow 'im like I told yer? You 'ear the man tell the cabbie where 'e wanted ta go?"

"You said to follow him to where he went. He went to the station. I didn't get close enough to hear him Nashey."

"You PC Fick?" asked Nashey with disgust at his man's dense behaviour.

Sergeant (Nash had got his rank wrong) Thick was a policemen who had found fame, or rather infamy, for his stupidity during the Lipski murder case a few years earlier. When the same officer happened to be the man to arrest 'Leather Apron', the first high profile Whitechapel murder suspect, despite there being no evidence whatsoever against the man other than vigilante-spread rumour, the sergeant's unfortunate surname was just too perfect.

"Fick Nashey?"

"Never mind."

Nash had to make a spur of the moment decision, to take over from Khan and forget about the slummer woman or to still make his appointment with her. He decided, against his better judgement, on the latter course.

"Alright, now get yerself back down to that taxi rank and start arstin' around about the gent what was... You come straight 'ere 'ave yer?

"Yes Nashey, straight, very sharp."

"Alright then, by the time you get back there, arst about the gent fare with the Derby 'at and the doctor's bag 'oo were a fare 'alf 'our ago. Crafty like. Tell 'oo wants to know 'e's a doctor and yer wife's a patient ov 'is and she's taken a turn for the worse and you gotta get 'im quick."

"Yes, Nashey."

"I got a see somebody now, so don't come back 'ere cos I won't be 'ere when yerve finished. Go back an' keep an eye on the 'ouse in Middlesex Street, case the gent comes back. Stay there till I get someone to take over from yer. You'll 'ave to stay there all night if I don't get nobody, or till the coppers move yer on. If I don't sees yer before, I'll sees yer in the Ten Bells openin' time tomorra. I know you don't like them sort a places, wiv the drinkin', but if I ain't there you wait." Lightening his tone, he went on with a wink. "I'll give ya a few winners for tomorra an' all."

With this, he got up and pulled on a once white vest now tinged with the blue of Rickett's Blue washing powder as might be expected of old clothing, but there were also pink streaks. Nash caught Khan looking at it.

"Yeah, I know. Bleedin' washer woman boiled an old 'ore's red smalls in with it by mistake. Poor cow ain't all there but I likes to give 'er the work. If she didn't take in washin' she'd be in the 'ouse for sure." He then donned the rest of his wardrobe, less his overcoat and half his trousers stock, to make him look less bulky and intimidating. "'sides, ain't like no one's gonna see it any'ow."

Khan started to get up to leave. He nodded at the grate.

"A cat Nashey. No dog?"

"Dogs don't catch mice and rats do they. They're all right in the pit a course, but they ain' so clever 'round the 'ouse. I likes cats cos they don't give a tinker's cuss about yer neiver."

Nash made his way towards Sookey's house, wearing his uncomfortable, thin stalking shoes. Something he never normally did when he wasn't working. But he thought they would look more respectable and less intimidating than his boots. He was irritating himself.

I'm chasing after some soppy tart who might know summin' about why 'ores don't bleed. An' what if she does? It's more important ta know who the Whitechapel murderer is, an' where 'e lives. I'm 'aving a sluish for some woman when I should 'ave been down Middlesex Street, keeping me eye on the cove meself. Now I've got that wrong un Shanks doggin' the killer when I should be doin' it. Good job I 'ad the idea to use 'im as well as Khan though. If there's anyfin' Shanks 'as been put on this world for it's doggin'. Least 'e won't lose the cove, an' I don't want nobody 'cept Shanks in on this pull more than I 'ave to.

Nash's thoughts turned to his impending meeting.

This bleedin' woman better be worf it.

He wasn't thinking about his black finger. The only thing he had on his mind was the blood of prostitutes.

Like somebody else I know, he thought sardonically.

CHAPTER 6:

"Now all is changed. Private enterprise has succeeded where Socialism failed...some independent genius has taken the matter in hand, and by simply murdering and disembowelling...women, converted the proprietary press to an inept sort of communism."
George Bernard Shaw, Blood Money To Whitechapel

On arrival at Sookey's house Nash was relieved to see Rose was not about. He wasn't in the mood to spar with her. On the short walk from his place he had been thinking about the man who was slaughtering women. The first of the newspapers carrying the double-murder story were already on the streets and Nash had been quick to read them. There had been no mention of James or Juwes (the authorities had suppressed the story, fearing anti-Jewish vigilantism, and had quickly removed the graffiti).

Funny 'ow that whitewallin' lark weren't mentioned. The crushers must a seen it above the bloody rag surely ta gawd. Praps some dog eat the droppin's and ran off wiv the rag. Spose it might jus' not bin found yet. The whitewallin's still jus' sitting there or some wag's scrawled summin' else over it. When it comes out I spose it'll be James the Jew this, that an' the ovver. I better go an' warn all the Jew-boys I know ta travel in packs for a while. But this maniac's doin' wot I fort 'e'd do, cour'esy a me now, but it ain' really 'im as is doin' it is it? More, it's the writers about 'im an' them likeness wallahs, photographists. I got a look out for them newspaper boys from now on. I'll 'ave to put the word about they ain' a be touched or 'ave no trouble.

Nash knocked on the door, looking down at the front step beneath his feet. It was dirty. He tutted to himself and shook his head ruefully. Even if you had lived in the area all your life, let alone arrived as an outsider, the first law of being respected by your fellow neighbourhood women was keeping a clean front step.

"She'll learn," he muttered to himself.

The door was almost immediately opened by the woman with the glistening hair.

"Helloo again Alexander. Please come in," she said smiling.

Nash had spent the five minutes he had spare after Khan had left, picking the little razors out of the peak of what he called his peak-blinder cap. It now looked an even more ragged affair than normal, though it was still in better condition than his billy pot hat. Having taken it off his head as he knocked politely at the door, he realised that not wearing either his overcoat or main pair of deep-pocketed trousers, he had nowhere to thrust it, so screwed it up in his right hand.

"You should not be using that hand at all sir. Let me take your cap," said Sookey still smiling.

Just as in their first meeting an hour ago, Nash was taken by the complete lack of condescension or scolding in her voice. There was none of the usual doctors' 'I know best' attitude.

"You will take tea with me Alexander?"

"Nashey, everyone calls me Nashey. Yeah tea'd slip down well."

Nash never drank other people's tea. They always made it too weak. But he wanted to have a look around before he had to engage in any further conversation, and hoped the woman would be too busy making the tea to talk for a short while. He was expecting her to reply with something along the lines of 'but Alexander is such a fine name', but she surprised him.

"Nashey it is. Please take a seat Nashey. I will not be a moment."

A large teapot hung over the fireplace like a witch's cauldron; the infusion inside it had been stewing awaiting his arrival. As Sookey busied herself with the tea, Nash scanned the room. He was seated on a good solid wooden chair, one of two in the room, the other being on the opposite side of the fine wooden table at which he sat. The first thing to catch his eye, he couldn't very well miss it, was a brightly coloured songbird in a cage on the table, flitting about and chirruping. Above it on the wall was an 18 by 9-inch framed motto 'East West Home's Best'. To the right of this was an archway through to a scullery, off which was the back door to the yard. He could barely see around the corner into the scullery but could just make out a few food tins. And he could hear someone rustling about in there.

On a shelf along the entire length of the wall opposite was a collection of shrubs and wallflowers in a series of jam and other types of jar. Beneath the shelf on the floor was a roll of fresh wallpaper, a bag of flour and several tins of condensed milk. Across the room next to the fireplace was an orange box, a soap box and a wet-fish box neatly piled on top of each other, no doubt ready to be broken up for firewood. There was no sign of a coal sack. A pair of button-up boots and a steel button hook lay next to them. The wallpaper on the front door wall behind him was peeling off in huge swathes. The front windows had newspapers over the panes, no doubt to keep draughts out.

"Somebody in yer scullery Sookey?"

"Oh that's Rose. She tidies up after me and keeps things in order. It is well she does, as I am rather ill at that sort of thing. She pretends to do so with bad grace, but I think she enjoys keeping an eye on me if the truth is told. I hope you understand but I could not receive a gentleman alone, so asked Rose if she had a mind to come in to sort some things out for me. She was delighted to when I told her who was coming. I think she looks forward to meeting you again. I believe you know each other."

Nash resisted the temptation to make the obvious joke about him being no gentleman.

"Yeah, me and Rose's parves 'ave crossed once or twice." He raised his voice. "Ain't that right Rose?"

But the third party didn't answer and stayed in the scullery out of sight.

She's earwigging every word though, I wager, mused Nash to himself.

Sookey put a cup of tea in front of him. She knew not to bother to ask about lemon.

"Do you care for milk or sugar?"

"Nah….er fank you," he added as an afterthought.

He noticed she didn't have any milk or sugar in her tea either. He nodded over at the tins of condensed milk.

"Looking at the amount of condensed you 'av in the place I fort sure you'd like it sweet and white."

She giggled and coyly put her tiny left hand over her mouth.

"Oh forgive me Nashey. Please don't think I make sport of you. It's just that I have the tins of condensed milk purely to make wallpaper paste. I would indeed have to be the most determined drinker of sweet white tea to have so many tins in my possession, would I not!?"

Soppy cow, thought Nash.

"Who told ya ta use condensed?"

"Why, Stan Martin, my good neighbour Rose's husband. He tells me that flour and condensed milk makes the best wallpaper paste."

No wonder all 'is chavvies is lousy, thought Nash.

He rehearsed the next sentence in his head.

Sound ya t's boy.

"Condensed does stick better than water but don't mind me telling ya, it attracts bugs an' all. You know the worse time for bugs in wallpaper? It ain' the summer like as you'd fink. It's blee.. blimmin' Christmas time. Father and the little 'uns use condensed to put the coloured paper loops up when mother ain' watchin' see."

Gawd, when's the last time I said blimmin'?

He remembered his mother blowing medicine down a newspaper funnel into his throat when he was taken ill once. He had just started his first job, as a 'nipper'; the boy who held the horse for his master and sat guard over goods at the tail end of the cart. His mother was desperate for him to go to work, knowing he would lose his job if he didn't.

"Blimmin' 'ell muvver," he said, at the disgusting taste of the powder.

She responded by cuffing him round the ear on almost every distinctly uttered word of her reply.

"Don't (cuff) you (cuff) come it (cuff) with (cuff) me (cuff) boy (cuff) and don't (cuff) you (cuff) dare (cuff) say (cuff) that (cuff) word (cuff)."

Fank Christ the ol' woman didn't have a bet'er way wiv' words, I could 'av lost me ear!

Nash was smiling at the memory. He had heard sentences with more words in them in his life, but none that had ever been so long in duration. He never did know whether 'that word' was blimming or hell.

"You smile sir? You make sport of me I wager."

"No, no what I says is true about condensed, you mark my words. You gonna strip the ol' wallpaper off?

She ignored his question.

"Then why do you smile sir?" she said with a knowing smile, still suspecting him.

There's that bleedin' 'sir' again.

He widened his eyes in mock horror.

"May I never move. I'm telling ya the troof. I was smilin' cos I was jus' finking..." He lowered his voice conspiratorially, nodding towards the scullery with a wink. "I wouldn't wanna be round Rose an' Stan's for Chris'mas. I'd be pickin' up a few presents what I didn't want."

They chuckled at this in unison. He was surprised that she had understood his joke, but he knew an honest laugh when he heard it. He had never met a woman who was so full of surprises, that was for sure. He repeated his question about stripping the wallpaper.

"No, I believe not," answered Sookey.

Gawd she's 'opeless.

"You should strip it so as to get rid of all the bugs as might be in the ol' paper – fleas, bed bugs, cockroaches and such. 'ere, I'll do the stripping for ya. Payment for you doing me finger see. But I ain't doin' the pasting an all. That's for you a do. Fair?

"That would be very satisfactory," replied Sookey with mock seriousness.

"And you do it with water," said Nash with a mild glare pointing his black finger at her, also in mock seriousness.

"Yes indeed sir. Now, let me have a look at that finger, before you lose the power to point."

Sookey administered to the finger. She had warned Nash that it would hurt and repeatedly apologised for the pain she knew she must be inflicting upon him. But he simply shrugged, and replied with a different succinct answer each time.

"It's gotta be done ain' it."

"It don't 'urt."

"I've 'ad worse dun a me"

"Get on wiv it woman." This time accompanied with a wink.

He showed no outward signs of the pain he must have been feeling. Sookey had never had such a brave patient. He was indeed a very tough man.

"I want you to take a sip of this whenever the pain gets particularly irksome," she said, proffering him a small dark bottle without a label on it.

"I told ya, it ain' that bad. What is it any'ow?" Nash asked.

"It's tincture of opium."

"Opium! 'ow the bleedin' 'ell d'you get 'old a that?!" spouted Nash, before realising what he had said. "Pardon me. It's just surprisin' a lady such as yerself would 'ave such a fing."

"It's not pure opium Nashey. It's laudanum. I get hold of it as you put it, easily enough. It's perfectly respectable, and if good enough for Mr Gladstone and Florence Nightingale, it's good enough for me, and you."

This woman could be very useful indeed, thought Nash.

The conversation continued easily between them over a range of subjects. He had learned that her songbird was a goldfinch bought from the Sclater Street bird market. There was some home-breeding but a lot of birds were trapped in Essex. He had told her he had a cat, thinking that she, unlike Khan, would like the idea of him keeping a cat rather than a dog. He kept it purely to keep the rats and mice down, and if it didn't eat vermin it starved as far as he was concerned. He wasn't wasting good money buying off the cat-meat man. She had been amazed that he hadn't given it a name.

"It's just a cat ain' it," he had replied with a shrug.

Sookey named the cat Doris and Nash promised he would call it Doris from now on, whilst thinking to himself 'soppy cow'. He had asked why she had so many flowers and flowering plants indoors.

"For the same reason I have the bird and the bright wallpaper, to give the place colour, to cheer up the gloom. Along with good coffee, that which I miss about my previous life is colour. The photographs of the newspapers' black and white world do not miss much in Whitechapel I fancy. I never go more than a week without getting something dan the Columbia Road flower market."

She had pronounced down as dan, trying to affect a Londoner's flat ow sound.

When the inevitable awkward question as to his line of work raised it's head, Nashey suddenly appeared to notice the cream coloured balls in the grate.

"Ay? Sorry gell I were miles away 'avin' a butcher's at them funny ball fings a yours. Like cricket balls wiv 'oles in. Never seen anyfin like 'em before."

"Oh, they are ceramic Nashey. They keep the heat in the fire. A clever invention is it not. I will be using them soon no doubt with the weather so inclement an' all."

It took all Nash's willpower to keep a straight face.

'Inclement an' all'. Gawd 'elp us!

He was also far from convinced of the validity of the ceramic balls.

They seen you comin' gell. Yerve been fed some ol' Codd's wallop down the market by a coster keen to unload some old Christmas stock ain't ya. But he kept his thoughts to himself, to keep the conversation where he wanted it.

"Yeah, I 'ave seen 'em. Down the frog and toad at the Sundee market. 'ere, I've finished me River Lea, where shall I put the cup?"

Sookey was bemused. She smiled uncertainly.

"Frog and toad? River Lea?"

She had not picked up on 'butcher's' but Nash's forced, artificial sentence had done the trick.

"It's the rhyming slang ov the costers. Frog and toad, road; River Lea, cup a tea."

It had the desired effect. Sookey was fascinated. The fact that she dropped the odd t, n or g, and turned th's into f's on occasion when she remembered to, in what was obviously a ruse to sound more like the people she lived among, made Nash think that she would be interested in the new rhyming slang. She would probably be keen to start using it herself. He was right. He taught her all the ones he knew.

'Ta'ers', meaning cold was her favourite because Nash teased her about her pronunciation, laughing with her that you had to say 'ta'ers', dropping the t, whereas she couldn't help but say 'taters'. She liked being teased. She liked sharing a joke rather than being the butt of one, and strangely she seemed to share a sense of humour with this brooding, menacing man from a very different walk of life. From Nash's point of view, this got the subject off his line of employment and the conversation flowed along very nicely thank you thereafter.

The Whitechapel murderer was never far from anyone's lips, but Nash wasn't sure how to broach such an unpleasant subject with a lady like Sookey. He bided his time and eventually manoeuvred the conversation adroitly to crime and personal safety in general.

"Yer shouldn't leave yerself alone in that gallery yer know. I could a been anyone. Yer came out that back room bold as brass when you 'eard me talkin' to meself about that funny pain'er. I saw yer were frightened ov me first up. An' yer were right ta be an' all. There's bad men about. Cut yer froat as soon as look at yer sum ov 'em." He then nodded his head to add gravity. "'specially in Whitechapel."

There was the bait. Now, would she bite?

"Indeed sir, these horrible murders are truly the work of the devil incarnate," she commented.

Nash was pleased with both himself and Sookey.

Good gell.

CHAPTER 7:

"Local street walkers are fleeing to the workhouses to escape the terror. If all the unemployed and other unfortunates could be induced to follow their example, a complete breakdown of the present poor law system would ensue."

Justice

Much juvenile prostitution was not for sexual deviants. Women could be hags at thirty, and the younger in age girls were, the less likely they were to be diseased, so men were drawn by the appeal of immaturity. This preference was so widespread amongst the higher-paying clientele that in a trade where once child prostitutes aped the appearance of adults, now grown women made themselves look like children as best they could. The most lucrative form of procuring was to supply a virgin to a heavy-spending debauchee. A virginally intact condition could be faked, and a bogus virgin would be passed off as a 'fresh Irish country girl'.

Kitty Johnson was a mature looking fifteen. She could pass for twenty. But this was no good thing from a business point of view. According to the law she was too young to have sex. According to some middle class sexual desires, she was close to being too old. She was already finding the better paying, more refined, cleaner customers more difficult to come by. She feared that she wasn't so far away from becoming like the poor haggard wretches she saw selling themselves to the roughest of trade for the price of a bed for the night in the lowest common lodging house.

Worse still as far as her immediate health was concerned, her fancyman, Harold Saville, was of the same opinion. He had witnessed her latest failure, when the man in the Derby hat rejected her without so much as a second glance. The ponce was furious. He had heard about the lucrative trade in procuring virgins and had plans for Kitty in that direction, but he was getting increasingly frustrated by her lack of enthusiasm for the job. And having been horrified to find that Kitty was planning a trip to a penny gaff on a Saturday night, he was then singularly unimpressed by her inability to temp the gent to hand over at least a small sum for a quick knee-trembler on a dark night. His fury had further increased when, instead of chasing after the gent, she had the temerity to just sit back down on her bench and start feeling sorry for herself. When she started blowing bubbles like some child, it was the final straw. It was now clear to him that he was never going to be able to pass her off as some young virginal Kate O' something from the bogs.

Saville had gone back to her home after the debacle and waited for her. The original idea was that he might as well have sex with her one last time before he beat her to a pulp and left her for good, but as the time passed he worked himself up into more and more of a temper. By the time she got home he didn't even wait for her to close the front door. He flew at her as she stepped in.

"I'll give you fuckin' bubbles!"

He attempted to punch her in the mouth as hard as he could, but his right fist came from such a long way back that Kitty had a fraction of a second to react. Flinching, her eyes closed, she brought her head down and threw up an arm, deflecting the punch a fraction onto the top of her head. It stunned her and she staggered backwards before losing her balance on her front step, causing her to fall flat onto the pavement outside. She hadn't passed out and although in some pain, had her wits about her. She opened her eyes and expected to see Saville's boot heading for her, but he was leaning against the door arch, with his right hand stuck under his left arm.

"Fuckin' 'ell!" he screamed through clenched teeth.

His knuckles had made solid contact with the hardest part of Kitty's head. Kitty had got to her feet by the time Saville's attention had shifted from his physical to his mental pain.

"Come 'ere you!" blared Saville as he started towards her.

Kitty didn't react. She stood still, staring back at the snarling Saville as he closed the ten feet between them. He stopped inches from her, untied his belt, ripping the leather from around his hips in an aggressive flourish.

"Yer got this comin' yer litt'e…"

Saville was cut off in mid-justification, when a brass heel stamped down on his stockinged left foot. He closed his eyes and screamed in pain, hopping away.

"Yer been brassed by a brass!" shouted a young woman's high pitched voice.

She had come from the side of Saville, and in his blind rage he hadn't seen her coming.

The pathetic hopping, groaning man was now an easy target, and a small fist, complete with a ring on one of the fingers, there for precisely this purpose rather than as jewellery, landed on the corner of Saville's mouth, skidding along his teeth, sending him reeling to the ground. The ring had ripped into the gum in the desired fashion, and blood seeped from his mouth.

"That's 'ow yer punch ponce!"

The owner of the brass heel and the fist grabbed Kitty by the elbow as Saville got up on one knee, spitting blood on to the cobbles.

"Come on gell, we gotta leg it! 'e'll be up to the scratch again soon enough."

Mary Kelly had been walking home from her long horrible Saturday night at work, when she happened to glance over from the other side of the street at the pretty young girl opening her front door. She had often seen her out and about but had never had cause to speak to her. Mary lived in the next court. She was impressed by her neighbour.

Blimey if she ain' fairer lookin' than me.

It was admiration rather than jealousy.

She deserves bet'er than that bastard of a bully she's got 'erself 'ooked up wiv.

When she had seen the girl stagger back onto the street, she instinctively ran to her aid, and arrived with perfect timing to deliver her strike. Kitty looked dumfounded at Mary.

"D'you 'ear me gell? Come on! Let's scarper," Mary implored.

Kitty smiled at Mary, hitched up her skirt and they ran off down the street together.

CHAPTER 8:

"All this hysterical cant will die down, and men, women and children will be left in precisely the same conditions of life as those which render these murders possible."

H.M.Hyndman

Nash had first come across Shanks when they were little lads. Nash was enjoying a snowball fight with his mates when he had been stunned painfully by a blow to the side of his head. He looked down to find at his feet the remains of a snowball with a big stone inside it. He glanced up to see Shanks only a couple of feet away laughing. He had wrapped the stone in a bit of snow and thrown it at Nash at point blank range when his target wasn't looking. Nash made eye contact with Shanks for a split second, smiling grimly.

I'll remember yer, don't you worry.

He then grabbed some snow, turned his back on Shanks and carried on playing with the rest of the gang.

A few years later, Shanks had been second in the pecking order of the Dorset Street teenage gang, and when its leader Freddie Boy Langton, had been sent down for robbery, Shanks had assumed he would take up the mantle. But young Nashey had other ideas, and his first impression of Shanks remained the same.

'e ain't worth the skin orf my nose. All piss and wind 'e is. The sort a cove 'oo fought wearin' nuffin 'cept a vest out on the street on the coldest day showed 'ow tuff 'e were. The type 'oo pretended ta know all there were a know about girls and knew fuck all. An' 'e picked on those 'e knew 'e could beat easy, like the meek lit'le Jew-boys. 'e might pick on those 'e weren't so sure 'e could beat an' all so long as 'e 'ad 'is mates be'ind 'im. 'e would always put that last boot in, when the gang had given some cove a good 'idin' and were scarperin'. 'e'd tap lads right on the ankle bone when the gang kicked a ball about. But only thems 'oo wouldn't kick back a course. 'e showed in'rest in everfin' everyone else were in'rested in cos 'e wanted a be part ov it, when 'e didn't have in'rest in nuffin'. An' 'e always 'ad to say summin' and pretend to 'it yer when 'e met up wiv the gang. ''ow are yer dog turds?' or some such, while frowin' pretend punches. 'e's tuppence-'a'penny. A wrong 'un.

Nash was a year younger and therefore a year later joining the gang (there was a lower age limit), but this was the only reason he was below Shanks in the pecking order as far as he was concerned. Nash had planned to move against Freddie shortly in any case. Pick a fight with him, knock him down, shake hands and that would be the end of it. Now he didn't have to. But Freddie had been a nasty bit of work, even by the standards of Whitechapel, and there was no telling what he and his gang were capable of, so the rival Adelphi Street gang wouldn't dare set foot in the Dorset Street neighbourhood. But word had spread round the slums like wildfire about Freddie being carted off to Pentonville by the authorities. It was not long before Adelphi Street gang members were seeing how far they could go in his old territory. Two of them had ventured onto Dorset Street in broad daylight and waylaid a little tot who was delivering clean linen to a customer of her mother, a wretchedly poor woman who took in washing.

Kinchin Lays (those who stole from small children) were the lowest of the low at the best of times, and for a rival gang to commit such a crime in Dorset Street was really 'takin' the rise'.

When word got back to Shanks he started rounding up what he considered his gang now, but Nashey was nowhere to be found. He was supposed to be working the station but he wasn't there. Shanks was doing a lot of shouting, mostly swear words, cant and blasphemies as his gang made their way to the corner of Adelphi Street.

"We're fuckin' kill 'em," was Shanks' call to arms.

And armed he certainly was with every small easily concealed weapon he could get his hands on. By the time they arrived at the corner of Adelphi Street, Shanks was alarmed that Nash still wasn't with them. He felt sure that Adelphi would be waiting for them around the corner, and he knew very well that Nash would make early inroads into the Adelphi boys and he himself could stick close to Nash's shirt-tails, thus keeping himself safe whilst appearing to be in the thick of the battle.

"Where's that bastard Nashey when you need im?!" he bellowed, with a tell-tale crack in his voice.

They turned the corner to find no rival gang. The street was empty of boys save for one blood splattered individual marching towards them head down below a glinting cap. It was Nashey. As he approached, the boys could see there didn't appear to be any cuts or abrasions on him. The blood was not his. He didn't look up or slow his stride as he mumbled to the gang.

"There won't be no more trouble with the Adelphi."

He passed by them, his face a mix of grim determination and incandescent rage.

"Where yer goin' boy?" enquired Will Roud.

"I got summin' for ol' Mrs Turner," replied Nash.

"'oo?" asked Shanks.

"She's the ol' woman whose washin' got swiped off the lit'le chavvie by the Adelphi," said Will quietly.

Nothing was ever said. Nash was the leader of the Dorset Street gang from that moment on, Will Roud moving up to second in command and Shanks dropping down to the lowest rank before quickly, quietly leaving the gang. The level of violence perpetrated on the leader of the Adelphi gang, who hadn't been one of the two who had robbed the little girl, assured there would indeed never be any more trouble from that quarter.

Years went by with the two of them living close to each other and following similar paths – crime. They even worked together on occasion, and there was never any apparent animosity between them, but though not apparent, and certainly unspoken, it was there nonetheless.

A month ago Shanks had visited the strange glossy haired slummer who he had heard could write genuine looking certificates he needed for a nice little fraud he had planned. He knew very well that she was as straight as an arrow, so he had given her a cock and bull story as to why he needed it.

"So thas why I needs these sirstifficates drawn up see."

Sookey had taken an immediate dislike to this man, and was pleased to conduct her business with him at her door, with Rose, who was talking in the street to some friends, only feet away, within easy calling distance. Sookey took a formal, unfriendly tone with her client.

"Very well. I am a little busy at Toynbee Hall this week and there is a rather a lot of work involved so I can have this done for you by Saturday. Shall we say a couple of bob Mr Shanks?"

Sookey was pleased that she had remembered to use local parlance for her charge of two shillings, though pronouncing 'a couple of bob' in perfect Queen's English rather than 'cupplabob' simply made Shanks snort contemptuously to himself. Shanks had been tipped off that the slummer was green so she would needless offer to do it for a fraction of the going rate, but he could still knock her down to half of whatever she offered. But being called Mr Shanks irritated him to the point that he forgot to launch into his rehearsed negotiations. He had introduced himself as Shanks when he arrived and she had assumed it was his surname.

"Yeah all right two bob it is, but it's Mr Mac Donald."

"Oh, Shanks is your er..." she hesitated. She had been about to say Christian name but then thought Shanks such an unusual name it was perhaps Jewish. "First name?"

"Nah, me first name's Niven. Shanks is jus' what they calls me. It's short for Longshanks see. Cos I'm tall see."

"Might I presume you are from good Scottish stock Niven? And that you have been given this name by some wag here in the East End," asked Sookey with a barely suppressed smile which was curling her lips and contorting her powdered cheeks.

What's the bleedin' 'ell's a matter wiv 'er. She should be in Bedlam.

"Me ol' man was Scotch. 'e weren't no good though. What ya mean wag?"

Sookey proceeded to give Shanks a brief history lesson about Edward the First.

⌒ ◆ ⌒

A month later, Shanks was standing at the station end of Middlesex Street, working for his old adversary Nashey. Standing in the cold, being paid by the day and given strict orders, he didn't like the idea of being Nash's servant. He was to keep an eye on a man 'as black as Newgate's knocker', who was in turn looking out for another man. He had never heard of such a thing.

"Don't move. Stay there till the black fella starts movin'. Then start walkin' slow to the station. When a gent passes yer, follow 'im. Even if 'e gets in an 'ansom cab, you gets the next 'un orf the rank after 'im. 'ere's some gelt to cover the fare just in case it turns out to be a fair way orf and 'ere's some wages an' all. I'll gives more tonight when I sees yer. An' before you arst, never mind what it's about. I got a keep it secret see. That's why I'm paying yer good money to jus' do as yer told and arst no questions."

Shanks wondered why he was being paid good wages and cab fares just to nose on some gent. He was also puzzled that he was the one being given the job rather than one of Nash's usual confederates such as Roud or one of the Carter brothers. And why was Nash in such a hurry to get away just now? Shanks had never seen him so jumpy. Shanks surmised that Nash was up to something, and that it was big, so he wanted to be part of it. He decided he would start asking around about Nash's movements, and also pay noses to watch him. He could certainly afford it, thanks to what he had been paid on account for the big job he had coming up in South London. But he preferred to think of Nash's wages to him being the money he was in turn paying out to noses to follow Nash. He chuckled slyly to himself at the thought.

He knew having Nashey followed would be dangerous but he determined to use men Nash could not possibly know, from Camden Town. And besides, the peculiar way he was acting, Shanks doubted Nash would be his usual suspicious self when it came to watching his own back. Shanks would talk to everyone Nash spoke to. Not his cronies of course, but men he wouldn't normally chew the cud with. He would find out what Nash was up to.

Social explorers, churchmen and politicians were quick to castigate the poor for what was considered to be feckless housekeeping such as purchasing food and services from street vendors, or from shops in small, expensive quantities. But if people didn't have enough money to buy the likes of cooking pans and utensils in the first place, they bought their food off the street. If they had insufficient to buy staples from shops in larger cheaper quantities, they bought 'tasters'; an "a'pence' of this, a 'pennyworth' of that. Nash had been brought up in such a household, and although he was much better off than his parents because he had no family to support, old habits died hard. He still bought three meals a day from street vendors, and spent as little of his income as possible on household purchases. He didn't even own a razor, other than the ones he kept as a weapon. He never shaved himself, preferring, to go for a shave twice a week at the shaving parlour. Why give yourself a latherless shave over a bucket of cold water in the yard in all weathers, when you could have two shaves for a penny ha'penny at the barber's.

Nash was walking to his preferred barber, well over on the far side of Whitechapel in a predominantly Jewish neighbourhood. His closest place was a squalid affair from where he had caught 'devil in the beard', a minor but irritating skin disease from the use of dirty razors. He hadn't used it since. There were numerous other places within a few minutes walk, all of which he had tried over the years, but every one of them grossly exploited their lather lads, who worked twelve hours a day, six days a week for five shillings a week. Hardly a week went by without Nash giving some street urchin a cuff round the ear for something or another, but he had a secret regard for them.

He remembered very well his own days at that age. He hadn't been a lather lad but his first job as a butcher's boy has been just as tough. Four shillings a week, work till nearly midnight some Saturdays, and then back in on the Sunday morning if there was still meat to sell; and never a kind word or deed from either the butcher or his wife. The day after he had fought with his father, the now homeless young Nash had resigned from the butcher's employ by piling as much meat as he could carry into a horsesack and making a run for it.

The barber shop he now used was run by a miserable but fair old man who treated his lads better than most. Nash walked under the haircutting and shampooing sign above the door and entered. It was his normal day for a shave but he had broken his usual pattern by having a shave just two days earlier, in readiness for his meeting with Sookey.

"Didn't expect you in 'oday," was the terse welcome from the proprietor. The barber continued, "Free shaves in a week. Got a fancywoman 'ave yer?"

"Don't your jaw ache?" came the sour response from Nash.

He always went to the barbers at a time when he knew it would be busy. He liked the wait. Nobody spoke to him or knew him from Adam. He enjoyed being anonymous for a change, just listening to the other customers. He usually stood waiting his turn but he had a lot on his mind, so he sat down on the waiting plank next to the wall, leaned back and closed his eyes.

Yes'dee's mee'ing with Soppy Sookey were a right waste a time wun it. Thas the trouble with them sort. They're so busy watching their p's and q's all the time it takes from now 'ill doomsday to get any sense out ov 'em. Mind you, yer got a 'and it to 'er, she were tryin' 'er best to talk like proper people even if it did sound queer 'alf the time.

He knew he could not have simply started discussing with Sookey why prostitutes didn't bleed like other people.

Gawd can yer imagine 'er ladyship's shock an' 'orror if I says wot I wanted straight out. 'Sookey, yer know doctorin' don't ya, so why don't 'ores bleed much? Is it cos they most likely all got syph?' So I 'as to go all round the 'ouses and finally gets me bit in when she says about as 'ow the killer ain' been caught yet. 'How can this monster walk through the streets with impunity?' she arsts. 'Well he ain' got no blood on him for one fing. He could walk right past a crush...policeman plain. Who's gonna suspect a respectable doctor?' I says. Course that were a mistake. Talkin' about a doctor took us right off the fred. 'A doctor?' she arsts. I then 'as to make up some ol' cock and bull story about why I finks 'e mus' look like a respectable doctor. 'They says the killer mus' be a doctor or least 'ave doctorin' skills ov some sort. An' he's got ta have a doctor's bag or summin' to carry the knife in ain' 'e? I doubts he can get that in no greatcoat pocket'. She flinches. I fought I says too much. 'I'm jus' surmisin' he mus' be respectable in his stamp cos he mus' walk right by the bobbies on the beat afterwards mustn't he? There's hundreds ov 'em all over the shop, plain clothes an' all so yer don't know 'oo's 'oo these days do ya'. She then turns all queer.

'The fiend has no blood on him you say? Pray tell, how do you know this sir? And I have doctoring skills do I not? You have shown interest in my abilities from the moment you first met me. You went to the trouble of seeking me out at the gallery when you could have simply waited for me to be at my home. Am I under suspicion sir? You must be plain with me sir, you are a detective are you not?'

Gawd 'elp us I fought I'd 'eard it all then. This woman's as soppy as a box o' lights. She's been reading too much bleedin' Sherlock 'omes an' Jekyll an 'yde. 'ow's she fink a slip of a woman like 'er could be suspected ov the crimes for gawd's sake. One ov the papers 'ad said it could be some woman mind. A midwife 'oo'd taken it against 'ores cos ov all the abortions she'd 'ad ta do'. This soppy cow must a read that an' all. I makes a quick decision to go along wiv it, without admit'in' to nuffin'. That way I can jus' tells 'er she must a got the wrong end a the stick when she finds out who I really is. It meant I didn't 'av to explain what I did for a livin' no more, an' I could press on with me questions without beatin' around the bush. I tried to make meself sound all official like, like a beak or like one a them arsewipes Anderson an' Warren sound in the papers. And I tried to sound me words even more proper.

'Madam, there is a belief that the murderer could be a doctor or at least have such skills. The wounds on the bodies suggest doctorin' knowledge. But there is somefin' you can help me with. The wounds have not bled as much as I would have fought. Could a disease stop blood sheddin'? Pardon me for putting such an inpolite question to a lady but may I be so bold as to arst you, could it be er...syphilis causin' it?' She don't turn 'air. 'Why no sir, certainly not. No illness could have such an effect. If there is little loss of blood there can be but only one answer. The injuries were inflicted post mortem'. Woss post mortem mean when it's at 'ome I finks! I sees Sookey is turned suspicious. 'The police surgeon will know of this will he not sir?'

Nash remembered gazing towards the scullery to avoid Sookey's perplexed stare, nodding sagely, while he tried to think of an answer.

The scullery! Shit! Rose! I forgot she were there! Crafty cow never made a sound once me and Sookey started jawrin'. She must a stopped doin' whatever work she were doin' and just sat there earwiggin'. Must 'av had a right chuckle to 'erself when I was trying to talk all proper. And soon as I leaves she'd 'ave gone straight an' told 'er ladyship 'oo I was I wager.

For a second he was furious, both with himself and Rose, but the anger was quickly dissipated by another emotion as he remembered the long chat he'd had with Sookey. They had chatted about all manner of things; personal things. He now felt strange; uncomfortable.

He felt a small kick on his right boot and opened his eyes to see the barber glaring down at him.

"'ere, cloff ears! Woke up 'av yer? You want this shave or don't ya?"

It was clear that Nash had been so deep in thought that he hadn't heard the barber call that it was his turn. Nash would normally have grabbed the old misery by the throat and muttered something appropriately menacing. He smiled at the old man through slightly narrowed eyes as he went through in his mind how he would normally respond to such lack of respect.

I'll give you a shave one day old man, real close it'll be, and you won't need anovver one.

But he was glad of the old man's intervention in to his thoughts; relieved to escape from them. And besides, nobody knew him in this neck of the woods. He didn't have any reputation to defend; no appearance to live up to. He kept silent and meekly got into the chair. He watched the barber's skill at resharpening the razor on his leather strap; not the most interesting of pursuits but it was preferable to closing his eyes again.

◈

Nash had decided Sookey Parsons was more trouble than she was worth. She had plenty of skills he could use, and it was obvious she had taken a shine to him so he could use that to his advantage, but he had other things on his mind.

The reason for get'in in wiv 'er in the first place were ta find out more about the killin's, and she's proved as much use as a pocket in a shroud. She'd 'ad some notion the killer must be killin' 'em before 'e knifed 'em. So 'e beats 'em to deff or strangles 'em or summin', and then starts cuttin' 'em up when they're already dead. I did 'ear one of 'em was knocked aboud a bit but I'm sure 'e' ain't gonna waste 'is time with all that lark wiv 'alf of London's crushers bearing down on 'im any minute. 'av you ever 'eard such a fing? Don't stand ta reason do it? Besides, to get back inta 'er good books I'd 'av to make up some ol' tripe about 'ow she's got the wrong end ov the stick about what I'd said to 'er about them questions about the syphilis. An' any'ow, she gets on me nerves. All that jawrin'. I was in 'er 'ouse for 'ours if yer please. Talkin' about everyfin' under the sun. She gets fings out a yer, crafty like. Bugger me if I ain' told 'er about me Ragged schoolin' 'fore I 'ad the fight wiv the ol' man an' joined the kidsman's gang. It ain' right people knowin' all yer business. It didn't seem that long mind, but it's a good job it's October so it gets dark and I was able to get on me way. If it 'ad bin summer I'd a bin there chinwaggin' till the cows come 'ome. An' I never did track down Shanks afterwards neiver. I'll 'ave to get 'old ov 'im after Khan now. Nah, when 'er ladyship ain' about I'm a man a few words and that's 'ow I likes it. I won't 'av nuffin' more a do wiv 'er if I 'as my way.

CHAPTER 9:

"Everyone should duly note that only a homicidal maniac could induce these poor wretcheds to prefer the 'bastilles of starvation' to the less dubious horrors of selling their bodies..."

Justice

The first letter signed 'Jack The Ripper', which had been in police hands for over a week, well before the last two murders, was made public through the newspapers. The crimes themselves had created a huge public outcry, but they were as nothing compared to the effect of the letter. A legend was born.

Nash walked into the Ten Bells looking for Khan. The pub was full of readers and listeners. The few semi-literate incumbents were stuttering out loud to the open-mouthed majority every gruesome word of the Ripper letter, murder scene interviews and police quotes, as well as any rumour the newspapermen had chosen to print. But there were faces and clothes, both too well groomed, who didn't fit. It transpired that they were reporters, dispatched post haste by their newspapers to get everything and anything they could from deepest, darkest Whitechapel.

A surge of adrenaline coursed through Nash. This was what he had hoped for. He was being proved right. A sense of well-being grappled with an underlying sense of guilt and foreboding, just as it had when he had allowed the killer, Jack The Ripper as he was know known, to get away Scot-free.

☙ ◆ ❧

Khan had not got very far. The cabbies had been more interested in belittling and abusing a lascar than giving out information. Khan had dropped Nashey's name in an attempt to get a civil response from the men. He thought one of them might know Nash and warn the rest of them to tell Khan what he wanted to know. This was the last thing Nash wanted. He needed to keep his interest in the man in the Derby hat a secret. But just as he was about to lay into Khan with his tongue for ignoring his orders, the Indian mentioned an incident that gave Nash pause for thought.

"But they stopped laughing at me when Leppy scuttled by Nashey. 'Gall on gis us a fit then Leppy-AY! Get them legs dancin' along the floor boy!' they were shouting after him. I took the chance to get away from them."

"Good to 'ear lit'le Leppy's out," said Nash with a nod of appreciation. "Last I 'eard 'e were in the Whitechapel union. Poor little sod. 'e's got an 'ead on 'is shoulders mind, when 'e ain't 'aving one a them fits."

Khan had seen from Nash's glaring eyes that he hadn't been pleased with him, so was relieved at Nash moving his thoughts to Leppy. To keep them there he quickly replied.

"Yes, Nashey, I walk with him. He told me he did so well as mortuary attendant someone spoke for him for job at funeral parlour. He's working there now."

Nash was bemused.

"Mortuary attendant?"

"He were chosen cos like you said Nashey, he's sharp when he's all there. When Polly Nicholls got dun in, there no mortuary in area to take her. So they did that cutting up of body they do to find how she die, in shed against workhouse in Old Montagu Street. They need mortuary attendant they call it, to clean, lay out body before doctor come, so Leppy do it."

"Did 'e now?" said Nashey with a far away look in his eyes.

Khan wasn't sure if it was a question or not. The words were a question but the tone and the eyes suggested otherwise. He played it safe.

"Yes Nashey, they did."

Nash didn't hear him.

⁓ ◆ ⁓

With Sookey a thing of the past, Nash had tried to give up thinking about why prostitutes didn't bleed much. After all, it wasn't so important in the swing of things. It was more curiosity than anything that had led him to thinking about it in the first place. It was not going to help him find out who or where this Jack The Ripper, as he now called himself, was. Or help him decide what to do about him the next time their paths met. Nevertheless, the lack of blood was an itch he couldn't scratch, so he had gone to the trouble of finding out where Tommy Newman, the epileptic, otherwise known as Leppy, was working these days. Nash thought it wouldn't do any harm to see if Leppy had any ideas about the blood. After all, other than a few policemen and doctors, he had more first-hand knowledge than anyone else about the body of one of the victims. If anyone could tell him something useful it was Leppy. But he didn't want Leppy to know he had anything but normal lurid interest in the killings.

Will Roud had done some nosing about for him earlier in the day, and armed with knowledge of Leppy's movements to and from work, Nash arrived on the street corner opposite the funeral parlour at the appropriate time, and didn't have long to wait for his man to appear. Not wishing Leppy to know he had been looking for him, the meeting had to appear happenstance.

"Leppy-AY!" shouted Nash as he crossed the street. "Fought yer were still inside the 'ouse. Good to see yer out an' about boy."

Leppy shook his head.

"Nah I've been out a few weeks now Nashey. 'ad a bit a luck for a change."

"Yeah? 'ow's that. You ain't still frowin' fits even when you're not frowin' 'em proper are ya?" asked Nash, referring to Leppy's previous occupation of bogus fit-thrower.

Leppy was an epileptic but didn't suffer the disease as badly as some. The occasional real attack had given him the knowledge and ability to fake many others in a believable manner. He mostly worked the churches and chapels. It was important to appear a decent-looking, neat, threadbare, hollow-eyed man, collapsing in convulsions, with limbs threshing and foam spewing from the mouth. On coming round he would tell the crowd which had inevitably gathered, of his tragic circumstances. He then produced papers apparently signed by a clergyman (actually forged by a screever) describing him as a man of good character, pious, industrious but prone to seizures that had reduced him to penury, and commended him to Christian charity. A collection would be taken. It was a living. Just.

Leppy grinned.

"Nah, got fed up wiv the taste a soap."

Nash frowned.

"Used to put soap shavings under me tongue to fake the foam," explained Leppy. "'sides, I was runnin' out ov places to do it. There's only so many churches and chapels ain' there? They only looks after yer once. Second time they shies away. I tried the boozers at chuckin' out time but all I got was a reviver. Yer can't live on spirits can yer?"

"Some try," said Nash sagely. "So wot were yer bit a luck then?"

"I 'ad a real attack see. Bad one it were. Worst I've ever 'ad. It were in that first particular, last munff. 'member, it were a real fick un, couldn't see yer 'and in front a yer face could ya. Nobody 'ad come near or by. Everyone jus' wants to get where they're goin' when the fog comes down dunt they. I were jus' comin' a me senses when a couple of lads rolled me. Took me last. Even yanked sum ov me clobber off me. Gave me a good 'iding an' all jus' fer the sport." He then added with gravity, "I'll know 'em again though."

"Let me know if yer need any 'elp boy," offered Nash.

"Nah, I won't need nun. Once I find out 'oo they are I'll visit 'em both, one at a time. Wrong uns like them won't be sa clever on their own. An' I won't be already down this time will I."

"That were yer bit a luck were it?" asked Nash sarcastically. "I wouldn't go ta 'urst Park if I was you."

"Funny sod ain't ya? Any'ow, I was in a bad way. 'ad nowhere go 'cept the 'ouse. But I was right as ninepence soon enough. The Whitechapel 'ouse is even worse than Poplar's. Full ov broken men waitin' ta die. I started 'elpin' out the nurses jus' for summin' a do. This doctor sees me and the next fing I know 'e's got me 'elpin' 'im. I was the only young, fit cove in there see. An' then, blow me if I ain't layin' out sum old 'ore for a post mortem as they calls it, not minutes after she's 'ad 'er froat cut. Turns out it's one a this Jack the Ripper's bits a work an' they got a cut 'er some more to find fings out. Not that 'e were known as Jack then a course."

"Post mortem?" queried Nash.

"That's what they calls it when they slices 'em up after deff for the inquest. It's I-tie for summin' a do with deff I were told. Dunno what they 'ave to start speaking I-tie for, der you Nashey?"

"I knows someone who's always speaking I-tie. If it ain't post mortem, it's hello," said Nash.

"Can't says I've ever 'eard that. Wassat mean nen?"

Nash was irritated with himself for getting off the subject.

"Never mind all that, tell us more about this layin' out business. So you got to see ol' Polly Nicholls while she were still warm ay? Must 'av been a right ol' mess. Blood everywhere I should fink?"

"'ow d'yer know it were Polly Nicholls?"

Sharp bastard you are Leppy, thought Nash.

"Yer said yer been out the work'ouse for a while, so it weren't the last two were it, an' Polly Nicholls were the one sliced up right by Whitechapel work'ouse so it don't take no Sherlock 'omes ta work out she must a bin the one yer layed out."

Leppy nodded.

"Yeah, never fort a that. Nah, she weren't that covered in blood funny enuff. Loads of 'oles, like a bleedin' pepper pot she were, but blood just oozed out of em' in a trickle so a speak. You could only just about a filled a small cup wiv the lot."

"Rum eh? Police doctor say anyfin' aboud it?" Nash was trying not to sound too interested.

"Well, I did 'ear 'im say summin' to the chief crusher about it when 'e arrived but they were talkin' quiet see, so as nobody could 'ear, so I must a mis'eard cos it didn't make no sense."

"Gall on," pushed Nash.

"Well 'e said as 'ow the wounds could av' bin administered as 'e puts it, post mortem. But the crusher shook 'is 'ead and said no, 'e must 'av 'eld 'er wiv 'is right 'and an' stabbed 'er and then slit her froat wiv the left. But what I sees as rum is the police doctor 'ad just done a post mortem on the body, so it don't make sense the wounds were post mortem do it? I must a mis 'eard."

"Yeah, must 'av," agreed Nash.

Praps that Sookey were worf keepin' in wiv after all.

CHAPTER 10:

"In our age of contradictions and absurdities, a fiend murderer may become a more effective reformer than all the honest propagandists in the world."

H. Davis, Commonweal

Sookey's monthly meetings for coffee with her friend Nora had started to become weekly ones. This was at Nora's request, with the conversations taking a distinct change in subject matter. The whole dynamic of the meetings had changed. Rather than Nora mostly holding court, with Sookey happy to hear all the gossip from her old world, Nora was now taking a much greater interest in Sookey and her life. Sookey had been both delighted and surprised by Nora's sudden interest in the East End in general and Sookey's work there in particular. A second cup of coffee was taken, and Nora insisted on paying for both. Sookey had been shocked to find Nora eager to broach the dreadful subject of the recent murders.

After they had their fill of coffee, they would continue their discussions whilst enjoying a stroll, and on their last walk Nora had asked Sookey if a couple of mutual acquaintances, Elizabeth and Rebecca, could join them the next time they meet. She wondered if Sookey would like to join them for luncheon. Nora deemed it wrong that Sookey should always have to make the journey to the West End for these gatherings. The least she, Elizabeth and Rebecca could do was to get a taxi cab over to the East

End for a change. She had made enquiries of Mr Thomas Cook as to whether there were any tours of the East End, but sadly there were not.

"It would appear it is easier to visit darkest Africa than darkest Whitechapel my dear," she laughed. "I think we will have to entrust you to be our guide Susan."

This had made Sookey uneasy. It would be awkward enough meeting Elizabeth and Rebecca again for the first time since her fall from grace, without having to worry about where and how to keep them and Nora entertained. There was also the problem of her attire; keeping up appearances for an hour in the West End was one thing, doing it for a day in the East End was quite another. It was fortunate that she was promised money by Shanks for the work she had done for him. It would pay to have her second dress cleaned. Another concern was that she and these women could easily bump into local people whom she knew; she liked to keep her past and present lives separate. But her reticence at Nora's suggestion was ignored, her friend easily brow-beating her into submission.

Sookey was not sure where to take them. There was a respectable Spiers & Bond refreshment room in Liverpool Street Station. The same company ran the Criterion Theatre, so it would probably suffice, but Sookey was concerned that the station was just where old and new lives might converge.

Nora meeting Rose; that would indeed be interesting, thought Sookey wryly.

Sookey had a stroll round the City of London, on the other side of the station. She knew that several new catering chains had opened premises to appeal to office-workers; one of these might be acceptable, though she would prefer it if Gatti Brothers, who ran a chain of respectable restaurants in theatres and the Adelaide Gallery in the Strand, had opened a branch nearby. She found a Slater's luncheon and tea rooms and an Express Dairy milk and bun shop, but feared they were not respectable enough. A chop house would certainly be respectable per se, but it would be full of men. Four women walking through the doors would turn the heads of the city gents whose sole domain it was, and there would surely be frowns and mutterings once the women had turned their backs to the moustaches, tipped hats and polite smiles. Much to her relief she eventually found an Aerated Bread Company tea shop, which she thought acceptable. She had been in one at London Bridge station a few years earlier, in another life.

The four women duly met, with Elizabeth and Rebecca far friendlier than Sookey could have hoped. There was none of the awkwardness she might have expected. After the initial inevitable small talk of West End life and the mutual acquaintances the four women shared, the subject was quickly moved along to the opposite end of the city. The women were keen to know all about Henrietta Barnett, and Sookey's involvement with her and the good vicar. They marvelled at Sookey's 'fascinating' life. Sookey retorted that it was very hard work and not without its many drawbacks. Her three new friends picked up on this remark to ask her about her safety, and from there moved the subject along to the recent murders. By this time they were coming to the end of a long meal, Sookey feeling not a little nauseous from the long forgotten feeling of an over full stomach. She was also intoxicated by being the centre of attention; having her lifestyle, which she had always assumed must appal her contemporaries, accepted and enthused over. She was enjoying herself immensely.

Sookey leaned forward solicitously, lowering her voice to a whisper.

"I have been interviewed by a detective on the matter," she muttered, referring to the murders which they had just been discussing.

Six eyebrows headed for the globed gas brackets which hung above. She considered the next sentence that had formed in her head. She pondered whether it was wise to continue for a moment before her excitement got the better of her and she blurted it out.

"I was a suspect. They thought I could be Jack The Ripper himself. Or dare I say herself!"

Three jaws sped in the opposite direction to the eyebrows. Sookey continued.

"All local doctors are suspects because the police believe that the injuries could only have been inflicted by someone with medical training. I was suspected because, I am not sure whether you are aware, I have certain medical skills acquired from my departed husband, a physician. And apparently, it is not impossible that a woman could be the murderer. The weakness of the poor wretched victims means a fellow woman could easily have overpowered them. The murders committed by a woman eager to cleanse society of the ills of ..."

She left the word 'prostitution' unsaid. She thought it too unsavoury for her audience.

Nora was a very effusive, confident woman. Sookey had never seen her lost for words; until now. The other two women had managed to slowly swivel their heads towards Nora, as if needing her to take the lead. Nora stuttered her way through several attempts at interrogative pronouns. Sookey got the gist and nodded with enthusiasm.

"The detective sought me out at my art gallery, at which I am Henrietta's curator, under the pretext that he required medical assistance for a hand injury, but it became clear that he was interrogating me. When I challenged him about it, he told me what I have just recalled to you. He is a clever scoundrel. A friend in Whitechapel, Rose, a rough diamond, who has been my saviour on many occasions, and without whose help I could not continue to live in the East End, such are its inherent difficulties for a lady of good breeding, believes him to be a bad lot."

She had to stop to take a breath. Her excitement was leading to a verbosity she had never believed possible of herself, certainly not in the company of Nora, let alone Elizabeth and Rebecca.

It is well I no longer wear a corset, I would faint for certainty, she thought cheekily to herself. She continued with her monologue.

"Rose believes this man to be a rogue; a violent thief if you please. Oh but his disguise is so fine. She is completely taken in. I have become friends with this gentleman, though he would chastise me for bestowing such a title upon him. We speak for hours about all manner of things. He is not well-spoken, or rich in the bank but he is not at all ill-looking."

She stopped suddenly, realising that in her excitement she had become far too wanton, perhaps even brazen. But the three women were far too stunned by Sookey's revelations to concern themselves with matters of female etiquette.

The day had ended with Sookey in a quandary. She was enjoying her newly raised status amongst her recently acquired middle class friends. But they were now keen for her to take them on a tour of the East End. She had initially responded to the request with enthusiasm.

"Why, most certainly. I can show you my vision of a future Whitechapel Art Gallery, and there's the library, of which we are so proud. There are some fine works on show in my gallery, which I know you would enjoy. I could introduce you to the Reverend Samuel and Henrietta, and we could perhaps time your visit to accord with a lecture or a recital at Toynbee Hall."

Nora smiled.

"That would be delightful my dear. Perhaps we could also take morning coffee with you at your er dwelling. And we would like to see Petticoat Lane of course as we have heard so much of it. Our cabman also suggested we should visit an eel and pie house for luncheon. And no tour would be complete without seeing a Cockney public house of course. But it is a serious excursion too is it not. We would like to see some of the poor wretcheds that walk the streets."

Sookey's ardour had been well and truly dampened.

CHAPTER 11:

"Whoever may be the wretch who committed these sanguinary outrages, the real criminal is the vicious bourgeois system which, based on class injustice, condemns thousands to poverty, vice and crime, manufactures criminals, and then punishes them."

H.M. Hyndman

On leaving Leppy, Nash had tracked down Shanks for a debrief. Shanks relayed that he had successfully followed the Derby-hatted gent to Euston station. He claimed that the gent had got a hansom off the Liverpool Street station rank, but so as not to lose him, he had to quickly flag down a passing growler, and being a fair distance to Euston it had cost twice as much as Nash had paid him. Nash was suspicious of the story. Cabbies were a fly bunch, and the boys on the rank wouldn't have let a passing growler swipe a fare from under their nose. But he wasn't in a position to contest it and had to pay Shanks the additional cost of the four-wheeler cab.

Shanks claimed that he hadn't managed to get close enough to the man at the ticket kiosk to hear where he was buying a ticket to, but he had followed him to his platform and watched him board the train. Shanks had actually seen the gent board the express service, but his enquiries into what Nash was up to had already led him to think that his best interests might be served by lying. He wanted to keep one step ahead of him. But Nash was a sharp one. He would have to be careful. He decided not to lie about what direction the gent travelled, but rather which train he got. That would cover himself if Nash later found out from another source that the gent went to Liverpool, whilst still keeping him in the dark if he didn't.

"It were the stopper ta Liverpool," lied Shanks.

Nash cursed inwardly to himself. He had not expected this at all, having assumed the gent was from the West End of London and no further. Shanks' news meant that the gent could have got off at any one of a number of towns between London and Liverpool.

"Did 'e 'ang about after 'e got 'is ticket?" interrogated Nash.

"Nah, bought a paper; that were it."

"'ow long did 'e 'ave to wait for the train ta go?"

"Not long."

"'ow long?"

"Dunno, five minutes or thereabouts I should fink."

"An' you saw the train go out?"

"Yeah."

"An' 'e couldn't 'ave dodged off it and on to anuvver train?"

"Nah. I 'ad 'em peeled sharp enuff all right."

"Wot time were it?"

"Gawd knows, didn't look at the clock."

"Did ya arst the porters what time the next Liverpool semi fast and fast was?

"Nah, why should I? Wot's all this about any'ow?"

"Don't matter, you did well boy."

"Nah, I mean wot's all this 'ole fing about. 'aving two noses work this gent."

"I told ya before didn't I, it ain't none a your bleedin' business."

Nash had finished the discussion at this point. He didn't trust Shanks further than he could throw him, but his story sounded about right. He had taken a calculated risk in using Shanks instead of someone like Will Roud. He was playing with very high stakes and if he got caught harbouring the killer, it was the noose for him for sure. He didn't want Will or anyone else he had any respect for involved. Hence he had kept Khan's involvement to a minimum and it was why he had Shanks do the main leg work. If anyone was going to get their neck stretched alongside him, it was going to be the wrong un.

Nash immediately set off for Euston to check on the timetables to see how soon after the stopper there would have been a faster train. He wanted to see if he could narrow down the number of stations at which the killer might have alighted. Taking the timings that Khan had given him for when the pursuit of the gent had started from Middlesex Street, and the time a cab would take to reach Euston, Nash had calculated the time Shanks and his quarry would have reached the station.

Nash's usual world was a compact one. Hoxton was about the furthest north he tended to travel, St Paul's the furthest west, both of which were within easy walking distance. But Euston was miles away. He thought about running it. It was no further than he would run round the marshes, but a runner on the street at night might attract attention. An inquisitive policeman might decide to have words with him. He looked down at his feet and cursed. He was wearing his uncomfortable dogging shoes, which he had worn the previous day for his meeting with Sookey, and slipped back on today without thinking.

I ain' goin' 'ome just ta get me boots. 'sides I'm in 'urry. Can't take all bleedin' night walkin' over a Euston an' back. It's the underground railway for me.

He hadn't been on the underground since his father had taken him as an excited young boy on the newly opened Farringdon Road to Paddington Metropolitan, the world's first underground railway. He thought about not paying his fare, but given the importance of his journey, he didn't want any trouble.

"Euston," was barked at the booking office clerk in Liverpool Street underground station.

"Closest yer can get direct from 'ere's King's Cross," was the equally abrupt reply.

Further information about alternative routings, including changes, were not forthcoming.

"Fruppence."

"Fruppence! I don't want first class. 'ow many classes is there?" demanded Nash.

"Free."

"I'll 'ave fird class"

"Yeah, I fought so, that's why I said it were fruppence. Second class is fourpence and first is a tanner."

"'ow many stops is it?" asked a Nash whose hackles were beginning to rise.

"Free. Stops Finsbree Circus then Farringdon then King's Cross, an' 'fore you arst, it's still fruppence wherever yer get off. It's fruppence fird class as far as yer like. Yer could 'av a nice little ride round the Circle all the way round London an' back 'ere if you 'ad a mind."

Nash didn't respond other than simply placing a thruppeny bit methodically in front of the clerk. A ticket was handed over. Nash slid it into his pocket before casually striding around to the side door of the booking office which he kicked open, before grabbing the waistcoat of the uniformed clerk and throwing him against the wall.

"Lucky I'm in 'urry lad. Now, 'ow often these fings run?"

"They're every ten minutes this time a night," squeaked the clerk.

Nash found the signs confusing at first but eventually made his way onto the correct, westbound platform. The smell and smoke made the air quality poor but at this station it wasn't much worse than the miasma above the surface. Nash had immediately forgotten the clerk's insolence and was deep in thought.

More bleedin' money out the door. Serves me right for put'in' on these soddin' shoes. It's bad enuff when I ast a wear 'em for work. This 'ol business is costin' an' there's the troof. I ain't dun hand's turn since it all started neiver. Money goin' out, nuffin' comin' in. I'll be in the work'ouse at this rate. Maybe I'll do a bit a work over Euston tonight while I'm over there. There won't be many crushers over there. They're all over 'ere lookin' for 'is nibs. Nah, best not, don't know the streets. Don't like not knowin' the streets.

A train of dark green carriages pulled in. Nash got in and noted how spacious and well lit it was. A quarter of an hour later he was in a part of London he had never ventured into before.

The timetable told a different story to that of Shanks. According to the timings, if Shanks had told the truth at least as far as the killer going to Euston and getting on a Liverpool train was concerned, he had lied about the train being a stopper. Nash spent the next half an hour in the station. He asked a porter if he remembered if the four o' clock to Liverpool fast train had left on time. It had. Had the three o'clock stopper been late leaving? No, bang on time. He then saw Freddie, a pickpocket he knew.

"FreddayAY!"

A tiny dark haired, hollow-eyed, pox-faced creature started running without even looking round to see who was calling after him. His pin-thin legs bowed badly from the rickets he suffered. He couldn't as much run as scuttle like a spider. Nash ran him down in a few yards and grabbed him as lightly as he could by the shoulder.

"It's only me, boy. Nashey. Not workin' Fenchurch Street these days?"

"Nashey," replied Freddie, with the far away vagueness of the starving. "No, they know me there dunt they, the bastards," he mumbled barely coherently.

"You talkin' about 'ow beloved police force Freddie? You shouldn't worry about them, they got bigger fish ta fry than you these days ain' they."

"'oo?"

"Jack The Ripper a course. Every crusher in the force is so busy chasing their tails cos ov 'im they ain' got time for the likes a you and me."

"'oo?"

Blimey, you are in a bad way ain't ya, yer poor little sod.

"You seen ol' Shanks about lately?"

"Yeah!" said Freddie with new found enthusiasm, his voice much stronger, pleased he could be of use to someone. "Saw 'im yestdee. Late artanoon it were. Late but still light I remember clear."

"Don't spose yer saw wot 'e was up to did ya?"

"Yeah, 'e were doggin' the gent I 'ad me eyes on at first. But the gent were too quick for both ov us see. I was up close to the gent by the ticket place but 'e cuts a right dash after 'e gets 'is ticket. I couldn't keep up wiv 'im so that was my chance gawn. Shanks got close to 'im but didn't do nuffin', an' left 'im to get on the Liverpool fast. He 'ung about to see the train orf. I remembers cos I fought it were a bit rum so I kept an eye on Shanks meself."

"Liverpool fast train yer say? You sure?"

"Yeah. I 'eard the gent buy 'is ticket. 'e were off to Liverpool all right."

"Speak to Shanks did ya, after?"

"Nah, fuck 'im, e's a wrong un that one."

"See you did 'e?"

"Nah, I saw ta that."

"'ere's a bob Freddie. Now, I could give ya nuffin' a course, or seein' as yer told me what I wanna know I could fank ya by givin' ya tuppence to get yerself a tightener wiv, and you'd be glad ov it wouldn't ya. But ere's a bob, not for wot yer told me but to keep yer trap shut should as 'ow if Shanks comes back round arstin' if I been 'ere, yer ain' seen me see. An' I'm givin' yer a bob instead a tuppence to tell yer that this is serious."

Nash grabbed hold of him, glaring into his eyes with menace.

"You ain't see me 'av yer boy?"

"Ain' see yer Nashey."

Nash had lied. He had given the pathetic human specimen a shilling for two reasons. One was because he knew it would keep him from the workhouse at least for another couple of days, and two, Nash knew Freddie would go straight and spend most of it on the quickest way out of town – alcohol. This meant he wouldn't be around in the station should Shanks come sniffing around again to cover his tracks.

◆

Shanks had gathered a lot of very useful information. Nash had been heard preaching to all who would listen about the killings being a good thing for Whitechapel; good for the East End; good for poor people everywhere. Nobody else appeared to agree with this controversial view, and Shanks thought that if it had been anyone else they would have got a facer on the nose. And if that hadn't been enough to shut Nash up, a good kicking up an alleyway would have done the trick. But who would attempt such a thing against Nashey?

Shanks had found that Nash had been asking around about the murdered whores, and had also spent a lot a time with the slummer, Soppy Sookey. One of Shanks' paid cohorts had found out from big Rose Martin that he had specifically sought her out. Rose had been only too pleased to pass on what she had overheard in Sookey's scullery.

"Sookey don't jus' do wri'in' an' all that sort of fing yer know, she does doctorin' an all, see. Nash wanted medical know'ow out ov 'er cos 'e finks as 'ow Jack the Ripper's sum doctor. And what's it to 'im if 'e is? What's 'e interested in ol' Jack any more than the rest ov us for ay?"

When this information was first given to him, Shanks was both puzzled and suspicious. He knew Nash must be up to something. He mulled it over in his mind whenever he had a spare moment. It took him a while but eventually came the flash of inspiration.

"Gawd almigh'y! The gent!"

He had got some of his facts wrong, but by default, Shanks had got it right. But it wasn't a concept to him that Nash could be choosing to let the killer go free for anything other than selfish criminal reasons.

Shanks had another brainwave. It was clear to him that Nash was going to blackmail the gent. That was why he had wanted him followed. He hadn't planned on the man being from Liverpool of course. He had been assuming that for the small outlay of a day's wages and a cab fare to the West End, he would have the gent's address delivered to him on a plate. Shanks couldn't help but be impressed by the plan. Blackmailing Jack The Ripper himself! Only Nashey would dare do such a thing. But the only problem with the blackmail idea was that it didn't explain why Nash was claiming that Jack the Ripper was good for the East End. Then Shanks' racing mind had more inspiration. Nash was going to work the police and the newspapers somehow. Claim the reward but first get the papers to pay him for information. That was why he was stirring things up by claiming 'Jack's good for the poor'; to help build up the frenzy in the papers. The bigger the story the more he would be able to extort from them. Play one newspaper off against the over. The timing would have to be good; the more information he gave out, the more chance the police could use it to arrest their man. Nashey would have to claim the reward at just the right time, when they still didn't have quite enough to go on to pounce. Shanks' imagination now ran riot. He had yet another revelation. Nash would attempt to extract money from all three! Blackmail The Ripper first, who was a gent and therefore no doubt worth a pretty penny, then get the newspapers to pay for snippets, then turn the killer in to the police for the reward. Shanks was convinced Nash was taking on too much. His old nemesis would get a taste of steel or have his neck stretched for sure. He smirked slyly at the thought.

But he could not think of how he could gain from all this at the moment, so thought it would be good to keep as close to Nash as possible. He had originally planned to use other contacts for his Aldgate post office robbery, but now he would use Nash. He had all the information he needed to break in, and the money was there every Friday night, so the job could be done in the early hours of any Saturday from now on, but he would stretch it out a bit. He wanted to see how things developed, and he wanted an excuse to meet up with Nash every week. The more the two men talked, the more chance he had of eking out some scrap of information that would be useful.

There was also the need to do something about that Sookey woman. Her work was of such high quality that he had been quick to use her many times recently. Unbeknownst to her, she had forged credentials, written illicit hard-luck petitions and letters of recommendation. Shanks' favourite use of her was as a 'gag-maker', namely writing begging letters purporting to be on behalf of survivors of shipwrecks. He had no intention of paying her so had simply agreed to whatever price she fixed, and had run up quite a bill. But he did not like what he was hearing about her spending time with Nashey, especially the news that they were having long talks together. It was his opinion that long talks were more personal than 'ow's yer farver'. The only thing long talks led to was friendship. And you didn't run up large unpaid bills with any friend of Nashey. No, this sort of thing had to be nipped in the bud before it went any further. He wanted Nash concentrating on the matters at hand, namely soliciting money out of the Ripper, the papers and the police; and organising the Aldgate post office robbery. It would also be good to get one over on the bastard, although getting his 'fancypiece' hurt was as nothing compared to what he was going to get over on him in the long run. All he needed was time.

⌒ ◆ ⌒

Shanks had been the one to call the meet. Nash was intrigued to know why. He suspected it must be something to do with the dogging of the gent to Euston. There was a fight going on outside the pub where Nash was about to meet Shanks. It was quite a brawl. Some local lads were getting the better of some sailors on shore leave. The crowd were giving plenty of vocal support to the locals. Nash spotted

Shanks. He was at the front of the crowd but rather than watch the fight and air his opinions like everyone else, he was constantly looking round at the crowd. Someone shouted his support for the locals from the back of the throng.

"Gall on kick the bastard."

This was Shanks' cue to turn round to the flaying bodies and shout in their ears from point blank range, shaking his fists for added emphasis.

"Gall on, fuckin' kill 'em," immediately looking round at the crowd again, beaming, like a little boy who had just done something good for his father.

Wrong 'un, thought Nash. You'll never be one a the crowd, one ov us, as long as yer got 'ole in yer arse. Little Sookey was more one of us the day she come 'ere than you'll ever be. Nash had always made it a point not to call him Shanksey. A nickname ending with a y usually implied at least a level of acceptance, even a certain camaraderie. And besides it would have detracted from the fun of calling him Shanks. He waited for the fight to die down enough so he could shout over the sound of the supporters.

"Shanks!" bellowed Nash. Shanks crooked his neck back to see who was calling him, and Nash continued. "I ain' got all bleedin' night. Come on, oud ov it."

Not withstanding the fight, which had spilled over from the pub just a few doors down, this pub was just about the quietest in the whole East End. It was run by a new landlord who had airs and graces. He wouldn't allow in to his establishment; prostitutes, paupers, Jews, actors, Irish, gypsies, pure collectors, cadgers and since Annie Besant had started stirring them up, the Bryant & May factory girls, whom he considered revolutionaries. The pub had lost its soul, not to mention most of its customers. Even the Salvation Army girls no longer stood outside to tell the clientele the error of their ways. It was too long between amens.

Nash ordered a couple of pale ales and looked into the large mirror behind the bar. Other than the words on the mirror, 'Dunville's V R Old Irish Whisky Belfast', all he could see was a foursome of old women shelling peas. The place was otherwise deserted. Shanks arrived at his elbow.

Don't worry Shanks I've already stood the round, thought Nash caustically, as he surveyed his surroundings without enthusiasm.

"Wot the bleedin' 'ell yer brought me in this dead an' alive 'ole for?"

Shanks beckoned Nash to the corner of the pub furthest from the pea-shellers.

"I got some work for ya. Fought it was the least I could do seein' as yer been givin' me work lately. Needed somewhere there ain't no ears flappin' cos I got fings ta tell yer see."

"Yeah?" Nash snorted with undisguised disdain. "Well I could do wiv sum work. I've 'ad a lot a costs lately," he said with enough sarcasm to impart that he knew damned well that Shanks had charged for cab costs he hadn't incurred.

Shanks carried on without appearing to understand the reference.

"Wiv all the crushers lookin' for ol' Jack, there's never been easier pickin's. I've 'eard tell smashers, buzzers, kinchins, snakesmen, cracksmen..."

"Yeah all right," interrupted an impatient Nash, "I knows all the ways a making gelt round 'ere. Now cut ta the chase."

"Well, I knows this post office what we can rob easy as anyfin'."

"An' which one are you, Pierce or Agar?" retorted Nash sarcastically.

Shanks didn't understand the reference to the perpetrators of the Great Train Robbery of three decades earlier, the most notorious crime ever committed against Victorian property.

"'oo?" enquired a puzzled Shanks.

"Never mind. So where is this sit'in' duck?" Nash remained unimpressed.

"Don't worry about that for now, but I 'ere tell it's got 'undreds in there one Friday night every two-munff. I don't know when the next night is, but I'll be gettin' tipped the wink soon enuff don't you worry. We could even give some old 'hore a good 'iding an' cut 'er about a bit over Spitalfields way, and get someone ta call out, "orrible murder!' an' all the crushers in London'll be over there sharp, leavin' the post office area empty fer us."

Nash repeated Shanks' words in his mind.

Give some old 'ore a good 'iding an' cut 'er about a bit.

It was all Nash could do to stop himself from beating the sorry human specimen in front him to a pulp right there and then. He looked at Shanks as if he was a piece of pure he had just found on the bottom of his boot.

"An' since when were we cracksmen? I 'it people for a livin', an' you do what you do. An' where'd ya get this from any'ow?"

Nash had suddenly narrowed his eyes, changing his expression from contempt to suspicion.

"Never mind all that. That's my little secret ain' it. I got new friends in 'igh places." Shanks giggled before holding up a hand in acknowledgement of his inappropriate behaviour. "Lit'le private bit a coddin' wiv meself Nashey. Any 'ow, they've set me up wiv this pull so as to prove meself fer a much bigger job in a while see. Might be able a get yer in on that an' all. But fer now, you got the contacts for what I needs for this post office pull."

So thas why 'e's offerin' me in. 'e's sum'ow got old ov sum gold-dust knowledge about a post office but he ain' got a bleedin' clue wot ta do wiv it. 'e would need a cracksman, a canary an' a crow for a start orf, and I knows 'oo ta use.

"Yeah I got 'em all right. An' I spose your job's ta slice up the old 'ore eh?" asked Nash with a straight face, knowing what the reply would be.

"Well no, I was finkin' that would be your job," came the confirmation.

"So I got a get all the troops an' do all the dirty work 'ave I? Wot you gonna do fer yer money?"

"I'm the only one what knows what post office and the date ain' I?"

So you're gonna do fuck all on the night. Yeah, that's about right for you ain' it Shanks, thought Nash.

"All right boy I'm in."

'Boy' was usually a term which implied a certain friendliness but it was always used by men when talking to someone their junior in age. Shanks was the older, but Nash had always called him boy from the moment he first joined the gang years ago. He knew it rankled with Shanks but he knew equally he would never say anything.

"Your stand."

Nash cocked his wrist to flick his empty glass towards Shanks. Shanks reached for it.

"'ere, woss that?" questioned Nash, nodding at Shanks' right forearm.

"It's a tat'oo. A ship's capstan. I went down Lime'ouse docks an' 'ad it done by sum ol' China woman. Nobody'll wanna muck me about now will they? All the sailor boys 'ave got 'em."

Typical, thought Nash. A wrong un trying to look tough.

"Didn't do 'em much good outside jus' now did it?"

CHAPTER 12:

"Surely the awful revelations consequent upon the recent tragedies should stir the whole community up to action and to resolve to deliver the children of today, who will be the men and women of tomorrow, from so evil an environment."

Dr Thomas Barnado

Nash did not like the idea of the post office robbery at all. It meant relying on and trusting Shanks, which was out of the question. It was also not the sort of crime he was used to committing, and he liked to keep within what he knew. The prisons were full of men who had bitten off more than they could chew. And committing any crime against property, and an official source like a post office of all things, was considered a far more serious crime than offences against the person. But he thought he would go along with it for the time being. He would recruit a cracksman and a canary, and Will Roud could be the crow.

The prospective cracksman's lair was over in Hoxton. Nash had just set up a meet with Will for the next day, and been to check on how Khan was doing on look-out duty across the street from the Ripper's door, before setting out to Hoxton via the other end of Middlesex Street. It was early evening but darkness was already gathering, with the first yellow-green hint of a pea-souper coming down.

Nash spotted Sookey as soon as she turned the corner out of Wentworth Street into Middlesex Street, just a few yards ahead of him. She was now walking in the same direction as him. He slowed his pace to make sure she kept well ahead of him. The last thing he wanted was to get stuck passing the time of day with her. And there was the little matter of the lie he had told, or more accurately, let her believe, when they last met.

Inspector Alexander Nash of the Yard, special nosegay. Gawd 'elp us. Least she won't be after me a do 'er bleedin' wallpaperin' now.

He noticed she wasn't wearing anything on her head.

If she ain' leavin' 'er front step dirty she's parading round the streets with nuffin' on 'er bonce.

He could just imagine Rose and the rest of Sookey's neighbourhood women tutting away at her back.

She'll learn all right.

Sookey crossed the road and turned right into Gravel Lane. He thought she was probably making her way to the shops along there. Nashey was going to cut up by St Botolph's, which was straight on, so he was pleased to have got rid of her. He could speed up now. But rather than simply look straight ahead he couldn't help but continue to look at Sookey for a few more seconds as she made her way down Gravel Lane. He didn't know why.

The street was crowded and noisy with horses, carts and hordes of unwashed humanity making their way over the cobbles, many of the latter shouting the odds selling something or another, before they disappeared down one of the myriad little lanes or alleys of the slums. It was therefore easy to follow someone up close, but equally easy to lose them if you let them get too far ahead. The only problem with following up close was if the person being followed suddenly stopped in their tracks.

Sookey had stopped to talk to a red-haired woman. Nash hadn't noticed who the red-haired woman was in the throng, but would have done soon enough had his attention not been suddenly drawn to someone else. Nash had earlier noticed that a man had crossed Middlesex Street immediately after Sookey and followed her down Gravel Lane, but on such a busy thoroughfare there were lots of people walking in all directions so Nash had not paid any notice to the man. But when Sookey stopped, the man stopped. Nash had never seen a man take so long to tie his boot-laces.

Bugger me if 'e ain' doggin' 'er.

It was none of Nash's business, but for some reason he couldn't put his finger on he felt compelled to cross the road and set off after the two of them. He immediately scolded himself, muttering under his breath.

"Bleedin' nose-ache you are Nash."

A few seconds after Sookey had left the young red-haired woman to continue her journey down the street, a small hand grabbed Nash's elbow.

"Nashey!"

He turned. Sookey had been speaking to Mary Kelly. Nash had known Mary for years, since he had caught her trying to pick his pocket. He had more time for her than anyone else he knew. She was the closest thing he had to a real friend. She could be relied upon too; he had once used her as a canary on a pull. He had also once taught her how to punch, ensuring she hurt the victim without hurting her own knuckles, a mistake a lot of men, who liked to think they were handy with their fists, made. She had told him on more than one occasion of instances where she had put his teachings to good use.

The more Nash liked a woman the gruffer he usually tended to be towards her at the start of any meeting. He barely acknowledged Mary, with the slightest raising of his head in an inverse nod, before bending to whisper, his mouth inches from Mary's left ear, barely perceptible over the din of hooves and wheels on cobblestone.

"'ere, I gotta pull for ya. Should pay a tidy sum, keep yer orf them streets fer a while I shouldn't wonder. Your fella'll be pleased an' all, long as yer don't tell 'im as 'ow yer got 'old a the gelt. But I'll have to see yer aboud it tomorra. Ten Bells noon."

He started moving away, nodding after the man who was following Sookey and wagging a thumb in his direction.

"In the middle a summin'."

He winked and put his right index finger over his lips to tell her not to respond. She would realise he didn't want an enthusiastically loud 'all right Nashey!' to be heard by the man, but it was Sookey's ears he was thinking about.

Sookey and her follower continued past the shops and into a warren of narrow, quickly darkening streets.

Where she bleedin' goin' at this time a night? An' wiv 'er not wearin' no 'at or shawl on 'er bonce an' 'aving that rouge on, this cove probably finks she's on the game. Probably waitin' for 'er a get somewhere quiet 'fore arstin' 'er for business. Soppy cow, she's gonna learn the 'ard way one a these days.

It was then that Nash spotted the second man following her.

Two of 'em? What the..? Gawd 'elp us, don't tell me the crushers are followin' 'er!

Sookey turned into a dark court that Nash knew.

'ere, this is where Shanks lives.

Intuition sent Nash's left hand into one of his overcoat pockets, and a moment later he was wearing his peak-blinder cap, complete with razors restored into the peak.

He was still mulling things over in his mind when the attack came. Sookey's scream was expertly muffled as the first man grabbed her from behind, his left fist being brought back towards himself, punching her in the stomach to knock the air for a scream out of her, the right hand further stopping any sound emanating by clamping over her mouth, and dragging her backwards into the darkest shadows. The second man dashed in and kicked her legs away from her with a hard boot to the right calf. The first man dropped with her to the floor, manoeuvring himself to lie on top of her, his right hand still clamped on her mouth, his left now beneath the right, pushing up into her throat.

The second man was just pulling out some rope from his pocket when Nashey's right fist thundered into the left side of his chin, and as the man spun around and down Nash pivoted and slammed his left fist into the man's testicles. The man crashed to the ground and lay still. Sookey's captor let go both grips to get to his feet, but he was only half up when Nash's right boot smashed into his mouth; teeth and blood splattering out. But Nash hadn't seen the third man.

A cosh landed on the back of Nash's head. He was badly stunned but he knew he had to stay on his feet at all costs. His legs were wilting and his vision blurring but he stumbled across the court and managed to swerve enough to hit the wall right shoulder first. This both kept him on his feet and turned him enough so he could see his attacker bearing down on him out the corner of his eye. The man ran towards Nash and momentarily steadied himself a couple feet from his prey to strike again with the cosh, but as he did so Nash delivered a straight left jab, catching the man flush on his Adam's apple. Nash hadn't had time to get any shoulder into the punch, simply extending his arm, so there was little weight behind it, but it was perfectly timed and the man recoiled, gasping for breath.

Nash's head was still spinning badly. He knew he might pass out at any moment and had to finish this quickly. He pulled off his cap and lunged forward at the man, who had his head bowed gasping, not looking at Nash.

Thas the last mistake you make today, thought Nash.

The man looked up just in time to see a brown blur flash across his eyes. Then there was another flurry, and another. Nash had backhanded, forehanded, backhanded his cap across the man's eyes in three lightning-fast strikes. There was a split-second lull in the action as the two men simply looked at each other, before the delayed reaction turned to horrifying pain. Small beads of red started to seep out of the gashes in and around the man's eyes, as screams of agony issued forth. He dropped the cosh as his hands came up across his face, blood escaping through the gaps between his fingers. The man's screams ended abruptly as he blacked out, and sunk to his knees before pitching forward onto his face. Seeing the blood flow, Nash muttered grimly under his breath.

"One fing's for sure, you ain' no 'ore are ya", with humour as black as the court they were in.

Sookey's first attacker was now up on one knee shouting something to his mate but his mouth was such a mess the words were indecipherable. Nash turned towards the man and made him an ominous promise.

"You need a den'ist dunt yer. I'll save yer the money by put'in' yer out yer misery."

He bent down to pick up the loose cosh, but the motion sent blood flooding to his head. He felt a wave of great heat pass through his brain and he crumpled onto the floor. He had passed out for a few seconds and was barely back in consciousness when a scream brought him back to his senses, at least to a degree.

The man he had been about to finish off was now grappling with Sookey, no more than a foot from his face. He had the cosh in his hand, and she had both her arms entwined with his. The man was weak with pain so she had been able to hold him back. Nash dragged himself onto his knees and planted his right fist into the man's nose. There was the sound of breaking bone, a spray of blood and the man went out like a light.

"Yer got a nose to match yer mouff now ain't ya," sneered Nash.

He looked across at the man he had hit on the chin and in the nether regions. He was pretending to be unconscious but was in such pain that he couldn't help but moan.

"Yeah you stay right there if yer know what's good for ya! Don't 'elp yer mates. Woss your name, Shanks?" shouted Nash with contempt.

Nash glared at Sookey.

"You 'armed?" he barked.

Sookey had recovered from the punch in the stomach enough to answer in a frightened high-pitched voice.

"By your leave sir I am not armed. The cosh was not mine."

Nash looked at her blankly for a moment before realising she had misunderstood him.

Soppy cow, he thought.

"No Sookey, I'm arsting yer, are you harmed in any way? How's that belly a yours?" he enquired in his best clerk's voice.

Sookey replied in her best Cockney voice, with as brave a smile as she could muster.

"Me belly does not..."

She grimaced and couldn't finish her sentence, but the two of them shared a nod and grim smile at each other.

CHAPTER 13:

"Nearly half a million pounds is yearly raised...by societies having their headquarters in London to propagate the Gospel in foreign parts...within cheap cab fare of that portion of Eastern London, which for many years has been known to have been in a social condition utterly devoid of the commonest attributes of civilisation."
Lord Sydney Godolphin Osborne

It was almost noon but Nash was only just surfacing. He had not risen from his bed all morning, and was only now up and about due to a need to pee. His head was throbbing from yesterday's events in more ways than one. The pounding headache from the coshing he had received was making it difficult for him to think, and he didn't appreciate a loud thumping on his door.

"It's Will. Yer told me a give yer a knock up just 'fore twelve remember."

"All right! Shut yer trap!" Nash bellowed.

He had completely forgotten. He had slept in his trousers and boots, having collapsed onto his bed with exhaustion on getting home. He now threw his vest, shirt and waistcoat, all of which had come off the night before in one go, back on in one motion. The overcoat followed and finally his tatty old billy pot hat. He no longer had a cap. He had removed the razors from it and dropped them down a drain, putting the bloodied cap on the head of an unconscious wretch lying in an alley, with his bucket of pure beside him. Pure collection was the lowest of all low jobs, done only by those who were one step from the workhouse or death.

"ere are boy, this'll keep yer bonce warm at least."

He grabbed a couple of weapons from his table, stuffed them into the deep pockets of his coat and marched out to join Will Roud no more than a few seconds after his door had been rapped. There was the usual lack of pleasantries, Nash starting immediately on the business at hand.

"I got a crow job for ya. I'm just off to see a canary in the Bells. You come an' all as then I don't 'as to repeat meself. I'll tells yer both at the same time what it's about."

Will just nodded and fell into step with Nash.

Gawd, you look rough, thought Will, but he wisely kept his thoughts to himself.

Five minutes later they were ensconced in a dark corner of the Ten Bells in Spitalfields with Mary Kelly. It was Mary's local. She lived only a stone's throw away in Miller's Court. She felt confident in her surroundings and she was in a good mood. She'd had her best ever night's takings, thanks to an old gent who had tried and failed to penetrate her, so she had gently taken hold of his member and caressed it until his release became apparent, speaking quietly with a mix of encouragement and foul-mouthed dirtiness throughout to get him there. This was way above and beyond the call of duty. She had been far more sensitive to an old man's needs than any normal street prostitute, and the old gent was well aware of this. His gratitude knew no bounds, as he gave her a half-sovereign and followed it up with a gratuity of a silk pocket handkerchief for her trouble.

Blimey, ten bob, and I'll be able a get anuvver free or four bob for the 'ankie an' all. Thas the best I ever bin paid, an' all for a three bob knee trembler.

Mary had previously negotiated a five shilling fee for penetrative sex, but would have given the little man hand release for a mere three shillings. She bobbed in appreciation.

"Fank yer very much sir."

This had seemed to embarrass him, and he quickly scurried off into the night.

"Christ you look bleedin' rough Nashey," said Mary, grinning broadly.

Will suddenly found something interesting to stare at on the other side of the pub, as Mary continued.

"Yer don't need ale by the look a yer. Let me go an' get yer some Godfrey's yer poor old sod."

This was an opium and molasses syrup cordial favoured by baby-farmers to sooth starving wretches.

"Don't you cum it, you saucy lit'le mare. I'll fetch yer a facer in a minute, then yer won't be sa clever will yer. Lit'le cow," retorted Nash.

His dark mood had immediately been lifted, first of all by the sight of Mary with her red hair, brightly coloured clothes and brass heels, propping up the bar when he and Will had walked through the pub doors, and then by this cheeky outburst. He had tried to keep a straight face and brought his right arm up and across his chest as if threatening to give her a backhanded slap, but he felt the upper parts of his cheeks quiver. He knew he'd let slip a slight smirk.

"Well I can't be an 'orse and a cow can I, make up yer bleedin' mind," she said, spotting the twinkle in Nash's eye and his little grin, so knew she was on safe ground.

"I can see I'm gonna 'ave to 'ave a word wiv that Joe a yours. 'e ain't keepin' you in 'and enuff. 'e needs to give yer a good 'idin' regular so yer show some respect to yer elders."

Nash was not looking serious, despite his best efforts to do so.

He saw Mary's bosom start to heave as she drew breath to retort, but he quickly jumped in, this time successfully losing his smile.

"Never mind all that, funny cuts, I got a job for ya. Canary work. An' cloff ears 'ere, yeah you back wiv us are ya?" Nash acidly queried of Will, "'e'll be yer crow."

Mary saw it was time to behave.

"Go 'ed," she nodded, "I got me lugs out."

Nash laid out the plan, as much as he knew it, offering them the jobs of canary and crow.

A cracksman, the skilled leader of a burglary, would have a kit which included specialist burglary equipment such as, if necessary, safe-breaking gear. If picked up and searched by the police, there was no innocent explanation for carrying such gear, and the purveyor would be arrested on the spot. No cracksman would ever run the risk of being caught with his gear on him. A canary was employed to carry it for him, to and from the job. It was usually a woman, as they were far less likely to be stopped by the police. A crow was a look-out, but the job involved far more than simply being another set of eyes. It was a skilled job. A crow would be an expert at a number of calls and signals – whistles, bird and cat noises; coughs, sneezes and flourished handkerchiefs; striking matches in a certain way.

Will and Mary were unimpressed by what little Nash had been able to tell them about the robbery.

"I'm tellin' yer that's all I knows," said a conciliatory, exasperated Nash. "Yer know what sort a cove 'e is, 'e don't trust nobody does he, so 'e ain't lettin' on till it's time, cos 'e's worried we'll go 'ed and do it ourselves wiv out 'im once we know."

"Yeah, well 'e's right there ain' 'e?" snorted Will.

Mary cut in.

"But why we got a 'ang about late every Fridee night just on the orf chance thas the night. Late Fridee's the only time I makes any money these days. Saterdees are startin' ta go right 'ome since that bastard Jack's last outin'. I got a livin' ta make yer know."

Nash wanted to get back at her with 'so do sum ovver trade!' But he and Mary had had many heated arguments about her being a prostitute, and this was not the time or place for another.

"Cos thas the way Shanks wants it. 'e's got us over a barrel so we 'ave to lump it. An' pulls like this 'as to be dun late. It's the only time the streets ain't teemin' wiv nose-aches ain' it. Any'ow yer ain' got a 'ang about this Fridee cos I already told Shanks I ain' got old a the cracksmen yet, so we start meetin' up next Fridee all bein' well."

The bickering continued but both Mary and Will reluctantly agreed to leave their Friday nights free from the 12th onwards.

＊ ◆ ＊

Sookey had not stirred from her house all day, and hadn't answered the door when Rose had knocked earlier. The previous day she had witnessed violence that she knew must exist in the slums, and she had certainly seen scraps of it. Only last Sunday two costers had almost started fighting when Sookey went to buy a scarf off one man, only for the next man to try and steal the sale by undercutting the deal. All was fair in love and war until the deal was made, but once the sale had been agreed, the losing coster should have conceded. He had almost got a punch on the nose for his trouble but the word 'almost' was crucial. There had been a lot of posturing, swearing and threats, but that was all. Knowing of something, and experiencing it in small ways like the quasi fight, was completely unlike seeing the 'real' violence that lurked down dark alleyways.

She had been amazed at the brevity of it all. From the moment the first man grabbed her, to the moment Nashey had sent his last victim into unconsciousness could not have been more than seconds. There had not been much she could do to stem the flow of blood from the cuts in the man's eyes, but she had at least managed to stop the blood coming from the cuts on his cheeks by applying pressure on the wounds.

Nash had wanted to get away. Head spinning, aitches were dropped.

"Come on, let's get out of 'ere 'fore any whistles start up."

"But he's bleeding to death Nashey. I must stop the flow of blood. Come, help me. Your hands are so much stronger than mine, you can apply so much more purchase."

"I ain't touchin' 'im. Attackin' a poor defenceless woman, 'e's a bleeding wrong un in more ways as one ain' 'e."

"Do you think these men are The Ripper? Perhaps that's why the police's efforts have been so hamstrung. They have been looking for one man, but it is indeed three."

"They ain't The Ripper. I knows 'oo The Ripper is right enuff don't you worry. Gawd if I ain't seen 'im wiv me own eyes, close as you are ta me now. I could a topped 'im there and then if I'd 'av 'ad a mind. But 'e's useful as 'e is see, for the time bein' at least."

Sookey loosened her grip on the man's neck as she swivelled around at this news, staring in wide-eyed astonishment at Nash. It was only when he saw her shocked expression that he realised what he had said.

Christ, this knock to me 'ed's loosened me tongue alright.

He avoided Sookey's eyes and made his way over to the man.

"All right, let me do it," he said, knocking her bloodied hands away and applying pressure on the deepest of the man's wounds.

He felt the need to keep talking. He didn't want to field any questions about what he had just let slip.

"Yeah, it's good if 'e lives right enuff. Yer can smash a man's body to pulp so 'e can't never work again and that's 'im orf to the work'ouse for good, or yer can smash 'is brains in and that's 'im off to Bedlam to be forgotten about, but unless yer actually kill 'im, nuffin' much 'appens. Some ol' beak sends yer off for a twelve-mumph pickin' oakum, where yer gets fed bet'er than in the work'ouse. But swipe a gen'leman's Hunter and it's orf to prison wiv yer fer years. Me ol' granfarver got sent off to gawd knows where on the ovver side of the world jus' fer a bit ov fencin' if yer please. Property's worth more than a man's worth. Course I were only actin' in self-defence, and savin' a good lady's life an' virtue an' all, so it don't really matter if this 'gen'leman' 'ere lives or dies, but best save 'im I spose, just to keep the crushers from sniffin' round."

Sookey's shocked stare had not changed so Nash continued in his verbosity.

"ere, the blood's stopped. And 'e's comin' round. 'e 'll live all right. But e'll start screamin' again that's for sure. 'ere, all free of 'em are comin' round now. Even the wrong un there. 'e 'll be countin' 'em in a minute," said Nashey with a wink, nodding over at the man he had punched in the testicles. "Let's scarper."

Nash didn't want any argument so he got up and pulled Sookey firmly to her feet and started to move away.

"But, what did you say of knowing who.." Sookey's question was cut off by Nash swaying.

"Quick grab me gell, I'm goin' again," he said in an urgent voice.

Sookey threw her left arm around his waist, nuzzled her head under his right arm so her chin was on his right breast. Nash didn't feel good but he was no longer feeling like he might pass out. He and Sookey left the court entwined like a couple of lovers and made their way home. They were both covered in blood but nobody took a blind bit of notice. It was a common enough occurrence for a wife to be helping her 'ol' man' stagger home, after he'd lost a fight or drunkenly tripped and head-butted the cobbles. They staggered home in silence, which was just how Nash wanted it.

$\qquad \Leftrightarrow \qquad$

Sookey had wanted to deliver Nashey to his abode, but he had insisted they go to her house first, and he walked home alone from there. She had hardly slept a wink last night. Her stomach ached a little, her calf and throat felt sore and she had been shocked by the amount of bruising to her neck. But it was not her injuries that had kept her awake. It was shock; but not the physical condition. And it was not the attack she had suffered, or the sight of the violence meted out to her attackers, which was the cause of her shock. It was partly her lack of shock at the violence. She imagined what the man who had dealt out the violence to her attackers would say to such thoughts.

"You're shocked at your lack of shock! Gawd 'elp us gell, that's Irish and there's the troof."

And then there were her feelings for this man. A few hours before venturing on her excursion to meet Shanks, she had endured a disgusting coffee with her friend Mary at Henrietta's coffee room. Mary had worn a rather whimsical look on her face as Sookey told her excitedly about her meetings and long conversation with a man called Nashey. And she had burst out laughing when Sookey had told her Nash was a policeman.

"'e ain' no crusher yer soppy cow. I 'eard 'e's started arstin' around about the murders for some reason. You must a got the wrong end a the stick there gell. 'e'd never say he were no copper. You must 'ave taken it on yerself an' 'e fought 'e'd joke wiv yer to let yer fink it, thas all. 'e likes a joke when the mood's about 'im. But yer 'ave to be careful ta catch 'im right. 'e can fall out wiv the stones, that one can."

Mary had gone on to tell Sookey that Nashey was an old friend of hers, though she had been unusually guarded about relaying much more information about him before diverting the conversation by embarrassing Sookey with the suggestion that she sounded like she was sweet on him. It was now clear to Sookey that Rose had been right all along about Nashey. He was a villain, not a policeman. Yet instead of being revolted by his way of life and let down by his duplicity (or rather a warped sense of humour according to Mary), she felt drawn to him more then ever. This was indeed shocking too. She had felt insecure all her life, but when she was with this man she felt safe.

People may be armed but they would be the ones to be 'armed.

She smiled at the misunderstanding with Nashey.

But it was not her physical safety per se that she was thinking about so much as her general well being. Until now the only time she ever felt safe was when she was engrossed in making her art, or discussing art in letters to her talented friend in Dieppe, but that was because she was no longer in the real world. This was the first time she had felt truly safe in the real world. In what the rest of society had now come to think of as the unsafest place in the civilised world, she felt secure for the first time in her life.

"'ow rum," she mused to herself.

CHAPTER 14:

"The very people who are now the most vehement in their denunciation of this .... demented murderer don't turn a hair when...thousands of women of the same class as his victims rot to death with syphilis in a Lock Hospital. Who cares too, how many young girls have their jaws eaten out of their heads by phosphorous in order that matches should be sold cheaper?"

H.M. Hyndman

Nash was shortly about to make another attempt at meeting the cracksman he had in mind for the post office robbery. He was just finishing his tea. It would normally be bread and something sweet from off the cart of a vendor on a Wednesday but he was enjoying a treat. It was a 'Sundee dinner' that old Granny Urlock had brought him just after he had got back from meeting the others about the robbery. The old lady had included his favourite, a pennyworth of pieces and pot herbs (carrot & onion). She had heard what he had done to save Sookey and wanted to show her gratitude. Sookey had saved her young grandson when the poor little mite had been very poorly last month. The old woman couldn't afford to heat the meal but Nash was delighted by the gesture. He had still been suffering with his headache from the coshing so didn't fancy it at the time, so it had sat on his table for an hour. He had just been round to the bakers and paid them tuppence to heat it up for him. He tossed the last morsel to the cat, which promptly ignored it.

"Choosey lit'le cow ain't ya! Woss your name, Marie bleedin' Lloyd?"

Mention of Hoxton's most famous daughter, sent his thoughts spinning off at a tangent. I wouldn't mind goin' to the local flea pit for a change. It must a been a twelve-mumph or more since I saw that Marie Lloyd up the old Paragon. Course she's too 'igh an' mighty ta perform in the Mile End Road these days. They says she earns six 'undred pound a week! Funny-looking tart she were an' all, wiv 'er buck teef and fin 'air, but she could 'old a bloody good toon and there's the troof. Good luck to 'er I says. Least one's escaped.

Spose I could arst Mary if she wanted a come wiv me. Mind you, 'er Joe wouldn't like it. Nah best not. Them two's 'as enuff bull and cows from wot I 'ear. Spose I could see if that Sookey wanted a go. It's bound a be up 'er street ain' it, featre, an' she'd fink it funny if I didn't come near or by after wot 'appened. An' any'ow I gotta keep in wiv 'er so as I can find out more about this post mortem lark, an' I got a make sure she keeps 'er trap shut about wot I said to 'er about me seein' the killer. Trouble is I don't want 'er finkin' anyfin' aboud it, like I want a be 'er fancyman or summin'. I seen 'ow she looks at me. I'll jus' says as it's cos she saved me from that feller's cosh and then got me out a there away from them crushers, an' as good as 'ome. A fank you, like standin' 'er a gin or doin' 'er wallpaperin' or summin'.

There was an urgent-sounding rapping on the door.

"Christ almigh'y! That soddin' door'll be on its last soon enuff! It's like bleedin' Regent's Circus round 'ere!"

❦

Joe Barnett (no relation to the reverend and his wife) was trying his hardest to make his way in the world, but it wasn't easy for someone who had committed the cardinal sin of not acquiring a skill. Unskilled men were ten a penny. He was in his mid-twenties and had already had a huge number of jobs, many of them seasonal, many of them done on the same day, dovetailed together the best he could.

He had told the census people back when he was eighteen that he was an unemployed porter, but this summer he had sold strawberries from a hand cart.

"Strawberries, all ripe! all ripe!" he cried till he was hoarse.

He stood next to an Italian who ran a Hokey-Pokey (ice-cream) stall in the park. Giuseppe's English wasn't very good so Joe would help him with his advertising.

"Hokey pokey, penny a lump, that's the stuff to make you jump!" was the cry on the Italian's behalf.

In return, Joe was able to keep his wares out of the sun, under the shade Giuseppe had rigged up on his stall to keep his ice cream cool. They looked after each other's carts when calls of nature were needed, and were a useful second pair of eyes against those who would steal anything from a cart that was left unwatched for a few seconds. On days when he couldn't afford the outlay to buy the strawberries, he might sell sherbet and water.

Unfortunately, it had been a freak summer. The weather had been awful. The only people to gain from it were the undertakers, sweeps, furriers, gas workers and coalmen, who hadn't been laid off in droves as they usually were in summer. It had even snowed one day in July. There had not been great trade in hot weather-related things such as strawberries and sherbet. Joe had therefore also sold ginger cake, milk, muffins, dead rabbits and cheap fish. Anything he could buy without too much initial outlay, which he could sell from his little hand cart or a simple tray, or in the case of rabbits by dangling them from a couple of bars over his shoulder, walking the streets with his wares on display.

The end of the summer had coincided with the start of the Whitechapel murders, which had led to a new job. Joe was now a newsboy. He would stand alongside several other such men (none were boys), each selling a different newspaper. He would hold an advertising board in front of him with the number of the edition at the top, with five headlines listed below. These were normally five different stories, but the murders were so dominant in the news that all of the headlines were now related to the killings.
Third Edition
WITNESS SAW MAN WITH FIRST VICTIM
ABBERLINE CONFIDENT OF ARREST
JEW WHITEWALLING CLUE DENIED
WEST END POLICE MOVE IN
SHERLOCK HOLMES 'LOOK FOR AMERICA LINK'

Joe was determined to make an honest living. He hated the fact that his sweetheart, Mary, was in league with local criminals, especially that menacing man Nash, and against his express orders she had started to make ends meet by part-time prostitution, which was increasingly becoming more like full time. He suspected that she also committed other crimes, but she would never admit to it.

The prostitution was a growing source of tension between them. Joe wanted Mary to live with him full time, give up prostitution and one day they would get married and become 'respectable'. But Mary was determined to retain her independence, preferring to live on her own at weekends in one tiny, filthy twelve foot square partitioned backroom in Miller's Court.

The single window was broken and the lock had been out of commission until recently when, thanks to the half-sovereign knee-trembler, she had treated herself to having the locksmith round. He had done a good job. She was now the proud owner of a front door key and a brand new good quality lock. It was her little fortress against the world. And after the post office robbery with Nashey, she was going to have the window man round.

There was just room for a double bed with a small table jammed up against it, on which Mary placed her solitary candle, matchbox and rouge. On warm summer nights she would throw her clothes in the grate. If it was cold enough for the grate to be in use, the clothes stayed on 24 hours a day. She had nothing else to her name. Joe was allowed to live there all week but she insisted that he 'buggered off' to his mother's at weekends. He knew full well why. It was Friday and Saturday nights that she would go out on the game.

Joe had just arrived at Mary's hovel after twelve hours on his feet selling newspapers. His feet and back hurt, and he was in a bad mood. Mary was home and the usual arguments were quick to start.

"You only keep this shit 'ole on so as yer can en'ertain yer men 'ere," Joe remonstrated.

Mary wasn't the most sensitive soul, and would rub Joe's nose in the fact that he barely earned enough to keep himself out of the workhouse let alone her.

"The day you comes to live 'ere proper's the day I goes to the work'ouse. Least I can get 'old a sum gelt when I 'as to, not like you. An' I don't come 'ome coopered every night like you neiver! If you loved me like yer says, you'd be me bully. I could get 'old ov a lot more gelt if I 'ad a ponce to look after me."

Joe was furious at such a thought.

"I ain't being no ponce! You're go the same way as them ovvers you will. Bleedin' good riddance to 'em I says. Ol' Jack's doing a good job. I 'ope 'e kills 'em all!"

"You..fuck..off!" shouted Mary, enunciating each of the three words well apart, slowly for emphasis. "You sound like fuckin' Nashey you do! I wouldn't be surprised if you were that bastard Jack! Nah, you ain't got the gumption 'ave yer. Even some old 'ore on her last could put you on yer aris."

Joe went red in the face with rage and took a step towards her, putting one hand on his belt buckle.

"Gall on, you takes yer belt off ta me and I'll give yer a taste of me life preserver," shouted Mary, waving a cosh that Nashey had once given her, along with a bit of advice.

"Any trouble wiv any ov your 'gen'lemen', an' yer puts this across their sneezer."

She kept it on her at all times, along with a small knife. She was confident she could look after herself. Mary grabbed her hat and shiny new key and turned for the door.

"I'm orf oud ov it."

She slammed the door behind her and marched off, expecting him to come running after her. He didn't.

Right, let's go and see 'ow ol' Sookey's get'in' on.

⌒ ◆ ⌒

Mary caught Rose Martin's eye as she approached Sookey's door.

"She in?"

Rose was standing on her own doorstep holding court with four other women, their collective entourage of nineteen children, four chickens and one dog, lined up along the side wall of her house. A couple of the smaller children were playing a game of 'tossing the pieman' but with a stone rather than a coin, and another couple of tots were passing the time by pushing, shoving and gainsaying each other. The rest sat or stood against the wall, silent, sullen, staring. The oldest child, a beanpole of a ten year old girl, stared wildly into space. Mary doubted she was 'all there'. She saw these feral scenes a dozen or so times a day and shuddered at the thought that she could one day end up like the Roses of this world. She would rather 'top meself'.

Rose knew Mary was a prostitute and as such beneath contempt. Rose didn't answer Mary's question, and just looked through her for a second with a scowl, before turning back to her four friends. It didn't really matter whether Rose knew if Sookey was in or not. It would not take Mary a second to knock on her door and wait. But she was not going to let Rose get away with the slight.

"'ere, cloff ears!" shouted Mary. "Cat got yer tongue 'as it? No lugs and no tongue, what a palaver for a jaw-me-dead like you. I should get down a Corton's to get summin' if I were you!" Corton's was the chemist on Whitechapel High Street. "ere, I'll arst your mate Nashey if 'is Doris 'as got yer tongue. I'll get it off 'er for yer if she 'as."

It wasn't the wittiest bit of a banter she had ever come up with, but she felt that something had to be said.

"Don't you fuckin' come it, yer little 'ore. I'll knock that old bounce out a ya..." was the start of Rose's reply.

Mary didn't hear the remainder of the sentence as she banged on Sookey's door and giggled to herself.

"'eard me that time right enuff didn't ya!" shouted Mary with a cocky self satisfied smile.

Sookey opened the door and saw Mary's smile and the direction it was headed.

"Helloo Mary. This is indeed a fine surprise." As an afterthought she added "and there's the troof," pleased that she had remembered to flatten the final syllable to East end proportions.

"I see you are on good terms with Rose."

"Ul yeah me and ol' Rose are right good mates."

Mary's sarcasm went unnoticed.

Got me tongue in me cheek there gell, shame ol' Rose can't do the same what wiv the cat 'aving it, thought Mary to herself with a sly grin.

Sookey busied herself with making tea while Mary sat at her table.

"I 'eard you and your fancyman 'av bin out givin' facers to all and sundry," Mary giggled. "An' there I was finkin' you were a real Mr Brownly. Yer wouldn't catch 'im lampin' that Jew kidsman feller, wossisname?"

"Fagin is the gentleman to whom I believe you refer Mary. And it's Brown-low. I fear that there are no such truly kindly people in real-life, but I thank you for the reference. I am pleased to hear you read Mr Dickens, Mary."

Sookey had said this with her usual lack of any semblance of being patronising.

"Ul yeah, never miss me liberee every week."

Again, the lowest form of wit fell on deaf ears.

"But pray tell, what do you mean fancyman Mary?" asked Sookey with mock seriousness, knowing exactly what her cheeky friend had meant.

"You an' ol' Nashey gave three 'erberts a good 'iding' is what I 'eard," said Mary.

"Mr Nash did indeed come to my rescue when three ruffians attempted to attack me. It was he who did the 'hiding', as you put it Mary. But I am intrigued by your use of the term 'fancyman', queried a coy Sookey.

"Just coddin' wiv yer gell. But 'ere, thems some nasty marks on yer neck an' leg, and I 'eard you got a fourpenny one in the belly an' all. 'ow are yer gell?" asked Mary seriously, showing genuine concern.

Sookey was disappointed. She wanted the conversation to stay on the subject of Nashey.

"I am quite well now thank you Mary. A punch knocked the wind out of my sails, but had no lasting affect. My throat and leg are near-recovered I am pleased to say. Here is the tea. It is Chinese, which you may not have had occasion to drink. I hope it is to your taste. I must confess I do not trust the Ceylon and Indian. The Indian tastes not a jot similar to the tea I had partaken of in India. And the Ceylon tastes the same as the Indian here. When I was in India I heard stories of dangerous colourings and flavourings being added to tea in England."

Mary gave an uninterested nod and thin smile.

Sookey became aware that she was boring her best friend, so took the chance to return to her preferred subject.

"Have you spoken to Nashey since the attack?"

Before Mary was able to answer there was a loud thumping on the front door.

"My, but I am popular. I have received so many visitors this day. It is my new found infamy," said Sookey with an enthusiastic raise of the eye-brows and a smile.

Sookey opened the door and two men immediately pushed their way past her into the sitting room. One of them was Shanks, the other was a man she didn't know, who was obviously in pain, head down with his hand clasped over his mouth. He had lost most of his teeth, one tooth was still just clinging to life, and there was much dried blood around his mouth but none on his clothes. His nose wasn't in much better condition. Shanks spoke on the man's behalf.

"'e needs 'elp. Jus' been in a factory accident. Left 'im in a right ol' state. 'is bloke jus' wants ta know if 'e'll be fit fer work tomorra ovverwise e'll find someone as 'oo is."

"I'll see if I can help, but he looks like he will need to go to the London Hospital, or at the very least see a fully qualified doctor," replied Sookey.

"Factory accident were it? Looks more like 'e's been given a good bootin' a me," said Mary with unconcealed suspicion in her voice.

She exchanged a glance with Sookey, who herself did not believe Shanks' explanation. The injury was clearly not new. It must have happened the day before, looking at the dried blood and the colour of the severe bruising, and the man had clearly changed his clothes since the accident. His original clothes would have been covered in blood. Shanks glanced at Mary for a moment and then turned to Sookey.

"'oo's yer monkey 'ere?"

"Oh, she is just a girl who runs errands for me. It is indeed lucky she is here, is it not. I will need her to fetch some bandages, ointments and the like from Corton's the chemists, so I am able to tend this poor man's wounds properly."

Inspecting the man's injuries, Sookey was now only a few inches from him. His smell was familiar to her. She found a pencil and a piece of paper and started writing furiously.

"Here you are Mary, please take this to Corton's in the High Street. As always, please read the note before you take your leave."

Sookey turned to Shanks to explain.

"I fear the poor chemist may not understand my hand. He commonly does not."

Turning back to Mary, she continued.

"Please check my hand is clear."

Sookey folded the paper over and held it blank side out towards Mary, before it was snatched from her by Shanks.

"I'll be the judge ov who leaves 'ere and wot 'appens."

Shanks was trying to ape the menace Nash would radiate in such a situation. He unfolded the paper and looked down at it. Sookey's anxious stare at her, told Mary that there was something incriminating on the note. Mary moved her hand slowly towards the cosh she had squirreled away. The note read:

'Mary, Fetch a policeman. I believe this is one of the men who attacked me last night'.

Shanks looked up and stared at Sookey for several seconds. He then looked at Mary for a similar amount of time, before turning his gaze to his injured friend.

"You read?" he enquired of him.

"Do me a favour," the man lisped.

Shanks leered as he passed the note back to Mary.

"Alright Mary monkey, bugger orf down ta yer chemists and be lively aboud it. I want you back 'ere sharp or it's trouble for you and your friend 'ere."

Mary snatched the note, and on reading it, the sneer she was about to give the man was swopped for a smile.

"I'll get back 'ere soon enuff don't you worry."

Sookey had not recognised the man to begin with. It had been so dark in that alley. And no doubt that was what the man had been banking on. But the injuries were exactly those which she would imagine the man would have, whom Nashey had kicked in the mouth. This, allied to his familiar odour, which she had smelt when he was on top of her with his thumbs pressed into her throat, convinced Sookey he was one of the attackers. But she was bemused.

What has Mr Shanks to do with all of this?

As soon as Mary left, Sookey busied herself rummaging around for things to help her dress the man's wounds. She broke the silence.

"I must apologise for not attending our meeting as arranged Mr Shanks. I was indisposed."

"I told yer before ain' I, it ain't Mr Shanks, jus' Shanks. I got your Mr Nash to fank for the name, and I got you a fank for telling me as why 'e gave it me an' all. I owes yer both all right. An yeah, I 'eard about your bein' 'indisposed'." There was undisguised contempt for the final word in the sentence. "Lucky Nash 'appened by when 'e did wun it? No tellin' what those free might a dun ta ya. Bad sorts everywhere yer look these days ain' there."

Sookey's right hand came up to her throat. There was an awkward silence whilst he stared at her intently with a sneering grin on his face. Sookey thought the time would pass better if she engaged in conversation.

"Do, do you have the er money you were to give to me last night Mr, er I mean Shanks?"

"Nasty bruise yer got there Sookey. Nah, you should 'av got it off me last night when I 'ad it. Ain' got it no more see. Got ovver expenses 'sides yorn yer know. You'll 'av to wait for it now wernt yer."

Shanks was enjoying intimidating this defenceless woman. He had never had the slightest intention of paying her the money he owed her. He had made an arrangement with her that she should call at his room for the debt, and he had fobbed her off with a tall story that he worked till late every night so the earliest she could come by was just after dark. She was never going to make the appointment. He had seen to that.

Small knuckles started rapping on the door.
"It's... me... Mary... Run as fast as I could."

She was panting from running to find help, and then running straight back to Sookey's. It had not been far but her one meal a day, if she was lucky, was not the regime of an athlete. She was very weak.

Shanks was inches from the door, about to open it a crack to check Mary was alone, when he was thrown back by the door being kicked open violently. Shanks stumbled backwards, only being saved by the table from falling to the floor.

"Gawd 'elp us, Shanks boy. Bloody door sticks dun it. Warped. Damp see. Needs a good kick."

Nash had the broadest of smiles. He was overacting. He glanced in the direction of the injured man.

"Yer just 'av to give sum fings a good bootin' when they need it dunt yer."

He turned to Sookey and continued.

"Jus' bumped in ta Mary 'ere comin' out a the chemists. She said she were runnin' errand for yer Sookey and I felt bad I ain' kept me promise ta do that wallpaperin' you arst me about a while since. So I fought I'd come round an' do it now if it's all right wiv you. I should get it done 'fore the light goes if I gets crackin' straight away. Yer can't wallpaper after yerve lighted the candles. What d'ya say gell?"

"That is very kind of you Nashey," replied a confused, relieved and highly stimulated Sookey.

She was feeling shocked at her lack of shock again.

A man wrecks my door with great violence and before I know what I am about, my chest heaves with relish and I feel easier than ever before. I can make no hand of it.

Nash continued in light vein.

"Can't swing a cat in 'ere. Some ov yers a gonna 'ave to bugger orf sharp so I can get on."

He took off his overcoat and started to peel up his shirtsleeves. Shanks and the toothless man noticed that the coat had made quite a clank when it landed on the table. There were obviously some heavy objects in the pockets. Sookey, for her part, had noticed the huge forearms and then the bulge of biceps in the tightening shirt. Mary noticed Sookey's glance and inwardly smirked, whilst keeping the straightest of dead-pan faces in what she appreciated was a tense moment.

Having turned to Shanks, Nash was suddenly no longer friendliness personified. His expression and voice-tone changed to dark and quietly menacing.

"It's time you went Shanks. Better leave yer boy 'ere mind. Poor sod looks like 'e needs some lookin' after."

It wasn't anything other than a demand with menaces. It was also a contract. Nash agreed to let the whole incident drop without retribution, without even a word said. It didn't do anyone any good falling out when they were just about to work together on the biggest, most lucrative crime of their lives. The pull was still on as far as he was concerned. And in return Shanks left alone. The man with the injury stayed. Just to make sure Shanks understood him, Nash continued.

"I'll be off to see that friend ov ours, Peter, when I leaves 'ere. Once I've seen 'im we'll be ready a do that bit of business we talked about. I got the ovver two friends already arranged."

A peterman was a safe-cracker. Nash thought that even Shanks should understand the reference. Shanks was furious but knew he was being let off lightly. He would have to deal with whatever Charlie let slip another time.

"Yeah, I'll be off and let yer get on wiv it," said Shanks, carefully avoiding making eye-contact with his mate. As he made his escape he shouted back over his shoulder with false bravado. "An' 'urry up and see that Peter, we ain't got all day yer know."

Nash smiled contemptuously, and turned to the injured man.

"Good mate yer got there ain't yer son."

"Dash it! I am quite done with Mr Shanks! What sort of a down-going man is he to see?" stormed a red faced Sookey.

But her ire was more aimed at Nash. Why had he let the man go without so much as a by- your-leave? Nash was aware of the situation.

"Sookey, you must be thinkin' why I didn't pitch it in red hot with Shanks?"

He had remembered his aitches; the first time he had done so in the company of others.

"You are indeed a nut to crack sir," replied Sookey, hands on hips.

"I'll tell yer anuvver time," replied Nash with a wink and the tiniest of nods. Sookey wasn't sure what he meant by these gestures.

"How that?" she queried.

Nash gave her an old fashioned look and allowed a tinge of exasperation into his voice.

"Don't stick out."

Sookey realised it was time to stop asking questions. Perhaps she would ask him again when they were alone. She smiled at Nash and turned to the injured man, her smile immediately fading.

"Let us see what ails you." It was the first time Nash had heard Sookey use the scolding, hectoring tone of the middle class.

She placed the fingers of her right hand none too gently on his chin and started to check for damage. He flinched and moved his head away from her roughly.

"Suffer me," said Sookey in a no-nonsense nurse voice.

"Never mind suffer me. What about suffer me!" lisped the battered and bruised man.

"Let 'er 'av a look at yer 'ounslows," interjected Mary wearily.

"'oo arst you a pipe up? An' who are you any'ow?" sneered the man.

It was a mistake.

"I'm the gell who's gonna take me friend Sookey 'ere for a lit'le walk. Get yer 'at Sookey, let's leave Mr Hounslow 'ere to 'elp Nashey with the wallpaperin'. I wouldn't be surprised if 'e 'elped Nashey wiv a few ovver fings an' all," said Mary with an exaggeratedly wide, false smile at the man.

Sookey's "oh, but.." was quickly quashed by Nashey.

"Good fought Mary. Six o'clock must a scarce rung out. Sookey, you were only tellin' me the ovver day you had to find somewhere to take yer lady friends on their tour. Why don't yer let Mary show yer the Sir Paul Pindar Tavern in Bishopsgate. Might be the sort a place you could take 'em. It looks ruff so they'll be excited right enuff, but it's full of Mary Anns, off duty coppers, slummers, laundresses, pea-shellers an' the like, so it'll be colourful for 'em but safe."

Nash shoved his hand in his right trouser pocket.

"Mary, 'ere's 'alf a sov. I dunno if they do grub, but if they do, 'av a good scoff the pair a yers. You look like yer could do wiv a good nosh Mary. When's the last time you ate summin', ay gell? But I want most ov that back in change, mind."

He pointed an index finger to show he was serious. Mary smirked back at Nash and then started ushering a bemused Sookey out.

Sookey put on her coat and started to leave.

"Where's yer 'at gell?" queried Mary.

"I haven't replaced my last one as yet. It 'went home' as we say here in the East End."

"Gawd 'elp us. We in the East End," Mary mocked, "never go out wivout no 'at or shawl on our bonce. It ain't seemly. The only time I don't is as when I'm invitin' custom, so they can see me lovely red 'air," she said cynically, pulling a face. "Now get this on sharp."

Mary perched her own hat roughly on Sookey's head.

As they stepped out of what was left of the door, Mary made sure her voice carried back into the house.

"'ope, ol' misery there's a carpen'er when 'e ain't attackin' women 'alf 'is size!" And she kept at full decibels for the benefit of others. "ere, look at the state a your front step. No wonder them ol' fishwives over there turn their nose up at yer."

The on-looking Rose et al tutted and looked away askance.

CHAPTER 15:

"The current unemployment meetings in Hyde Park…and the Whitechapel murders…are both effects of the same cause."
Justice

The alcohol broke down her barriers. Sookey was well aware that everyone in the vicinity must be inquisitive about their strange middling neighbour. Being a charity worker was one thing, but living in the East End full time? Earning a living in Whitechapel? Living like we do? Dressing the same? Trying to be like one of us? Sookey was ready to tell someone some of the story, though not all. She would give Mary a potted history of her recent problems, editing out and précising down the more painful details. She would start by telling Mary of her nemesis, that most despicable of women. Most of the information she relayed had come out at the trial.

Dinky Smith had had an ingratiating but likeable manner which, it transpired, gave way to feral ferocity. She had worked for some time at fairs and circuses as a fake fortune-teller, supplementing her income with any confidence trick she could pull off. She had successfully wheedled her way into the heart of an apothecary's assistant, from whom she gained knowledge of dispensing. Armed with such information, she was quick to start making up potions and concoctions to sell at her fair or circus booth.

"Problee worked the markets an' 'orse race' meetin's. Penny gaffs an' all I shouldn't wonder," offered Mary.

"But it was as a trickster, what you would call a magsman I believe Mary, where Dinky's true talent lay."

The woman used an ability to charm the gullible into trusting her whilst she relieved them of whatever she could. She had worked on a young, apparently naive and avaricious attorney, John Beck, with a view to getting him to invest in a non-existent cosmetics business. The plan was to get him to hand over the money, and then disappear. Dinky had impressed Beck, not just with her sales ability, but with the ease with which she handled tricky cosmetic ingredients such as arsenic, white lead and antimony, but she had been a little too blasé with said items and had been stricken down with self-poisoning.

"Serves 'er bleedin' right, I 'ate magsman," sneered Mary. "It's a shit'ouse crime. Bash me over the 'ead, stick a knife in me if yer will, but don't take the rise out a me. Yer got a be a wrong un ta be a magsman."

During Dinky's time laid up, Beck had rushed the deal along, renting and handsomely fitting out a little shop in New Bond Street. The money had been invested without a penny going into Dinky's pocket. The shop was called Beauty from the Orient, and Beck had advertised widely. His message to ladies was an enticing confectionary of the exotic and sensual.

"Oo-ah!" Mary was shocked at Sookey's candour. "An' what's an encitin' confectionary when it's at 'ome?"

"An attractive mixture. Various powders, oils, washes and soaps were stocked, and reference to the usages in the harem proved a telling attraction."

"Harem?"

Mary had never heard the word. Sookey was a little embarrassed and wished she hadn't mentioned it. Ignoring the question, she told Mary that New York Spring Water was Madame Smith's big seller. It had actually been just an infusion of bran in hot water.

"Gawd 'elp us, there's one born every minute ain' there."

Mary was shaking her head in disbelief. Sookey sighed in agreement.

Considering Madame's supposed great outlay in bringing this water from far off climes, two guineas a bottle had not been excessive, and was among the least expensive of her wares. Those who wished to have the ultimate in ablutions could invest in a 'Turkish Toilet Cabinet' as supplied to the sultana herself, costing from 20 to 150 guineas.

"Give over! I'm in the wrong game 'ere ain' I gell?"

Seeing Mary was incredulous, Sookey was quick to make a point.

"Yes, indeed Mary. I would prefer you even a magsman than…"

"An 'ore. Yeah I know. We've 'ad this talk ain' we? Now get on wiv yer story."

Mary had suddenly become very serious. Her whoredom was the one subject which was off limits as far as she was concerned, even with her friend Sookey. Suitably chastised, Sookey relayed further trial revelations.

Dinky was no mere saleswoman. The very notion of make-up carried a hint of impropriety. If used at all, it was supposed to be purely a means of assisting nature, allowing slightly older women certain latitude. The business was directed primarily at such ladies, who were also wealthy and not too straight-laced. There were also gentlemen clientele who bought the sort of presents that could only be given to women with whom they were intimate.

"But wos all this got a do wiv you livin' 'ere in Whitechapel ay?"

Sookey's audience was obviously less than captive. Sookey winked, one of her many new skills acquired in the slums.

Dinky had also run a house of assignation, where lovers could meet in secret. The beauty enterprise, with its bathing and treatment amenities, provided ideal cover. Business boomed precisely because its reputation was questionable. There had been an enticingly risqué quality to the luxurious little shop.

"Ay?"

Sookey guessed what Mary was querying.

"Risqué is a French word. It means…saucy. A touch of it sold cosmetics well you might say." Sookey then gave a sad little sigh. "And then Dinky met me."

Sookey had been the widow of an army officer. She had spent much of her adult life bored in a loveless marriage in India. She was a faded beauty; years of tropical sun had left her with a brown tanning of the skin which was most unflattering. All the women she knew back home in England had fine pearly white skin. Her once beautiful looks had withered. But now back home with the freedom of single status, she wished to regain her lost glamour, and a little romance would not have gone amiss. As a young debutant, her nickname had been Sookey; she had recently started calling herself by the name again. Withering brown Mrs Susan Parsons was dead; enticing white Sookey had returned. And though not very rich, she had owned a modest property and had £4,000 invested, which was a tidy enough sum.

Sookey paused from her story for a moment, expecting Mary to issue forth with a show of shock at her fellow slum-dwellers' wealth. But the audience was well and truly captive now. Mary waited in silence for the next instalment.

Sookey's self-deception had made her an easy target. Having relieved her of £150 for cosmetics, Dinky had plied her with expensive treatments. It transpired that on a couple of occasions whilst on the premises for these treatments, Sookey had encountered Lord Aylesford, a rakish bachelor. The two of them had flirted, and around this a great fantasy was woven. Sookey was given to understand that the nobleman was greatly attracted to her. He had even had the temerity to peep at her through a spy-hole (purpose-built) while she was having an Arabian Bath and had fallen madly in love. He wanted to make her Lady Aylesford, but unfortunately it was crucial for family reasons to keep the connection secret for the moment. Any public recognition was impossible; they must communicate only through Madame. Thus the wooing was carried out by love letters through Dinky. Sookey had been robbed of every vestige of sense by the letters she received, and Dinky for her part was thrown into a frenzy of avarice. There appeared nothing she could not make Sookey believe. By Lord Aylesford's wish, his beloved began further treatments, before being required to purchase expensive jewellery in keeping with her new status, which Madame would keep safe for her. Lord Aylesford was in temporary financial embarrassment due to all his immediate funds being ploughed into philanthropic ventures to aid the poor. Sookey was proud to assist. Madame introduced a lawyer, a role played by John Beck under an assumed name, who arranged for Sookey's capital to be disposed of through him for charitable works. In just five months, they had bled her dry.

The lover's letters had been well written and showed sensitivity and insight. Sookey had treasured them. But their author, a clerk, had demanded ever increasing amounts from Dinky, so his services were dispensed with. Lord Aylesford suddenly became barely literate, and Sookey finally became suspicious. Financially ruined and terribly disillusioned, Sookey confessed the whole sorry business to her relatives, who were not deterred by fear of scandal. Dinky duly came to appear before the Recorder of London.

In the witness box at the Old Bailey, Sookey, gaunt from grief, remorse and shame, cut a sorry specimen. The defence counsel had a field day. How could anyone have been deceived by such abject balderdash? Was it not plain that the woman had poured away her money buying gratification for her lewd appetites? The case caused a good deal of scandal, not to say entertainment. Sookey had become a figure of fun and there was loud laughter in court at her expense. Lord Aylesford joined in the merriment. Dinky was sentenced to five years at her majesty's pleasure.

"Course we both knows someone 'oo'll see to 'er when she gets out, if yer wants.'

It was a quiet, desultory response from a shocked and sad Mary.

"No, no Mary, I want it never more be heard of. It was in my previous life."

This was where Sookey decided to end her story. The tale of how she made the journey from the courthouse to living in the slums would be for another time. And she could see from Mary's shocked silence that she had probably had enough for one day too.

CHAPTER 16:

"We call on her servants in authority to close bad houses."
Henrietta Barnett's petition to Queen Victoria, signed by 4,000 women 'for the labouring classes of East London'.

Nash walked into the pub that he had recommended. It was crowded but the two women had managed to snuggle into a quiet corner. The pub did not serve food so they had imbibed on empty stomachs. Mary had successfully moved the conversation on from Sookey's troubled history to lighter matters. Mary's latest outrageous, funny remark had Sookey giggling, with her right hand over her mouth in shock, shaking her head as she laughed.

"Still 'ere spendin' me money I see. Couple of respectable young ladies like you should be careful drinkin' this time a night, you'll 'ave the bug 'unters doggin' yer 'ome."

It was a usual brusque Nash welcome, and he hadn't been prepared to sound his aitches in something as public as a pub.

"Let me stand yer a drink out yer own gelt you old bastard," chortled Mary.

She got up from their table and joined Nash at the bar. She lowered her voice to a conspiratorial whisper.

"You get what yer want out ov ol' misery?"

Nash returned her gaze with an appreciative nod.

"Mind you don't cut yerself. Yeah, I got it right enuff."

"Yer didn't get no wallpaperin' dun I wager," replied Mary with a knowing look.

"Funny cuts. Nah I didn't. Well I suddenly fought, I can't leave Sookey wivout a workin' door can I, so I went an' got that little Jew-boy locksmiff. The one you told me did a good job fer you. 'e 'ad a look and 'e's gonna cum round wiv 'is mate who does carpen'ry tomorra. I've just left your mate Rose keepin' an eye on the place." And then as an afterthought he added with a grin and a nod. "She speaks 'ighly a you."

"Yeah I know. Me an ol' Rose are great mates. Jus' like 'er and you. Took yer an 'our ta do that did it?" queried Mary sardonically.

"Charlie, that were ol' misery's name, an' me 'ad a lit'le talk."

"Come an' nen, tell us, what were all that wiv Sookey about?" asked Mary winking.

"Nose-ache," retorted Nash as he tapped Mary's nose gently. "You mind yer own."

He got his beer and they rejoined Sookey.

Sookey saw Nash tap Mary's nose and a wave of jealously pulsed through her. She smiled a slightly false smile as they sat down.

"Prey tell me plainly, where did the two of you first meet?"

Sookey didn't like the conspiratorial glance and grin the two of them shared. Mary started to speak.

"'e.."

But Nash immediately talked over her.

"Her ladyship here," he was back on his best behaviour with his speech now they were ensconced in a private little nook of the pub, "tried to pick me pocket if yer please. I'm mindin' me own business, on me way ta see a friend who lived down by the Victoria an' Albert, when before I knows what I'm about, this one's got her hand in me wes'cutt." Nash's wide-eyed mock horror turned to a grin. "It is well I catched her straight mind. If she gets half away down the street her days would have been numbered when I catched up with 'er."

"If I'd gets away a yard, I'd 'ave never more bin 'eard of. 'ow were you gonna catch the likes a me?" she snorted back with an equally broad grin.

Sookey was beginning to wish she hadn't asked. She started to feel like an outsider, but then had a brainwave.

"I once paid a figure, it were stiff and there's the troof, to be received at a party to raise funds for charitable causes, attended by Queen Victoria herself. She was enquired, lest her opinion was ill, what she thought of the new museum being named for her and the prince. Her answer: 'We are not amuse-eum'."

She looked for a flicker of recognition of the joke registering in the eyes of Nash, but was disappointed.

"Yeah, I spose she would think it choice if they never arsted her permission," he said seriously. There was a short silence before Nash continued, "I should pay yer fer that door. I jus' bin ta see a tradesmen to sort it out. Two of 'ems comin' round tomorra. I had ta run round all over the shop at this time a night to find someone, so I never had a chance ta do that wallpaperin' after all. I've pushed the door to, so as yer just needs to give it a bit ov a yank when yer gets 'ome. Rose's keepin' an eye out."

Sookey insisted that she would pay for the door and made the obvious appreciative noises. She then asked the names of the men, how much she should pay them, whether he knew what time they would be arriving and assured Nash that there was no hurry where the wallpapering was concerned. She wasn't sure whether she should say in a light throw away fashion that she could probably do the job herself shortly, so he needn't feel obliged to come back to do it, but thought that Nash might take this as a slight. She left it that she would receive him another time to do the job. It would also be another chance to see him.

The doctor in her brought an enquiry after the man with the mouth injury. Nash gave her the vaguest answer he thought he could get away with.

"He was gone out short after you. I had a little talk with him about the whole business before I let him clear orf. He didn't know you from Adam. Him and his two mates were just gettin' paid a bit of bunts by their bloke. No doubt this gen'leman'll be expectin' a visit from me. He won't be disappoin'ed."

Sookey didn't pursue the conversation further as she thought it best to leave things to Nashey. She was disappointed that such a joyous evening had turned so serious, and that she had been the one to spoil things. But she reflected that these things had to be discussed. Mary then took up the conversation and soon had the mood lightened again, good naturedly arguing with Nash.

Sookey had come to realise that 'leg-pulling' as people called it was an important aspect of human relationships in the slums. It was often a sign of close friendship, though she had also seen fights start when the recipient of the critique had taken exception to it. She had seen Rose and her husband Stan have rows that spilled onto the street on more than one occasion which had appeared to start from banter. She found it difficult to ascertain when, and to whom, one could use such humour and had steered clear of it. She was pleased to hear that Mary and Nashey's argument was not over something insignificant or trivial. It was a worthy, if rather colourful, argument about who was the toughest, Bill Sykes or Magwitch. It was a joy to her that people brought up with nothing but an all too brief schooling before the need to work had thrust them into premature adulthood, had read, been read, or at least heard of such stories. She felt that her work at Toynbee Hall, and that of others such as the Ragged schools for the poor, was making a difference. It was not so long ago, at the time Oliver Twist and Great Expectations had been written, that there would have been a terrible irony in that none of the real life characters in such a story would have ever heard of the book, let alone be able to read, or argue over it. She felt a moment of peace.

She looked around. The 'Pinda' as it was called, was a squalid place. It may have had the glitz of an old gin palace once, but over the years the mirrors and bright lamps had been smashed or cracked and replaced with nothing but advertising boards that had got filthy with smoke. The gaiety of purple painted walls and huge drapery of a few decades ago had become a filthy stained, pock-marked crumble, and the curtains had long since rotted with damp and disappeared. The smell and pall of stale tobacco, mildew and unwashed humanity hung in the air, and the customers were just as Nashey had described them. A middling slummer sticking their head through the door might see a den of iniquity, but these people were too weak, too broken to be part of that sort of scene. These people were simply hiding, trying to escape, albeit temporarily. She appreciated that she was completely out of place, a fish out of water, and she was all too aware that she turned disapproving heads with her middling manners and accent, yet she had never felt so at home.

"...Mary, I'm tellin' yer, 'e shouldn't a used some soppy little sod like Oliver ta break in frew the winda ov that rich gent's 'ouse, 'e should 'ave used one ov the boys like the Artful Dodger."

Nash was far more impressed with Magwitch than Sykes. Anyone who could escape from the infamously horrendous prison hulks, thankfully some years since scrapped, was alright with him. He continued his critique of Sykes.

"An' 'ow is it a crowd a ruffs followed the coppers after 'im in Jacob's Island. Them Bermondsey boys 'ates crushers same way we does. They wouldn't 'ave believed a word the crushers said about some murder, so 'e must a bin a wrong un for 'em ta chase after 'im. An' if 'e were spose ta be so bleedin' tough, 'e wouldn't 'ave let sum pawsey little fightin' dog give 'im up would e' now?"

Before Mary had time to answer, an increasingly happy, confident Sookey felt it was time to make her debut as a 'leg-puller'.

"I dare say Mary, that is why Nashey owns a cat rather than a dog."

She had a broad self-satisfied smirk on her face. Mary let out a little giggle, though she hadn't found the joke very funny. But Nash's expression darkened in an instant.

"I don't owns a cat. If it don't catch mice it starves."

He leaned forward to within inches of Sookey's face.

"It is well for you I ain't Bill Sykes. Lest you forget, just cos I lets 'er take the rise," he said giving a brief nod sideways at Mary without taking his intimidating stare from Sookey, "don't mean nobody else can."

The blood drained from Sookey's face. She was ashen. She glanced nervously at Mary for support, but her friend was suddenly finding her shoes an interesting topic for inspection.

Christ almighty gell, yer gone an' dun it now ain't ya. I told yer ta be careful with 'im. There's rules, limits ain' there.

But after a second of shock, Mary knew she had to defend Sookey. She wasn't going to let even Nashey upset her friend. She raised her head defiantly and was about to say something when Nash flicked his gaze at her and gave the tiniest, quickest of winks. Mary was taken aback. Sookey was avoiding eye-contact, staring at Nashey's chest.

Nash lifted a finger and gently applied pressure to Sookey's chin, raising her head to bring her eyes up to meet his. His face collapsed into a broad grin.

"Gell, ain't you amuse-eum?" He started to laugh heartily. "If old Queen Victoria herself heard that joke, she'd have yer carted off to the Tower fer sure, an' she'd be right to do it an' all. I 'ad to get me own back for the 'distress of the mind' as you would call it, caused me there gell!"

Sookey was wide eyed by this time, and swivelled her head slowly to look at Mary. Mary had much the same expression as she twisted to look at Sookey, and then burst into laughter.

"Gawd 'elp us, 'e 'ad yer there proper didn't 'e gell!? I was just about to tell 'im what for an' all. 'e 'ad a bleedin' cheek. 'e would a got a piece of me mind I can tell yer. An' a facer I shouldn't wonder!"

"Would I now?" interjected Nash with mock aggression.

"Yeah, I says!" said Mary, folding her arms across her chest in defiance.

The colour which had drained from Sookey's face moments earlier had now surged back, and she felt a huge blush in her cheeks. Mary saw the reddening and was tempted to make a joke along the lines of her having even more rouge than usual, but felt better of it. A memory of the people laughing at her in court came into Sookey's mind, and she felt anger course through her, but when she saw the warmth of the laughter of her two friends, and realised they were laughing with her, not at her, the anger was washed away by a torrent of well being.

"You trifle with me for sport sir. Be off with you and make haste! I am done with you!" she said with tears streaming down her cheeks.

The water had formed as sorrow but fallen as joy.

～ ◆ ～

Sookey realised that the cruel joke at her expense had been an important moment. She had never felt so accepted, and the conversation flowed easily between the three of them until Mary suddenly informed them that she had something else to do and started to leave. Sookey was surprised as Mary had not previously mentioned anything to this effect. She enquired politely if it was anything interesting, but Mary just fobbed her off.

"Nah, just remembered summin' I got a do thas all, nose-ache."

Sookey thought it was most unlike Mary to be so vague. She shrugged and made arrangements to meet Mary at Henrietta's coffee room the following morning.

Sookey and Nashey continued enjoying each others company in the pub for a while, before Sookey suggested they retire to her house. She wanted to speak with him on a delicate matter best not discussed in public. Having arrived there and made tea, she was not at all perturbed by being alone with this man, though she feared what Rose would say. Sookey had just finished telling Nashey about the wonderfully joyful tea-pickers in India, who always seemed to have a smile on their faces despite doing a back-breaking job for long hours. She had described the job. Nashey hadn't realised that tea was grown on bushes. He had always assumed it grew on trees like other leaves.

"Sounds bet'er than the Bryant & May factory or the sweated trades any day a the week. Reckon Mary'd be a good tea-picker if there were such a fing 'ere. Keep 'er orf them streets an' all."

Sookey agreed and the conversation took on a more serious note, discussing Mary and her line of work for a while. Sookey then took the opportunity to introduce the subject which was the purpose of her asking Nashey round.

"Our paths keep crossing Nashey."

Nash simply nodded. They were only five words but he was already on his guard. Sookey continued.

"I am glad to have this opportunity of serious discourse with you. The man Shanks…"

She left the words dangling in the air to see if he would pick them up. He was only too pleased to oblige her.

"Rum sort a do, wern it. He were up to no good a course but I let 'im go cos 'e'd 'ave only made up some tall story. Better to get the gen after from his mate wivout the teef. It ain't right a course, and I'll sees Shanks pays for what he's done, don't you worry."

Sookey had been over the whole episode in her mind a number of times but couldn't fathom any of it.

"Forgive me Nashey, but what has he done? I am lost on it. He asked me to visit him so that he could pay the debt he owed. I am then attacked by fiends in the very court in which he lives, and oblige me if he doesn't visit me at my dwelling with one of the very men who attacked me. And he possesses a threatening demeanour to boot. If Mary hadn't been there I don't know what would have become of me."

"She's one ov the best alright. Do anythin' for anyone she's a kinsman wiv, and tough as ol' boots she is inta the bargain. She'd have seen ol' Shanks and his mate off wiv that knife and cosh ov hers if need have bin."

There was unusual affection in Nash's voice.

"Are you and Mary sweethearts Nashey?" asked Sookey with a cheeky grin.

She knew very well that they weren't, but she wanted to hear his response. She feared he would say something along the lines of 'no, mores the pity'. But his reply was far worse than she could have imagined.

"Nah, I don't goes in for all that sort a fing," he said uncomfortably.

There was a brief pause before he regained his composure.

"'sides, she wouldn't be on the game if I were her ol' man. I'd knock her over before I'd let her do that. And not just fer herself neiver. It's a dishonour on a man see."

He had pronounced the aitch in 'dishonour'. Sookey beamed. She loved the effort he was making. Nash continued.

"Young Joe Barnett's her feller. He's a right enuff young scamp, but one word from him and she does what she likes. He needs to take her in hand but he ain't the man for it see."

"Barnett?.."

But before Sookey could carry on with the obvious question, Nash held up his hand.

"No, 'e ain' related to the vicar. Queer ain' it?"

"It is not queer Nashey, it is what is called a co-in-cid-ence," said Sookey slowly, with an enthusiastic smile to ensure she did not sound patronising.

It worked. Nash was impressed just as he was when he first met her, by her ability to educate him with knowledge without sounding like the old harridans who used to teach him in his Ragged school.

"Queer word for a queer fing," said Nash with a smile.

Sookey returned the smile and carried on.

"Like you, Mary is book-read from Ragged schooling and I have given her further tuition. When she is back from a visit to her sister in the north, I will enquire of Henrietta if there could be a paid position for Mary as my assistant at Toynbee Hall. All Hall workers have to date offered their services freely, but only middling people are in such a situation and we do not always offer the fittest of things. We need a girl like Mary. And it isn't just the moral question. She needs to get off the streets with this fiend still undetected. Can you not chastise her Nashey?"

"Chastise Mary? Easier said than done gell. I've been on at her since the first killin'. She don't listen ta no cove. Tell yer what I will do mind. I knows a crusher who likes a bit ov dropsy. I'm gonna see if 'e can get 'old ov a police likeness ov one of them murdered women for me. See if I can scare her that way. But you should try her an' all. She might listen to a slum... educated, much cleverer, much older lady like you."

Sookey knew very well that she was someway less intelligent than Mary and she wasn't sure she liked Nashey saying she was a 'much older lady'. She was only thirteen years older after all. But she appreciated him stopping himself from calling her a slummer. She didn't care for the term.

"I think your suggestion of a police photograph is the fittest. But allow me to correspond with my friend Walter in Dieppe. The painter whose work you did not regard? In a recent last letter he told of seeing such a photograph in a local newspaper if you please! It would seem their stomachs are stronger in France. I will request he dispatches an edition post haste."

She was surprised at her own moral turpitude, not to say her candour. She was shocked at her lack of shock; again. She glanced across at Nashey, who was blinking back at her with a mix of surprise and something else which she couldn't quite put her finger on. Perhaps it was what she hoped. They shared a joint chuckle, and then there was a brief pause as they looked at each other. Nashey broke the spell.

"Yeah, I'll do that tomorra. But let's hope you get her that job in the Hall, and then she'll be off the streets anyhow."

"Yes indeed," replied Sookey.

But that's all she said and there was another pause while they exchanged glances.

Nash was keen to reignite the conversation.

"Don't fink I've forgotten ta do that wallpaperin' ov yours," he said with an earnest nod.

Sookey realised the moment had passed and that she had been sidetracked from her original concerns of Shanks' behaviour.

"Nashey, perhaps you could come to the Hall and give a lecture on the art of wallpapering!" she said lightly. But before he could reply she went on, changing voice and expression to great seriousness.

"Did Shanks have me attacked? For what purpose? Why did he bring that man to my house? He must surely have known the game would be up soon enough?"

Nash had all the answers but he didn't want to disclose them, or how he had acquired them.

"I shouldn't put much mind to it gell. Coves like Shanks don't look further than their nose. The prisons an' workhouses are full ov 'em. He jus' wanted to get out ov paying yer what he owed yer. Got hold ov some ruffs to give yer a good 'idin' and their pay was gonna be whatever they could snatch off yer. Probably told 'em you were well-heeled and as likely to have some finery on yer worf havin'. It all happened in the pitch dark so when one of 'em started up about his mouff, Shanks fought it'd be funny to go round and get you to sort him out. Finks that's funny, cove like him, an' not havin' to pay yer like a proper doctor were jus' bunts. You said yerself he told yer he weren't gonna pay yer no more, and his freatenin' yer were his way ov telling yer not to arst for the money again."

He saw from Sookey's frown that she was finding it slightly difficult to believe a man could be so stupid.

"See, criminals ain' like they are in some book are they. Sherlock 'omes wouldn't take no time to catch Shanks would he? So books has to have clever sods as the criminals dunt they so as they's hard to collar." Sookey still had a slightly quizzical look on her face, but he could see he was wearing her down. "I tells yer, give me two famous criminal cases in London. Not the Ripper a course. Two ovvers. Gall on."

Sookey enjoyed these sorts of conversations that she had with Nashey. She remembered the long chat they had about the costers' rhyming slang.

"Very well."

She pondered for a minute, pursing her lips and narrowing her eyes in concentration.

"The Fanny Adams and the Franz Muller cases. There sir, pray enlighten me," she said with a whimsical smile.

"Blimey gell, sweet Fanny Adams, that must be a score and more year ago. I don't even remember it meself, only what stories I've heard tell. What made yer fink of that?"

"It was precisely a score and ten years ago. I was the same age as Fanny. It was such a shock to my parents. I remember not being allowed out to play in the park, even with my governess, for a year thereafter."

Nash thought to himself, little Fanny were eight if I remember right, so you're fifty eight are ya Sookey? Yer looks younger.

"The bastard who did fer her, took her away in front of her two sisters, so they told the crushers 'oo he was, and then when the police poked around in his house, they found his diary with "I murdered a little girl today" written in it. I arst yer. Didn't need no Sherlock 'omes on that case did they? An' Muller, he murders someone on a train and leaves his own hat behind, which was real unusual so everyone knew it was his, next to the body, and then when the police catches up wiv him, bugger me if he ain't wearing the dead man's hat. Even the tecs they got on this Ripper case could have twigged that one."

Sookey shook her head ruefully.

"The whole business does not command itself to reason, but you have convinced me Nashey, I will forget about Mr Shanks."

Yeah, but I won't, thought Nash solemnly.

CHAPTER 17:

"At length our masters are aroused, and behold! A Royal Commission is enquiring into the particulars of the housing of the poor."

H. Davis, Commonweal

Men with similar characters and dispositions can often be the best of friends or great rivals or sworn enemies. It is sometimes all a matter of fate; how, when and where they first meet, the circumstances, the foot on which they get off. George Lusk was not unlike a more respectable version of Alexander Nash. The two men had not got off on the right foot.

Lusk had stolen a prospective girlfriend off Nash when they were young men making their first forays into the world of romance. Though stolen isn't really an accurate term. More, he stole a march on Nash. The two boys had both been making their way along the Ratcliffe Highway, on the Saturday 'Monkey Parade', where all the young men and women of the area paraded up and down in front of each other. With the bravado, not to mention the social pressure, a thirteen year old can only experience at the head of a group of mates faced with members of the opposite sex, Nash was chirping cheeky remarks and offering his love and devotion disguised as insults, to the girl of his dreams, Daisy. But he had taken her first coy rejection too literally. While he was licking his wounds at the back of his group as one of his mates took up the cudgels with Daisy's friend, Georgie Lusk, from another group of lads, moved in and made a quick killing with Daisy. Nash had lost the girl of his dreams.

They never did like each other after that. Nash was the sort of man Lusk used to be but he was trying to leave his past behind. He was a successful builder nowadays. Lusk 'fancied 'isself' as far as Nash was concerned. Their last meeting had ended with Nash telling him so, contempt written all over his face.

"I remember you when yer used to chew bread for our ducks!"

Lusk, along with the rest of the world's population, had never been employed as a duck's bread-chewer, but he understood very well what Nash was saying in his 'arse-about face' way. But that had been some time ago. Although they lived in the same square mile, their paths rarely crossed.

Lusk had opened the door with undisguised lack of enthusiasm, and greeted Nash with "Yeah?"

Nash made it clear he was equally displeased to see him.

"Still gettin' that gang ov navvies in frocks togevver are yer George?"

Lusk was the self-appointed head of the local vigilante mob, who had taken it upon themselves to do what the police couldn't, and bring the killer to justice. Nash agreed with their ideals, and if it had been anyone else other than George Lusk at their lead, he would have joined them. Their first abortive attempt to catch and no doubt beat to death the man they knew to be the killer ended in miserable, embarrassing failure. One John Pizer, nickname Leather Apron, was their target. He was their man on what they considered was the overwhelming evidence against him; he was violent towards women, owned a big knife which

198

he liked to flash about, was a butcher by trade so had the knife skills, and the surname told you the rest. The police had managed to get to Pizer first, arresting and then questioning him only to find he had a cast iron alibi for the last murder, and relayed this to Lusk, with a warning about his future conduct.

The incident had been reported in the newspapers and Lusk's name given. Soon after the double murder and the publication of the first Jack the Ripper letter, a box had been delivered to Lusk, inside which had been a kidney and a note purporting to be from the Ripper. The kidney was supposed to be that of poor Catherine Eddowes. The police took it seriously at first but eventually concluded that it was a joke played by a medical student, though Nash suspected that a newspaper hack was laughing up his sleeve somewhere. Lusk had become the celebrity of the day. He used his new found notoriety to put forward the idea that small, hard men should dress up in women's clothing and walk the streets at night, ready to give The Ripper more than he bargained for. Nash thought this most amusing. Lusk cursed his sarcasm. Nash feigned innocence.

"I was gunna volunteer but fought I might be too big for ya. An' now yer like that..."

"Damn your eyes Nash, what you after?"

Nash turned his gravest expression on like a tap.

"I wanna know why I shouldn't follow you into a dark alley one night, and come out the ovver end on me own."

Lusk was bemused.

"Ay?"

"I 'ear tell one a your lads as 'ad all 'is teef out. 'e's gonna 'av a new gas stove put in."

Nash laughed grimly at his own joke. Lusk now understood.

"Yeah I 'eard about that. Case a mistaken identity, as the new police term goes it. Lucky yer were there wern it? I 'eard one ov my boys an' two ov 'is mates, dunno 'oo they were, fought that funny slummer woman might be the Ripper. She's got the doctorin' 'know 'ow an' the killin's started up sharp after she come to live in Whitechapel. They say the Ripper could be a woman dunt they? Thas why the police ain' got a clue see. They ain' even lookin' for the right sex!" He laughed nervously, before adding an afterthought. "They were jus' gunna take 'er down Liverpool Street police station. Thas all. Lads ay?"

There was another nervous chortle.

Nash had not been told anything he didn't already know. He had prised this much out of the man with no teeth in Sookey's front room with nothing more than a punch in the testicles and an arm-lock which had threatened to have the man tickle the back of his own neck. He didn't doubt the story. Charlie no-teeth would have told him everything, he was that petrified.

"I spose finkin' Sookey, thas 'er name case you 'adn't 'eard, is the Ripper ain' much more fuckin' stupid than finking some Jew-boy butcher's the killer jus' cos he likes 'urtin' women. Most men round 'ere knock women about when they've 'ad a few dunt they. Some when they ain' 'ad a few neiver."

Nash darkened his stare even more, leaning forward to within a few inches of his old adversary's face before carrying on.

"But your boy tells me you put 'im up to it, an' the ovver two were your boys an' all I 'ear. So I 'av to 'old you, not 'im an' 'is two mates to account see. And they got a bloody good 'iding, so what to do wiv you? It's only fair."

Lusk folded.

"It weren't nuffin' ta do wiv me. This cove Shanks comes an' sees me. 'e tells me this Sookey woman's the Ripper an' 'e can prove it see. 'e says as 'ow you saw 'er do the last one but you're keepin' yer trap shut cos you want the papers to keep goin' on aboud it, so yer don't want 'im, I mean 'er, caught."

This shook Nash. He hadn't expected this. He had thought Shanks probably just wanted to get out of paying Sookey the money he owed her. Was this a, what was that word Sookey taught him, co-in-cid-ence? Did Shanks invent the story about Sookey being the murderer just to get her beaten up badly or even killed? Or did he base the story on the truth, just replacing the Derby-hatted gent with Sookey? That would mean Shanks knew something.

But 'ow? Nah, it mus' be a co-in-cid-ence. 'e must a jus' wanted Sookey in 'ospital or in the ground so 'e didn't 'ave to pay 'er.

Nash was unconvinced by his own argument. He started to mull over in his mind how Shanks could know anything, but Lusk interrupted his thoughts before he got very far.

"Wass 'appened ta me boy any'ow?"

"I told 'im they 'ad good den'ists south of the river. I suggested he went an' found one, an' 'is 'ealth 'd be a lot betta if he stayed over there an' all."

Yer never say nuffin' straight do yer Nash? thought Lusk silently.

⌒ ◆ ⌒

Questioning Lusk about the attack on Sookey had not been top of Nash's agenda. He didn't really know why he had gone to see Lusk when he had other more pressing, more important things to do. Sheer curiosity, he supposed.

Lucky you ain't no cat ain' it Nash, he cursed to himself.

But now Nash was at his most important venue of the day, and he was in new territory. He had never had cause to visit a local grocery shop. It was owned by John McCarthy, who was also a slum landlord, renting out many rooms in the vicinity. Nash had got his name from Mary. He was her landlord. McCarthy was behind the counter, resplendent in immaculate clean white apron down to his knees. He glanced up smiling at what he thought was to be a new customer. His expression changed as he saw who had just walked into his shop.

"Mary Kelly told me where a find yer," said Nash.

McCarthy was well aware of who Nash was and who his friends were.

"'ere, I don't want no trouble. She ain' paid 'er rent. I told Tom to arst 'er for it that's all. 'e didn't 'it 'er or nuffin'. I got a dog in the back."

"It is well Tom didn't 'it 'er then, ovverwise me an your dog 'ad be fallin' out wouldn't we?" said Nash with a scowl. "That is after me, Tom and you 'ad fallen out first."

The man quivered as Nash's right hand came out of his pocket. The expected cosh wasn't there, just a handful of coins.

"'ow much she owe?" asked Nash as he started sorting through his change.

"It's a sov at the end a next week. She won't 'av paid for a munff or more" replied the relieved grocer, letting out a deep breath.

Nash looked up from his palm and sneered.

"I didn't arst yer 'ow much she owed next week."

"It's three weeks, four bob a week. That's .."

"I knows 'ow much it is!"

Nash tossed a half-sovereign and a two-shilling piece across the counter, both coins bouncing to hit the apron before falling to the floor.

"I seen that room you've got 'er in. Your rent's stiff fer it. She 'as to walk the streets to pay you," said Nash with undisguised disgust for the slum landlord in front of him.

McCarthy wanted to answer with 'thas the goin' rate, take it or leave it, an' I ain' interested in 'ow she gets the rent so long as she does', but he got a mental image of himself laying on the floor in a pool of his own blood. He didn't say a word as he scrambled on the floor to pick up the money, and hoped the huge man in front of him would perhaps just knock a bowl of apples over and maybe steal something, just to make a point, and then walk out.

He took longer than he need have to rescue the coins, out of sight behind his counter, waiting to hear Nash's heavy boots creaking out the shop. He eventually got to his feet to find Nash just standing there looking at him.

"I didn't come ta pay 'er rent see. Lucky yer spoke ov it ain't ya. Thas bunts fer ya. But woe-betide you if Mary tells me it ain' so a course. But now to the purpose. Mary tells me yer 'av more places fer rent in the area. She says yer offered 'er a bigger room in Middlesex Street for a cuppla extra bob a week, just shy ov a twelve-mumph back. Place wiv the rag in the winder. That right?"

McCarthy was both relieved and wary. He was appalled by the thought of having Nash as a tenant. Who would collect the rent?!

"It's rented out. All me rooms are rented out."

Nash had not known that The Ripper's bolt hole had been the one Mary had mentioned when Nash had asked her if she knew if her landlord had any places in Middlesex Street. She had just said that her landlord had offered her a place there, but he hadn't gone into further details because she wasn't interested at the higher price; she could barely afford her present hovel. He knew it wouldn't be easy to coax information out of McCarthy, and he couldn't very well get it out of him with his usual tactics. Inflicting injuries on Mary's landlord was a sure way to have her booted out on the street.

He had thrown in the rag in the window just to see McCarthy's reaction. It was now clear he was the Ripper's landlord. That was a bit of luck, though given that McCarthy rented out so many rooms in the vicinity, perhaps it wasn't so much luck as the odds having been in his favour.

"I didn't arst if it were fer rent now," retorted Nash. "I knows it ain'. I wants to know 'oo yer've rented it to. An' before yer says, it's none of me business, I'm tellin' yer different."

Nash was pleased with the original misunderstanding with McCarthy about Mary's rent. McCarthy should be pleased to have had his rent paid to him, and had already shown himself to be easily intimidated.

"It'll cost yer," said McCarthy.

Nash smiled inwardly. He had him.

Nash looked about the shop with interest, rather overacting.

"Good shop yer got 'ere. See yer got them new bananas and tomar'er fings from one a them funny cun'ries. I 'ear they give yer a cancer. Bet this shop brings in a pretty penny mind?"

The threat was not lost on McCarthy. He already had twelve shillings in his pocket from this man, he better not push him too far. He had heard what Nash had done to those three boys of George Lusk's. And they were tough bastards themselves.

"Reach us anuvver four bob towards Mary's rent. An' it saves 'er the trouble a paying me next week then dun it. Poor girl. Must be 'ard for 'er."

Nash resisted the temptation he felt to tell McCarthy where he could stick his concern for the 'poor girl'. He just fished in his pockets for a couple of florins.

Before he brought out any money, he made sure he brought out a knife, a cosh and a marlin spike first, and laid them matter-of-factly on the counter. He handed over the money and started to replace the weapons back in the cavernous pockets of his overcoat.

"Gives me the name S.E. Milbrac. I arst 'im what 'is first name was an' 'e said 'e prefers initials. Laughed 'is head off at that 'e did like he was coddin' wiv 'isself. Bleedin' escaped from Coney 'atch if yer arst me. Gent 'e was mind. Big gold watch an' chain. After I told 'im the rent, 'e says as 'e'll pay a stiffer figure if I keeps meself scarce, an' if anyone arsts anyfin' I 'old me tongue. Puts the rent in the post to me 'ere at the shop if yer please, lest anyone sees 'im about. Spose 'e uses it a take 'ores and don't want nobody nosing about. Saves 'im doin' it up against a wall eh!" he laughed, and then thinking of the 'poor girl' who was Nash's friend, quickly returned to a serious countenance.

"Ain' right though is it Mr Nash?"

"Nah, it ain' right," agreed Nash solemnly. "When did 'e take the room?"

"Middla August."

What were thought to have been the first two murders, of Emma Smith and Martha Tabram, had taken place before this date. Nash was consequently very surprised at the date.

"Ay? You sure about that?"

"Yeah, I remember plain it were the Saturday after the second murder."

"You been in the room since?"

"Nah, if he suspected I'd lose a stiff paying tenant wouldn't I."

"Gis the key. I ain' gonna take nuffin'. I'll make sure 'e don't suspect."

"Leave orf, if I ain' doin' it you ain' doin' it."

"You forget what me and my friends do for a livin'. I knows people who can crack a case wivout a sign no cove's bin there."

"Nah, I got too much to lose. You can't afford wot 'e's paying me."

"If yer don't gimme the key I'll crack the case wivoud it, and I'll do it so as 'e knows someone's bin in. You loses yer stiff rent any'ow."

Nash changed his tone to a more conciliatory, conspiratorial one.

"I tells yer the troof John. I'm gonna gain out a this. 'e's a rich gent after all. Nuff said. You don't 'ave to know more. But I'll pass on some bunts to ya. I won't beat about the bush. There's Jacks in it for ya. No more, no less."

Jacks was five pounds. Nash was making a deal he couldn't afford. He realised now that he would have to go ahead with Shanks' post office robbery, no matter what happened. McCarthy guessed that Nash must be confident he could find something of note in the room. Blackmail was his guess. Five pounds was a lot of money. He smiled with sly enthusiasm.

"I'll go and get me spare from out the back. Jacks it is."

Jack's it certainly was. Nash didn't know the word 'irony' but he felt it nonetheless.

CHAPTER 18:

"Under any civilised conditions it would have been impossible for these monstrous crimes to have been committed."
George R. Sims, Sunday Referee

Nash finally got around to tracking down the cracksman he needed for the post office robbery. Having called at his cellar slum to find he had just missed him, Nash was in no mood to simply hunch his shoulders and return home. He asked around in the suspicious-minded tight-knit enclave, and it was some time before he found someone willing to tell him anything. He was eventually told that his quarry had gone to a nearby tavern to watch the ratting.

Rural blood sports still flourished thanks to their enjoyment by the ruling classes, but the authorities had clamped down on all but one of the urban ones – ratting. There was far less pity for rats than any other animal so the authorities did little to interfere. Consequently, although Nash was an unknown face in the pub, he had no problem gaining admittance to the ratting upstairs. He mounted the filthy open staircase, the banisters having long since rotted away, to arrive in what was once the upstairs parlour of the landlord; dropped his shilling into the hat of the proprietor and entered the ratting room.

The dog 'pit' consisted of a small circus, six feet in diameter, fitted with wooden rims to chest height. Over it the branches of a gas lamp lit up the white painted floor and every part of the pit, as well as the faces of the men leaning over the rim, their features filled with the unique far away stare of the fervent gambler's excitement and anticipation. The men with the inside information; the men who knew they were going to win. At least, so they thought. Nash recognised the type. He saw them in large numbers at horse-race meetings. He wondered where these men came from. They seemed to appear from nowhere. He never saw them on the streets, or in the pubs, or anywhere else for that matter. Their clothes were an indeterminate mix that gave up no clues. They spent money wildly, never buying individual drinks, always buying by the bottle.

The action was about to start, and the audience who had been too late to get a pit-side view were clambering on tables and forms. The dogs were tied to the legs of tables. The English terriers were very excitable, raring to go, whilst the bulldogs and Skye terriers were sleepy. The rats were then brought forward in rusty wire cages. All the dogs were now excited and ran out to the length of their leashes, barking and almost choking themselves in their eagerness to get at their prey. There was no smell of drains from the rats, which suggested these were not sewer rats.

The atmosphere was building. The noise climbed as shouted bets were offered and accepted, roll-ups hurriedly trodden out underfoot, hob-nailed boots scraped along the rotten wooden floor as the last few men gathered around, pushing and shoving for the best view from the back of the throng. Corduroy-trousered costermongers, soldiers enjoying the freedom of unbuttoned uniforms, coachmen still in their livery and assorted tradesmen in aprons and the like, jostled for position.

The first event was an eight minute affair. More than enough rats were to be let loose. How many could Billy kill in those eight minutes? Nash had spotted John The Blackguard in the crowd. He was a renowned animal catcher. If something moved on the Essex marshes, John caught it and sold it. He did well selling songbirds to market tradesmen – starlings, blackbirds, thrushes, finches; but his greatest ability was catching sewer and water-ditch rats. Nash wanted to ask about for the cracksman before the first event started, after which the din would preclude any conversation. John wouldn't know Arthur but others would.

He turned to the man next to him, a costermonger. The coster had just placed a bet with the urgent near-panic of the betting man who had waited till the last possible moment before declaring his interest in the belief it would gain him an advantage as he weighed the odds and possibilities, and was now worried he wouldn't get his money accepted. His bet had been based on what he believed to be an astute analysis of the weight of the first dog.

"Wot rats they got?" Nash enquired, just to break the ice.

"Country barns. Dogs 'll be alright tonight," came the confident, curt reply, meaning that the dogs would not suffer canker from getting infected mouths from sewer rats.

Rats caught in country barns were the most esteemed. Nash nodded with apparent satisfaction.

"Good. Seen Arfur Phillips about 'ave ya?"

The man's demeanour changed from indifference to suspicion. He looked Nash up and down as if he was something that had just oozed from beneath the brush of a crossing-sweeper.

"Wossit a you if I 'ave?"

Nash leaned forward to within a few inches of the man's face, with the darkest of expressions on his face.

"Ain' you 'eard, every crusher's walkin' their plates off lookin' for ol' Jack. They ain' gonna find 'im in 'ere are they?" The pub was notoriously anti-Jewish, and all its clientele would have been convinced the Ripper was a Jew. "I'll fuckin' find 'im meself," shouted Nash above the growing clamour, the emphasised first letter of the swear word spraying spittle on to the man's cheek.

The coster was treated to a parting sneer before Nash switched his attention to the search for Arthur. He would be easy enough to spot. Nash just had to look for a dog-end wagging up and down from the corner of a grizzled mouth. Arthur had that knack of being able to speak, shout, spit and do his full gamut of facial expressions without ever having to withdraw his thin saliva-sticky rolled-up cigarette from his mouth.

Nash pushed his way around the outer boundary of leaning, shouting bodies and eventually saw the cracksman. Arthur was close to the front. Nash was not going to be able to get to him, so he grabbed an old chair that was up against the wall, tipping onto the floor a huge decrepit Old English bulldog that had been curled asleep on it. It had no ear flaps, a sure sign that it had once been a fighting dog. These vulnerable appendages would have been sliced off before its first fight. The dog gave the most perfunctory of growls in protest, but it was more meek complaint than threat. It had tasted the end of a boot often enough to know its place. Nash issued a threatening 'grrh, gidoudovit' of his own at the dog and made himself comfortable. A switching ferret peered at Nash from inside the cage next to the chair. The odd ferret would be thrown in to the pit to kill rats just to add a bit of variety to the bill for the paying customers.

There was not much to hold Nash's interest as he looked about the place. Along one wall were a cluster of black leather dog collars and large square glazed boxes which held the stuffed bodies of past champion fighting and ratting dogs. Pride of place was given to Bruce, a six-pounder who held the record of almost two hundred rats killed in the designated time. A row of mutoscopes lined the back wall. They were primitive 'What the Butler Saw' machines, with photographs of women undressing, showing underclothing and sitting in highly suggestive postures and nude. Each machine had a placard above it with seductive titles 'How Shocking!', 'Naughty! Naughty! Naughty!', 'Very Spicy!' Nash returned his gaze back to the ferret, deciding it was more interesting.

The first contest of the evening came to an abrupt end when the time-keeper shouted 'eight minutes up' and his assistant dived into the seething mess of dead bodies to haul out the frenzied dog.

The din changed from a raucous shouting of encouragement at, or cursing of, the dog depending on where the shouter's bet was laid, to a mix of quiet murmurings of excited anticipation and loud sworn oaths and arguments, as the count was made.

"Firty nine!" came the shout, followed by a huge wave of abuse from the majority.

It was clear the big money had been on the dog killing at least forty rats in his eight minutes. The sweating dog, shaking with exhaustion and over-excitement, its coat caked in the fur and blood of dog and rat, was taken away by its owner. The man cursed the dog for embarrassing him by killing fewer than expected.

"Yer turned felon!"

But Nash noticed the man didn't kick the dog as he might have expected. Nash got to his feet, lightly kicking the cage of the ferret.

"'ope you do better boy."

The dog-owner had disappeared into a side room. Nash had to pass the room as he was making his way round towards Arthur Phillips' twitching cigarette. He pulled the curtain back and saw the dog owner on his knees, dressing his charge's wounds as the dog tucked in to beef tea with, judging by the bottle at the man's side, a touch of brandy in it.

"You're a good 'un you are, Billy, I'll fetch yer a warm bath when I get yer 'ome," whispered the man with affection.

Nash let the curtain fall and quietly moved back into the bestial throng.

The cracksman spotted Nash making his way towards him.

"I jus' 'eard you were 'ere lookin' for me," he said, nodding back over his shoulder at the surly coster Nash had encountered on his arrival, who was looking on with a scowl.

Nash leaned into Phillips, and whispered in his ear.

"When yer finished 'ere I got summin' for ya."

Phillips gave a sly enthusiastic smile.

"I got money on the next 'un. Then I'll be wiv yer."

The next event was the grand match of the evening. 50 rats – could Wee Jasper kill them all in the allotted time? The proprietor of the pub owned the dog and had made a big money match with his son, who had bet him the dog wouldn't be successful. Billy's victims were gathered by their tails and flung into the corner, and the floor swept.

Some were still just alive, squirming their death throes in the moving pile.

Seemingly to add a bit of showmanship to the grand match, the fifty new rats were not in rusty cages, but one big flat basket with an iron top, like those in which chickens were taken to market. The proprietor's son, daringly thrust his hand into the basket, picking up the biggest ones first from the seething black mass, and flinging them into the pit. Within a few minutes all fifty were in the pit, huddled together in a cowering mound. Nash thought they looked like the heap of hair sweepings in his barber's shop after a heavy Saturday's trade. They were sewer and water ditch rats. This became apparent from the sudden smell of latrine. The basket had actually been used instead of the cages to mask the smell for as long as possible. Nash suspected the proprietor's son had kept this knowledge to himself. It might take Wee Jasper just that fraction longer to subdue sewer rats. The odds had changed. Nash glanced over and sneered as he caught the eye of the sullen costermonger who had been so sure they were country barn rats.

Rats disliked wind, which sent them scattering. The throng shouted as one.

"Blow on 'em!"

The dog's second blew at them as if extinguishing fifty candles. A bull terrier in a fit of excitement was brought in by a boy.

"Lay 'old closer to the 'ead or e'll nip yer," advised the dog's owner.

The boy handed Wee Jasper over to the second, who jumped into the pit with the dog. As soon as the terrier was let loose, he became calm, in a business-like manner and rushed at the rats, burying his nose in the mound till he brought one out in his mouth. In short time, dozens of rats with broken necks were lying, bleeding on the floor; the white paint of the pit, stained red. One rat was now hanging on to the terrier's nose, and he couldn't shift it by tossing his head so he dashed it against the side of the arena. The dog nosed the rat kicking on its side as it slowly expired. Too much time had been wasted on one rat.

"Dead un, drop it!" shouted the second.

"Time!" shouted the time-keeper.

Wee Jasper was picked up and held, panting, staring at the three rats left alive. One of the filthy wretches commenced cleaning itself, one hopped about, the other sniffed at the trousers of the second. The proprietor had lost and he wasn't a good loser.

"That dog won't do for me! 'e's not my sort! 'ere son, you can 'ave 'im if yer like. I won't give 'im 'ouse room!"

A shower of ha'pennies were thrown into the pit by successful punters as a reward for the second.

Nash glanced over at the costermonger again. He wasn't throwing coins. Nash couldn't resist verbally kicking the man while he was down.

"Ay-ay, trouseys! Win on them country barn rats did ya?"

Arthur had a new roll-up between his lips. Like the appearing and disappearing gambling set, Arthur's fags were one of life's mysteries. Nash had never seen him make a new roll-up. They just seemed to appear. Nash also noticed he always seemed to have a day's silver beard growth; never clean-shaven, never more than a day's growth, another mystery. The two men left and made their way to a quiet pub where their conversation wouldn't be overheard. Arthur wasn't in the best of moods having had more money than he could afford on Wee Jasper. Nash explained the job.

Arthur was an escaped convict. He had melted his pewter cocoa mug over the gas light in his prison cell and moulded it into keys cut from lock-impressions made in pieces of soap. Pewter is soft and moulded like this apt to bend or break in a lock when turned. It had taken all of Arthur's considerable expertise to get the keys to work. The keys had gotten him out of the cells and into the prison church. He had worked away at the floorboards in the church for weeks whilst knelt in prayer in the same pew. He was able to get a floorboard out and get under the chapel floor. He had crawled to a point where a narrow opening had been cut for ventilation in the prison wall. It was a tight fit but he was only a small man and he squeezed through to freedom.

He now lived a very compact life, rarely straying far from the deepest of rookeries in which he lived, where no policeman feared to tread, and only came out of his lair to work, and even then only if it was really worth his while. He never worked with people he didn't know. There were too many informers about for his liking. Consequently he didn't like the sound of Shanks or his job.

"'ow am I supposed to know what tools to bring if I don't know what the job is till I'm on it? An' what 'appens if the crushers get 'old a this Shanks. He sounds like 'e'd turn us all in sharp."

Nash tried to sound reassuring, though he was far from happy with the arrangement himself.

"Bring all yer tools. I'll 'ave the canary slip round ta yer every Friday night till it 'appens. An' don't worry about Shanks. He don't tell me where or when the pull is, so I don't tell 'im 'oo I'm using on the pull. An' 'e won't see yer till we split the money up at the end, and then you'll just be some feller in a dark alley. 'e wouldn't knows yer again from Adam. An' me an' 'im's 'ad a sort ov understandin' since we were lads – 'e don't piss on me an' I let him alone a do whatever 'e does. 'e pisses on me, 'e only does it once.

Be sure cracksman 'e's more scared a me than anyfin' Old Bill can frow at 'im."

Arthur's mouth had opened so wide when Nash had suggested he take all his tools, that he almost dropped his dog-end. It clung to his lower lip by the merest speck of saliva.

"Canary! If they got a take all me tools, they'll 'ave to be a bleedin'.." He tried to think of the name of a really large bird but couldn't think of one. "Like one a them big fings they got in the zoo from one a them funny cun'ries!"

"Vulcha," proffered Nash with a chortle, but the laugh was a dry one; the situation was not funny. "I got a gell in mind 'oo…"

"Gell!?"

Nash had been cut off in mid-sentence. Not something that happened often but it was understandable on this occasion. Arthur was aghast.

"Since when could some slip of a woman carry all my tools!?"

Nash thought of a certain nineteen stone rent-book sandwich-making woman he knew who could carry all Arthur's tools and probably Arthur as well at the same time.

"Wot you laughin' at?" asked Arthur tartly. Nash hadn't realised that his mental image of big Rose Martin carrying Arthur's tools over one shoulder and Arthur over the over had shown on his face.

"Nuffin'," he replied sternly. "Gells makes the best canaries, you knows that. You've always used gells in the past ain't ya, so I dunno wot yer chirping on about. This girl's doin' the job an' that's the end ov it. An' before yer arst, never you mind why. I tell yer what I will do mind. I gives yer two canaries. Got an old Indian fella we can trust."

"Gells and Indians, gawd 'elp us!" came the not unexpected reply.

But there was something in the exasperated cry that confirmed to Nash that despite all the shortcomings of the plan, Arthur was in.

Fank christ fer Wee Jasper's clingin' rat I says.

⌒ ◆ ⌒

With the robbery finally organised, Nash was pleased to be back at the more important task at hand. He had taken Will Roud with him, telling his accomplice he was breaking into a gent's love-nest to find something incriminating with which he could blackmail the man. Nash nodded to Tom Carter briefly, a reliable and trustworthy if rather dim young lad he used for simple skulduggery assistance on occasion. Nash dropped a step behind Will and put a finger to his lips, telling Tom not to speak. Tom was alternating shifts with Khan selling matches across the street from the Ripper's bolt-hole. Nash and Will then strolled matter-of-factly over to the door with the coloured rag on a stick above it. Nash slipped the key into the lock and opened the door.

He nodded at Will and made to walk in when Will grabbed him by the shoulder.

"'ere, stop right there."

There was nothing on the floorboards other than a soup of filth such as rat droppings, save a large dirt encrusted mat just inside the door. Such a hovel certainly wouldn't usually have a mat to clean boots on. Will held his left index finger up in a motion to Nash to stay where he was. Will knelt down on the crumbling front step and leaned in to the room, gingerly peeling back towards him, between right thumb and index finger, the far right corner of the mat. A layer of dirt had been swept under the mat, and it was clear by its uniformity that is wasn't random housekeeping. Will craned his neck and peered up at a perplexed looking Nash.

"Wot the bleedin' 'ell you up to?" enquired Nash.

Will gave him a tired look in response.

"It's a trap ain' it. When 'e gets 'ere 'e checks to see if any cove's been in 'ere. They'd leave a footprint in the dirt as they stepped in see. Yer wouldn't step in wivout steppin' on the mat would ya. Dunno why 'e'd go a the trouble mind. It's like 'e's expectin' someone. Wot sort a gent is 'e? Clever bastard, right enuff."

"That makes two a ya then dun it," was Nash's gruff praise for his friend. Will's query was not going to be answered; the conversation was finished as far as Nash was concerned.

Nash would have to bend to get in through the small door as it was. He didn't like the idea of taking a running jump over the mat in a crouched position. If he didn't clear the mat he would leave a tell-tale bit of boot mark, not to mention the heads that would be turned in the street looking at his antics. He grabbed the door around its edge and used leverage on it to awkwardly step over and around the mat. He almost stepped on a box of matches and as he stretched to make an extra long step to avoid them he felt his left groin give out a sharp little twinge of protest.

"Christ I'll do meself a mischief at this rate. I'm gettin' too old for this lark," he mumbled under his breath.

"Wot?" asked Will.

"Shuddup and keep 'em peeled," came the reply through a slamming door.

Even though it was the middle of the day, there was only just enough light in the room for Nash to see his way about. The room was not unlike his own; small and spartan. There was an uncomfortable-looking bowing bed, with an incongruously smart, expensive coat on it, an assortment of bits and pieces on top of a decaying table, an old chair, and not much else. There was no sign of any ashes in the fireplace or a coal sack.

The fire ain' even been ligh'ed, thought Nash with incredulity given the unseasonable cold weather they had been having.

But the contents on the table were quite different to those in Nash's place. Instead of an array of weapons, there was an array of small bottles, tins and jars, plus various written materials were strewn about, both on the table and on the floor. The first thing to catch Nash's eye was a copy of Punch dated a week before he first came across the Ripper. It was folded back showing a page that had a cartoon on it. The cartoon was of a policeman blindfolded and surrounded by four leering villains.

The cartoon joke read:

'Turn around three times, and catch whom you may.'

The word 'may' had been underlined in red crayon, and across the rest of the page had been written in the same crayon:

'Ha! Ha! You are just shy of halfway to naming old Jack. You could build a house of it!'

Nash spotted a little tin that held a red crayon, a piece of chalk and some cotton strands. Next to it were a pile of prints. The top one was obscene; far more lurid than anything you would see in a mutoscope. Nash didn't want to touch anything. He assumed the rest of the pile was similar. He dropped to his haunches to read a piece of paper on the floor. It was a poem. Nash read a couple of lines but it was meaningless drivel as far as he was concerned.

Christ almigh'y. Wossis mean? Sookey'd know.

He thought about trying to memorise the lines but forgot about the task when his eyes were drawn to the red crayon which obliterated the rest of the poem:

'Michael you are so clever. My brother is so clever. clever.'

Nash grimaced, and got to his feet. This wasn't getting him anywhere.

He decided he had to take a chance and move some of the papers on the table to see what else he could find. Beneath the copy of Punch, which he had been careful to keep folded exactly as it was as he moved it, was a photograph. It was of pretty young woman. She looked quite a bit like Mary but there the similarity ended. This woman was very well dressed; obviously a middling sort. Nash flipped over the photograph half hoping that there might be a red crayon hint to who it was. There was no red crayon but there was more than a hint of who the woman was:

'Florrie. The Whore,' was written neatly in black ink.

Nash replaced the photograph and the copy of Punch. He went over to the bed and patted the pockets of a long dark coat with astrakhan collar and cuffs. Nothing.

Until now he had not bothered to look at the bottles and tins. He didn't think they would be of much interest. He took a glance at them. There was a bottle of 'bone black' (purified animal charcoal) which Nash knew was used to counter the effects of arsenic and strychnine. Next to this was an unmarked brown-glassed bottle full of drops. Nash had no way of knowing he was looking at three hundred grains of arsenic, enough to kill everyone living in Middlesex Street with something left over. He considered whether he should take an example away with him.

Mary knows that chemist feller in the Whitechapel Road. 'e gives 'er stuff she mixes up to make that white muck she puts on 'er face. I could arst 'er to arst 'im if 'e knows what this is.

He decided he wouldn't risk leaving any sign of his presence. Nash looked through the other tins, bottles and jars. They all contained what appeared to be medical compounds of one kind or another. Some were still in the original bottles in which the chemists had prescribed them.

It was clear that the Ripper was a 'self-destroyer', a drug addict, in need of pain-killers and various concoctions to fight liver, headache, constipation and stomach ailments. Nash also recognised a potion that his depressed mother used to take, for her 'nerves'.

'ope they do you as much use as they did 'er yer bastard, thought Nashey bitterly. One fing I can promise yer, you'll need more than pills to 'elp yer when I've finished wiv yer. But lucky fer you, yer ain' served yer purpose enuff yet.

He looked over at a writing implement he had seen in use.

"Not by a long chalk," he said out loud.

A piece of neatly folded paper fell onto the table.

Shit! Where's that dropped from?

Nash thought it must have been resting up against the tin. He worried he might not replace it in the right spot. He might as well look at it now the damage was done anyway. He looked down at his hands and decided they were clean enough to risk unfolding the paper. It was on high quality notepaper, but what might have been the headed, top of the page with useful addressor and addressee information, had been ripped off. Nash cursed. The letter was about a deal being struck regarding the supply of something only referred to, in return for services rendered, again not specified. The signature was incomprehensible. Another curse. Although apparently a business letter, it was addressed informally:

'My Dear James.'

"James won't be blamed for nuffin'," scoffed Nash.

CHAPTER 19:

"The victims have forced innumerable people who never gave a serious thought before to the subject to realise how it is that our vast floating population, the waifs and strays of our thoroughfares, live and sleep at night and what sort of accommodation our rich and enlightened capital provides for them."

Daily Telegraph

Sookey had seen a lot of her increasingly close friends Mary and Nashey in the week after the fateful joke in the Pindar, but she wasn't going to see them today. She was busying herself in Toynbee Hall and her make-shift art gallery all day, preparing for her guided tour of the slums for her new good-weather friends. She told herself she needed to distance herself from Mary and Nashey to concentrate on the difficult job at hand. She was to take her tour group for mid-morning coffee with Henrietta Barnett at her coffee rooms, where they would see the poor wretches who availed themselves of the facilities. Sookey was then going to show them a Dr Barnardo Free Day school, where six hundred hot breakfasts and four hundred hot dinners were offered four times a week.

There was certainly no denying that Thomas Barnardo was doing a fine job, but when she had met him she found that she did not care for the smooth Irishman very much. She did not like the way he called his boys 'cases' and she had heard rumours of financial improprieties and cruelty in his homes, and of faked, or 'schneid' as Mary called them, photographs of desperate children.

Given that Nash had clearly benefitted from his schooling, Sookey had once asked him if he would be willing to try to influence boys to go along and learn a trade at a Barnardo school. She had been surprised at his reticence.

"Wot's the use a teaching boys skills when there ain' enuff skilled work ta go round in the first place. They'll jus' be frown on the scrap 'eap with every ovver cove. That ain' no cure for what's wrong with this cun'ry. They got a sort out men not having no work first, but none of these chari'ies try ta do anyfin' to sort that out da they? It ain' no good givin' people linctus against cancer is it, yer got a find a cure for it ain't ya?"

She had not really understood what he had meant at the time, but she was beginning to. There was certainly something wrong with the economics of the country. Unemployment was certain, due to a surfeit labour market. Charities were treating the symptoms rather than effecting a cure. She wished she understood politics and economics, but it had always proved beyond her.

She had decided not to ask Barnardo to receive her guests at the London Hospital. Apart from her aversion to him, there was a rumour that all the doctors at the London Hospital were Ripper suspects. The supposition that the killer must have anatomical knowledge, which had been held by the police after the disembowelment of the third victim, Polly Nichols, had become accepted to the point where baseless, unsubstantiated theory had become fact. It was rumoured that as well as Barnardo, Frederick Treves, who had done so much to rescue the poor wretch Joseph Merryck, 'the Elephant Man', from the clutches of a dreadful penny gaff, was being shadowed by detectives, as was Dr P.E. Halstead.

Sookey did like Frederick Charrington, who had done marvellous work against drink and vice. He had given up his family fortune from a brewery to work in the East End. It had made Sookey feel guilty that it had taken her social disgrace in her old world to send her to the slums to do her bit. It would have been so much better if she had come to Whitechapel with her reputation and more importantly her wealth intact. Think of all the good she could have put that money to. But there was a rumour that Frederick had hired Jack the Ripper in his fight against prostitution. This was surely not so, but she felt it best, on balance, not to introduce her friends to Frederick.

Sookey remembered the shock on her friends' their faces when she told them she had been suspected of the crimes. She couldn't help but smile at the memory. What a soppy goose she had been. Soppy Sookey. It was only a few weeks ago but so much had happened since. She felt she had learned more about people in a month than the rest of her life put together, thanks to Nashey and Mary.

After the coffee rooms, she would show her group Toynbee Hall and her embryonic art gallery. Whilst at the Hall, she was going to have them sit in on a lecture she was going to give personally, on calligraphy, to the Association for Befriending Young Servants. They were to have luncheon in a public house. She had asked Mary to show her around the quietest, safest, least boisterous establishments in the vicinity, but in some ways they were more shocking than the rough ones. They had been full of broken people, one step from the workhouse, who just sat there staring into their drinks and coughing and wheezing with the latest illness.

She decided that the Sir Paul Pindar tavern in Bishopsgate, where she and Mary had got a little tipsy that evening when they were spending Nashey's money, would have to suffice. With a bit of fortune it would have the same mix of characters - women shelling peas, a couple of worn out prostitutes whom her friends would be sure to be both shocked and pleased to see, and some off duty policemen glad to hide somewhere, away from the taunts and insults of all and sundry due to their failure to catch 'ol' Jack'.

Her friends insisted that they spend the afternoon on a walking tour of Whitechapel, including seeing some of the sites of the murders, the idea of which Sookey found most distasteful. They were then to finish with tea at her humble abode.

She was dreading the afternoon. It was far more into the unknown, and who knows what sights and sounds they might see and hear. And then there was the little matter of her home. Rose had shown her how to clean her front step and had helped her wash everything that was washable at the baths. Mary had helped her distemper the scullery and generally clean and tidy inside the house. The broken glass in her windows had been mended, and she had scrubbed the ground-in filth on the other window panes so the glass glistened in the sunlight for the first time in a decade. She had bought the best cakes from the Aerated Bread Shop and expensive tea from British Tea Table in the Strand. But her home still smelt of the slums. It was a slum. There was no escaping that.

CHAPTER 20:

"These are just the days when apathy to the condition of the lowest classes is fraught with danger to all the classes."
Lord Sydney Godolphin Osborne

Nash had confirmed to Shanks that all was in place earlier in the week, but had not informed him about the extra canary. There was no need for him to know. Nash had changed his mind about using Khan as the second canary, having charged him with other duties.

Khan and Tom Carter were, between them, keeping the Ripper's door in Middlesex Street under surveillance eighteen hours a day. The only time the door was not watched was between one and seven in the morning. Nash thought it unlikely the Ripper would arrive at such time, especially as if, as Nash suspected, he was arriving by train from Liverpool. The last train arrived before midnight. It was also difficult to keep a man standing in one spot in the early hours as there was no reason for him to be there and the policeman on his beat would be sure to become suspicious and move him on. Once the Ripper had turned up, that was another matter. Nash would have to have several men taking it in turns to keep the place in view at all times, the best way they could. But from now on Nashey was going to replace Khan on his Ripper duty with Tom's brother Jem.

The new idea was for Khan to follow Shanks at all times. Shanks could meet up with the general manager of the Post Office himself and Khan wouldn't know who he was from Adam, but Nash just wanted to know if there was anything he could get from having Shanks followed. Any snippet of information might prove useful. He would keep Khan in reserve for the post office job, in case he needed him for something at the last minute. At the very least Khan could keep an eye on the wrong un throughout the night of the robbery.

A second canary had been volunteered by Mary; her new young friend Kitty. Mary had found Kitty a new place to stay, the night she had rescued the youngster from the ponce, by knocking up her landlord in the middle of the night. He had put Kitty in a room sharing a bed with a prostitute her own age, who was pleased to have her rent halved.

Kitty was already known to Nash. Mary had enlisted his help in retrieving Kitty's things from her abandoned room. The girls were fearful the pimp would be laying there in wait for them. When the three of them had reached her door Kitty gave Nash her key and cowered behind him nervously, looking away down the street as if she were contemplating running away. Mary stood confidently with hands on hips next to the door and scolded her young charge.

"You ain't in no danger 'ere yer daft mare."

Nash had used Kitty's key and walked in with Mary right behind him. Kitty heard a bellow from a voice she recognised, a few thunderous running steps from heavy boots on floorboards, some other brief noises she didn't recognise and then silence. Mary stuck her head back round the doorframe and motioned to Kitty with an irritated sideways nod of the head.

"Come on, we ain' got all day. Get yer aris in 'ere and tell us what yer wanna take wiv yer."

Kitty peered in and gasped. The ponce lay flat out on the floor, eyes closed, motionless, dead or unconscious, she couldn't tell. Nash stood over the prone figure, reaching down and rummaging through his pockets to see if he had anything on him worth taking. He didn't.

"'e weren't sa clever when 'e 'ad more than a lit'le gell a deal wiv were 'e," sneered Mary.

Kitty grabbed her things quickly.

⌐ ◈ ⌐

Nash was looking forward to the look on Arthur's face when he turned up with two very young, slightly built, highly made-up women, who were bound to be laughing and cavorting about. He had made a little bet with himself that the dog-end would come right out of his mouth and hit the floor. He would see Arthur cigaretteless for the first time. But Nash lost his bet. The fag drooped precariously on the lower lip but stayed in situ.

A large case and a small box were at Arthur's side. He looked the two girls' bodies up and down closely, but there was no hint of lust in his eyes. Nash was quick to explain.

"They 'ad ta be gells after all, cos the crushers fink every cove with a bag on 'im late at night's ol' Jack. A man wouldn't get 'undred yard in some spots carryin' summin' without 'aving crushers on 'im. An' thems bein' 'hores is good an' all. All the coppers'll be followin' them finking ol' Jack might jump out at 'em at any minute, and that leaves you free and clear dun it?"

"Yeah, good enuff," conceded Arthur.

He could see that far from being a hindrance, having a couple of head-turners was ideal. He smiled at his new cohorts.

"Alright ladies, 'ere's what I got for ya. I got twirls, rope, rod, jack, brace & bit with blades an' drills, glass cutter, chisel, jemmy, dark lan'ern, set a betty's, an outsider, petter-cutter, special cutter an' a Jack-in-the-box. And they're all swaddled good an' all."

He looked at Mary, the larger of the two petite women, and nodded at the large suitcase.

"You got a takes that lot, if yer can get it orf the ground in the first place that is."

Mary opened her mouth to protest but Arthur was expecting it and quickly interjected.

"I'd keep quiet if I were you. You're the lucky one gell."

He turned to Kitty and pointed at the small bag.

"Now here's a brand new fing. 'ardly anyone's ever eard ov it see. Soup we calls it, but its real name is Nobel's nitro glycerine."

He paused and looked earnestly at Kitty.

"'ow old a you gell?"

"Old enough to be an 'ore," replied Kitty. She was picking up Mary's spikiness.

"So you'd be at least eight then would ya?" retorted Arthur wearily, showing more disgust with the world than sarcasm against Kitty.

"I'm fifteen if yer mus' know."

"Very well, young Kitty, what you 'ave there is sort of explosive, an' it's quick tempered like somebody else I know. It blows yer ta smivvereens soon as look at yer if you ain' careful wiv it."

Nash was the first to react.

"Give over, Arfa! I ain't lettin' 'er carry that. We'll 'ave to go wivoud it, and make do the best we can. Kit'y'll 'ave to take sum ov Mary's gear any'ow."

"Give the soup ta Shanks," said Mary with a mischievous smirk on her face. "'e don't even know Kitty 'ere's on this job does 'e? Tell 'im I'm 'avin' ta carry an 'ole case a tools cos ov 'im an' 'is secrets, an' this 'ere box a stuff's too much. Tell 'im it's an American augur. Sounds impor'ant dun it rather than just anuvver name for a bib an' brace. Tell 'im it's made a glass so yer gotta be careful wiv it and 'e can be trusted wiv' it more than some slip of a gell."

Nash and Arthur looked at each other and smiled grimly.

CHAPTER 21:

"We ask each undergraduate as he develops an interest to come and stay in Whitechapel, and see for himself. And they come, some to spend a few weeks, some for the Long Vacation."

Henrietta Barnett

Sookey's lady friends had piled off a growler, but she was surprised to find a man alighting with them.

"This is Mr David Lloyd-George, Sookey. He is a friend of mine who is very interested in the work you are doing here in Whitechapel, so I invited him along. I hope you do not mind," said Nora taking Sookey by the arm and guiding her away a few feet before whispering conspiratorially.

"He's Welsh but terribly bright. My husband says he will go far. Politics and all that. Needs to keep him on side, you know the sort of thing."

Sookey looked at Nora. She did mind. She minded a lot. She was nervous enough as it was, without dragging a 'terribly bright' young man, who no doubt had an agenda, around the slums of Whitechapel.

"Pas de tout, pas de tout!" cried Sookey with a cheery wave of her left arm.

It was the best thing she could think of on the spur of the moment to get back at Nora. She knew her friend didn't understand a word of French. Nora looked at her with a slight tilt of the head and an expression that said 'what are you talking about, please don't embarrass me in front of this man by misbehaving', but she said nothing. She held her smile and waited. Sookey just smiled back at her, waiting.

Lloyd-George came to Nora's rescue.

"Que je suis contents de vous voire!"

Sookey would normally have been impressed and complimented the man on his French, even though he had a wincingly poor accent. But she was no longer the shrinking violet, the Soppy Sookey who Nora no doubt still believed her to be. She feigned being rather disconcerted at the temerity of the man's words. After all, he should have waited for Nora to introduce Sookey to him before he responded 'how pleased I am to see you'. At the sight of Sookey's raised eyebrows and look of dismay, Lloyd-George felt it congruent to continue, but his French was more hesitant this time.

"Que vos... er... voisins sont...er...gentils."

Sookey was genuinely taken aback this time.

How kind your neighbours are? Perhaps he did not quite mean to convey this? His French is poor is it not. I suppose he means how kind everyone here in Whitechapel has been to take in poor old Sookey. No doubt he has heard all about what that terrible woman did to me.

This time Nora reciprocated, rescuing Lloyd-George.

"Why, I need to take the two of you to task," said Nora with friendly mock admonishment. "I haven't finished introducing the two of you and you are off in foreign climes together."

Nora's voice was higher pitched than usual and Sookey saw that her friend's neck was a mottled red. She had never seen that before. Having won this little skirmish, Sookey felt good about herself, smiling as she resumed speaking in English. Lloyd-George smiled with some relief and introduced her to his Welsh accent. The other two women, who had not said a word since they stepped out of the cab, threw in some small talk. Normal service had been resumed. Everyone was charming to one another.

The first half of the tour had gone to plan. Sookey had chosen a route either side of Toynbee Hall and her art gallery which avoided the most overcrowded courts that teemed with the most pathetic of the poverty-stricken. There were two reasons for this; she didn't want to shock her friends even more than was inevitable; and she spent much of her time in these courts administering medical care, so being recognised and approached for help would have been likely. On this occasion she wanted to be as inconspicuous as possible. But she couldn't relax; they were about to arrive at the pub.

"This is the Sir Paul Pindar Tavern in Bishopsgate Without. I am afraid I am a dash poor guide, as I know not who Sir Paul Pindar was or what indeed Bishopsgate is without!" said Sookey lightly.

Her audience laughed but Lloyd-George introduced a note of seriousness.

"It is clearly not without the worst poverty I have ever seen."

The group mumbled sad agreements at the sentiment.

"I fear you have not seen the worst of it sir," replied Sookey with gravitas. The group stood in silence, nodding heads bowed.

A crowded bus hurtled by, making a terrific clatter on the cobbles. The driver on its top floor, wedged in the gap between advertising boards, swore loudly at his horses, breaking the sad spell. Sookey looked up at the driver to view a sea of Nestles Milk advertising placards festooning every square inch of the bus. She was aware the others were following her gaze.

"I am afraid you will not be able to partake of Nestles Milk where we are about to go ladies and gentleman," she said with a wry smile.

The others were relieved at the change of atmosphere and laughed a little too heartily.

Sookey returned to being a tour guide.

"Look about you. On the second and third stories of the public house there are fine two hundred year old bow windows. I believe the front of the tavern was originally part of Sir Paul Pindar's mansion."

The 'fine' windows were caked in soot and a large banner reading Barclay Perkins Stout fluttered across them in the stiffening breeze.

"What are those men doing?" asked Nora.

Next door to the pub, two men, one struggling with a large awkward-to-carry camera, the other grasping the accoutrement that came with it, ran hurriedly under the pull-down shade of Louis Harwitz' picture frame manufacture shop. They were hoping it would hide them.

"They are a newspaper reporter and his photographist. You can scarce look about you without seeing one of these many teams making haste to create photograph work and report on this area since the murders started."

The women lowered their gaze to the ground and put their gloved hands to their mouths at the mere mention of the word 'murders'.

Sookey had spotted what was happening and she was keen to avoid it.

"I believe them to be just sheltering from this accursed wind. The photograph equipment is a difficult beast to control I think. Allow us to adjourn for luncheon inside," she said, motioning for them to walk across the street to the pub.

The women started to follow her but Lloyd-George stayed put, still looking at the men.

"Are they welcome here?" he asked.

"Indeed they are not sir," replied Sookey. "It is believed that local people are shown to be rather morose in photographs because the reporter asks them to be straight-faced so the image is not blurred. This is indeed so, but if you look at the images, there is no welcome in the people's eyes. There is a difference between straight-facedness and sullenness is there not? Come we must adjourn, the ladies are waiting sir."

But the astute Welshman was looking down the street.

"Local leaders create and mould opinion here? They are the assessors and makers of the common conscience? The church is abandoned? Leaders' beliefs and prejudices seep through the slums and condition minds? But at the moment, lower orders bring forth a common emotional upsurge with illegal deeds their leaders allow, but which propriety forbids them to perform themselves? I have heard of attacks on Jews, Ripper suspects, and now perhaps..."

Sookey had already seen what Lloyd-George was looking at. A small gang of young men were walking determinedly up the street. They were still fifty yards from the cowering newspaper men, but she could already hear the obscenities. Sookey looked round at her guests. Lloyd-George was rubbing his chin in deep thought. The women had just spotted the gang too and Sookey noted the panic in their eyes. She smiled reassuringly.

"I do believe Mr Lloyd-George is not hungry. More's the pity for they have fine fare here. He seems keen rather to view the progress of our local cricket team. They are a little boisterous at times I fear. But such is the way with young men in Whitechapel. Let us make haste to The Pindar as we call it."

Sookey had said 'Pindar' in a flat Cockney accent. She had hoped it would amuse her friends, but it fell on deaf ears. They were too busy squeaking and scurrying towards the safety of the pub. Sookey had been dreading taking them into the pub, but was now only too relieved to get them through the doors.

☞ ◆ ☜

Nash was at home, and had just been interviewed for the third time by the police since the murders had started. The last two visits had been just since the double murder night. Every able-bodied man who lived in the area had been interviewed at least once but there was growing police belief that the murderer occupied a single room or empty warehouse somewhere between Middlesex Street and Brick Lane.

Nash lived alone; lived close to all the murder sites including almost next door to one of them; and was known to the police as a violent, nasty bit of work who was often out on the streets late at night. If he had been Jewish, known to have any medical knowledge or knife skills such as butchering, he would have been a suspect.

But it was well known that Nash did not like knives. He considered using one beneath contempt. Before the murders started, he had carried a knife as a last means of defence should a bunch of the constabulary jump him on a job, but he never had cause to use it, and had ceased carrying it recently for fear of being stopped and searched by the police. He didn't miss it. If you needed a knife to get the better of someone, you weren't much of a man as far as Nash was concerned. It had always made him smirk that some thought themselves tough because they carried a knife, and weren't afraid to use it. But he thought it was the sort of sly crime that men like Shanks would commit.

Nash had been amazed to be questioned by the police about his friendship with one Sookey Parsons. It seemed that her ridiculous belief that the police suspected her of being involved in the crimes had not been so far fetched after all.

Nash had true alibis for all of the nights when the murders had taken place bar the double killings. Some years earlier he had tracked down one of his sisters, who he had not seen since his fight with their father, and had kept in touch with her ever since with the odd visit. She was now married to a Surrey Docks lighterman, and lived over the water in The Blue in Bermondsey. They had backed up his story that he had been visiting them on the night of the third murder, and he had been in public places such as ratting and other gambling dens at the time of the first two and fourth murders. It was ironic that such a night owl actually had more cast iron alibis than men who simply slept in their beds each night. Will Roud remained his weak alibi for the night of the double murders.

But he was finding the interviews increasingly difficult, as he came to know more about the murders and who was perpetrating them. There was a lot more to lie about, to leave out; more he could get tripped up on. The first two visits had been easy. Sir Charles Warren, the man with overall responsibility for the Ripper investigation, had flooded the East End with West End police. They had no knowledge of, or contacts in, the East End. The wool was pulled over their eyes at every turn. However, this last pair of policemen had been spry enough, though this had not stopped Nash from using his usual contemptuous, sarcastic manner when speaking to the police.

As they were leaving Nash could not resist a passing shot.

"'bout time they gave ol' Abberline the boot ain' it? 'e ain' got a bleedin' clue as 'e? In more ways as one!"

The more senior of the two policemen gave a matter of fact response.

"I dunno. 'e's a good boss right enuff. 'e shouldn't quit just yet."

The infamous first Jack The Ripper-signed letter had started with 'Dear Boss'. 'Boss' was an Americanism. The letter had also claimed that the killer would not 'quit'. This was another colloquialism from across the ocean. Neither term was in general usage in Britain. It was considered to be a possible clue to the killer's identity. Conan Doyle was one who believed there may well be an American connection. The police hierarchy were less convinced, but this sergeant seemed to be.

For once in his life, Nash was blissfully innocent, which stood him in good stead.

"Ay?" was his honest, vacant reply.

"Thas wot 'orses eat ain' it?" snapped the more junior officer.

It was the second time in a few days he had heard this joke at his expense. The first time Sookey had said it with a purse of the lips and that little sideways glance she did when she thought she was being funny.

"Cheeky cow!" he had retorted with a grin.

It was the first time he had sworn at her, even in jest. She feigned shock with her right hand covering her mouth, but the glinting eyes gave her away.

It was a good memory but you would not have known it from the sneer Nash gave the little ferret of a man he wanted to slam up against the wall.

"Time you got 'im back to 'is barrel organ in it?" Nash enquired of the senior man.

The men left soon after.

Nash was sitting at his table thinking about this when there was an official sounding thump, thump on the door.

They're back! Shit! I must a let summin' slip an' they've picked up on it, ain' they.

"It's Will!"

Nash blew out a large breath and flung open the door.

"Wot the 'ell d'you want!?" was the less than enthusiastic welcome afforded Will, but it was water off a duck's back to him; he had known Nash a long time.

"Yer told me a tell yer if I ever 'ear about any trouble with newspaper fellers? Gawd knows why. They got a bleedin' cheek if yer arst me. I'd..."

Will was cut off in mid rant

"I ain' arsted yer 'ave I, now 'urry up an' tell me wot's 'appened."

"Well, a couple of them newspaper fellers are just about a get a good 'iding from young Briggsy an' is mates. I fink they might a bin put up to it by Lusky."

"Do yer now? Yer know I went ta see Mr Lusk a while since. About that ovver lit'le matter when 'is boys attacked lit'le Sookey. I'm gonna 'av to go and see 'im again. I won't be as friendly this time mind."

Will didn't know what was going on.

All I knows is ever since you bin knocking about wiv that doctor tart Sookey, yer been actin' right queer. Woss it got a do wiv you if Briggsy wants to give a couple of bleedin' newspaper coves a good kickin'. Bastards deserve it, showing the world an' 'is wife all what goes on round 'ere. They should keep their sneezers out and leave us alone like normal.

"Yeah Nashey, I'll come wiv yer if yer like," was Will's reluctant offer.

Nash arrived just as Reg Briggs had the camera above his head, about to smash it to the ground. Nash was impressed the young lad could lift such a heavy, awkward thing so high.

"Put that fuckin' fing down!" bellowed Nash at the top of his voice. "And do it gentle an' all. And the rest of ya, leave 'em go."

Reg was the leader of Whitechapel's largest street gang. It had a different name from Nash's day but it was essentially the same affair. Nash didn't want young Reg to lose face, so he was prepared to let him shout the odds, even give Nash some lip, but he couldn't afford to let newspaper staff be fearful of entering the slums. They were, after all, his mouthpiece.

Nash didn't want to hurt anyone but he would if he had to. He had brought a selection of weapons. He eased out of one of his deep pockets, a monkey's fist. It was the least dangerous implement he owned. A pathetic weapon by his standards, which he hoped would have the desired effect of telling Reg that he didn't want any trouble. The weapon, if you could call it that, was an idea he had got from a lascar off the boats. It was a length of rope that fed into a mushroom ball of very tightly woven rope, the ball covered in red lead paint. It served a similar purpose to a policeman's tightly rolled up raincoat. It was like having a soft truncheon. The lead paint gave it a top heavy feel and you could swing it fast, but it was only rope so he could hit someone with it hard without doing any real damage.

He could also throw the implement some distance with a quick underarm whip and it would land noiselessly, not giving his position away.

"Fuck off Nashey, this ain' got nuffin' a do wiv you. They got it comin', keep comin' round 'ere gawping at us frew this fing like we were beasts in the zoo. Writin' stuff about us. Tellin' the 'ole world about Whitechapel."

The important thing from Nash's point of view was that Reg had lowered the camera, and the rest of the gang had stopped their attack on the two newspaper men. They had the men pinned to the wall of the shop and were raining blows at them but fortunately had barely made contact with anything soft and painful yet, the men's arms, elbows and knees having taken the brunt of what was largely a posturing attack without their leader. It was lucky that vicious little Reg had busied himself with the camera rather than the men. Nash had arrived just in time. Once the men had gone down, the boots would have been in. The wrong uns in the gang, having been at the back when they were facing someone who could fight back, would have waded in. Nash was hoping Reg was astute enough to realise the situation. It was a quid pro quo. Reg saves face with his mates and the community at large by standing up to Nash. Nash keeps the newspaper men safe.

"On yer way son," said Nash quietly, with the shortest of winks that only Reg could have seen.

He left the 'fuck off while yer got the chance' unsaid but trusted Reg would effectively hear it nonetheless. While Nash's left hand dangled the monkey's fist, his right slipped on a glinting new cap before being stuffed back deep in his pocket, fingering something lethal.

Reg was not the leader by chance. He knew the score. If he rushed at Nash with a shout for his mates to join him, his trusted lieutenant Bill would be at his shoulder quickly enough, but others would hesitate and there would always be one who would stand frozen to the spot till his mates had done the dirty work, before rushing back to enjoy the spoils when it was safe to do so. They would get the better of him in the end by sheer weight of numbers, but Nash would wreak severe damage on those who attempted the first blows. Reg spat down at Nash's feet.

"Wot you protectin' 'em for any'ow?"

Nash looked down at the oyster of spittle, and then back up at Reg, with the grimmest of smiles.

"Cos they keep comin' round 'ere with their cameras takin' them pictures ov us and puttin' 'em in their papers. Writin' stuff about us. Tellin' the 'ole world about Whitechapel. Now yer as wise as ever ain't ya?"

Reg was getting ready to leave. He fired his passing shot.

"You're orf yer 'ead you are. Ever since you took up wiv that fancy screever tart a yours. She'll 'ave yer in Coney 'atch 'fore long, you see if she don't."

Nash just looked at him. Quite a crowd had gathered. Nobody had ever spoken to Nash like this, least of all in public, least of all in front of a baying congregation.

An' I don't like Sookey bein' talked about like that neiver. I'm gonna 'ave a word wiv you boy anuvver time.

But for now, he took it. It was a small price to pay. Reg turned round to his gang.

"Come on lads, let's leave this ol' Mary Ann to look after 'is little mates 'ere."

The gang moved off and Nash wandered over to the newspaper men.

"Sorry about that boys. Always a few young scamps shoutin' the odds ain' there? It was all kid stakes really. They wouldn't 'ave 'urt ya. Ain' 'urt yer 'ave they? Gear all right is it?"

242

Nash went on a charm offensive and explained to the men that they would be completely safe from now on, and so would all their colleagues in the press. He would see to that. He was what you might call an unofficial neighbourhood leader.

They were joined by a Welshman who introduced himself as Lloyd-George. Nash would normally have been very aloof, if not down right suspicious of and aggressive to any stranger, especially one who spoke with a strange accent, but the man interested him.

'e's a gent a sorts, but there's a working man's stamp about 'im an' all, an' I can see 'e ain' no slummer.

And there was a sparkle in his eyes which told Nash he might be genuinely interested in why Nash had just behaved as he did.

"Alexander Nash, Lloyd, hello."

Nash thrust his huge hard hand into the one proffered him. The two newspapermen were eager to get away from the scene of their near-mishap. They left Lloyd-George and Nash to discuss the newspaper coverage of the murders and the effect they were having in introducing the troubles of Whitechapel to the world.

The women were eventually joined by Lloyd-George. The pub was now full with an excited crowd, discussing what they had just seen. But the tour group had been alone in the pub save the staff for a while. Everyone else had left to view the rumpus outside the shop next door. Sookey had been relieved at the exodus. Up until then the air had been blue courtesy of an off-duty soldier with a loud voice entertaining a small knot of drink-buyers with a tall tale of derring-do in far off climes in the name of Queen and country. He appeared to believe that the eff word was compulsory at least once in every sentence.

The women had originally expressed an interest in visiting an eel, pie and mash shop, but having had Mary take her into one the previous week, Sookey had decided that a pub would be a safer option for a meal. Sookey had dealt with most things the slums had thrown at her, but the sight of the eels within the glutinous substance in the tubs on the counter as they entered, had made her feel quite queasy. The cold lavatory-like tiling and the hard wooden stalls, facing each other railway carriage-style, which were always full enough with customers to ensure the group would not be able to sit together, were another drawback. The disgusting looking green liquor, complete with dubious bits in it, which Mary had recommended she have on her pie, probably as a joke knowing her though she feigned innocence as she giggled at Sookey's horrified face, was the final straw. They would eat in a public house.

The whole group had just eaten fish and chips. The pub, which didn't cook food, had imported the meals from a passing street vendor. The group were delighted with the newspaper crockery and human cutlery. It was just the sort of local colour that they had been hoping to experience. Sookey had indigestion. She had suffered from verbal diarrhoea in her attempt to speak continually to try and drown out the soldier's swearing. She had even told them the only two non-crude jokes Mary had ever told her, in an attempt to explain Cockney humour. Both involved rice pudding. Both were excruciatingly unfunny to sophisticated middle class ears. Mary had been told them as a young girl by her father one Sunday afternoon, the only time in the week when he was not either exhausted from work or aggressive from the alcohol inside him.

None of the group had wanted to bring up the subject of what was happening in the street outside. They had all guessed it was something unpleasant. But with an awkward silence having settled on the group as a result of their tour guide having finally run out of things to say, Sookey panicked. Any conversation was better than none.

"Mr Lloyd-George, pray tell us plainly sir, of what was that commotion? It is well you stayed, lest we would never receive report."

Lloyd-George was taken a back by such candour.

"Madame, I am without relish to do so."

Sookey continued to prompt him.

"The crowd around us seem in high spirits from the event. I believe there were young scoundrels ill favoured towards the newspaper men?"

Lloyd-George was warming to this woman. She was not the sort of sycophant that he usually had to waste his time charming. She was nothing like her friends, and he was somewhat pleased to report on what he had seen, if the truth be known.

"Well, the ruffians were attacking the poor men in most villainous way, and the camera was about to be smashed beyond repair, when before I knew what I was about, a man hove into view from out of the ken. He stuck out with the leader of the ruffians. I can make no hand of it, for he was no policeman and was a solitary man against many so they could have sent him to his account, but it was clear as a transparency that for all their bluster, the gang were wary. He was a big man. He didn't pitch it in hot. He issued forth threat by mere presence. That and strange villainous weaponry! The whole affair was over in but moments."

Sookey had to ask, but she already knew the answer.

"Did you hear of this man's name sir?"

"Yes, I introduced myself to the man. Chap by the name of Nash. Called me Lloyd. Thought it was me Christian name! I did not correct him. He did not appear to be the sort of chap one corrected."

A warm glow of pride coursed through Sookey.

"You state it was over readily sir. But you were some time after us?" enquired Nora.

As she was asking this, Rebecca was whispering in Sookey's ear.

"You appear to have a flush my dear. What ails you?"

Sookey waved her away dismissively.

"Oh, such events give me distress of the mind. It is well they occur rare. It is a trifle. There, it is gone I fancy."

She missed the start of Lloyd-George's reply to Nora.

"… when I relayed to him that I had recently joined the Liberal Party and become alderman on Caernarvon County Council, he called for 'coves like me to lift the shadow of the workhouse from the homes of the poor'. Quite eloquent for such a man what? He even suggested we tax those who had more than enough to pay for those who did not."

"Good gracious! Socialism!" and other similar utterances came from all the women but one.

"You do not seem as shocked by Mr Nash as others sir," opined Sookey.

Lloyd-George looked seriously at her.

"There was a time I would have joined the good ladies in their gasps madam, but my eyes are opening. I must hold you to account for this Hogarthian picture of appalling degradation seared into my mind," he said with mock censure. "I am not a man for Mr Hyndman and his socialists I fancy, but though a proud liberal," he leaned forward and continued in little more than a conspiratorial whisper, "I hold at least some respect for my Fabian brethren madam."

Aware that this was not the time, nor place for such serious discussion, he brightened and turned to Nora.

"My fellow Welshman, Sir Alfred Danes, who I believe will soon become the new Superintendent of the Metropolitan Police, has also promised me an expedition here. I fear he will not be as charming or informative a host as your Mrs Parsons."

"You do me an honour sir," responded Sookey formally before changing to a knowing smile.

"I trust you did not convey your association to Mr Nash? He cannot be taken with the police force. I fear he would give you short shrift."

There was a nod of fearful agreement.

"That, I shall not like to witness madam. He is also a salesman I fancy. He has asked, well, insisted, that I give a talk at your Toynbee Hall. I had told him that I spoke at Temperance Society meetings in Wales you see. And that I had a rather, how shall I put it, fiery delivery."

"You know this man Nash, Susan?" asked Nora incredulously.

Sookey's spirits dimmed.

"He is the man I spoke to you all of once before. He is not a policeman as I thought."

She found her head bowing in embarrassed surrender, until Mary flashed into her mind.

Keep yer bleedin' 'ead up gell. Yer always lookin' down. There ain' nuffin' down there 'cept your ugly feet and summin' for the pure collector. Look 'em square in the eye an' tell 'em ta fuck orf oud of it.

Sookey raised her head defiantly.

"Mr Nash is far better than any pol...crusher. He is a very fine man. If messrs Warren, Anderson and Abberline and their cohorts were so fine, the Whitechapel maniac would have been brought to book and women would be safe to walk the streets at night."

She turned her head from Nora to Lloyd-George and without taking breath continued.

"Monday November the 12th would suit. Shall we say three o'clock sir?"

She had no idea if the Hall was free on the twelfth. She had no memory for such things and badly needed help to keep abreast of what was happening and when. It was one of the jobs she had in mind for Mary. It was also rude of her to assume that Lloyd-George could make himself available at whatever time suited her. But she had been determined to end her little speech on a suitably indignant, independent note. The other women shared nervous glances at each other before turning their gaze to Lloyd-George.

"I believe the 12th at three o'clock would be acceptable. I hope to see Mr Nash there," smiled Lloyd-George.

He, for his part, had no idea if he had a prior engagement. He had so many these days he would need to check with his diary, back in his hotel room, but he would be at the Hall as agreed. He was only twenty five years old but was already a politician who knew the importance of doing what he promised.

CHAPTER 22:

"The real point to be complained of is the low rate of payment earned by …women."

Clementina Black, TUC

Henrietta Barnett had initially refused Sookey's request for an employed assistant. The sixteen 'settlers' who worked and, Sookey apart, lived in Toynbee Hall, were not only unpaid, they actually contributed to the Hall's coffers to be there. The Hall expected its workers to be young members of the social elite, there to receive education, whilst they themselves provided education to the less fortunate. It was a symbiotic relationship. The hope was that these future politicians and captains of industry would in turn enlighten others in the ruling classes about the need to improve the living conditions, health and education of the poor. Whitechapel residents would in turn be expected to use the education they received at the Hall to improve their lives through self-help. The Barnetts were not there to provide direct employment for them.

Sookey's timing had, however, been exemplary. Henrietta had been about to ask Sookey to take on a greater workload. Henrietta had arranged with Charles Ashbee, a leading designer and entrepreneur, that he would set up a Guild of Handicraft. It was to teach primarily metalwork – jewellery, enamels, hand-wrought copper and wrought ironwork. But such an enterprise needed far more space than could be assigned to it within the confines of Toynbee

Hall. Sookey's art gallery was still in its very early stages, and had plenty of room. But it was very much Sookey's project. She had found the building in which it was housed in Angel Alley, around the corner from the Hall, off Whitechapel Road, and most of her army widow's pension was being spent on its conversion, upkeep and rent.

Henrietta had felt uneasy about asking Sookey to donate much of her space to the new guild; and then she was going to have the temerity to ask her to oversee the new project too. When Sookey approached her about a paid assistant's position, Henrietta had felt even more perturbed by the thought of a young local woman working at the Hall. But when Sookey responded to her rejection by offering to fund it herself, Henrietta saw a quid pro quo. She agreed that Sookey could pay a local woman out of her own pocket to be her assistant, on the understanding that Sookey took over the running of the Guild of Handicraft, which was to be housed temporarily at least, within her art gallery space. And this assistant was not to set foot in Toynbee Hall or speak to any of the settlers.

A little white lie had been told about Mary's present occupation. Henrietta had seen Mary often enough with Sookey in her coffee room, so Mary's penchant for loud clothing and even louder make-up was explained by the fact that she presently worked at a stage costumiers. It was expected that the staff had to make the customers feel at home by looking something like them. The worldly-wise Henrietta didn't believe the tall tale for a second, but she knew a bargain when she saw it. The deal was struck. Mary Kelly, respectable local shop girl, was hired.

Sookey had a lot more money coming in these days so she could afford it. She thought it strange how suddenly, a few weeks ago, everyone she did some work for, whether it be as doctor, writer or private tutor, paid up immediately and never haggled about the price. Until then, most people had fobbed her off with excuses and promised to pay the following week but never did, and even those who did pay had always negotiated her original price down to the smallest of fees. Even the repellent Shanks had got someone to drop off on his behalf the considerable sum he had owed her. She was relieved he had not brought it in person.

Sookey had tried to lie to Mary about the situation, but Mary had seen straight through her as always. Sookey could never get away with a lie to Mary. All her attempts at 'leg pulling' in response to all the jokes Mary so successfully played on her, always ended in failure.

"'oo's payin' me?"

Mary had narrowed eyes, chin raised and arms folded across her chest. Sookey answered with enthusiasm.

"Oh, there is a fund at the Hall, out of whose coffers you will be remunerated. I believe it is money Mr Toynbee himself left in his will for precisely such purpose."

Mary did not understand a couple of the words in the sentence but got the gist. She always knew when Sookey was lying. Her eyes would flutter.

"Yeah?" said Mary with unhidden scepticism. "You're payin' me ain't ya?"

The eyes started fluttering again.

"I assure you Mary…"

She was interrupted before she got any further.

"It's alright yer know, I'll take yer money as long as there's a full day's work ta be dun mind. I ain' takin' no chari'y see. I knows yer can afford it, so I don't fill guilty takin' it."

Sookey gave up her pretence.

"Oh, very well Mary, you see straight through me like glass as always. I do not know how you do it. I will be your employer." A frown then surfaced on Sookey's features. "Mary, you say you know I can afford it. Do you have any idea why people pay me what I am owed these days when they scarce used to."

Mary felt the urge to grin, but managed to keep a straight face.

"Ul yeah, I know a good reason why, right enuff."

She was well aware that Sookey's friendship with Nashey was becoming generally well known in the neighbourhood, and it was not advisable to effectively steal money from friends of Nashey. Sookey was looking at her enquiringly.

"It's cos yer been accepted by everyone see. Yer one ov us now ain't ya gell," she lied.

Sookey was not sure what she was more delighted by; Mary's acceptance of her position, or her own acceptance by the neighbourhood. But when she thought of what Mary did to earn a living at present, she knew there was only one answer. She clapped her hands in joy, but then her expression changed. She needed to assert her authority. She decided to adopt her best school marm voice.

"Very well Mary. Good. I will see you at nine o'clock sharp on Monday morning, and be sure to be on time. I won't abide tardiness. Your first job is to help me prepare for Mr Lloyd-George's visit, and then we have to get to work on Mr Ashbee's Guild of Handicraft. They are both very important men. There is plenty to do, and there's the troof."

As soon as she had finished with 'and there's the troof' she was exasperated with herself. She should have ended the sentence at 'do', and saying 'troof' made it even worse. She wouldn't be able to assert her authority if she was going to speak as if she was in the pub with Mary and Nashey.

For all Sookey's funny little ways, and her extraordinary naivety, Mary respected her enormously. Consequently she managed to keep a straight face despite having an overwhelming desire to snigger at Sookey's little speech. She thought about doing a little bob to her new employer, but thought even Sookey would realise Mary was 'taking the rise'.

"Yes Sookey," she said seriously. "You can rely on me, don't you worry."

She even managed to stop herself finishing the sentence with 'gell' as she would normally. A boundary had been set.

$\diamond$

Sookey went to visit Nash to tell him the good news about Mary. She had never been to his home. She had never been to Mary's home come to that. If she met either or both of them in anywhere other than a public place it was always at her house. She felt it was time she saw Nash's place. She knocked on the door.

"'oo's there!?" came a less than friendly bellow.

"It is Sookey, Nashey."

She waited whilst she heard much rustling and general moving about. She couldn't help but listen intently, and gave herself a start when her ear touched the peeling paint on the door. The fog meant there wasn't the usual noise of horse's hooves on cobbles to hide sounds. What was he doing in there? She had to wait a full minute before the door opened.

"I was just on me way out gell. You were lucky a catch me. I'll walk wiv yer mind. Yer shouldn't be out on yer own in this yer know."

And with that he closed the door behind him and joined her. There was silence as they set off, with him trying to remember what middling sorts said in this situation. He didn't want to say what he usually said to anyone, 'what the bleedin' 'ell d'you want?'. Then it came to him.

"To what do I have the pleasure?"

Sookey smiled wistfully and with a slight nod was the embodiment of formality.

"Good morning Mr Nash. I trust you are well this fine day?"

It was a pea-souper. She had been extremely unwise venturing out in it, and had done well just to find his building without getting hopelessly lost.

Were she being a funny cuts? Yeah, course, she were coddin'.

He went with the joke.

"Indeed madam, it is glorious don't yer know. Where might we be orf to, to make most of it?"

"Fought we'd go down the booza for a tightener me old cock," she said, still in her most formal, middling tone.

He looked at her in astonishment and they both burst out laughing. They didn't go to a pub. He apologised for not letting her in to his place but explained that he was a little embarrassed at the state of it. They agreed to go to hers, but not before she scolded him for still not letting her see Doris.

"'oo?" he enquired innocently, which was met with the appropriate look.

Safely out of the yellow-green pall, Sookey told Nash over a cup of tea the good news about Mary. Nash was delighted. It led them into hours of discussion on a wide range of topics, and apart from an awkward ten minutes when they had argued passionately about Nash's idea that the Ripper was a good thing for poor people everywhere, the conversation flowed wonderfully.

The disagreement about the Ripper had started to make Nash feel uneasy, but rather than change the subject completely, which would have been a success because Sookey was keen to move the conversation on too, he stayed on the subject of the killings, introducing inappropriate levity. He laughed as he told Sookey about his latest visit from the police, and that they had questioned him about his relationship with her. He also relayed what Mary had said when he had told her about it.

"'ere, you're the perfect double act you two are. Villain Nashey 'ere gives 'em a tap on the loaf, then along comes ol' Doc Parsons to cut 'em up."

But Nash had seen that Sookey didn't enjoy the joke. She was sensitive to the fact that it was all very well laughing at the police, but their stupidity meant that a maniac was still on the loose and likely to kill again.

Nash had looked at Sookey and thought what he thought twenty times a day, every day since the night of the double killings.

If only you knew the killer were on the loose courtesy ov your good friend Nashey. Let loose to kill again; to show 'em again.

It was the costliest advertising campaign ever devised.

The subject was changed by Nash picking up on Mary's use of the rhyming slang for head.

"Loaf of bread - head. 'ere, yer never did work out what 'ta'ers' meant did ya?"

He told her about 'potatoes in the mould – cold'. Sookey brightened with relief, and was all too pleased to mock scold him for not allowing her to know what it had meant when they had first met. Pronouncing 'ta'ers' correctly for the first time, she told her tutor that she thought the term could have derived from Mrs Beaton. This saw the conversation drift to culinary matters and thankfully off the subject of the killings for the rest of a joyous morning.

Nash had talked about himself in more detail than during earlier conversations. Sookey heard about his fondness for history when he was at the Ragged school; mock censure and shared laughter had ensued when Sookey admitted she had let the cat out of the bag to Shanks about the origin of his nickname. Nash later told Sookey about his family; working for a kidsman; becoming the leader of a boy's gang; his full time adult occupation of violent crime was scaled down to one of part-time petty pilferage to make ends meet due to the lack of work about. She didn't need to know any different.

Sookey felt a real bond with this man, and when he asked her what brought her to live in Whitechapel, she told him. It seemed right for her to tell him about her former life. Aware that when she had originally told Mary about her nemesis Dinky Smith, it had been too verbose for her friend's short attention span, she abbreviated the story for Nash. Like Mary, Nash had interjected his comments at various stages. He didn't like magsmen either, not that he had ever had one of them try anything on him.

"No, I dare say they would not Nashey," she had said knowingly.

When she reached the same point at which she had stopped with Mary, he asked the obvious question.

"But how did you get from the court to here?"

Sookey hesitated for a moment and then told him.

Sookey explained that she had lost everything – financially and emotionally. Both her own family and that of her in-laws were furious with her. They had endured a great deal of shame and embarrassment by association, and were substantially out of pocket too. They felt it incumbent that Susan should become financially independent. They were cutting her off; effectively cutting her out of their lives. She must start a new life. Gain employment. Gain self-respect. They would see her at Christmas no doubt.

Employment opportunities for middle class women were very limited. The only position that was readily available to them was governess. But it was a lonely life, living apart from the servants and a social outcast from the middle classes who scorned those of their sisterhood who had to lower themselves to work for a living. A governess was casteless. But there were a huge number of such women, so there were hundreds of applicants for each position and the law of supply and demand ensured it was lowly paid - £20-£35 a year or even just board and keep and maybe a cast-off dress from her ladyship. A teacher could be an alternative, although it was more an upper working class role. Women were popular with primary school governors because they worked much cheaper than men, but they were not considered to teach older age groups because of their inability to keep order amongst the bigger boys.

Sookey's life in India had been a cosseted one, but she alone among the officer's wives had dared venture into the local village with just a lone servant for guidance and protection. She had seen at first hand the harsh realities of extreme poverty.

After the trial, she had struggled to come to terms with some of the emotions she was feeling. Not the obvious ones of great sorrow and the like, which were terrible but understandable, but another imperceptible feeling that she couldn't quite put her finger on for some time. Part of her felt ...what? Unlike the other feelings, it was positive. Then in a moment of epiphany, it came to her. She felt alive! It was a sort of intoxication. Her mind had a clarity that she had never experienced before. She had always felt dull, and that she had been striving for something all her life, without ever knowing what it was, and certainly never finding it. She could have the most enjoyable day, the most pleasant experience, yet she never felt completely content. There had always been something missing.

But now, for the first time in her adult life, she had known exactly what she wanted to do next; what she was going to do, and not what someone else told her or what society deemed appropriate. She was going to live in the slums full time, but not as a slummer. She had worked there before with her middle class friends. Part time; very part time; the latest thing to do. Let's do our bit. No, this time she would be of the slums; one of us, not one of them. Accepted for what she did; what she was. And she now had little to her name, so she wasn't just 'slumming it'. She belonged there.

She felt a different, better person. Like the dull part of her brain had died and been replaced with some wonderful new drug. The worst events of her life had in a terrible way, been the best thing that had ever happened to her. She was reborn.

And now people came to her for help and advice with their three r's as well as all their medical problems, and she was a scribe for everyone from the most reputable lawyer's clerk's offices down to the poorest of wretches. She had finally found her niche in life.

Not that he knew Ovid's or Machiavelli's expression, but the end did justify the means as far as Nash was concerned.

"Wot happens in the long run makes up for wot goes on along the way I says. In a queer sort a way that litt'e cow's dun yer a favour ain't she gell. If I met her I wouldn't shake her hand mind, rather I'd give a facer to be chompin' on, but I'm fankful to 'er anyhow so a speak."

CHAPTER 23:

"The increase of the population can only be accounted for by the fact of the labouring classes crowding themselves into those houses which were formerly occupied by tradesmen ... which now are let out into tenements."

John Liddle, Medical Officer of Whitechapel

Maybrick's drug addiction was now overwhelming him. His health was declining to a point where his increasing intolerance to cold meant he could not face another night in his Middlesex Street bolt-hole. It had a fireplace but he was ignorant of how to light a fire. He had never stayed in the room whilst his servants lit one. He thought it must be simple enough but he was not prepared to take the chance of setting the place alight. Even a minor mishap could have a policeman knocking on the door when he saw smoke issuing from the room. Furthermore, he had no inclination to buy or order coal, wood and any of the other things he would need. He avoided entering any shops because he felt that if he just came and went without so much as a by-your-leave, he was invisible.

Maybrick was also increasingly paranoid. He was convinced he had been followed to Euston Station when he had left Whitechapel after the last murders, and he had also read a newspaper report that one line of police enquiry was that there could be a link to the north of England. It was only one of hundreds of lines of enquiry but Maybrick believed the police could be closing in. The idea of being caught excited him after a fashion, but it also appalled him. He decided that he would need to change his tactics. He would rearrange his work schedule the week of his next sojourn and travel down to London a day earlier, taking a less direct, less obvious route from Liverpool to Euston. And he certainly could not afford another incident like the one he had with the man and his pony-and-cart in Duffield's Yard on the night of the double murder.

I thought the little yid eyed me. That would be most ruinous to my little game. But no mention by the fool Abberline. And the nag near trampled me as I stood over the whore Liz Stride. Astride Stride. Ha! Ha!

From now on he would spend his evenings in London at his brother Michael's house in the West End. Despite being jealous of his more talented poet-brother, Maybrick was closer to Michael than any of his other siblings. He felt at ease in his home, not to mention warm. He would have to take his bag containing amongst other things his trusty knife, to his brother's. It was not so much of a risk. The bag would always be locked and nobody would dream of looking in it. But he would not take the bag with him on his next venture into Whitechapel. It was too obvious a thing for the police to be looking for. He would have to carry his knife by some other method.

He would tell his brother he would not see him in the morning, because he would be leaving at the crack of dawn to catch the first train to Liverpool; an important business meeting beckoning in the afternoon. An hour after the household, including the last-to-bed servant had retired, he would slip out of the house. After committing his crime he would escape into his Middlesex Street bolt-hole until the inevitable commotion had died down and the coast was clear, and then calmly wander off to find a hansom; not off the rank at Liverpool Street station this time; Fenchurch Street would be safer.

⌒ ◆ ⌒

Sookey had treated Mary to new clothing, more suitable for working for Toynbee Hall. She was to look the epitome of respectability in her new dull green ensemble, of cloak buttoned to the neck with just a hint of white blouse showing above, and a matching green ankle-length skirt. The brass heels were gone too. Mary thought it rather too uniform-like for her liking, but she looked forward to seeing Nash's face when he saw her. She didn't look unlike a Salvation Army girl. She had her 'amen' ready for him and guessed what his colourful reply would be.

But Mary was wearing her prostitute's garb and make-up one final time. She could not very well back out of the post office robbery now just because she was going to work for Sookey next week.

Nash had noticed how the police, both plain clothes and uniformed police on the beat, had been attempting to follow prostitutes, hoping the Ripper would tackle one and get himself apprehended. The view that the Ripper could be a woman was never a seriously held one by the police. It had been just one more sensationalist piece of journalism to sell newspapers. But after his questioning by the police about Sookey, Nash believed the police were taking the notion with more than a pinch of salt. Thus, a woman canary was not such a good option after all. The whole point of a canary being a woman was that the police did not suspect them of being up to no-good in the early hours as they might a man so did not stop and search them. The last thing they could afford was for police officer William Thick or one of his mates to stop a woman thinking she might be the Ripper, only to find she had every cracksman's tool imaginable on her.

Mary had, therefore, changed jobs from canary to crow, though she would not signal a warning in the usual manner because she didn't have the whistling skills. She needed to keep an eye out for the police, and be a decoy if and when necessary. As soon as any crusher showed up, she was to ensure he saw her and, it was hoped, follow her. She would lead him away from the robbery area. Nash had also employed Khan to stand by. If the crusher didn't show signs of following Mary, Khan was to approach her as if he was a customer and they were to start off together in the hope the policeman would now follow them. If he still didn't, Khan had to pretend to start to get rough with Mary. That should certainly do it. If the worst came to the worse Mary would cry out "murder!" Even Thick and associates should respond to that.

Will Roud was to take his chance as the canary. If stopped by a crusher, Will would cosh him and make a run for it. Young Kitty needed to shadow Will, and if he had to 'scarper' she was to grab the tools and get rid of them as quickly and quietly as possible. She would immediately lighten the load by putting all the small stuff down the nearest latrine. Nash had not told Arthur this part of the plan; he thought ignorance was bliss.

Mary had spent the afternoon and early evening with Sookey but she was now at home. A neighbour at the end of her tether, Lizzie Albrook, had drifted in for a shoulder to cry on. Lizzie was a part-time prostitute but had stopped a month ago after the last murders. Without the extra income street-walking afforded her, she was destitute and starving. Mary sympathised with the poor wretch.

She thought back to the row she had with Nashey last week. It was as well Sookey had not been there; some ripe language having been tossed back and forth as voices got louder and louder, even before Nashey had gone too far.

"...people in 'igh places is startin' a take notice I'm telling yer! Council and government coves are goin' on aboud it in the papers. Children in common lodging 'ouses, the 'omeless, abandoned chavvies, the 'ousin' ov the poor, gettin' rid a the rookeries, rebuildin'. They didn't wanna know till ol' Jack got ta work did they? Didn't hear nuffin', didn't see nuffin'!"

He was immediately annoyed with himself for calling the maniac 'ol' Jack'. Mary had already been red in the face before this latest outburst. She glared at Nash with disgust.

"Six women lay dead and buried, and 'orribly murdered at that, with their fuckin' froats cut! You tellin' me thas right are ya!? Are ya!!? And there's the likes ov Lizzie, and there's loads ov 'em like 'er! In a terrible state she is cos she's too scared ta work the streets no more! Dyin' on the streets like dogs they are! They got a work, or it's the 'ouse or starvin' a deff and they usually choose starvin' dunt they! The only money they get is off cowsons wiv their cocks out. No ovver bastard's gonna give 'em nuffin' are they?!"

Nash had known he was losing the argument. He had lost it with himself often enough this past month. But he carried on regardless, becoming abusive and raising his voice to a shout as a line of defence.

"What d'you know of it any'ow! Thas why the murders is doin' good yer stoopid lit'le 'ore! Showin' thems that's in charge they got a do summin'! They ain' been listenin' for three-score year, but now they are alright!"

Mary was incandescent. She had never been so furious in her life, and she was getting more and more angered with every word that spewed out of Nash's mouth. She started to speak quietly, slowly.

"Some ov us 'av tried doin' the work they gives us. Phossy Jaw. Yer seen that 'ave yer? Yer fucking face falls off. I walk the fucking streets, knowing every time I pick up some disgusting, sweating pig, he could have a knife waiting for me."

She had pronounced her g's as she ground out the words in the clear enunciation of cold, determined rage, but her voice had suddenly cracked and become shrill on the word 'knife'.

"You ain' got no fuckin' idea wot thas like 'ave yer cunt!"

She hit him with a right cross, her little fist smashing into his teeth.

He must have seen it coming. In her fury she had brought her arm back way too far. But he stood there and let the fist hit him. She waited for the retaliatory blow. She wanted him to hit her. She wanted the bruise, the cut, the badge of honour staring at him the next time they met. She would have won. One more man exacting violence on a defenceless woman. But it didn't come. He just walked off, blood oozing out of his lower lip from where her ring had hit home. She had never seen him so furious but strangely she wasn't at all intimidated. The rage in his face did not seem to have been levelled at her.

She flexed her hand at the memory. One of her knuckles still hurt. In her rage she had forgotten to hit him in the cold, calculated manner in which he had trained her. She had hit him as hard as she could, but the memory hurt more than the hand.

That had been after last Friday night's meeting. Their fourth meeting and still no sign of Shanks' pull. She had not seen Nash since. Both had spent time with Sookey on different occasions but they had managed to avoid each other. Mary had told Sookey about the row with Nash, even telling her what her parting comment and action had been. Sookey was not at all shocked at the swearing or violence but was visibly upset by Nash's views.

"I have had similar conversation with him. He is a nut to crack is he not? I sometimes wonder what sort of a man he is to see. He is a rum cove when it comes to these horrible murders. And he claims to know the identity of the Ripper if you please! He has seen the man, plain as day! He let this slip when suffering from a blow to the head when he rescued me from those ruffians. I have since tried to broach the subject with him but he insists he was not of right mind. But I saw his eyes Mary, and I tell you indeed he was."

Mary was astonished.

"I'll 'ave it out wiv 'im on Friday when I sees 'im, you see if I don't."

Sookey grimaced and told Mary she didn't think that was a good idea. She changed the subject.

"You see Nashey every Friday night. Am I not to be invited?"

"It's business Sookey, nuffin' a do wiv you. But now I'm startin' work for you, I won't be meeting up wiv Nashey no more on Fridee nights lessen it's jus' ta drink, and you're invited a course."

Mary had already told Nash that if the job did not take place this coming Friday, he would have to find somebody else. She was fed up with Shanks wasting their time, and besides she had a new job to go to on the Monday. She didn't need or want to commit crime any longer.

After Lizzie had left, Mary lay on her bed singing loudly, a typically sentimental Victorian ballad, 'Only a violet I plucked from my mother's grave'. She was maudlin, hungry and weak, not having earned enough to eat properly for a week. It would be easy to fall asleep.

"The pull's on!" Shanks delivered the news with excitement and enthusiasm.

He went on to relay all the information Nash needed to commit the robbery including the type of safe it was. Nash knew nothing about safes but nodded sagely.

"You need ta take that glass stuff I gave yer ov Ar.. Peter's for a safe like that." Nash had taken the precaution of not calling the cracksman Arthur whenever speaking of him to Shanks. "Me an' Peter gets down there and looks out for Will. You makes yer own way. If yer see us collared by Old Bill, make yerself scarce down some empty alley then smash this ta smithereens on the ground. Then scatter off."

Nash gave a sly, wicked smile at Shanks, who mistook it for grim determination.

"Will do Nashey."

Nash got to Arthur's. All but one of the gang was there. Nash gave them the good news and passed on intelligence gathered by Shanks about elements of the job.

"You all know what ta do now, so gall on scarper. Where's Mary?"

Kitty mumbled apologetically.

"Late."

Mary had been late the first two weeks; the first time through picking up a customer for a quick knee-trembler who had taken the devil's own time to reach his climax. She had to give him a bit of oral extra to get him there in the end but the bastard wouldn't pay her any more. The second week she had fallen asleep and been awoken by Nash thumping on her door.

"Just as well it ain' fuckin' on ain' it," was the opening line of a deluge of abuse delivered from no more than a few inches from her down-turned face.

She made sure she was on time the third week.

"Fuck 'er. Can't wait for 'er now. Kitty, get some rouge on and get down there and do what Mary were gonna do. Khan, if Will 'as any trouble, you back 'im up like Kitty were gonna do."

The three of them started to scuttle off when Nash remembered how Khan did exactly what he was told and no more.

"Khan, yer still got'a pretend yer a customer if needs be. Ov Kitty's instead ov Mary's see."

Khan nodded his understanding and left with the others.

Nash relayed to Arthur what Shanks had told him about the type of safe that was to be dealt with.

"You know it cracksman?"

"Enuff. Won't need no nitro."

"Shame," commented Nash.

Arthur gave Nash an old fashioned look.

Shanks' information had been surprisingly good. Nash and Arthur were to break into a warehouse in Duke Street, just around the corner from the post office, then make their way onto the roof. This was adjacent to the roof of the post office, which had a trap-door big enough for a man to get through.

It had all gone smoothly. They had met up with Shanks and Will with the gear. Arthur was puzzled to see Shanks with the nitro, and quickly told him he needn't have brought it after all. Shanks had been quite amenable about this, relieved as he was to have an excuse to leave.

He agreed to keep the gear at his place till Will picked it up from him the following morning.

Nash and Arthur duly made their way to the trap-door. Nash had a jemmy ready but it wasn't locked. As Nash climbed through the trap door, his concentration on the job in hand was broken by a flash of memory – his argument with Mary over Bill Sykes' housebreaking prowess.

"No need for young Oliver tonight," muttered Nash, just audibly.

"Jus' bleedin' well get in there will yer, leavin' me out 'ere like two ov eels," said the old cracksman, now taking on the role of leader for the first time. The cigarette between his lips was unlit. He didn't smoke at work.

They made their way gingerly down some stairs in the pitch dark before Nash felt they were sufficiently distant from any windows to light a match. He spotted the door into the office that Shanks had told them would contain the money, and forced it open. More matches allowed them to find £3 in a quickly jemmied open drawer, which was actually the postmaster's own money he had left there. There was no sign of any other money.

"Free bleedin' sovs! That bastard Shanks! Where's the fuckin' safe?"

It was clear from Arthur's tone that Nash was going to have to stand in a queue if he wanted to give Shanks a good hiding when they got back.

"Down 'ere!" shouted Nash, having taken a flight of stairs off the office.

He forced the door and they were into the cellar. There stood Arthur's safe behind a barred entrance. Arthur got to work on the bars while Nashey was match-man.

Arthur took a length of rope and a strong metal rod, passed a double loop round two bars, inserted the rod between strands and turned it end over end, twisting up the rope and drawing the bars together. The bars became bent enough for him to slip through, but Nash was too big to get through the small gap. He passed the matches to Arthur, who struck one and a second later threw a horrified glance at Nash.

"It ain' the safe Shanks said. It's a Bramah-locked plate. We need the fuckin' nitro!"

"I'll do for the bastard!" replied Nash solemnly as he turned to go back.

"Jus' coddin' wiv yer. It ain' the safe 'e said alright. It's easier." Arthur was beaming at his own joke. "I'll 'ave it open in no time."

"It's as well you're the ovver side a them bars cracksmen," came the response through gritted teeth.

He handed Arthur his dark lantern and his petter-cutter drill with an old fashioned look. Nash held a lit match while Arthur lit the dark lantern. The lantern threw a spot of light the size of a shilling from an oil-fed wick, and Arthur used it while he clamped his drill to the keyhole of the safe, allowing powerful leverage to be applied to the cutter, which was made of hardened steel. It bit a small opening over the lock through which the wards could be manipulated. It was highly skilled work to use the tools effectively and quietly. Arthur was earning his share. As good as his word, the safe was open in double quick time. Nash passed Arthur a jemmy and a chisel and he got to work on a locked compartment within the safe. But despite some tips proffered by Nash, he couldn't budge it.

A heavily sweating Arthur got back through the bars and took hold of a small jack worked with a ratchet and pinion. It opened a larger gap in the bars which Nash was just able to struggle through. Arthur sat down, exhausted. Nash still hadn't forgiven the old man for his inappropriate joke.

"Should a used that in the first fuckin' place shouldn't ya!"

Nash got to work on the metal of the compartment and his greater brute force did the trick. He wrenched it open and hauled out a huge wad of something. When the light hit it they saw it was stamps. Nash grimaced at Arthur and threw them on the floor with disgust.

"Give over! What yer expect in a bleedin' post office yer soppy sod," said an exasperated Arthur. "Reach us a match."

He bent down and licked his filthy fingers for grip. Under match-light he rifled through the pages and then started counting on his fingers before giving up and asking Nash.

"'ere, wots a fousand fivepences?"

Nash had to think for a while himself. He eventually came up with an answer.

"It's a bit more than a score. Don' arst me 'ow much more mind."

Arthur proceeded to quiz Nash on ever increasing amounts and numbers, and asked him to keep count. He reached the last sheet of stamps.

"Wots all that come to then?"

"'bout two 'undred and seven'y pound."

The two men nodded at each other and Nash scrabbled to pick up the loot and stuff it into his extra large overcoat pockets with enthusiasm. Arthur said what Nash was thinking.

"No need for Shanks to know about these. 'e's only interested in the money ain' 'e?"

Nash smiled approval at the old rascal, before turning to try another larger compartment which was rather easier to get open. It contained sovereigns, half-sovereigns and a large assortment of smaller value silver coinage. There was more counting by match-light.

"'bout fifty pound," muttered Arthur as he looked uncertainly at Nash. At least it was cash this time, but they had expected more. It joined the stamps in Nash's coffers. There was a locked drawer which, despite all Nash's most violent efforts, was proving difficult to budge. The sound of weaponry on buckling metal was echoing round the empty post office. Having had no success at attracting attention with his repertoire of whistles and animal calls, Will's urgent whispered cry tried to make itself heard above the din.

"Nashey! Arfa!"

Arthur thought he heard something, tapped Nashey and put his right index finger to his lips.

"Nashey! Arfa!" The two men froze to the spot. The voice continued.

"It's Will."

The two men dashed up the stairs two at a time to find a head dangling through the trap door.

"Pack it in, I can 'ear yer from the street. There's too many crushers for us all ta deal with. There's one 'aving a drag on 'is pipe fifty yard down Mitre Street; 'e 'll be 'ere sharp enuff."

The three of them retraced their steps over the roof. Will had left the spare tools in the warehouse while he went to fetch his confederates.

"Leave 'em," ordered the old man with resignation.

Arthur was sad at leaving his tools but knew the chances were too high that Will would get stopped. He could no longer ask Will to do something he was not prepared to do himself. The constable would have finished his quick drag by now and might be on his way from the far end of the square towards the warehouse. He might be about to spot the signs of break-in. He might be looking towards the warehouse at the very moment when three heads popped out.

The three men were steeling themselves to leave the premises. Nashey held coshes in both hands. He would normally have led the three of them out of the warehouse and dealt with whatever came at them, but he was badly weighed down by their bounty. If it came to a straight running race between them and the police he was carrying the top weight of a gold cup winner, and the going was getting decidedly heavy. The coinage also jangled noisily as it slid around in his pockets with every step he took.

"You makin' enuff fuckin' racket are ya? Didn't yer bring nuffin' to wrap it in?"

Arthur was starting to realise he was working with amateurs.

"Didn't fink." Nash was furious with himself.

Will saw the glum expression. He knew this state of mind. There was nothing more dangerous than a Nashey annoyed with himself. He thought he had better stop Arthur from saying anything more.

"Both of yer shuddup. I'm the crow now. An' now I earns me share. I lead. Any trouble, I scarper and the crushers chase after me. You go second Arthur. Nashey, you go last an' easy. Wait for me signal."

With this Will emerged into Duke Street. The stench from the open slaughterhouse next door assorted his nostrils. It wasn't the sort of street you walked down unless you had to, and Will was pleased to see that policemen obviously had sensitive noses. The street was empty save a wretch lying in the gutter.

He made his cat-call, the others emerged and they started to walk quietly towards their agreed meeting point with Shanks. Shanks had tried to insist they split the takings up in the alley where they were due to meet, so he could see he wasn't being fleeced, but Nash had shouted him down, insisting the money be split behind closed doors in the post office. If he wanted to be in on the split, he could make his way over the roof with them if he wanted. He didn't want. The annoying irony now was that due to the necessary speedy evacuation of the post office, they would have to do exactly what Shanks had wanted all along.

Will was passing the wretch in the gutter, when the man's left hand came out and grabbed Will around the ankle. Crusher! thought Nash and moved towards the man, cosh at the ready. He thought the man might have a beat-policeman's whistle on him; he had to get to him before his target could curl his lips around it. A panic-stricken whisper issued forth from the gutter.

"You took yer bleedin' time didn't ya!"

It was Shanks. He had been lucky Nash had been the third man, and lagging a few yards behind. Another second and Shanks would have lost consciousness, possibly for good, but he had the temerity to complain.

"I've 'ad to lie 'ere like two ov eels. Couldn't 'ang about could I. Crushers everywhere yer bleedin' look. Look at the state a me!"

He was not supposed to meet them there in case any police had spotted him loitering. All three of his fellow robbers were furious. Nash wished he hadn't stopped himself when he had heard Shanks' voice.

"That's nuffin' to the state you'd be in if I'd a jus' coshed yer lights out!"

Arthur moved quickly into the conversation. This wasn't getting them anywhere.

"It took a while cos we 'ad a lot a sums ta do."

Shanks took this to mean that they had been successful. He displayed the excitement of a little boy.

"'ow much yer get any'ow?"

"Fifty pound."

Shanks' expression changed from excited to crestfallen to undisguised suspicion, in a moment.

"Fifty!? I were told four 'undred."

Nash and Arthur looked at each other grimly. Nash took one step towards Shanks before Arthur stepped in between them.

"Tell a lie boy, it were fifty free wern it Nashey?" He laughed in an attempt to defuse the tension. "We forgot them three sovs bunts we got out a one a the drawers. There were a bit ov the safe we couldn't get open in time cos we 'ad ta scarper sharp. Must 'av had your ovver gelt in there see."

Arthur realised he was being rather defensive, when he felt quite the opposite towards Shanks. His expression and tone of voice changed.

"It were your idea ta do a pull with 'alf a London's constabulary on the doorstep wern it Shanks? An' now we're gonna get our pawsey collars felt while we're standing 'ere like cods in a trance!"

The four men shared a sheepish glance before nodding agreement and scurried off around the back of the slaughterhouse. There were many such buildings in the vicinity, and the name Aldgate had for decades been synonymous with slaughter. It still was, though more so nowadays; it was part of Whitechapel.

When telling him the pull was on, Shanks had briefed Nash as to the regular habits and foibles of the policemen on the relevant beat. PC Crisp passed by the post office every fifteen minutes, and would stop in a dark spot for a quick illicit draw on his pipe roughly every twenty minutes. Aldgate post office was on Mitre Square, where Catherine Eddowes had been killed, so there was a plain clothes officer on patrol in the vicinity too. Shanks had spotted him during his surveillance work over the preceding weeks. Nash had relayed this intelligence to Kitty and Khan who, completely untrained and unskilled in the job of crow, proved to be surprisingly good decoys. They successfully led both the uniformed and plain clothes officers away from the post office during the robbery.

When PC Crisp had got too close to the post office for comfort, the novice crows rather overacted a negotiation, with Khan, probably the gentlest man in the whole of Whitechapel, pretending none too convincingly to threaten Kitty. But it worked a treat. Both policemen followed them. Kitty and Khan chose purely at random to lead the policemen east, till they decided to lose them in the New Road. If they had led them north towards Thrawl Street and lost them around there, which they could just as easily have done, one or both of the policemen might have spotted a gent in a Derby hat, who happened by a little later.

Nash walked down Aldgate High Street towards his home. He passed the junction with Middlesex Street and glanced up it as he always did whenever he passed it these days. It had become a habit. It was nearly half past five Saturday morning. The place would be a hive of costermonger activity on a Sunday, getting ready for the market. The night he chased after the Derby-hatted man flashed through his mind. Yes, it had been a Saturday night/Sunday morning. But Saturday morning was the quietest part of the week – the Jewish Sabbath had just begun. The streets were deserted.

Ten minutes later Nash would have seen a man he recognised, dart quickly into a house he knew. The man forgot to check his mat trap. Nash's slight groin strain had been acquired unnecessarily.

❧ ◆ ❧

In the past few days Nash had been so busy with the arrangements for the robbery, he had not thought about anything else. But now he was trying to get some sleep only for his mind to be racing; flitting between thoughts of the robbery, Mary and Sookey. He would have expected the robbery to still be in his head, and angry though he was with Mary he was eager to clear the air with her, but he was puzzled that thoughts of Sookey kept forcing their way into his mind. And they were not specific thoughts like those of the events of the previous night. They were just random. One moment he was remembering the money he had made last night, and the next he was thinking about Sookey's previous life.

Poor little cow's 'ad it 'ard alright. Not 'ard like me, but no bet'er for all that. I never fought a people like 'er 'avin'.. Spose I never fought about people like 'er at all come a fink ov it. Jus' people ta rob ta get me own back. That turd ov an 'usband. There's worse fings than knockin' yer old lady about ain' there. Takin' 'er somewhere worse then 'ere! On purpose, when yer don't 'ave to! Then 'e don't 'ardly speak to 'er an' she ain' got 'ardly no ovver bugger to talk to neiver. No wonder she talks ser much now! Then those bastards see 'er comin', she loses everyfin', everyone takes the rise out ov 'er and she ain' got a soul in the weld to 'elp 'er. Then she comes 'ere on 'er own an' 'as to put up wiv the likes a Rose an' 'er mates looking down their noses at 'er, an' then she 'elps everyone, an' never a bad word. She even 'elped Shanks…

As the gang had been about to split up and go their separate ways after the robbery, Shanks had made a suggestion to Nash about Mary.

"Give 'er a good 'iding when yer see 'er."

A glowering Nash made it clear he wouldn't be following the advice.

"Mind yerself Shanks. We still ain' talked about that lit'le matter of Sookey an' your mates 'av we?"

The wrong un shrank back into his overcoat, and professed his innocence.

"They ain' no mates a mine Nashey, he jus' knocked on me door cos 'e knew me and it 'appened right where I live see. I took 'im ta Sookey's cos where else was I gonna take 'im?"

Shanks had darted a glance at Arthur looking for a sympathetic nod, but all he got was a look of contempt and a twitch of the roll-up.

Every relationship of any kind that Nash had ever had, ended with violence, occasionally physical, more often than not verbal. He was not going to let his friendship with Mary die that way. He was going to see her the next morning and would break the ice by handing over her share. He had insisted Mary got paid. Shanks had asked why she should. Nash was about to reply when Arthur replied for him.

"Cos you've sodded 'er about the past munff thas why yer lit'le shit'ouse!"

An affronted, "'ere!" was all Shanks could muster in reply. Nash looked at the old man with renewed respect.

"I bet you were a right 'andful when yer were younger wunt yer."

Nash's thoughts meandered from one crime to another.

I wouldn't be gettin' any older if that cowson 'ad got to me wiv that cosh. Fancy Sookey 'oldin' 'im orf. An' she'd already bin 'alf strangled and 'ad a fourpenny one in the belly. Or Derby Kelly as she now tells it. She likes 'er coster rhymin' that one. She's a funny cuts. Not like Mary's funny, but she makes yer laugh right enuff. 'We are not amuse-eum'. I arst yer! And she takes my coddin' wiv 'er an' all...

The money had been split up into varying sizes of share. It had been taking too long for Nash's liking while Shanks and Arthur counted every penny under a gas light as Nash stood guard.

"Christ almigh'y, don't count every mortal fing. We ain' got all night. Jus' chuck me all the small stuff and you two can sort out the rest tomorra when the dust set'les. It ain' enough to worry about. Arfa, let Shanks take some a your share fer now. 'e won't be able a get one over on yer; yer knows 'ow much it all is dunt ya."

Nash had forgotten to call the cracksman Peter in Shanks' presence, but nobody seemed to notice. Nash glared at Arthur, a look that said, 'we got £270 pound worth ov stamps in me pocket, so don't get us nabbed by the crushers worryin' about the odd sov 'ere or there'.

Arthur understood. He nodded, and Shanks was also in full agreement, his devious mind immediately thinking about how he could make more than his share out of the arrangement. Nash took his own, Mary's, Khan's and Kitty's shares; it was all in sixpences, shillings, florins and half-crowns.

Least none ov us'll be caught tryin' ta pass orf large gelt...Could a done wiv Sookey reckonin' them stamps up. An' she knows more about over fings than them teachers they got in schools, an' yer keeps yer lugs out when she's tellin' yer fings an' all. She's clever and soppy as a box a lights at the same time. Never known anyone like 'er...

Nash would let them have their shares when he next saw each of them. He had hidden the stamps in a special little hide-away under his floorboards. He would fence them and give half the proceeds to Arthur, and share his half with Mary, Will, Khan and Kitty.

He decided to keep the coinage on him but bundled it into every sock he owned, removing those he had on, before returning the money to his pockets. That would stop the clinking somewhat. He would tell Mary he was keeping some of her share back to make a point to her about not turning up for the pull, but would let her have it as a surprise present at Christmas. She would have probably spent the rest by then. He knew she had plans to move to a bigger, less disgusting place, which was going to cost her.

She should set'le down wiv that feller ov 'ers. I used to fink she could do bet'er. Needed some cove ta take 'er in 'and, look after 'er, get 'er orf them streets. 'e's a bit young for 'er, and 'e ain' tough enuff for round 'ere, but...

CHAPTER 24:

*"I always believe in people being improvable; they will not be
improvable without improved dwellings."*

Octavia Hill

It was mid-morning and Nash was deep in slumber,
having finally dropped off only a couple of hours earlier.
He was awoken by a thumping on his door. He groggily
stumbled to the door. Before he had a chance to ask who
it was, it became apparent.

"Nashey! Nashey!"

It was Tom.

"'e's come out the 'ouse!"

"Ay? 'oo?"

Nash wasn't fully awake yet.

"The gent! 'e's scarpered!"

"Wot yer on about, come out the 'ouse? When did 'e
go in?"

"'e ain' gone in, 'e jus' come out!"

Nash's senses flooded back into him. The Ripper must
have arrived in the early hours when there was nobody on
duty, which means there must be a good chance he's been
up to his old tricks again. Now he was getting away again.
Nash had slept in his clothes all bar his boots and overcoat,
both of which he threw on in double quick time. As he was
putting on his boots he shouted up at Tom.

"Where's 'e now?"

"Dunno. I left 'im ta come 'ere. 'e 'eaded fer the station."

"I bet 'e did," muttered Nash.

He rushed past Tom and shouted over his shoulder.

"Get back there in case 'e comes back. If he does, stay there. If 'e goes off again, dog 'im."

Nash thought of something and skidded to a halt on the slippery cobbles. He dashed back, thrust a hand in his pocket and came up with the smallest sockful of silver coin, which he gave to Tom.

"If 'e takes a cab, you take one after 'im. 'ang on to 'im no mat'er wot. An' if I'm not about, tell Will what yer find out."

Nash turned and ran off without seeing Tom's face. Standing there with a silver-filled sock on his palm, his face was a picture. Nash was not confident his orders would be adhered to.

Little bastard'll problee go straight ta the booza wiv it. 'e's never had so much in 'is mitts in 'is life before I wager. Still, can't 'elp that now.

He ran full tilt to Liverpool Street station and scanned the cab rank while he got his breath back. There was no sign of the gent. He thought about asking the cabbies if they had seen his man, but decided he didn't have the time. He shouted at the first hansom driver on the rank.

"Euston station. There's an extra tanner in it for yer if yer don't 'ang about. Got a train ta get."

"Gis a bob and I'll give 'im the whip good for yer."

The driver was nodding at his poor, underfed, overworked horse. Nash didn't have time to comment. He nodded and jumped in.

On arrival Nash sprinted into the crowded station and looked about him. There was still no hint of his quarry as far as he could see.

Cove like 'im 'd travel firs' class.

He could find the next train to Liverpool and simply run straight on to it, pushing aside the porters, but he couldn't afford any trouble. He thought it better to buy a ticket. He ran to the booking office.

"Firs' class Liverpool," he bellowed.

The ticket clerk looked Nash up and down with contempt. Villainous looking men with three days beard growth, bloodshot eyes and filthy clothes do not travel first class.

"Single or return?" he sneered.

Nash remembered the little uniform at the underground station he'd had trouble with. He vowed to keep his temper in check no matter what the provocation, and simply get this ticket quickly and quietly. He gave a warm smile back at the sneer.

"There an' back if you please good man."

I'll give 'im 'good man', thought the clerk.

"Yer comin' back today or anuvver day?"

Nash smiled again.

"Today, thank you."

The clerk's sneer turned to a patronising smile.

"Yer know 'ow much first class is?"

Nash dug into his pocket and pulled out a sockful of post office cash, and tipped it in front of the clerk. Nash replaced the smile with one of his more threatening expressions and leaned closer.

"I don't want no comments. Fink that'll be enuff do yer?"

He completed the transaction without further problem, though the clerk got in a parting shot.

"While you've bin stood 'ere the Liverpool train's jus' leavin'. Platform five it is."

Nash ran flat out. He was nearing the platform when a porter stepped in front of him.

"'ere, where's yer ticket?" he asked aggressively.

Nash shoved his ticket under the man's nose, and immediately flew up several social classes as far as the porter was concerned, whose face cracked into a broad smile with a soft voice and lighter accent to match.

"Thank you sir. Liverpool is it? You'd be better getting the fast. Express only takes five hours. Platform one in half an hour. This is the stopper. Take a lot longer. Yerve got time for a nice cuppa tea down there."

The porter was nodding towards platform one, opposite the entrance to which was a branch of Spiers & Bond refreshment rooms. Nash looked along the station towards the café.

"You seen a gent, moustache, gold watch, Derby 'at?"

The porter showed either puzzlement or suspicion in his face, Nash wasn't sure which.

"It's me guvnor see. I should a bin 'ere ta meet 'im 'alf 'our ago. Got held up by a young lady, yer know 'ow it goes." He flashed a conspiratorial wink at the porter. "Dunno wevver 'e's getting' the stopper or the fast. 'e don't like 'angin' about. 'e might a got the stopper."

The porter seemed satisfied with the explanation. He rubbed his chin and looked down in keen concentration.

"Can't say as I noticed wot 'e were wearing but there were a gent with a moustache walked past down towards Spierses jus' now."

Nash nodded the closest thing to a 'thank you' that the porter was going to get and marched off towards the café, moving as quickly as he could without breaking into a run. He peered in through the window. No sign of his man, but it was crowded; he went in to get a closer look. Heads turned and a silence dropped, as this dangerous looking man moved among the tables with no apparent thought of sitting down, his eyes darting this way and that. What villainy was this man about to commit?

An obviously well dressed man sat with his back to Nash. No hat. It was no doubt hanging with his greatcoat nearby. Nash spotted an empty table opposite the man and calmly made his way over to it. As he sat down he glanced casually in the man's direction. The man had a moustache, gold watch and chain. Nash immediately got up and walked towards the man. He continued on past him and out of the café. The man didn't have the face he last saw under a light, chalking on a wall, five weeks ago.

The well dressed man didn't look up. He hadn't been aware of the menacing man who had just inspected him. But everyone else in the café most certainly had. Had Nash left the door open he would have heard the gush of exuded breath and nervous chatter that followed his departure.

A porter's whistle blew. The stopper was about to start away. Nash had a flash of clarity.

'e wouldn't 'ang about havin' a bleedin' cuppa tea would 'e now? 'e'd want a get away sharp. Don't matter 'ow long the soddin' train takes!

He started sprinting, but the train was already moving. He felt the weight and bulk in his stuffed pockets making it difficult to sprint as quickly as he wanted to. He brushed past the friendly porter. The train was still twenty feet away but it was already almost at his running speed. He was barely gaining on it, as he screwed his face up into a demonic grin and sprinted harder. There was a distant cry.

"'e's first class!"

An arm shot out of the guard's van.

"Reach me yer 'and!"

Nash thrust his arm up and grabbed hold of a uniformed sleeve. The sleeve pulled and Nash jumped in unison. He was aboard.

At just about the same time that Nash's feet hit the guard's van floor, a hansom pulled up outside Euston station. The man who alighted checked his gold watch. He had just spent an hour scratching a woman's initials into the inside of his watch-cover. It was the sixth set. He was running out of space. It was thirty minutes till the express departed. He remembered the refreshment room at which he had breakfasted once before. He was exhausted from his night's work. A beverage and something to eat was the order of the day.

Maybrick's growing paranoia had led him to be extra vigilant about his movements away from Whitechapel. He had walked to Fenchurch Street rather than Liverpool Street station, where he had taken a cab to St Martin's in the Field's, before flagging down another hansom in the Strand to take him to Euston. It had taken a bit more time but he felt it was worth the inconvenience.

Nash had walked along a station platform past several carriages each time the train stopped before hopping back on the train when it was about to depart. The porter checking tickets had given him a puzzled frown when coming across him in second class. A man who looked like he should be in third class if anywhere, travelling with a first class ticket but sitting here? The respectable looking young lady sitting alone in the carriage with Nash at the time looked decidedly nervous. She had decided she would change carriages at the next stop, but was relieved to find the man was only too pleased to move on himself. Nash had moved up and down the train without seeing his man.

Nash arrived in Liverpool after a tediously long journey, just as his quarry was walking through the front door of Battlecrease House, the half mansion he shared with his wife Florrie and their young children. The express had run to time. Nash's stopping train had been overtaken as it sat in Rugby railway station.

Nash waited at the station, checking to see if his man stepped off a later train. On one occasion he went to the cab-rank to ask if anyone had seen a gent with a moustache and a Derby hat. His gruff tone and cockney accent had not been well received by Liverpudlian cabbies. One had sent him on his way with a two-fingered salute. This gesture was new, derived from an older gesture involving a v sign above the head which meant cuckold. The new gesture had not infiltrated the slums of the East End yet. Nashey hadn't seen it before, but he guessed it meant something along the lines of sex and travel.

He bought several snacks off different street vendors who plied their wares in the station, engaging each of them in conversation, being careful to be friendlier than he had been with the cabbies. He had given each of them a more detailed description of his prey. Added to gent, moustache, gold watch and Derby hat were age, height, build, hair colouring and suit. But it was still rather vague and could fit many. One vendor said there had been such a man, get off the express a while ago, but she didn't see which way he went. This helpful woman was at least useful in telling Nash where in the city such a well-heeled man might live, and where that was in relation to the station. Nash thought he might come back there some day soon and have a look around. But he didn't want to do it now. He wanted to get back to London to see what had happened. When the last train of the day back to London came in, he got on it.

Nash had only slept a couple of hours the previous night and this, added to the stress of the robbery and his tough day since, was catching up on him. His mind had been racing on the train so sleep was difficult to manage, and the only time he had been on the verge of dropping off, a guard had woken him with a little foot tap to his feet, demanding in no uncertain terms to see his ticket.

As soon as the train had stopped for the first time, a couple of passengers had been along to the guard to complain about a ruffian sitting in first class. Nash had paid for it so thought he might as well sit in first class. It had been worth being woken up to see all their faces when he produced his ticket. The second class carriage closest, quickly filled.

Nash realised that had the Ripper killed again, it would take a while before it was reported and the news would not have reached Liverpool by the time he left it, so the fact that there was no talk of it on the station or on the train didn't mean anything.

He was so exhausted and deep in thought when he got off the train that he didn't notice the headlines or the cries of the newsboys on the station. He should have noticed; should have gone over to them and bought a paper for all the details, but he didn't want to. Out of sight; out of mind. The news would filter through to him quickly enough, tomorrow morning. No doubt from the first person he spoke to. Nobody would be talking about anything else. If the Ripper had struck, Nash had a woman's death on his conscience and he wanted to wait till tomorrow to face up to it. He walked head down out of the station. He had spent enough on transportation for one day and he hadn't risked picking oakum for years to waste his ill-gotten gains on cab or underground fares, so he trudged the miles home. It was well into the early hours by the time he collapsed on his bed. The streets had been deserted, which was very strange for a Saturday night, but he hadn't noticed.

For the second night in a row he fell asleep thinking of his friend Mary. He was looking forward to seeing her.

She wouldn't appreciate him being his first port of call on a Sunday morning. She liked her lie-in. After all, she didn't usually get to bed till late on Saturday nights. He would call round to see Will and then Sookey, and get any news from them.

⁘ ◆ ⁘

Mary's thoughts had drifted to Nashey. The last civil conversation they had enjoyed was a brief spell of welcoming banter last Friday, before the row, when he arrived to tell them that the job was again not happening. She was just finishing telling Arthur, Khan and Kitty one of her rice pudding jokes.

"… you got any cold rice puddin'?, nah 'e says, come back tomorra it's 'ot today."

Kitty thought it most amusing. The others just nodded appreciatively. Nash made a typical mock grumpy entrance.

"For someone 'oo ain' got enuff to eat 'alf the time, yer spend enuff bleedin' time talkin' aboud it."

"'ere look what the cat, Doris ain' it, dragged in," retorted Mary, remembering that Sookey had recently told her that Nash's cat now had a name.

She guessed, correctly, it would be a source of embarrassment to him.

Mary was smiling at the memory of Nash's colourful reply when Christ Church Spitalfields struck one o'clock. She was due to meet the others at two in the morning. Not wishing to risk falling asleep, she got up and peered through her sole, tiny, broken window. She would be relieved when she had the money from the robbery to pay a 'winders-man' to come and stop that draft.

'ave to arst ol' Khan if he knows somebody. 'e used ta be in that game.

She could see down the street a short way, and spotted someone she knew coming along. She grabbed her key, locked her door and ventured out.

George Hutchinson was a regular customer of Mary's. Nash had met him once and immediately labelled him a wrong 'un. Mary had educated him to the reality of her situation.

"Beggars can't be choosers Nashey."

"George!" she called.

After a few words of mutual welcome, they strolled out of her court and turned right into Commercial Street. George had no money on him and was roaring drunk, but was after a quick knee-trembler on credit. He wouldn't take no for an answer and an increasingly irritated Mary now wished she had stayed in her room.

"'ere, I told yer, I ain' on the game no more."

"Yeah, it bleedin' looks like it."

George was looking at what was for the world to see her prostitute uniform of brightly coloured dress, lace up boots and caked on make-up.

"I pays yer. I always pays yer dun I. Tomorra."

"I'm late for summin'."

Mary put her head down and quickened her gait to get away from him down Thrawl Street.

"The favours I dun you in the past."

George had the temerity to have incredulous disappointment in his voice. The only 'favours' he had done her was pay her a pittance for pounding away at her up against a wall every Saturday night.

"Fuck off George! I'll 'ave Nashey on yer."

The threat brought the required response. He stopped in his tracks. He gave her a look of contempt and turned away, lifting a leg and letting rip a huge raspberry of a fart as he did so.

"Don't tear it I'll take the piece!" said a cultured voice.

Mary looked round and burst out laughing.

"Twist!" she chortled as George disappeared somewhere into the shadows.

The man started laughing too, though he had no idea what he had just said. He once heard someone say it in a rough pub when a similarly large audible fart had been fired off. Judging by the merriment that had ensued, he guessed it was very crude. He had no idea what Mary's reply meant either.

"Was that scoundrel trying to rob you my dear?" asked the gent, putting a hand round Mary's shoulders in protective mode.

"In a manner a speakin'." She shrugged his arm off. "But don't get no funny ideas. I ain' workin' ta night see. Got summin' a do urgent."

She started to move away.

"Oh quite so, quite so. I am in a hurry myself. Even if you had been working I have no time. Shame. I have a particular liking for girls with red hair. And you being such a pretty little thing, if I had the time I would have offered you a sovereign, two with the comfort of a room."

The most Mary had ever earned from a client was the half-sovereign with the silk handkerchief tip that the pathetic little man who couldn't penetrate her, had given her recently. She only got a fraction of that from the working classes which made up most of her clientele these days, and George paid her even less. He had the temerity to demand a regular client's discount. At least it was over with quickly enough with him. She calculated George worked out around a ha'penny a thrust.

Shov 'a'penny! There's a joke right enuff. But this ain' no bleedin' game. On the game - there's anuvver joke. Fank Christ I ain' got a do this no more.

She snorted to herself with disgust as she peered into the darkness.

You're there somewhere ain't ya George, gawpin' at me. Nashey were right about you wern 'e.

She wanted to get rid of the gent and be on her way. She would make him a ridiculous offer which he would refuse and they would go their respective ways.

"Yeah a cryin' shame, and there's the troof. Still, even if you 'ad time, it'd 'av to be five sovereigns. There ain' no fairer than me on the street these days is there, an' yer got a make it werf me while see, makin' me late for me impor'ant meetin'. I ain' doin' it for no less."

He winked at her.

"Very well, if you have a room?"

Mary hid her amazement, simply nodding in agreement.

"Alright my dear come along, you will be comfortable."

She looked him over. The gold watch and massive gold chain he carried showed her that he would indeed have the five sovereigns on him. He was a genuine gent alright. She felt confident she had nothing to worry about with such a man but she looked down to make sure he wasn't carrying a doctor's bag. She couldn't be too careful. He carried just a small parcel with a strap around it. It would take some unravelling.

'ardly 'andy place to keep yer knife. One move fer it and I'd 'av me own knife out quick as yer like. 'e don't look like no Jew-boy neiver. An' any'ow, ol' Jack likes it on the street dun 'e.

She was safe enough. She took him by the arm and led him back to Dorset Street. The arch and passage into Miller's Court was so narrow that only one person could walk down it at a time. He followed her down it gingerly in the pitch darkness. She unlocked her door, lit a candle and threw her hat on the bed.

"I weren't coddin' about 'aving somewhere a get to yer know. Reach me that gold watch a yours."

The man did as he was told. She brought the candle to it. It was half past one.

"I got a be gone be two. I can't be late see. Yer only got jus' shy ov 'alf 'our, thas all," she said, nodding for him to look at the watch face.

"That's longer than I normally get my dear. May I ask your name?"

"Mary Kelly. You should be honoured yer know, you're me last ever customer."

The man smiled, nodded and took off his Derby hat.

CHAPTER 25:

"Modern society is more promptly awakened to a sense on duty by the knife of a murderer than by the pens of many earnest writers."

The Lancet

After a short, fitful night's sleep, Nash walked round to see Sookey. There was no answer to his knock. Rose Martin was cleaning her step. She got up and walked over to him.

"She's not in Nashey. She left yesty and ain' come back. She's at the 'all. She left me a note. Pushed it under me door, she did. Yer wanna come in. Stan's in. 'ave a nice cuppa River Lea?"

Nash was taken aback. Rose didn't speak like this to her best friends, let alone him. She had made it clear on the increasingly frequent occasions that their paths crossed that she did not like him, disapproved of Sookey's friendship with him and didn't like the influence he had over her easily led neighbour, for whom she had come to have a grudging respect. Nash was puzzled. It wasn't just that she was being friendly and speaking gently. There was a certain tone to her voice; a certain expression in her face.

It's like she were talkin' ta some lit'le chavvie or summin', tryin' a keep 'im easy. Rum, and there's the troof.

He decided to give a brief smile and a nod.

"Nah, that's alright gell. I gotta get down the market meself. Maybe I'll knock into 'er down there."

As he started to turn away, Rose called after him.

"Yeah, yer will most likely. Gawd bless yer boy."

Nash walked away perplexed. 'Gawd bless yer boy'?

He didn't want Mary to be the first person he saw today. He wanted to know what happened yesterday, if anything, before he spoke to her. It was clear that if the Ripper had just killed again, he couldn't do anything but keep his thoughts to himself about the advantages of having a maniac on the loose, killing women. He would have to agree with whatever she said and say he was sorry about their falling out. When the time was right he would joke with her.

"'ere, you wait till I tell your new employer what yer called me. She'll be givin' yer the boot fer sure."

And she would be sure to pay him back with interest.

"I've already told 'er, don't you worry. I'll call yer more than that next time an' all, and give yer anuvver facer in ta the bargain."

He was smiling to himself as he made his way to Will's. He would drop his share off, see if Tom had been to see him and ask if anything untoward had happened yesterday.

"NasheyAY!"

It was old Bert Walker. He lived in the same tenement as Khan. He ran up to Nashey, breathless.

"It's your Sookey, Nashey!"

Nash had got as far as answering, "'ere, she ain't my Sook.." when he saw the pain in Bert's eyes.

That were it! Pain. It were pain that 'ad bin in Rose's eyes, only worse, much worse.

"She's jus' collapsed down the Lane," puffed Bert.

Nash feigned indifference.

"Daft mare's been workin' too 'ard by the sound ov it. Forgot'en to eat I spose, then she puts 'er stays on under 'er Sunday best an' before she knows what she's about she's tastin' the cobbles."

Bert simply blinked.

"Ain't yer gonna see to 'er, poor lit'le cow?"

Nash pulled a face.

"They would a picked 'er up by now wouldn't they. She's probably made a bob or two an' all, people finkin' she's some ol' leppy!"

Bert didn't appreciate Nash's attempt at humour, and simply looked at him silently in consternation. Nash felt awkward, and thought he better say something more.

"I'm goin' that way any'ow. I'll see she's alright."

Bert nodded and put a hand up as a gesture of leaving.

"Gawd bless yer lad."

Nash made his way towards Petticoat Lane market, marching quicker than he would have liked to admit.

Everyone's blessin' me today. Wos a mat'er wiv 'em all. They been to bleedin' church or summin'? Ol' rev Barnett mus' 'ave bribed 'em ta come to 'is Sundee sermon at St Jude's.

⌒ ◆ ⌒

At the same time Nash had been kicking his heels in Liverpool, Sookey was spending her Saturday giving her home a thorough sorting out. She took down from the wall her framed motto 'East West Home's Best' and replaced it with another, 'Home is the best where all is best'. Coal was collected from its sack and put in the fireplace, ready for lighting; wood likewise. Having dangled some sticky foul-smelling paper traps to kill bed bugs, Sookey then got out her lime and whitewash brushes and carbolic soap to lime-wash her bedroom with the aid of Klenzit Kleener. Next, boot blackening was on the agenda, followed by washing. She didn't want to go to the wash-house; others would be there. Every bit of clothing, bar what she stood up in, plus her only bed sheet, were hand-washed in cold water then hand-wrung till her weak wrists ached.

It was November; time the Christmas bunting came out. Sookey hung up the two Chinese coloured paper lanterns she had brought from her old life, and set about making others with the materials she had. After all, they were only paper and wire. But the job proved too difficult and she wasn't in the mood to stop and work out what she was doing wrong. She turned her attention to her front step. It was still in reasonable condition from when she and Rose had cleaned it for the visit of her friends, but she cleaned it again. Rose stepped outside to bash a filthy mat against her wall but as soon as Sookey heard her neighbour's door creaking open, she darted back inside.

It was now late enough for her to be sure nobody from Toynbee Hall would make an appearance to discuss the Guild of Handicrafts in her art gallery. Having walked dark, deserted streets to Angel Alley, she completely rearranged her whole art exhibition. Sookey had originally liked the new piece that her friend Walter had sent her from France. It was interesting; full of thought-provoking power. It had pride of place in the gallery. But there was something distasteful about the prone female form which grabbed your eye. She took the picture down and relegated it to the floor of the back room, facing the wall. Her own work had been neglected of late, so a long session of candlelit sketching was entered into before cramp got into a malnourished knuckle. She returned home.

Retrieving the wallpapering materials, Sookey made a paste which was hopeless, but carried on with grim determination. She measured and cut with the precision of an artist but her control of the paper was as poor as her paste. The early hours were spent trying to put up a single piece before Sookey gave up and used the paste to hold together more Christmas bunting. She put her old green felt Father Christmas, another relic from another life, on the table as the glow of dawn took over from her dying candles.

Toynbee Hall had religious services first thing Sunday morning. Sookey had turned her back on God; the slums had seen to that. She went to Petticoat Lane market, careful to avoid people she knew.

❧ ◆ ☙

It was easy to spot her. A crowd had gathered around but was just starting to drift away as she showed signs of recovery. She got to her feet just as Nash arrived. He was about to launch into a typical Nashey greeting in front of others in such circumstances.

What the bleedin' 'ell you been up to? Got any gelt from people finking you're a leppy? 'ope you didn't land in no pure. You'll 'ave to spend it all on soap gell!

But one look at her face and he could see such humour was out of the question. It wasn't the embarrassed, flushed face of someone with too tight a stays. She looked terrible and was trembling. It looked like she hadn't slept for a week, her normally beautiful black glistening hair was dull, matted and twisted, and there was no trace of her famous, infamous doll-like make-up. She was staring at the people around her wildly.

"Sookey?" said Nash enquiringly.

Sookey swivelled her head and looked at him, blankly for a moment before focussing.

"Nashey."

She stumbled into him, her face plummeting into his chest, his arms automatically enfolding her.

"Come on, let's get yer 'ome and get some grub inside yer gell."

She pulled away from him a couple of inches and gazed into his eyes. There was no pain there at all. Where had he been? He didn't know.

"Yes Nashey, get me home."

They walked entwined, staggering a little like partners in a three-legged race. They didn't say a word. They were both remembering a similar walk they had shared a month ago, only it was Nash's turn to support Sookey this time.

As they appeared at Sookey's doorstep, Rose gave them the shortest, saddest of smiles before retreating into her home. They stepped through the door and into Sookey's living room. Nash looked around in shock. The place was a shambles, crammed with all sorts, and smelt much damper than usual. He found it difficult to manoeuvre her through the sea of washing, peeling wallpaper and bunting, so picked her up in his arms and carried her through to her bedroom. He had never been in any part of her house other than her front room. The bedroom was as shocking in the opposite way to the living room. It was empty save an incongruously expensive looking brass bedstead and mattress. Evidence of the carbolic spring-clean was still in the air. Nash laid her gently on the bed. He took his huge coat off and put it over her. Not knowing that the pockets were bulging with post office cash, she was amazed at the great weight of it.

"I'll go an' get yer some grub," he said quietly, with a reassuring smile.

As he started to lean back up and away from her, she grabbed his shirt collar and stared up at him with tears welling up in her eyes. She hadn't cried since she heard the news but she was going to now.

"Suffer me to tell you. It is well it is me. It doesn't command itself to reason. Our dearest friend Mary. She is murdered!"

She only just got the terrible last word out before she started sobbing uncontrollably. Nash lowered himself onto the bed, staring incredulously at her before looking away. He started to shake. The trembling fingers of his right hand roamed aimlessly across his face. Sookey regarded Nash. The effect of her words had been even greater than she could have imagined. He was staring into space like a madman. She sat up, placed her head over his right shoulder and held him. He felt her convulsions, the liquid from her eyes and nose making the back of his shirt wet, as she heaved for breath between the sobs. It was the natural reaction to great loss. He just stared; the natural reaction to a different, equally powerful emotion.

∾ ◆ ∾

The two of them now laid together, heads sideways on the mattress, facing each other, a few inches apart. She had just finished telling him everything she had heard; the facts, the conjecture, the rumours. Nash had gone into denial. It must have been the boyfriend. He would go round there and kill the little bastard. Sookey shook her head sadly. No, it was the fiend. She couldn't bring herself to say the name that everyone called him by these days. It had been confirmed by the police. The wounds were rumoured to be horrific.

They started to reminisce about their dear friend, talking over all the things they had shared together. Sookey laughed and cried in equal measure. Nash couldn't cry; couldn't laugh.

Sookey was just coming to the end of another bout of sniffling laughter when she looked into Nash's eyes with the deepest of stares and he reciprocated. She leaned across and took him in her arms, hugging him with all her might. It was the first time Nash could remember ever being hugged. He hugged back. They stayed in that position for some time. Sookey felt the crying before she heard it. Nash's body started to rock with convulsions and then the tears poured out in a torrent of guttural sound. Sookey didn't react. She stayed just hugging him, feeling it would be too personal to share the moment any more completely with him.

When he had finished she brought her head back in front of his, looking at the miserable, puffy red face in front of her. She smiled the kindest of serene smiles at him and gazed at every little nook and cranny of his face for a full minute before lowering her lips to his.

His coarse four days of beard growth rubbed painfully into her chin. The pain thrilled her. She wanted it. Pain was emotion. A mental image of her husband's regime flashed into her head. He would always shave. Not for her benefit, but for his. He didn't want the servants sniggering at her flaky chin. But the present wasn't for thinking about other people; this was just two frightened people helping each other along the path. She felt a heady mix of embarrassment, nervousness and expectation. Her heart was seemingly pounding out of her chest. Was she about to faint again? She didn't care.

They kissed gently, uncertainly, flinching slightly as they butted noses whilst attempting a minor change of position. She had her right palm resting on his huge torso. Her thumb brushed against a button and without thinking she slipped it open, tucking her hand beneath his shirt. She felt thick coarse chest hair. A pang of shock at her own brazenness flashed through her, so she freed herself from the embrace. She stared up at the big face and saw he felt as awkward as she did, which was strangely reassuring.

Nash couldn't hold her stare for more than a second, looking to the side for a moment before returning to her. He repeated the gesture. She reached up and held his chin firm so he had to hold his gaze at her. Her fingers drifted away as she stretched her neck up and their mouths came back together a little too hard. There was a clink of teeth, and they pulled away from each for a moment in shock, sharing a chuckle of embarrassment before returning hesitantly to the matter at hand.

He suddenly felt intimidated for the first time in his life. Sookey had achieved something nobody, not the toughest of men, had ever managed, and this with the gentlest of weapons; a loving smile burning into him. This wasn't as he had heard about such things, when in his youth it had been the most popular topic of conversation among the boys in the gang. And it wasn't the impression he had got when nodding sagely at his fellow men in the pub, talking about 'ow's yer farver'. The thirty year old Nash's only previous sexual experience, with anyone else at least, had been back on his sixteenth birthday, with a dollymop. The quasi-prostitute had been paid for by a kidsman, in a moment of rare generosity in appreciation of his young charge's pickpocketing successes. The dollymop experience had been an empty one, young Nash had chosen not to repeat. He had been popular enough with the local girls, and had embarked upon the fumblings of a testosterone-driven male adolescent, but they hadn't gone well. He came to decide that it would be safer not to pursue the opposite sex in future. He had only once been tempted to change his mind, but had hesitated to make his feelings known, losing the girl to another; and it was against his code of behaviour to try and woo her away from this rival, though he was confident he could have.

Nash and Sookey now lay there, on a bare mattress, beneath his heavily weighed down coat, both of them fully clothed, right down to his huge boots. They kissed and cuddled; caressed and hugged. They stayed like that for some time before Sookey motioned with a tug of his shirt, for him to take his clothes off. She nodded at him, and started to unbutton herself. Not a word was spoken.

Nash got to his feet and felt a mix of panic and embarrassment as he hobbled around the room trying to unburden himself of his boots, which were imprisoning his trousers. He needn't have been so self-conscious, as Sookey had her head buried under the coat. He had to cede to the strength of his laces, his fingers scrambling dementedly at the things to let him free. He finally managed it and ducked quickly under the cover of the overcoat.

All Sookey's sexual experiences had taken place in the dark, under bed covers, under bed clothes. A short burst of staccato movements and it had been over. The man had achieved his release; the purpose achieved.

Ten years married, Sookey knew very little. Her mother had never told her a thing. The disastrous, painful in every sense of the word, wedding night had been a voyage into the complete unknown. There had been the giggling conversations with her fellow girls at school, but no real, accurate information had been gleaned, and the subject had certainly never been broached in the polite circles of her adulthood.

There had been a much more recent conversation about sex with someone who had experienced a lot of it, but Sookey forced this memory from her mind, kissing

Nash reassuringly as he rejoined her. Their union was that of two teenage virgins. A lack of expertise compensated for by desire, longing and a fondness for investigation. She had guided him to feel her clitoris, but his huge rough fingers lacked the desired knowledge and finesse. After much awkwardness they found a rhythm, only for him to accidentally slip out of her suddenly. His embarrassment and resultant fumbling attempt to re-enter led to a slight softening of his erection until she kissed him passionately and whispered something loving in his ear. His confidence and hardness returned.

When they had finished, she still awaited her first orgasm, but she was far from disappointed. She had not reached the mountain peak but she had at least reached the foothills, rather than the sea-level of her marriage. It had been splendid indeed. As was he; as were they.

CHAPTER 26:

"Since the recent calamity in the east of London, several benevolent persons have come forwards to provide night shelters for the outcast men and women."
Dr Taylor to the Sanitary Committee of Mile End district

Emotions had run high. It had been the most emotional day of her life. Nashey's too, she suspected. But it was another day and Sookey wasn't sure what her relationship now was with him.

She was desperate to see him again; to laugh and cry with him; tell him more things about herself; hear more about him. Lay with him again. But they hadn't made finite arrangements to meet again. They had both hesitated at their moment of parting and left things unsaid. They would no doubt bump into each other again soon enough. It had been easier that way at the time. They had both been drained, exhausted. A moment of awkwardness was easier to deal with than a moment of revelation.

Should she go to visit him? Wait for him to visit her? Did she need an excuse to pay her respects? There were the funeral arrangements? No sooner had Sookey thought this than she was horrified by herself.

I want excuse to visit Nashey and immediately think of poor Mary's funeral as a tool by which to do it. What sort of a woman am I to see?

Mary had always paid the first penny she had earned every week into her funeral club. If it was a choice between the funeral club and a pennyworth of food to keep fed, she went hungry. There was only one thing that scared the people of the slums more than the workhouse, and that was having a pauper's funeral. There was never to be a pauper's funeral for Mary Kelly.

Sookey had liaised with the necessary people and overseen the arrangements.

Polished elm and oak coffin with metal mounts and a brass plate:

'Marie Jeanette Kelly, died 9th Nov., 1888, aged 25 years'

Four pallbearers (she hoped Nashey wouldn't mind not being asked; she felt it would be disrespectful to Joe Barnett); coffin to be carried in an open carriage drawn by two horses with two coaches to follow from Shoreditch mortuary to Leystonstone Roman Catholic cemetery.

She needed to walk round to see Nash, amongst others, to let him know what was happening. Sookey decided she would visit others first, and leave Nashey till last; it was more appropriate.

❦

Nash had just got back from Bloomsbury, where he had fenced the stamps. Nobody in the East End could handle such high value, not to mention high profile goods. The robbery would normally have made the local newspaper; maybe even a small column in one of the nationals. But taking place as it did at the same time as another Ripper murder, it was big national news.

The police were now an even greater laughing stock than they had already been. How could a gang have ransacked a post office not much more than a stone's throw from where yet another horrible murder was taking place, and the hordes of police in the area had not seen a thing? PC Crisp had seen a black man acting suspiciously with a young pretty prostitute, though not the one killed admittedly. Perhaps the killer wasn't a Jew after all. A black man was an obvious alternative. An inaccurate description of Khan was added to the long list of Ripper suspects.

Sir Charles Warren had finally been forced to resign from his post of Commissioner of Police; an abject failure. Nash knew he had to be very careful because all known fences would be under heavy scrutiny from the police, who did not take kindly to being made to look fools. If they couldn't catch the Ripper, they would at least nab the post office robbers.

There were receivers such as certain shopkeepers, kidsmen, pub-keepers, lodging house-keepers, whom Nash knew, but he suspected that they tended to hunt with the hounds and run with the hare; they might be informers when it suited them. And turning in the post office gang to a very grateful police force would certainly suit them. Such men dealt with dangerous men like Nash on a regular basis so were careful not to openly help the law, but the police menaced them as well, so they had to play one off against the other the best way they could. Nash knew he could not trust any of them. And the reward being offered was another reason for a normally trustworthy type to turn informer. The only fence he trusted enough was his old partner-in-crime Taff Hughes. He had been a kidsman in Whitechapel but the high number of police in the area these days had sent him off to a new lair in Bloomsbury.

Nash had once saved Taff's life when they were young, toshing for anything of value they could find in and around the sewers that fed into the Thames. Taff had been overcome by gas, an occupational hazard, which was the reason toshing was always done with a mate. He had been lying head down in watery human detritus with a gang of huge rats starting to nibble at him when Nash had found him. He might have drowned if he had been lucky. Nash had hauled him out and back to the safety of the river. Choking from the fumes and stench, exhausted from the monumental task of dragging someone almost as big as he was through ankle deep detritus and water by the back of their shirt, Nash had collapsed with his load into the river, ensuring he kept his friend's face up, out of the water. On his knees and gasping for air himself, he had then slapped and splashed the boy until he had come round. Taff had always been suitably grateful. He wouldn't turn his old mate in if he turned out to be Jack the Ripper himself.

Taff had fallen awkwardly when he had passed out, and the wound sustained had got infected, no doubt from the filth; the rats' nibbling and Nash's admittedly much-needed dragging, probably hadn't helped. Taff had eventually had a leg off in the London Hospital in Whitechapel.

This was the second most feared building in the vicinity. Only the shadow of the workhouse brought more anguish. Taff had entered the hospital not expecting to come out, so it was with relative relief that he escaped its dreaded walls with no more than a leg lost.

Nash arrived at the kidsman's new abode in Bloomsbury to find Taff's disability still didn't stop him from being a nasty bit of work. A couple of his young thieves had just returned home empty-handed, so Taff had removed the strap that held on his wooden leg and was flogging them mercilessly with the strip of leather. Taff was very pleased to see Nash, though not half as much as the young lads. They made them themselves scarce as the two old partners talked about times old and new.

Back in his own lair now, Nash was thinking of Sookey. He was confused. He had always avoided this sort of thing for precisely this reason. It made strong men weak; decisive men dither. People could get to him though Sookey. Imagine if Shanks found out; being more than just friends with Sookey was just the sort of thing the wrong un might try to exploit. But Nash couldn't help but give an ironic snort. Had it not been Shanks who had first thrust them together? Nash found it difficult to believe that any of this could have happened but for that attack on Sookey.

His normal thought processes would then have taken him back to Shanks having had Sookey attacked, but they didn't on this occasion.

Who would have thought it; him and a woman like Sookey of all people. He couldn't wait to see her again; but what could a woman like her think of a villain like him? They had both been so upset and one thing had led to another. But that was then. The moment had passed. She would probably be ashamed of him now, not to mention herself. What was he supposed to do?

He had a full wash down in the yard and then started to tidy his room up. He remembered his mother, hands on hips in astonishment, once seeing him wash behind his ears for the first time, when he was about to go on his first monkey parade.

"Gawd 'elp us, I fought yer were growin' cabbages back there. I spose there's a first time for everyfin'!"

Nash didn't own any cleaning implements save an ash-pan and brush for the fire. He was making do with this for all jobs, when he saw Doris peering at him with that look of superiority and inscrutability that only cats can summon.

"Christ, let's go and see 'er and get it over wiv."

Nash grabbed the cat by its scruff and was on his way.

Nash arrived at Sookey's to find there was no answer. He thought he would knock at Rose's to ask her if she knew where Sookey was, but before he did so decided to shove the cat out of sight into one of his extra large coat pockets. Rose was telling him that Sookey was doing the rounds about the funeral and was probably on her way to see him at his place, when a little white head popped out of his pocket and miaowed.

A few minutes later, Nash and Sookey bumped into each other en-route. Neither had the confidence to say they were just on their way to see the other. Nash thrust the cat at Sookey as an ice-breaker. It had the desired effect, and after a few minutes of small talk, they were laughing with each other and had fallen into step, heading for Nash's.

They spent the rest of the day together, with Sookey helping him finish his cleaning job, before they went to Sookey's for Nash to rescue Sookey's attempt at wallpapering. By the end of the day it was clear to them both that they were 'walking out' together. The confection of tears and reminiscences were still there, but they now realised that they were an acceptable, natural part of their relationship, not the foundations of it.

⌒ ◆ ⌒

Nash had lied to Sookey but he could not tell her the truth. He was haunted by that look on Mary's face, the last time he saw her; the look of contempt and disgust when he had told her why the Ripper's killings were a good thing for the common cause. He could not face that expression being etched across Sookey's features, as it surely would if he ever told her the truth. He had invented a concoction of truth, half truths and lies.

Nash had told Sookey that he knew where the Ripper stayed when he committed his crimes. He had found the body of poor Catherine Eddowes, and had fled for his life in fear of being thought the Ripper. As he fled he had seen a gent on the streets, carrying a doctor's bag. He had not thought anything of it at the time. Horrified by his grisly finding, and concerned that some unknown eye-witness might have seen him in the vicinity of the murder and given the police a description, he had made it his mission to find the killer himself.

He was only one man but he was in a better position to do so than the hordes of West End crushers that witless Warren had brought into Whitechapel. What did they know of the East End? And the police were despised by local people. Nash, on the other hand, had been able to glean far more information from the witnesses than Inspector Abberline's detectives had managed. The Jew with his horse and cart, who had almost fallen over the killer seconds after he had murdered Liz Stride, had described the man Nash had seen. The description fitted the gent he had seen perfectly. Unlike the police, he knew what his quarry looked like and had been face to face with Jack the Ripper.

It had been clear to Nash that the killer had to have a bolt-hole in the vicinity of the murders. A killer covered in blood could not roam the streets of the most overcrowded neighbourhood, of the most densely populated city in the world, undetected.

"'member when I first come ta see yer in that art place? It wernt ta get me black man's pinch seen to. It were to find out from yer about the blood see. I couldn't see as how he could get away wiv it, wot with the streets now crawlin' with crushers. I had a mooch about all the killin' places and worked it out as he had to have a bolt-hole somewhere between Middlesex Street and Whitechapel Road or thereabouts. But Whitechapel Road's too big and well lighted, and the courts is overcrowded with people sleeping rough, so he'd never be able to come and go unnoticed. So I went to see all the landlords in the area. Sumfin' ol' Abberline's boys didn't fink ov I wager. I had a bit of luck. Mary's landlord.." He stopped, looked down and frowned for a moment at the mention of her name. "He tells me about a gent oo's rented a room off him these past two munff since. I arst him what he looks like and it turns out he's the spittin' image of my man. I gets a spare key off him by givin' him a bit a bunts; that's summin' else I can do wot the crushers can't, see. They expect people to jus' tell 'em. Anyhow, I gets the key and lets meself in. That's when I finds the clues. The police didn't have a clue in more ways as one."

Sookey had listened in shocked silence until now, but she couldn't wait any longer to ask the obvious question.

"But Nashey, why didn't you tell the police of your findings?"

"I did tells 'em", said Nash convincingly; he had rehearsed thoroughly. "But I had to be careful see. I couldn't say about findin' poor Cath Eddowes could I? Trouble were, they was gettin' too much help in some ways. One of 'em told me they got hundreds of clues from hundreds a people every day. It all had to be checked. My help was just in wiv everyfin' else see. And why should they take much account ov a cove like me? Don't spose they even checked the place in Middlesex Street neiver. Couldn't a dun."

Nash went on to explain about the clues he had found in the bolt-hole; the drugs, Florrie, Michael, James, 'catch whom you MAY', 'just shy of halfway to naming Jack', 'you could build a house of it'. His version of events did not include watching the killer chalk on a wall, so he omitted the 'Juwes' clue. He continued that he had Khan and the brothers keeping watch over the place as much as they could. But it had turned out that the killer only used the place after his crimes, not before, and the devil had slipped into the bolt-hole in the early hours after Mary had died (another pause), when Nash's men hadn't been on duty.

He then gave her a factually correct account of his wild goose chase up to Liverpool. She asked him how he knew the man lived in Liverpool, and he explained how on one occasion Shanks had followed him to Euston Station. Sookey had then asked how Shanks had come to know this man.

Nash remembered his mother scolding him on more than one occasion when he had been caught out in an obvious lie. "Liars (clip), need (clip), good (clip), memories (clip) yer lyin' (clip) lit'le (clip) sod (clip)." She was right.

He diverted the question by telling Sookey how he had found out that Shanks had lied to him about the train to Liverpool. He then went off at a tangent telling her more of the story behind her attack by the three men. He was relieved when she didn't repeat her earlier question.

CHAPTER 27:

"The riots of 1886 brought in £78,000 and a People's Palace; it remains to be seen how much these murders may prove worth to the East End."

George Bernard Shaw

In the weeks after Mary's death, Nash suffered from depression. He would wake up in the early hours. There was none of the usual grogginess of awakening. As soon as consciousness returned, he was wide awake. His sleep-starved mind collapsed into unconsciousness readily enough every evening, but his demons woke him as soon as they could. He was putting this sleeplessness to good effect. He had come to realise that the Ripper always struck at weekends nowadays. The last five murders had all been on a Friday or Saturday night. Nash knew it was probably the only time a working Liverpool gent could get away to London. He now had men keeping watch on Middlesex Street twenty four hours a day, whilst he spent every Friday and Saturday laying in wait at Euston station. When the trains stopped running he roamed the streets suitably armed, ready to end the reign of Jack The Ripper.

Nash's mind started to try to heal itself by transference of blame. He could not stop thinking about Mary, and the part Shanks had played in her death. As far as he was now concerned, she would be alive today if Shanks had been straight with everyone. Nash became obsessed with thoughts of Shanks' guilt rather than his own.

He remembered an incident from their youth. There had been a fight in North Greenwich with some South London lads who had come across the water. They claimed North Greenwich was their territory because they were Deptford boys and anything with the word Greenwich in it belonged to them, even if it was north of the river. And besides, their New Cross football team played their home games in North Greenwich. Nash had not been there, having been otherwise engaged on some pickpocket work for a kidsman. But many of his gang had, and been given a beating due to being badly outnumbered. A bloody Will had told Nash of the taunts they had endured as they had to 'scarper with our tails between our legs".

Nash had returned to the scene of the crime with numbers and serious weaponry. The Deptford boys were nowhere to be seen. He decided that if they were going to invade his side of the river, he would do likewise. Nash and his gang didn't know South London at all. They stumbled through Rotherhithe and Bermondsey, eventually finding their way to Deptford, and got plenty of looks from surly young individuals, but their gang prey was nowhere to be seen.

They decided to try to set fire to one of the platforms on New Cross Station. That would warn South London boys not to set foot north of the river. Shanks was the one member of the gang not there, Nash having made a point not to take him along. Although the police had been quick to descend upon them, all bar the none-too-fleet of foot Nash and little Harry had escaped. Fortunately for the two held in custody they had been caught before having a chance to inflict any real damage, otherwise it would have been off to prison for committing the cardinal sin of harming property. They were up before 'the beak', successfully pleading for mercy thanks to a masterful performance by Harry, the big-eyed little innocent of the gang, when in walked Shanks. He told the magistrate that he was a member of the gang and had been at the station but had been lucky enough to escape. He admitted to a crime he didn't commit to gain what he thought would be greater respect. It had the opposite effect of course. He had no idea. He was a wrong un.

If he could admit to something he didn't even do, what might he say if the police ever got hold of him about anything he might be up to at any given point in his petty criminal life? A wrong un like him would crack in an instant; tell them everything about the post office robbery. And then there was the little matter of the attack on poor Sookey. She could be lying in the next grave to Mary. He was going to have to do something about Shanks.

꒰ ◆ ꒱

There was an agreement between all who worked on the Aldgate robbery that they would lie low till after Christmas. Nash was therefore surprised when he got a visit from Shanks. He had another pull. This made Aldgate small in comparison. It was easy work too. No real skill was involved, no security to overcome and no risk of capture. Nash snorted.

"There's always risk."

But Shanks continued undeterred. It was such a delicate matter that nobody else could be in on it. The utmost secrecy had to be maintained. It was going to be just the two of them. It was a job way out in the sticks.

Nash had no intention of ever working with the wrong un sitting at his table ever again. It was all he could do to stop himself ploughing a huge fist into the man's face where he sat. No, on second thoughts, it would have to wait till he stood up; punching someone when they were sitting down is the sort of thing Shanks would do. But Nash held himself in check and let the man talk. Curiosity had got the better of him. And besides, he might find something out to his advantage.

Shanks told him it was to be arson. Set fire to something big in such a way that the whole lot went up. But his employers were powerful, important men. They stood to gain a great deal but they couldn't afford any mistakes, and the men who did the job had to be able to disappear into the night, never to be seen or heard of again. That's why they were paying such big money for such a simple job. On being told what he would be paid, Nash could not help but show startled enthusiasm. He knew Shanks would be keeping a high percentage of the money being paid for himself, so the large amount being offered to Nash showed what a big job it was.

"Ware'ouse is it?

Shanks gave him a snivelling clerk's smile.

"In a manner a speakin'."

"Insurance? 'ave to be a bleedin' ware'ouse to be worf the sort a money you're talkin' about. Woss it got in it any'ow?"

"Never you mind."

"When and where?"

Shanks looked uncomfortable.

"I can tell yer the when this time, but I ain' telling yer the where till we get there on the night."

"Again! After last time!"

Nash threw his chair back violently, rushed round the table, grabbed Shanks by the throat and started to squeeze. Shanks started to gurgle and change colour, before he managed to blurt out one urgent sentence. It was barely decipherable.

"Crystal Palace! We burns down the Crystal Palace! Debt trouble!"

This brought Nash out of his near trance and back to his senses. He released Shanks immediately, and stared wildly into space as the half strangled man dropped to his knees, wheezing and coughing as he grabbed at his throat. Nash stomped to the door, flung it open, grabbed the coughing man up by his coat collar and flung him out the door.

"Gall on fuck orf oud of it. Come round 'ere again, I'll top yer!"

When he had calmed down sufficiently to think straight, Nash thought about Shanks' proposal. Nash sifted the information through his mind that Khan had given him after he had followed Shanks in the lead up to the Aldgate job. When he had given Khan the job, it had been with the intention of him digging up a clue to who the inside man was in the post office who must have fed Shanks the information. Nash had told Khan that if Shanks met up with anyone who looked a bit different in any way from the usual low ranks Shanks fraternised with; a clerk, a gent, anyone like that, he should follow the clerk rather than Shanks after they go their separate ways.

Khan had followed such a man. He was a middling sort. Not a gent but prosperous enough; a senior clerk perhaps.

After the meeting, the middling man took precautions against being followed, getting a cab before walking for a while, eventually being picked up in a growler by a gent. The two of them rode around in a circle, before the middling man alighted.

Khan had used his initiative for once, deciding to follow the gent in the cab, which Nash was annoyed with at the time. It had cost Nash a lot of money. Khan was in a cab himself of course, and had followed the gent for miles, south of the river.

Ended up in the back of beyond in some Gawd forsaken place 'e did. What were it called? Catford, that were it. Least the soppy sod got 'old ov the cove's address.

Nash had taken the information gleaned from Khan to a private enquiry agent, who had managed to find out some details of the man who lived in Catford. There could have been a legitimate reason why Shanks and a south London gent had a mutual middling acquaintance, but Catford was only a stone's throw from Sydenham, where the Crystal Palace was located. Co-in-cid-ence? Nash didn't think so.

⌒ ◆ ⌒

All the words whose spelling he wasn't sure about had been written down on a piece of paper in random order. Nash was confident he knew how to spell his own words but he was borrowing some from Sookey's vocabulary, so asked her to check them. 'Sincerely' and 'blackguard' had been wrong. He could understand sincerely being spelt as it was but blackguard?

Sookey was curious as to what he was up to, so was quick to tell him of the sir and sincerely rule. Is it to someone of your acquaintance sir? He tapped her gently on the nose and said, 'nose ache'. She remembered the scene when Nashey had tapped Mary in a similar fashion. Sookey lowered her head sadly. Nash mistook this for her being a little 'vexed' as she would put it, at not being told what he was up to.

Dear Mr Burgess

I am writing to tell you of our mutual friend, Mr Niven MacDonald, what you might or might not no as Shanks.

319

He telled me of your little plot to burn down the Crystal Palace. He is telling it all over the shop. All that money. He is giddy with it, and that is the truth. To the purpose, I trust you will make haste to wrecktify this situation by ending your interest in this scheme and this blackguard, lest I be forced to tell my good friend P.C. William Thick. I am sure he would be most vexed and his intelligence grow apace. It is well you restrain Shanks or your days will be numbered. I tell you plainly, your secret is safe with me if you forsake Shanks.

Yours Sincerely

Mr Alexander Esq.

Nash did not like what he had done. It was a conniving sort of thing to do. Writing a letter just to get one over on someone was the sort of thing Shanks would do if he could write. Nash doubted the letter would ever be read by anyone other than a manservant in any case, and he would throw it away thinking it to be a hoax, not wishing to burden his master with it.

Nash had sent the letter primarily because writing it had made him feel better, just as he had to admit to himself the near-strangulation of Shanks had too. It was the pleasure he had felt with his hands round Shanks' neck that had so horrified him.

After he had told Sookey of the violence he had used on Shanks, he had never seen her so angry.

"Have you not seen enough!" she shrieked at him.

In her anger she had tried to insist he should not use violence, but he reminded of her the time he had saved her from three villains.

Nash considered the letter as a piece of non-violent mischief against Shanks. The wrong un would be furious when he found out from his employers that he was no longer required for the Crystal Palace pull. And the best of it was that he would know who was responsible for doing him down, but wouldn't have the nerve to do anything about it. Nash half hoped that he would. It would give him the excuse to deal with Shanks once and for all. Either way, he had promised himself that he would put the wrong un out of everyone's misery when the time was right. He had not forgotten what Shanks was responsible for.

The following day Shanks was found dead, with his throat cut in a court off Little Somerset Street.

Nash felt almost nothing. No shock, no pleasure, no remorse, just a pang of concern. Could Shanks have told his employers who he was planning to do the job with? Nash doubted he would have told them. They wouldn't have wanted to know. The least they knew the better. And Nash had rejected the job. No, he couldn't see Shanks confirming who his accomplice would be at least until it was certain. But might they have got it out of him before they killed him? Nash made enquiries about the death. Shanks had left the Hoop and Grapes pub in Aldgate High Street only minutes before his body was found. With the number of police around these days, killers on the street had to be quick. Nash felt he was safe, but as a temporary precaution took to wearing his peak-blinder cap and carrying his most lethal weapons at all times. If any paid assassins followed him into a dark court, they were going to earn their money.

As concern for his safety receded, it was replaced by a darker malaise. With the death of Shanks, came the end of Nash's subconscious transference; there was nobody else he could blame now.

⤙ ◆ ⤚

When a prostitute was strangled in Clarke's Yard, High Street, Poplar, there was no abdominal mutilation so cries of it being the Ripper were muted amongst the newspapers, though Nash's interest was aroused. Nash decided to take another look inside the Middlesex street bolt-hole. It was empty. The drugs, the magazine, everything was gone. Even the mat trap had been kicked to one side. Looking at the webs and dust, it appeared that nobody had been there for weeks.

After a little unfriendly persuasion from Nash, Mary's landlord confirmed that the rent had stopped being paid. Mc Carthy could so easily have moaned to Nash that it was the second lot of rent he had lost in quick succession, and what chance did he have of ever renting Miller's Court again now. He was very lucky he didn't.

Nash buried himself in the hunt for his prey. Every newspaper article read, every bribable policemen paid, every witness questioned. He used his robbery proceeds to pay for his fixation, employing the Carter brothers, Tom and Jem, as information gatherers. And with scrutiny of the Middlesex Street bolt-hole now abandoned, the two of them also helped Nash cover Euston Station every Friday and Saturday waiting for the Liverpool trains to arrive.

Nash no longer saw much of Will and Khan as they now had legitimate full-time work with plenty of overtime. Khan worked long hours for the Whitechapel and St. Georges Board of Works. He was part of a gang of men working within the huge budget of £2200, the third largest expenditure allowance in the district, putting in more and more gas lamps with double the illuminating power of the few previous ones. They were also being trained to start working on the installation of electric light. Will had building skills and he had got a job with George Lusk, of all people. Lusk had never had it so good. The well-to-do slum landlord Henderson family, who had done very nicely thank you for decades from the rents of the poverty stricken in Wentworth Street and surrounds, had been keen to dispose of all their property, tainted now as it was by the murders. Lusk was one of the builders charged with the job of demolishing their rookery and then building Stafford House, which was to be new, decent housing for the poor. When he was finished there, he had work on the demolition of part of the foulest of all the rookeries, Flower & Dean Street. Reverend Barnett's 4 Per Cent EE Dwelling Company had bought the north east side of this site and was going to employ Lusk, amongst many others, to erect the Nathaniel Dwellings, which was a huge undertaking that would eventually house 800 of the poor in 170 new apartments.

The Ripper fixation, along with his robbery proceeds, meant Nash no longer committed any crime, which was a great source of pleasure to Sookey, though her man had one scare, when Francis Horarti, who was working for Taff, was arrested in possession of a hundred and twenty 5d stamps. But young Frankie must have been more afraid of Taff than he was of the police. He took his sentence and kept quiet.

News of Nash's interest in the Ripper eventually filtered down to the ears of the police, and of course he wasn't able to offer them the alibi that he was ransacking Aldgate Post Office at the time of the November murder. But the police were so inundated with possible clues and information that one man showing an even greater interest in the murders than everyone else, was not seen in itself as particularly worthy of special attention. They had a number of men investigating the five main suspects, and many more delving into the huge second division of suspects, whereas Nash was way down in the depths of division three along with a black man thought perhaps to be Indian, and a gent with a doctor's bag who, when arrested, had given his name as one S.E. Milbrac.

Nash had become convinced that all the Ripper's murders had taken place on Friday and Saturday nights. The third to seventh (Mary's) murders had all taken place on those days of the week, and the more he found out about the first two, which had not, the more he became convinced that they were not the work of the maniac. Martha Tabram may have been killed by a soldier, and Emma Smith had been robbed, which wasn't the Ripper norm, and three young villains may have perpetrated the crime. And most significant of all, the two women had been killed in April and August, before the Ripper had rented the bolt-hole in Middlesex Street. He also dismissed the Poplar strangulation, which had taken place on a Thursday night, as common violence against some poor woman trying to earn a living. There had been numerous attacks of such kind in the past few years and there would no doubt be more in the next. Nash was convinced his destiny was to meet the gent in the Derby hat one last time, on a Friday or Saturday night.

But Nash's mind was in turmoil about how exactly to deal with the killer when he caught up with him. It was natural to want to bludgeon his quarry to a pulp. He could finish him off by strangulation, and mutilate the body in the same way the killer had done to his victims, before dumping it, along with the knife and doctor's bag, on the steps of Liverpool Street police station with a sign pinned to it stating 'I am Jack The Ripper'.

Another part of him thought that if the death of poor Mary, and those other mothers and daughters, were to be of any meaning, it was important that the Jack The Ripper legend remained. If the world found out who the Ripper was, he would be just another murderer in a long line of them. The people who had been forced to face up to the problems of the poor these past few months, would suck in a large breath of relief and Whitechapel would be left to return to how it had been before the murders began. Whereas, killing Jack in a different way, quietly, would mean he would never be caught. If the killer were never caught, he would live on in the minds of the middle classes. The publicity, guilt, social investigation and improvements would continue. Nash was thus considering killing the man dispassionately, without fuss, quickly and quietly, making sure there was no evidence left on the body to suggest the murdered man was the Ripper. The knife, the doctor's bag and its contents, and anything else of note would be removed; the gold watch and chain and any other valuable item taken, to make it look like a robbery. The gent will have been the victim of some dastardly East End villain.

The problem was that Nash's code of correct behaviour believed the right thing to do would be to avenge his friend.

I got a do the right fing by Mary. She'd want me ta get 'er own back on the bastard for 'er. Every punch would be fer 'er and I'd tell him that an' all as I did it. I can't use Mary's deff to 'elp me wiv my ideas. It wouldn't be right.

But he also knew the right thing to have done was to have killed the man when he had the original opportunity back on the night of the double murder. Nash knew that he had sold his soul that night, and there was no going back now. He would kill the man quietly. The legend of Jack the Ripper would live on.

Lil Brewer was on the autistic spectrum. She was considered an imbecile, but had hitherto managed to avoid being locked away. Plenty with better mental health than Lil had been carted off to South London's 'Bedlam' or one of the other mental hospitals hidden away in the countryside so society could turn their backs and forget about them. But in Whitechapel, such was the level of physical atrophy in the human specimens that roamed the streets that it was difficult at times to ascertain whether someone's appalling condition lay in physical or mental problems. Many broken men and women in the workhouses showed classic signs of mental illness only to be written off as the undeserving poor.

Lil got free lodging in the lowest of common lodging houses in return for cleaning out the disgusting latrines. She slept in her single set of rags (one couldn't call them clothes), in a box room next to her stinking workplace. She fed herself by prostitution but her autism meant she was only just barely able to let her body be entered, her neck craning away in disgust. She was also unable to make eye-contact or make conversation with her clients. She made them feel exactly how every man should have felt each time they used a woman's body.

Thus, Lil was not a whore to whom customers returned a second time. She was wandering aimlessly along Wentworth Street, when she was approached by an obvious gent. Her usual clients were the lowest of debased men, either straight off one of the boats or from one of the lowest common lodging houses. She had never been approached by a gent before.

"Are you working tonight my dear?" asked James Maybrick, just arrived via cab from his brother's house in the West End.

"Pooka Sullivan 'ad no sense, bought a fiddle for eighteen pence, and all the tunes that 'e could play were ta-ra-ra-ra-boom-de-ah," came the unexpected reply, followed by Lil wrenching her bosom out of her dress.

Ignoring this strange behaviour, Maybrick engaged in conversation.

"Eighteen pence. One shilling and sixpence. A fair price. Shall we adjourn to this dark little nook over here?"

He moved to guide her arm at the elbow but she shrank away from him, only to walk unguided into the alley he had proffered. No sooner had she arrived in the gloom, and Maybrick dropped the package he was carrying and thrust both his hands around Lil's throat, thumbs together pushing as hard as he could into her larynx. She immediately went limp, her tongue flopped out of her mouth, and she stared the stare of the already dead. It was like strangling a rag doll.

"Look at me, you fucking whore! Look at me!"

Maybrick, eyes ablaze, took one hand off Lil's windpipe to slap the side of her face in an attempt to get her to look at him. But despite his efforts her eyes looked around and wide of him. Maybrick strangled his victims with a broad, madman's grin on his face. As they started to pass out he would become sexually aroused. It was their eyes rolling back, their moment of expiration he enjoyed rather than the sadistic enjoyment of inflicting pain per se. He wanted their last sight on this earth to be of his face enjoying killing them. It was personal; very personal. He would then silently address his wife, asleep in bed beside her lover, two hundred miles away in Liverpool.

"This is you Florrie! I am down on whores! Kill the whore!"

But Lil would not make eye-contact; would not put up a fight for life. What was the point of killing something which was already as good as dead; there was no life to extinguish. Maybrick took both hands off her throat and grabbed her at the sides of her head in a vice-like grip.

"Take yer 'ands orf 'er."

It was a steady controlled voice. A big rough-looking man loomed out of the shadows. Maybrick spun round with the mad staring eyes of a cornered animal, allowing the rag doll to drop to the floor. The tall man, now standing still just a few feet away in the darkness, both hands in deep overcoat pockets, cut an intimidating figure, yet Maybrick breathed a huge sigh of relief. No uniform, no truncheon, no whistle. The man was clearly not a policeman.

Maybrick kept his eyes on the man as he slowly lowered himself into a straight-backed crouch. There was an eerie silence save for the sound of Maybrick's knees cracking. He felt for the package he could see out of the corner of his eye, still not removing his gaze from the big man, picked it up and slowly raised himself back up. The man continued to stand still, watching him.

Maybrick's problem was that whilst Whitechapel had lots of closed-end alleys and courts which were ideal for his purposes, affording him optimum privacy, it meant that he always had to leave by the same route by which he arrived. And now this big man blocked that route.

Lil broke the silence with a series of coughs and rasping intakes of breath as she regained consciousness. The noise moved Maybrick to action. He slowly, carefully felt in a pocket and withdrew two sovereigns. He tossed them onto the ground, next to the alley wall, a few feet to the side of the man. To retrieve them the man would have to move, and give Maybrick a chance to flee past him. It was too dark for the man to have been able to see what type of coins they were, although the type of jangle hinted that they were substantial pieces of metal.

"Sovereigns," confirmed Maybrick quietly.

The man could just as easily attack Maybrick first, and pick the coins up afterwards. Or perhaps the man had other things on his mind other than money. It was a move borne out of desperation.

But Maybrick's luck held. The man moved for the coins and Maybrick pumped his creaking knees. He was past the man in a second and with only a package rather than a doctor's bag to carry, he sprinted into the main street. He was a poor human specimen in every sense of the word, and within yards was gasping for breath. As he started to slow, he craned his neck. He stopped running as he saw nobody was chasing him.

A lascar, just off a ship at Limehouse docks, had been out looking to give a prostitute some business. He had seen Lil earlier and remembered her from a previous encounter. He had not wanted to repeat it, but there wasn't another woman to be seen on the streets so had retraced his steps looking for Lil. Anything was better than strapping a skate to a mast. In the darkness the lascar hadn't seen Maybrick's gold watch and chain; didn't see the man was obviously a gent who would have valuable things on him. Had he done so he would have tackled the gent to the ground and used his sailor's knife if need be. But the lascar had been too busy considering Lil. He saw her apparently black eyes staring blindly at him. The white's of Lil's eyes were no longer white, the blood of the strangled having filled them. Not for the first time, a man preoccupied with other thoughts had chosen to allow Maybrick to escape.

The following night, Maybrick's near nemesis was in a rough pub in Limehouse. He told his drinking cronies of his good deed, saving a woman from being strangled. It was the only time he told the story before getting back on board his ship and sailing off, never to return to London. One of the men in the pub, Wilf Bagnall, was a drinking acquaintance of Nash. A week later the two men bumped into each other and had a couple of drinks together. They swopped a few stories but Wilf didn't happen to mention the tale he had been told about a woman almost being strangled by a gent.

A further week later, Nash heard that poor Lil Brewer, whom he knew of and seen about, but never had cause to speak to, had finally been put away. The Chinese whispers of the grapevine had changed the story slightly.

"She'd 'ad a good 'iding from some cowson. An un'appy customer I'll wager."

"Poor lit'le cow," commented Nash, before the conversation moved onto something else.

Lil was never heard of, or discussed again. There was to be no co-in-cid-ence.

CHAPTER 28:

"Within six years Jack the Ripper had done more to destroy the Flower & Dean Street rookery than fifty years of road building, slum clearance and unabated pressure from the police, Poor Law guardians, vestries and sanitary officers."
Jerry White (historian), Rothschild Buildings: Life In An East End Tenement Block 1887-1920

Maybrick's failed sixth attempt to kill in Whitechapel was a sign of his fading mental and physical powers. His health was deteriorating fast; an underactive thyroid left him tired, lethargic and depressed; muscles ached; and he suffered from moxoedema, severe gastro-intestinal trouble, a liver complaint, headaches and dyspepsia. He was only free of pain on some mornings and was rarely anything but irritable. Tobacco or alcohol left him numb down one side, a furred tongue and sore hands.

He was furious with himself for almost being caught by the big black man. He hadn't kept his concentration; hadn't been careful. He should have spotted the man, who could so easily have been one of Abberline's men. Maybrick had lost confidence, and now read in the newspapers that one of the police's theories was that the killer travelled down to London by train. It was one of many theories, and all the others were hopelessly wrong, but he saw it as a sign that the net was closing. He would not go to London to kill again.

Maybrick had made his first killing in Manchester, and returned there to claim his seventh and final victim. But the memory of the horrific mutilations he had perpetrated on Mary haunted him. He had nightmares, and when faced with the body he had just strangled the life out of, he hesitated and then left the scene. It was strangulation and nothing more, and it was in Manchester. There was nothing to link it with Jack The Ripper.

As Maybrick's health drained away, so did his appetite for murder. He finally became self-aware that he was quite mad, and took to his bed to await his fate. On the eve of his death his anger abated, and he even had thoughts of rapprochement with his long-loathed wife, 'the whore', whom he was about to divorce. In killing whores he had killed her. Her neck the target of his angered thumbs on one unsuccessful and seven successful occasions, her body the recipient of his plunging knife on five, he now confessed to her that he was Jack The Ripper.

Florrie Maybrick was aware that she was to be left a relatively small sum in her husband's will. She was certainly financially better off with him alive, but their marriage had been effectively over for some time. They lived separate lives within the same house, save the odd outbreak of open hostility. He had hit her on occasion, but that was as nothing to the horror of divorce; divorce by reason of her infidelity. It hung over her like the sword of Damocles. Her affair would become public knowledge. She would be shamed, ruined. But far worse, parted from her two children.

The drugs which he took to such excess, that so befuddled his brain and were the source of all their problems, could ironically now be her saviour. They were killing him. She could start a new life, albeit in much humbler surroundings. Perhaps even start working. There was much charitable work to be done in the slums of Liverpool. She had heard of the deeds of women such as Henrietta Barnett in Whitechapel. In such a place! A fine woman indeed.

Having called her to his bedside and confessed, Maybrick was in such torment of mind and body that he pleaded with her to send him to his death. He informed her that there was enough arsenic secreted around the house to kill fifty men or more, and that she only need but kill one.

Florrie rushed to all the places he had told her contained arsenic. She found them all locked and out of harm's way; her children were safe. She was pleased to hear the confession. It was nonsense of course, but showed his mind had gone and no doubt his body would quickly follow; she would soon be rid of him.

James Maybrick finally went to hell, dying of severe gastro-intestinal failure. His body was found to have a significant amount of arsenic in it, and the police were called in by the dead man's suspicious brother. Having forged Maybrick's signature on a new will, and destroyed the old one while his brother's body was still warm, Maybrick's brother had good reason for wanting his sister-in-law to be discredited. He couldn't be sure what she did or did not know of the genuine will.

The police had graduated from the Whitechapel school of stupidity. A few puzzled frowns and barbed comments from the brother turned their heads. Their suspicion metamorphosed simple everyday household objects into clues. Innocent behaviour was turned into scraps of evidence. This was woven into the fabric of a case against the wife. She was arrested, charged and sent for trial. Guilty of the heinous crime of infidelity, Florrie was found guilty of murder in a court of law.

Nash was like a bear with a sore head first thing in the morning, whilst Sookey could be irritable and argumentative when she first got home after a long day at Toynbee Hall. The two of them were from such different walks of life that they did so many things so differently. Nash had a disgusting way of clearing his throat first thing in the morning; he smothered all his food with 'gear oil' as he called it; Sookey thought the strong brown relish horrible. His housewifery skills were non-existent, and he didn't see the point of cleanliness in the home. He saw the numbers of women in the slums whose lives were dominated by the need to stay clean. They seemingly spent every spare minute scrubbing something or another, but they still died young.

As for Sookey, she could not complete the simplest task that involved the use of any reasonable level of common sense.

"Trouble with common sense is it ain' sa common is it gell?"

Nash had philosophised this as he put his arm round a distraught Sookey, after she had made a terrible mess trying to cook a concoction involving a cod's head and 'pairings' from the tripe shop. Nash had been relieved to see it go on the floor, if the truth be told. He had seen it going. Could he have reached out and caught it as it toppled? If it had been one of his favourites, he would have dived to catch it, and if he had been too late he would have thought nothing of picking it up off the floor and eating it.

Nash would let the odd 'bleedin', 'bloody' and 'soddin' slip, and blasphemies were commonplace, but Sookey was well aware that he would use much more colourful language when she was not around. She felt this was just part of the wider problem of him never feeling able to be completely himself with her. She would protest to him that he should be with her as he was with others, but he would shrug this off with a little chuckle.

"All men needs two lives gell; free or four some'imes. Salt ov the earf at work, then go home and knock their ol' lady about. Bastards six days a week, then keep the nippers 'appy like a funny feller on the boards on Sundees."

The two of them were fortunate enough to be able to retain two homes. They would have found living together impossible, just as so many couples in the slums did who had the sorrow, loathing and bruises to show for it.

Sookey and Nash spent most of Sunday and the early evenings of Monday to Thursday, together. Their relationship had grown closer, mentally and physically. Sookey now enjoyed sexual fulfilment for the first time in her life. On one occasion as her breasts slowed their heaving and her blood slowed, a post-coital clarity of thought took her back to Mary. She remembered the only time they had discussed sexual matters. Mary had assumed it was a taboo subject with someone like Sookey, and for her part Sookey had thought the last thing Mary would ever want to do, was talk shop.

"Nah, ain' no such fing. It's an ol' wives tale I'm telling yer. I've 'ad more men in me than I've ad' hot dinners. Well I ain' 'ad that many 'ot dinners I spose," she said with a sad, laughing sigh, "but, any'ow, I'd 'av 'ad one by now wouldn't I?"

Sookey had laughed as Mary continued.

"I did enjoy a good apple mind, while I 'ad some piece ov filth poking away at me the ovver night. Gawd it was tasty. It's the closest I've come ta one I tell yer gell!"

The two women had then swopped tall or perhaps not so tall tales of what they had heard being done by various women to pass the time, while men did what men did.

Sookey told of how Rose claimed to knit. Mary burst out laughing.

"Gawd 'elp us you wait till I see 'er!"

"No Mary! That is in confidence!"

Mary didn't know what the long word meant but she understood nonetheless. How could she not. Sookey's face was a picture. Mary stared mock innocently, enquiringly at a crestfallen Sookey, before the two of them collapsed in laughter.

Back in the present, Sookey's reminiscing smile faded.

"It is no laughing matter; none of it."

⁓　◆　⁓

Sundays were the one day of the week when Sookey had something of a regular routine these days. She would head for the market to buy fresh produce for Sunday lunch and then buy a newspaper. Being such a poor cook, she felt that the freshest possible ingredients were required just to make a meal edible, let alone appetising.

There had been cooking lessons with Rose, but the tutor herself displayed limited culinary skills. Rose's mother of seven (with six more lost in infancy) had rarely enjoyed the sort of cash-flow that would have allowed her to buy the pots, pans, cooking utensils, crockery and cutlery that might have led to the acquisition of such abilities. And if your mother didn't teach you to cook, nobody else was going to do it. On the occasions when there was enough money in the family purse to afford more than the scraps that led to the rent-book sandwich incident, Rose spent it on meat for her husband and the odd treat for her family's sweet tooth.

Sookey would cook a Sunday lunch the best she could in time for Nash's return. She wouldn't see him from Thursday evening to Sunday morning. He would always be quiet when he arrived late Sunday morning, after catching a few hours sleep back at his place. Not morose, but subdued and distant, exhausted from lack of sleep, frustrated and disappointed that his prey had yet again not appeared. Sookey thought it was time he gave up his quest. It was obvious the monster was no longer at his work. Gone to his account in hell, or put away in a mental institution.

At least, the meal would cheer him up. Not the food so much as the leg-pulling about her cooking. But Sookey didn't have the savage ripostes of Mary and was sensitive about her shortcomings, so Nashey more often than not tried to stop short of being cruel with his humour at his lover's expense.

They would spend Sunday afternoons doing as little as possible, recuperating from the rigours of the week. When he wasn't trying to track down the Ripper, Nash was working legitimately for the first time in his life, and he was finding it exhausting. He had got work in a couple of pubs in the area, Mondays to Thursdays. The amount of rebuilding work going on had brought a lot of tough men into the area looking for work, and when they found it they had plenty of wages to spend in pubs. Someone had to keep the drunks in check, so Nash had got work in the Princess Alice next to Toynbee Hall, and just along the street from there in the Commercial Tavern. In between them was the Ten Bells. He had turned down work there. It was too close to home.

Sookey had once entertained the thought of the two of them going for a ride on one of the new velocipedes. They were quite the fashion. Everyone was trying them, and her friend Walter had brought back the latest Peugeot bicycle from Dieppe.

"You ain' gettin' me on one a them fings. Bleedin' deff traps they are."

Sookey thought it most amusing that a man who usually feared nothing, was afraid of a couple of wheels and pedals.

Nash would have first read of the newspaper. Rose had educated Sookey to the fact that it was a man's right to eat meat on a Sunday, no matter if it couldn't be afforded, and he must have first read of the Sunday newspaper too. Sookey would therefore leave it on the table for Nash to pick up and start reading as soon as he arrived home, whilst she put the finishing touches to the meal. He was a slow reader, and certain stories would be commented on and then a discussion or friendly argument ensued, so Sookey usually had to finish her reading by candlelight.

The murders were the one newspaper topic never discussed; not even touched upon. It was a taboo subject between them. And Nash would only read the relevant section of the newspaper on a Monday morning after Mary had left for Toynbee Hall.

But Nash needed to talk it over with Sookey. He needed her reassurance.

Wot Mary go and do that for when she had work ta go to? There were the pull an' then the 'all on the Mondee. She knew it were too dangerous. She should a let sum ovver old 'hore… sum ovver muvver's daugh'er…she'd still be alive today if…

He needed her forgiveness; and Sookey's.

⟨ ◆ ⟩

There was a chill wind so Sookey was huddled up. She had filled her gardening trug, a relic from her previous life which had been pressed into service as a shopping basket, with the ingredients of a fine Sunday lunch, and now headed for a newspaper. She walked towards the newsboy head down against the elements and it was only when she scrambled in her pockets for the change to pay for the newspaper that her head came up to focus on the man proffering the paper towards her. She saw that it was Mary's old sweetheart, Joe Barnett.

The last time she had seen him was at the funeral. The enormous tearful crowd that had gathered to pay their respects, and the mass of carts, vans and tramcars, had completely blocked the streets. The strength of feeling for a young woman few of the crowd would have known, but whom they knew lived on her own in poverty, with few friends and forced to walk the streets to keep out of the workhouse, had taken the authorities completely by surprise. They still didn't understand. They had to quickly mobilise large numbers of police to keep order. Bowed heads, hats and caps in hand, lined the six miles to Leystonstone, but the police had ordered the carriage driver to whip the horses so they almost galloped much of the route, much to the disgust of the throng. The police failed Mary to the last. She wasn't even allowed dignity in death.

Joe was one of the few Sookey had allowed to attend the grave, whilst hundreds were locked outside the cemetery gates. She had exchanged a few pleasantries with Joe after the ceremony, before she left him alone at the grave.

And now his head was also down against the cold wind, not looking her in the face, so it was with relief she realised he probably hadn't recognised her. She didn't want to engage him in conversation. There was nothing to say. She abandoned her usual 'helloo' and made sure she handed over the correct money, took the paper without a thank you and quickly darted away, folding the paper neatly, precisely into quarters to make it more manageable in the wind.

Her eyes caught one word of headline on the quarter of the paper facing out, as she positioned the paper carefully in the trug so as not to get it dirty from the vegetables or bloody from the meat. BRICK. On getting home she extracted the newspaper from the trug and opened it up with a view to pushing out the wrinkles caused by her tight folding into quarters. She flipped the newspaper over and glimpsed another word of headline. MAY. She opened the paper out. MAYBRICK.

Sookey stared at the word for a full minute, before reading the rest of the headline and then the article beneath. On finishing it she looked around for her hat. It was nowhere to be seen so she grabbed her shawl, only to find the hat was on her head all the time. She had not taken her coat off either, so she was ready to leave. Sookey walked to her art gallery to pick up a red crayon. She was only in there a few moments before returning home via the railway station, where she bought a copy of every newspaper.

As soon as she was through the door, she put the newspapers down and set to work on the original wrinkled newspaper. Using the crayon, she underlined boldly the first three letters of 'Maybrick' before circling the last five letters, writing next to it:

'YOU COULD BUILD A HOUSE OF IT'.

She then took off her outer clothes, slipped on her pinny and got to work on Sunday lunch. As soon as she heard him coming through the door, she stopped what she was doing, and faced him. Nash started to nod a greeting but was immediately taken by the strange expression on Sookey's face. He hadn't seen this stony look before. Without her eyes leaving his, she picked up the top edge of the newspaper and pulled it up six inches before putting it back down again. Nash looked quizzically at her but didn't say anything. He picked up the newspaper, and within a few seconds she saw his expression change to the same as hers. The cause celebre of the day was the murder of one James Maybrick. It was all there: James, May-brick, arsenic, strychnine, a cuckolded gent with a much despised wife Florrie, a poet-brother Michael. Sookey drifted to his side. They looked at each other in stunned silence for a moment before he wrapped his arms around her and she buried her face into his chest. She started to cry. He didn't.

Nash could no longer deflect his mind to the hunt for the Ripper. He was left with history; with guilt. Scholarly articles, written by wise men, important men, upholding the same views as Nash could always be found in the next few years. Nash sought them out. He tried to gain solace from these quotes in his darkest hours, but would any of these men, these *men,* have written such things if they had been responsible for one of those deaths? He knew the answer, and he knew that he would to have to live with that answer to his grave.

AUTHOR'S NOTES:

This novel has been carefully researched. The dialogue is accurate as far as I deemed feasible, but some of the criminal fraternity's speech was so full of swear words that if accurately repeated, would have detracted from the reader's enjoyment. When swear words are used, 'bleedin'' and 'soddin'' often replace the harsher swear words that would have been spoken in reality. Likewise, the slang and colloquialisms which would have actually been used, if reproduced in full colour as it were, would have made the dialogue too difficult to follow. Hence words and phrases such as 'soppy' and 'taking the rise' have been used. It is hoped the glossary of terms will help with any language difficulties in the dialogue.

The characters' names are a mix of the real life and the invented. Their personalities are from my imagination, with the exception of the Ripper's, which is based on a diary purporting to be that of James Maybrick, a wealthy Liverpool cotton merchant. The diary, if genuine, gives irrefutable evidence that Maybrick was Jack The Ripper. He liked his pathetic little jokes, and died, after a long self-induced illness, six months after the last Whitechapel murder was committed, with his wife Florrie being found guilty of his murder on the flimsiest of evidence. Mary Kelly was the Ripper's fifth victim in Whitechapel (thought to be his seventh at the time). She was a pretty young red-haired woman who bore a passing resemblance to Florrie Maybrick. Her boyfriend was Joe Barnett, no relation to Reverend Barnett, who along with his wife, Henrietta, ran Toynbee Hall amongst other philanthropic ventures. All the policemen, including the wonderfully named William Thick, and other officialdom were real life characters. George Lusk was the leader of the local vigilantes. John McCarthy was Mary's landlord. Taff Hughes was a one-legged kidsman. George Hutchinson was witness to Mary's meeting. with her final customer. A young Lloyd-George was shown around the murder sites, where his passionate concern for the poor, which later saw him introduce practical welfare legislation such as the Old Age Pensions Act, was no doubt fostered or increased. Nashey and Sookey are inventions.

Some of the more far-fetched sounding events really did take place; some of the more believable did not. Aldgate post office on Mitre Square was robbed, but truth was stranger than fiction. I moved the robbery to the night of the fifth murder for dramatic purposes (the only liberty taken with history), but it actually took place on the same weekend as the double murders, one of which, that of Catherine Eddowes, actually occurred in Mitre Square.

Maybrick was probably the man whom records show was arrested and taken to the local police station where what appeared to be a doctor's bag, was not searched, and he was freed to go on his way. A description of the man seen over the body of Liz Stride by the eye-witness with the horse cart was a remarkably accurate description of James Maybrick, yet this was discounted as evidence by the police.

Sookey's court case was based on a real affair whereby a wealthy middle class woman was robbed of everything by a confidence trickster. The real woman was far more stupid than Sookey; the real events would have been thought unbelievable by modern readers.

Jack The Ripper killed and mutilated five women in Whitechapel. Maybrick's diary tells us his sixth attempt was thwarted, and his first and last (seventh) murders, perpetrated in Manchester, did not involve mutilation. Strangulation was the cause-of-death on each occasion, the Whitechapel mutilations being post-mortem, which was no doubt why nobody ever saw a man roaming the streets covered in blood. The police failed to appreciate this.

They didn't have a bloody clue.

GLOSSARY OF TERMS:

Aris	- Costermonger rhyming slang: Backside. Aristotle-bottle-bottle & glass - Arse.
Bastille	- Workhouse.
Beak	- Magistrate.
Bedlam	- Bethlem Royal Hospital. Mental institution in Southwark.
Billy pot	- Tall hat. Working man's equivalent of a top hat.
Black man's pinch	- Blackened, badly bruised finger.
The bloke	- Foreman. Became modern usage in 20th century.
Bonce	- Head.
Brass	- Prostitute.
Brownhatter	- Male homosexual.
Bull and cow	- Row (argument). Costermonger rhyming slang.
Bully	- Prostitute's procurer. 'Ponce'.
Butcher's	- Costermonger rhyming slang: Butcher's hook - Look.
Chavvies	- Children.
Chops	- The sides of a man's face.
Cloth ears	- Mildly derogatory term for someone with hearing problems.
Codding	- Joking
Codd's wallop	- Codd was brand name; wallop nickname for type of drink.
Coney Hatch	- Colney Hatch mental institution,

mispronounced Coney.

Coopered	- Tired (a person) or scuppered (a plan).
Cove	- Man. Modern equivalent 'bloke'.
Cowson	- Bastard.
Cracksman	- Safe-breaker.
Crusher	- Policeman.
Derby Kelly	- Costermonger rhyming slang: Belly, stomach.
Dollymop	- Prostitute paid in kind by having money spent on them.
Dogged	- Followed.
Dogs are barking	- Feet are aching.
Don't your jaw ache?	- Sarcastic question to someone talking too much.
Dropsy	- Bribery.
Easy	- Calm.
Facer	- Punch in the face.
Fancyman	- Boyfriend.
Farthing	- Quarter of a penny. Coin.
Fittest	- That which fits best (i.e. Darwin's 'survival of the fittest').
Florin	- Two shillings. Coin.
Fourpenny one	- Punch.
Frog and toad	- Costermonger rhyming slang: Road.
Funny cuts	- Mildly derogatory term to person being amusing or sarcastic.
Gelt	- Money.
Gin palace	- Large Georgian pub.
Growler	- Four-wheeler taxi cab.
Gyppo	- Derogatory term for gypsy.
Half-crown	- Two shillings and sixpence. Coin.
Half-sovereign	- Ten shillings. Coin.
Hand's turn	- Day's work.

Hansom	- Two-wheeler taxi cab.
Ha'penny	- Half a penny. Coin.
Hounslows	- Costermonger's rhyming slang: Hounslow Heath – Teeth. Became
	- Hampsteads in 20thC. (Hounslow Heath now Heathrow airport)
Hunter	- Type of gold watch.
Ivories	- Teeth.
Jaw-me-dead	- Someone who talks a lot.
Jawing	- Talking.
Kidsman	- Criminal who ran gang of children pickpockets.
Kid stakes	- Pretending, bluffing.
Lamping	- Punching.
Loaf	- Costermonger's rhyming slang: Loaf of bread - Head.
Loony bin	- Derogatory term for mental institution.
Lugs	- Ears.
Magsman	- Confidence trickster.
Marketing	- Shopping.
Nose	- Person employed to gather information.
Nose-ache	- Inquisitive person.
On the mace	- On credit.
Out of the ken	- Out of the blue.
A Particular	- Thick fog
Pawsey	- Term for anything frustratingly unpleasant.
Peeler	- Policeman.
Penny gaff	- Crude, poor man's theatre/ freak show in temporary premises.
Picking oakum	- In prison. Picking oakum (ship's rope) was job given to prisoners.
Pitch it in red hot	- Argue heatedly.

Plates	- Costermonger rhyming slang: Plates of meat - Feet.
Pop shop	- Pawnbroker's.
Pull	- Criminal caper.
Pure	- Dog excretion. Collected off the streets to be used in tanneries.
Queer	- Strange, unusual, ill.
Ratting	- Dogs killing rats as organised blood sport.
Regent's Circus	- What is now Piccadilly Circus.
River Lea	- Costermonger rhyming slang: Tea. 'Rosie Lee' in 20th century.
Rum	- Strange, odd.
Scarper	- Run away.
Screever	- Writer. Criminals would use it to mean forger.
Sluish	- Wash.
Slummer	- Middle class worker in the slums.
Smalls	- Woman's underwear – knickers, drawers.
Snakesmen	- Burglars.
Sneezer	- Nose.
Stamp	- Appearance.
Stick out	- Argue.
Stiff	- Expensive, overpriced.
Suffer me	- Let me.
Tail	- Prostitute.
Taken	- Taken ill.
Taking the rise	- Making fun of someone.
Tanner	- Sixpence. Coin.
Tart	- Dismissive term for woman. Rarely used as meaning prostitute.
Ta'ers	- Costermonger rhyming slang:

	Potatoes in the mould – Cold.
Tightener	- Alcoholic drink – a short.
Top	- Kill.
Toshing	- Searching sewers and river mud at low tide for anything useful.
Tossing the pieman	- Tossing coins, predicting which side up they would fall.
Tuppence ha'penny	- Derogatory term; someone only worth two and a half pence.
A twelve-mumph	- A year. Pronounced 'mumph' not 'month'.
Union	- Workhouse.
Weasel	- Costermonger rhyming slang: Weasel and stoat - Coat.
Went home	- Wore out.
Whitewalling	- Writing on a wall with white chalk.
Woodbines	- Brand name cigarette.

Lightning Source UK Ltd.
Milton Keynes UK
26 July 2010

157461UK00001B/1/P